The Engineer von Satanas

FROM THE SAME AUTHOR

The Adventures of Saturnin Farandoul
Chalet in the Sky
The Clock of the Centuries
Electric Life

The Engineer von Satanas

written and illustrated by
Albert Robida

translated, annotated and introduced by
Brian Stableford

A Black Coat Press Book

ISBN 978-1-61227-425-6. First Printing. August 2015. Published by Black Coat Press, an imprint of Hollywood Comics.com, LLC, P.O. Box 17270, Encino, CA 91416. All rights reserved. Except for review purposes, no part of this book may be reproduced or transmitted in any form or by any means, electronic or mechanical, including photocopying, recording, or by any information storage and retrieval system, without permission in writing from the publisher. The stories and characters depicted in this novel are entirely fictional. Printed in the United States of America.

TABLE OF CONTENTS

Introduction

L'Ingénieur von Satanas by Albert Robida (1848-1926),
here translated as *The Engineer von Satanas*, was originally
published in Paris by La Renaissance du Livre, with a copy-
right date of 1919. It is, in one sense, a radical break from the
series of novelistic images of the 20th century that the author
had published previously, but there is another sense in which it
completes a peculiar trilogy introduced by the two shortest
items in the earlier series, both entitled "La Guerre au
vingtième siècle," and both translated here, by way of introduction to the present text, as "War in the Twentieth Century."

The first of the two versions of "La Guerre au vingtième
siècle" that Robida published appeared in the 27 October 1883
issue of the magazine he edited, *La Caricature*. The second
version, which accompanied a different set of illustrations,
was published as a book by Georges Decaux in 1887; a fac-
simile of that edition was issued in 1991 by Jules Tallandier,
who had inherited the address from which Decaux had operat-
ed. The inclusion of the two stories here as a preface to
L'Ingénieur von Satanas illustrates the origin of some of the
ideas that he redeveloped in the latter text, and the manner in
which, although the detail of his anticipations had only been
slightly modified to take aboard the innovations of the previous thirty years, his attitude to the prospects in question had
shifted sufficiently to replace a tone of wry black comedy with
one of furiously bitter criticism.

I have also included two stories by other hands as appen-
dices to Robida's novel, both of which illustrate similarly
proximate imaginative reactions to the Great War, and which
have marked affinities with Robida's work in spite of very
considerable differences of narrative method. The first of
them, "De la pluie qui surprit Candide en son jardin et d'un
entretien qu'il eut avec divers personnages" by the poet

Adrien Bertrand (1888-1917), here translated as "The Rain that Surprised Candide in his Garden" [omitting "and a conversation he had with various people"] appeared in a collection of four stories, all written while the author was dying, entitled *L'Orage sur le jardin de Candide, romans philosophiques* [The Storm over Candide's Garden; philosophical fictions], published by Calmann-Lévy in 1917. The second, *Comment Paris a été détruit en six heures le 20 avril 1924 (le jour de Pâques)* by the journalist Louis Baudry de Saunier (1865-1938), here translated as "How Paris was Destroyed in Six Hours," [omitting "on Easter Sunday, 24 April 1924"] was originally published as a pamphlet by Ernest Flammarion in 1924.

The 1883 and 1887 stories of 20th century warfare were not the first such images that Albert Robida had produced. In the course of his long chronicle of the *Voyages très extraordinaires de Saturnin Farandoul dans les 5 ou 6 parties du monde et dans tous les pays connus et meme inconnus de M. Jules Verne* (1879)[1], each of whose five parts takes up where one of Jules Verne's novels left off, in the interests of parodic exaggeration, Saturnin Farandoul and Phileas Fogg end up on opposite sides in an intense war fought in America between the North and South of the Disunited States of Nicaragua, in which heavily armored "locomotives of war" (i.e., giant tanks) mount fearsome charges, gigantic cannons launch unprecedentedly powerful shells, "submarine cavalry" mount a daring raid to capture the transatlantic cable, and chloroform bombs play a crucial role, before the climactic battle takes place between two fleets of war-balloons.

Many of these images crop up again in the 1883 version of "La Guerre au vingtième siècle," which is mostly set in Africa, partly as a joke about the potential future of colonies that become independent go-ahead "young nations," and partly in order to distance its slaughter from Europe. The story is

---

[1] tr. as *The Adventures of Saturnin Farandoul*, Black Coat Press, ISBN 978-1-9355453-61-0.

set in 1875, twenty-five years after the main action that Robida had developed in his massive satiric account of *Le Vingtième siècle* (1883), which was in press when the story in *La Caricature* was published and was heavily advertized in the subsequent issues of the periodical, so it could not have disrupted the imaginary history of the novel, but it neverthe-less leaves the society described therein untouched. The casu-alty figures cited in the story are horrific, but by no means world-destructive, and only affect the "young" nations—the bark rather than the heartwood of the envisaged world civiliza-tion.

Unfortunately, the account of the Australo-Mozambiquan war of 1975 is incomplete, because of the very strict space limitations of *La Caricature*, in which only four pages could be devoted primarily to text, and even they carried two or three illustrations each, in addition to those included in a special pictorial pull-out section. The later phases of the sto-ry are drastically abridged, either cut down from a longer text in order to fit, or, more likely, written while the typesetting was in progress, under enormous pressure from the rapidly-shrinking available space. It would undoubtedly have been a better story had Robida had more scope to develop it, and might well have featured even more speculative materiel. Four years later, however, when the second version of *La Guerre au vingtième siècle* appeared, in a format that was much gen-erous in terms of available space, the author elected to fill the extra space with more elaborate illustrations; the text is only a thousand words longer than the text of the earlier story, alt-hough it extends over forty-two pages, and the conclusion is only slightly less clipped.

The second version is set mostly in Europe, and is specif-ically dated 1945, five years earlier than the main action of *Le Vingtième siècle*, but it is equally careful not to disrupt the history of continuous progress set out in the definitive novel. All the images of mechanical and chemical warfare featured in the earlier version are deployed again, but there is also the key addition of an "Offensive Medical Corps" dedicated to biological warfare, as well as the less fortunate addition of military mediums deploying Mesmeric "fluid." Like all the other devices, however, the Offensive Medical Corps is used in a farcical spirit, in spite of the devastatingly murderous effects credited to it, and the list of diseases developed as weapons by the Offensive Medical Corps of the short story makes an interesting contrast with the nastier list credited to the Offensive Medical Corps of *L'Ingénieur von Satanas*. The 1887 story also alters the narrative strategy of the 1883 version, reducing the narrative distance between narrator and reader by liking its narrative viewpoint more closely to the consciousness of the hero.

The Offensive Medical Corps appeared again, in a marginal role, in Robida's sequel to *La Vingtième siècle, La Vie électrique* (1892)[2], whose hero is a reservist in the Chemical Artillery, called up in the course of the plot to take part in elaborate training maneuvers simulating a hypothetical invasion, while his father is an industrialist whose factory is working on new development in the weaponization of diseases. Much more attention is paid in the description of the hypothetical battle featured in the plot to the tactics of deployment of chemical and biological warfare than in two short stories, but the fact that the battle and its hypothetical casualty figures are unreal blunts the imagined horror considerably, and does not interfere unduly with the hectic comedy of the plot, the main satirical targets of which are the overly stressful pace and excessive complication of technological civilization.

The enemy nation with which France goes to war in the 1887 version of *La Guerre au vingtième siècle* is carefully unnamed, although the description of crossing the border between the two leaves little doubt that it is Germany—a diplomacy that contrasts strongly with *L'Ingénieur von Satanas*, written immediately after four years of the Great War and understandably replete with angry anti-German rants. The prin-

---

[2] tr. as *Electric Life*, Black Coat Press, ISBN 978-1-61227-182-8.

cipal different between the earlier texts and the later one, however, is not the sudden flowering of a blame culture but the replacement of a farcical tone that is relatively breezy with a profound and sincerely embittered grimness—a shift greatly assisted by a further decrease in narrative distance, by the employment of a narrative strategy that takes the reader into the consciousness of the first-person narrator, to eavesdrop on his thoughts and dreams as well as following the development of his realization of the situation he discovers in Europe in 1929, after fifteen years of absence, stranded in the vicinity of the North Pole. Indeed, the narrative distance becomes so close that the temporal standpoint of the narrative voice frequently becomes confused.

The most interesting thing about the shift between the 1887 and 1919 accounts of twentieth-century warfare, however, is that it was not produced by any new awareness of military possibility; although the novel calls a tank a tank instead of a "locomotive of war" and makes its "airborne commandos" heavier-than-air craft instead of miniaturized souped-up dirigibles, there is nothing in the military technology of its image of warfare in 1929 that had not featured in the author's earlier images of war in 1975 and 1945. What had crucially changed, as a result of the experience of the actual war of 1914-18, was Robida's realization that that he had been more accurate in his anticipations than he had supposed, and far more than he had wanted to suppose.

We now have the privilege of looking back from a viewpoint considerably beyond any of the dates cited in Robida's accounts of hypothetical twentieth-century warfare and civilization, and we can see that so far as events are concerned, his score as a prophet is zero, exactly similar to the score of every other prophet throughout history (except, of course, that who made "prophesies" after the fact and falsified the dates). If, however, we consider anxieties rather than actual events, we can see that Robida was a very remarkable and far-sighted prophet indeed, not only because he anticipated fears about chemical and biological warfare in the 1880s, but because he anticipated in 1919 fears that were to become central to British scientific romance in the 1930s and an important subschema of American science fiction in the 1950s. In that respect, *L'Ingénieur von Satanas*, which was not much liked at the time, because it made exceedingly uncomfortable reading in 1919, and was almost forgotten thereafter, is most definitely a classic of futuristic fiction, ten or thirty years "ahead of its time"—depending on whether one uses British or American units of measurement—and whose "time" is not yet over, because the threat that it describes still exists and still serves as a significant motor of anxiety.

In fact, British writers were not slow on the uptake with regard to the revelations of the Great War, and Edward Shanks's *The People of the Ruins* (1920) and Cicely Hamilton's *Theodore Savage* (1922) both produced similar imagery within a couple of years of Robida's text. There was then a steady trickle of such works throughout the 1920s, before the boom in such text in the 1930s elevated the imagery in question to the dominant note of scientific romance in that decade. That interim was occasioned by the fact that Robida's anticipation of a resurgence of German militarism was delayed in the real world until Adolf Hitler made the threat painfully obvious. With the aid of hindsight, however, we can see that, although Robida's timetable was inaccurate, his conviction that the armistice of 1918 had not ended the Great War at all, but merely postponed its resumption, was fundamentally correct.

Consideration of that fact also helps to explain one of the fundamental differences between the French genre of *roman scientifique*, the British genre of scientific romance and the American genre initially called "scientifiction" and subsequently renamed science fiction. The U.S.A. was immune for a long time to the anxieties prevalent in European varieties of speculative fiction because the Atlantic and Pacific oceans seemed to place it well out of range of the kinds of saturation bombardment that might destroy civilization. That kind of anxiety only provoked very weak echoes in American science fiction of the dominant note of British scientific romance in the 1930s, thus liberating the sciencefictional imagination to see the future largely in terms of a new phase of American colonialism that would replace the once-Wild West, now comprehensively domesticated, with the "final frontier" of space.

For that reason, while apocalyptic future warfare was the dominant note of British scientific romance in the period between the two worlds wars, it played such a minor role in American science fiction that even when the USA revealed the superweapon that opened up its own vulnerability to annihilation in 1945, the anxieties stimulated by that revelation had such a long way to travel that it was only gradually, over a period of a further forty years, that anxiety gained the upper hand over soaring optimism in American futuristic fiction—which had, in the meantime, colonized European literary marketplaces so successfully that French and British science fiction overwhelmed, overtook and displaced the native traditions in the meantime, albeit always retaining a much more noticeable alarmist undertone.

Within that historical pattern, *L'Ingénieur von Satanas* is, if not a pivotal work, at least a work that posted a very significant flag of discovery, marking a magnetic pole toward which many future imaginative travelers were to navigate. Because it was the first to reach that pole, it shows certain elements of naivety, but it also shows certain elements of raw pain that could only be dulled by repetition and revisitation. Those are stark, both in terms of telling details of the circumstances in which the survivors of the holocaust live, but also in the novel's conclusion, not so much in the character of the *deus ex machina* that provides the plot with the sense of an ending but in the true, unrecorded climax that is carefully left beyond the end of the text. That deliberate exclusion, which might seem perverse to some readers, was partly calculated to make the enormity of the "final solution" to the problem of "Prussianism" more appreciable by suggestion than it could have been by illustration, and partly in order that, in spite of the horrendous casualty figures implied by the story, the score of deaths actually described within it remains a highly conscientious and somewhat contrived zero.

As noted above, the primary reason for including two further stories in the present volume is to illustrate other close-range reactions to the Great War by French writers who found imaginative fiction an appropriate medium for dramatizing their anxieties. Adrien Bertrand was one of the earliest casualties of the war, in which he volunteered to fight as soon as the Germans invaded, even though he was a committed pacifist who had been active for some years in promoting that cause as a journalist. He went straight from cursory basic training into the front line, where, two months later, in October 1914, shrapnel from a shell-burst penetrated his chest and damaged his lungs. The injury was mortal, and there was no prospect of a recovery, but its lethal effects were not swift, and it took him a little over three years actually to die, confined to bed the entire time. As a poet and journalist by vocation, he naturally used that interval of agony to write, and won the Prix Goncourt in 1916 for his one and only novel, *L'Appel du sol*, which describes the horrific experiences of a group of soldiers during the early months of the war. Thereafter, he only wrote short stories, probably because he had no confidence that he could finish any long work that he started.

The story included here is the longest of the four that he completed, and by far the most far-ranging in its method and ambition. A *conte philosophique* in the very heart of the Voltairean tradition, it introduces the hero of *L'Appel du Sol*, recreated immortal after his death from wounds sustained in battle, to a group of other immortals—archetypal literary characters rather than real historical individuals—in order that they can discuss the significance in human affairs of war in general and the Great War in particular. If the argument seems a little slight and abbreviated in places, that is surely forgivable as well as understandable, but the story is by no means a work that is only remarkable for having been done at all; it is done well, with plenty of red meat for mental nutrition, and its con-

14

versations make a interesting surreal comparison with the exemplary conversations on the same theme that Robida's narrator has with Dr. Christiansen and Jollimay.

Like Adrien Bertrand, Louis Baudry de Saunier was a journalist, but whereas Bertrand was a socialist and pacifist whose writings were primarily political, although they clearly reflected the fact that he was a poet too, Baudry de Saunier's career was shaped by his passion for the bicycle, and he became a prolific writer on the rapid development of that technology and the sport associated with it in the early 1890s. From there it was a very short step to tracking the development of automobile technology and its associated sport, and from there to take in aviation and the development of flying as a pioneering and sporting endeavor. During the Great War he expanded his fascination to take in artillery technology and wireless technology, and afterwards such topics as the various potential uses of electricity and aluminum, thus remaining one of the leading popularizers of new technology of his era. He only wrote one work of fiction, which arose, like *L'Ingénieur von Satanas*, from the conviction that the armistice of 1918 had not really ended the war, but had merely postponed its continuation, similarly with the supplementary conviction that when it did recommence, it would do so even more destructively.

The most interesting element of Baudry de Saunier's story, however, is not what it has in common with Robida's but the dramatic contrast in its narrative method, which, far from looking at "Prussianism" from a horrified distance, adopts the strategy of looking at, no less disapprovingly, it from the inside. Like Robida, Baudry de Saunier sets out to produce a striking image of the symbolic "ingénieur von Satanas," but attempts to make it even more striking by allowing him to tell his own story, in a long diabolical gloat. In terms of his nationality, of course, that figure is now hopelessly out of date, but in terms of his profession, he is still very much alive as a bugbear, and as scary as ever, Nowadays, he is a "genetic engineer" attached to the Offensive Medical Corps rather than

15

the aviator that Baudry de Saunier elects to make him, but the fundamental principle remains the same, and twentieth-century versions of Robida's Dr. Christiansen do not have to modify the good doctor's fundamental argument regarding "that slut Science" at all.

Unlike Robida's narrator, of course, modern readers are unlikely to be so easily converted to Dr. Christiansen's point of view; the century that has elapsed since the Great War has made us, in spite of our anxieties, somewhat more complacent than Robida or Baudry de Saunier felt entitled to be in its immediate aftermath. We are far more likely to side with the valiant dead-but-immortal heroes of Adrien Bertrand's story, determined in their hope that life can and will go on, and that Candide's symbolic garden can be replanted, if only we can all pitch in, like Mr. Pickwick, Faust and Achilles. There is, after all, no alternative. Wherever we might stand intellectually, however, there is no doubt of the continuing relevance, in the twenty-first century, of the five texts in this volume. Their juxtaposition increases that relevance synergistically. In term of their anxieties, they were ahead of their time, but in terms of provoking thought, they have only become more urgent.

This translation of *L'Ingénieur von Satanas* was made from a photocopy of the Renaissance du Livre edition made by Jean-Marc Lofficier from a copy of the book supplied by Marc Madouraud. I am very grateful to both of them for enabling me to translate an exceedingly rare text of particular interest.

The translation of the 1883 version of "La Guerre au vingtième siècle" was made from the copy of the 27 October 1883 issue of *La Caricature* reproduced on the Bibliothèque Nationale's *gallica* website.

The translation of the 1887 version was made from a copy of the 1991 Tallandier reprint of the book. The translation of "De la pluie qui surprit Candide en son jardin et d'un entretien qu'il eut avec divers personnages" was made from the copy of the Calmann-Levy edition of *L'Orage sur le jardin de Candide, romans philosophiques* made available by the University of Toronto to the Internet Archive Digital Library at *archive.org*.

The translation of *Comment Paris a été détruit en six heures le 20 avril 1924 (le jour de Pâques)* was made from the copy of the Flammarion edition reproduced on *gallica*.

Brian Stableford

Albert Robida: *War in the Twentieth Century* (1883)

The Australo-Mozambiquan Conflict
The Events and Chemical Operations of the War

The new era has arrived. The old established order of things has collapsed, at the same time as the antique dominatrix of the world. Europe, ravaged by the martial monomania of her populations, has allowed the scepter of the world to slip from her senile hands, and the vigorous and healthy peoples of young continents are preparing to pick it up.

The struggle today is between young Africa, overflowing with sap, exuberant with youth, and adolescent Australia.

America, the daughter of Europe, as Europe was of the great ancestor Asia, is growing old, and from now on has been thrown out of the lists; the future belongs to the nations constituted by the vast territories of Australia, or the almost virgin lands of great Africa, the mixture of a hundred diverse races, newly melted, so to speak, in the crucible of nature.

Africa and Australia have come, arms in hand, to dispute the scepter of the world, in a first collision, which has stirred the African continent from the Cape of Good Hope to Lakes Nyanza and Tanganyika, bloodying the banks of the Mozambique, the waves of the Indian Sea and the clouds racing above the Mozambiquan and Australian plains.

It is an accurate summary of the terrible events of the great Australo-Mozambiquan War that we are going to condense in a few pages, accompanying our story with a certain number of sketches collected on the terrestrial, aerial and submarine battlefields, as many by trustworthy eye-witnesses as by myself, who has had the honor of participating in the entire campaign in the capacity of volunteer aide-de-camp of the Colonel-General of the Mozambique Torpedo Corps, and who, as a result of my conduct, has been mentioned in dispatches six times in three weeks.

The Causes of the War

Everything has changed since the last century closed the era of ignorance and barbarity. Once, among the ancient peoples of the little corner of the Earth still called Europe on maps, war was only waged between adjacent or not-very-distant neighbors. There were no points of contact, no motives for war, and, above all, no means of waging it more distantly, even if anyone had wanted to.

Science, shrinking distances, removing obstacles, cutting isthmuses and perforating mountains, has created points of contact between the most distant peoples, and permitted all communications amicable or otherwise. Immense progress!

No more barriers! No more separations! Instead, commercial and financial relations between peoples, giving birth to entirely new motives for war. Peoples no longer fight nowadays for frivolous and sometimes chivalrous motives, such as the protection of a weak ally or the defense of principles of liberty, but for serious, solid reasons, most often resounding, such as advantageous commercial treaties, the opening of markets, favorable custom duties, speculations on the Stock Exchange and the regulation of financial accounts.

The Australo-Mozambiquan War had no other origin than an immense coup on the Stock Exchange. Taking advantage of the temporary embarrassment of the great African nation, caused by the great expense of the completion of its railway network, making a further eight hundred thousand kilometers available to traffic, not to mention the enormous impetus given to other public works, a group of Australian bankers was able, by means of skillful maneuvers, to cause a panic on the Mozambicoville Stock Exchange, and bought a colossal quantity of 2½% bonds at 35.75. When the operation

20

was complete, the Australian government, interested in the scheme and acting in the name of the syndicate, demanded via diplomatic channels the reimbursement of the bonds at full value, which would have produced a net profit of eighteen and a half billions.

The Australian demand provoked a legitimate surge of indignation throughout Africa. On 15 April 1975 the President of the Republic responded with a formal refusal and immediately convened the Parliament at Livingstonia, the political capital of the great South African Republic, situated in a strong position at the extremity of Lake Tanganyika.

17 April 1975. From this day forward events will progress rapidly. Second Australian note.

Australia repeats its demand for the eighteen billions and raises another question. The Mozambiquan Parliament having raised its import duties on merchandise from Australia several years before, in order to prevent the crushing of African markets, is summoned to abolish those duties completely.

Australia gives Mozambique three days to respond, and warns that a refusal will constitute a *casus belli.*

18 April. Call to the flag of all men capable of bearing arms. The Mozambiquan taxpayers are invited to pay three years taxes in advance.

"What is the Fatherland?"

"It is the place where one pays one's taxes."

The best Fatherland must be the one where one pays the least, in money or in military service. Unfortunately, the more one progresses, the more one pays, in both fashions. We fear that the men of the twenty-first century will be tormented by the fatherland's collectors or recruiters from weaning to the age of seventy, the age at which one will be put into the reserves.

Those are the slight inconveniences of civilization. In the barbaric centuries, the times of armies of twenty thousand men, one was acquitted much more cheaply. Everything increases, the consumption of human flesh as well as other contributions.

The Mozambiquans do not murmur. Six months before, in order to claim a little liberty hindered by a Ministry, they had had a Revolution. This time, at the first appeal, they rally as one man to the offices of revenue, customs and excise, in nature or recruitment.

19 April. Review, at Livingstonia, of the troops of the active army. Call up and mobilization of all the chemists in the territory.

Review at Mozambicoville of the four divisions of the torpedo corps.

20 April. Response of the South African Republic to the Australian Republic. The Australian demands are flatly rejected and the revision of customs tariffs refused.

The Australian ambassador leaves in a war balloon of the Australian squadron. It is war; it only remains to wait for the official declaration.

Mozambique prepares energetically to sustain the struggle. She has complete confidence in her forces. A well-planned system of torpedoes defends her coasts and the Zambezi, her great river, against the attack of the Australian submarine naval forces. It is absolutely impossible for the enemy ships to carry out a disembarkation without running into three narrowly-spaced lines of torpedoes.

Everything is prepared to repel a submarine attack and submerge the assailants. Unfortunately, an aerial attack has more chance of success; all militaries are aware of the extent to which the unexpected enters into the schemes of aerial warfare. How can one anticipate in advance the precise location of a descent, and how, even if the location were to be divined, can sufficient troops be transported there to the descent efficaciously, without removing them from another location, on which the adversary might precipitate his flying squadron?

And in fact, the Australian air fleets have, in recent times, been raised to a high degree of power, and are commanded by engineers of the greatest merit.

The Great Council of War

Engineer Marshal Blick, the commander-in-chief of the Mozambiquan forces, an old warrior curbed by sixty-five years of studies in his laboratory, meets with all the chiefs of the army aboard the admiral balloon *Ravageur*: the Engineer General of Military Railways, the energetic Balister; Dr. Clakson, commander-in-chief of the aerial squadrons; General Turpin, commander-in-chief of the land army, an old moustache whitened in a hundred combats; Colonel Engineer Barbarigo, commandant of the perforators; Engineer General Coloquintos, commander-in-chief of the torpedo-carriers of the line, flying, subterranean and submarine; and finally, Engineer Eugene, the commander of the mobilized chemists.

After three hours of secret discussion, the defense plan prepared long ago by the great Engineer Marshal Blick, has been adopted, save for slight modifications of detail, and the engineers have departed at top speed to take up their posts at the head of the troops.

21 April. The Light Aerial Squadron, reinforced by all the available aerial scouts and dispatch-vessels, has departed for an observation mission. Overseas, a squadron composed of the lightest balloon scouts has to reach the coast of Australia in order to track the enemy preparations.

The greatest activity reigns in the arsenals. The mobilization of railway troops is carried out with an extraordinary precision; in 13 hours 45 minutes, all the contingents have arrived at their posts with the officers, engineers and electricians of the reserve, fully assembled. The locomotives of war receive their garrisons and charge their electric accumulators. The locomotives of the active army are speeding along the iron roads inland and along the coast; the huge blockhouse-

23

locomotives and fortresses have reached the important strategic points.

22 April. The submarine army is still at anchor off Mozambique aboard submarine frigates, on the surface. It has set up its advance posts six leagues out at sea. Off the foremost protrusion of the coast, at a depth of twelve meters, strong patrols are scouting the passes and submarine dispatch-boats are extending reconnaissance at a distance; at the first signal, the submarine forces will be able to set off for the threatened point.

23 April, 7 a.m. A telegram brings the Australian declaration of war.

7:50. A series of frightful detonations bursts forth at sea off Mozambicoville; jets of water are launched to enormous heights, clearly designating three lines of conflagration. They are the torpedoes blowing up. Engineer Marshal Blick, returning from a nocturnal aerial reconnaissance in his admiral-balloon, is nearly hit at a altitude of three hundred meters by a column of water and rocky debris.

The Australian attack has followed closely on the heels of the declaration of war.

The Mozambiquan engineers were tranquil, the dispatches of the aerial observation fleet over the Australian coast had simply announced a concentration of troops in Melbourne and a few ports.

The Australian government, having decided on the war, had very secretly sent out a strong submarine division even before sending the first note. At the very moment when the declaration of war reached Mozambicoville, the commandant of the Australian submarine corps received his instructions via a special wire connected to the first international telegraphic islet in the Mozambique Channel.

Six volunteers commanded by Engineer Electrician Pipermann slipped between the enemy posts in the torpedo-launch *Fuse*, destroying a Mozambiquan patrol by means of an electrical discharge, and came to attach an electric conductive wire linking the three coastal torpedo systems.

Immediately informed, the Australian admiral, sacrificing the brave men of the *Fuse* in order not to lose the fortunate opportunity, had activated his electrical battery. All the torpedoes disseminated over a distance of twenty leagues had blown up simultaneously. Two frigates and eight dispatch-boats, surprised by the immense conflagration, perished along with forty or fifty merchant ships, belonging for the most part to neutral nations.

23 April. Complications in the South. The Australian Atlantic Squadron, which was believed to be in America, comes in violation of human rights and treaties to land a corps of troops in the neutral territory of Kaffiria.

Port Natal has been taken by a nocturnal surprise attack. The Kaffir troops only put up feeble resistance, and King Nelusko III has contented himself with registering a protest by means of a note addressed to the diplomatic corps. The Australians, arguing links of origin between the founders of the former English colony of Port Natal and Australia, have proclaimed the annexation of Kaffiria to Australia, while announcing the intention of respecting the rights of Nelusko III if he will resign himself frankly to recognizing the suzerainty of powerful Australia.

That sudden conquest of Kaffiria gives the Australians an excellent base of operations and provides them with the key to the South-East African and Timbuktu-Congo-Cape railroads, and thus the entire Mozambiquan network.

The Statesmen of Mozambique now see the danger present for their neighbors, small neutral countries, too weak, if necessary, to compel respect for their neutrality by overly powerful and, above all, inadequately scrupulous nations.

24 April. The Australians have already received reinforcements at Port Natal by the submarine route. The Kaffir

25

war locomotives, filled with Australian troops, have crossed the Mozambiquan frontier and have taken possession of the mountain passes after a fierce combat.

Six hundred thousand Australians left Melbourne last night by maritime, submarine and aerial routes.

Engineer Marshal Blick has rallied all his army corps in order to confront the enemy. The initial reverses, far from diminishing the courage of the Mozambiquans—on the contrary—stimulate the martial ardor of the engineers and soldiers.

25 April. Bad news from the South. The Australian locomotives are making the most of their advantages, crushing under their number the few mobile fortresses spaced out along the frontier, from which forces had been withdrawn. They have reached the great plains and hastened their progress over the roads and tracks toward the passes of Monomotapa. Their objective is Zumbo on the Zambezi, where the Timbuktu-Congo-Cape intersects with the major Mozambiquan lines of the Lakes.

Engineer Marshal Blick has gone to met them with eight hundred mobile blockhouses, a hundred and fifty thousand men of the railway infantry, and a strong aerial division.

For his part, Engineer General Coloquintos, with a superb submarine corps, is heading up the Zambezi in a submarine flotilla in order to collaborate with the defense of the Zambezi lines.

The Battle of Zumbo[3]

26 April. The Australians, stopped during the night by the aerial squadron's rocket-torpedoes, mounted a vigorous offensive at four a.m. The great mass of mobile blockhouses was launched against the Mozambiquan mobile fortresses, in

---

[3] The subheadings that I have treated as chapter titles disappear from the text hereafter, presumably as a space-saving measure.

spite of the frightful fire vomited by the six hundred railway artillery pieces and the aerial squadron's two or three hundred pump machine-guns.

In less than twenty minutes, the Australian right wing was repelled and almost pulverized, but a division of reserve blockhouses commanded by Adjutant Engineer Flaghurst, the savant professor of the Military University of Melbourne, replaced the destroyed locomotives and launched a vigorous assault on the breathless and badly damaged Mozambiquans. The Mozambiquans, who had thought that they were already victorious, were forced to retreat.

At five a.m., at the moment when the great Engineer Marshal Blick advanced in his admiral-balloon to clear the damaged mobile fortresses and bring forward in the midst of the debris the intact blockhouses and armored wagons, the Australian railway artillery, recognizing the Engineer Marshal's flag in the smoke, directed all their fire at the balloon.

The Engineer Marshal, excessively scornful of the danger, leaned a little too far over his armored poop, and was hit full in the body by one of the superdynamite shells that the Australians' new cannons sent forth with a simple two-gram cartridge. The illustrious Engineer Marshal was killed outright; all that was found of his remains were a few buttons from his uniform.

Disorder spread through the Mozambiquan lines. One after another, fourteen engineer generals were killed. The aerial squadron sacrificed itself and resolutely engaged the enemy in order to give the railway artillery time to reorganize. In the meantime, the fortresses retreated and formed up again in front of the great tunnels of Zumbo. Two companies of Mozambiquan perforators, arrived that same morning, penetrated the immense embankment of Zumbo, with a dozen electric borers traveling at two kilometers an hour.

The Mozambiquan perforators soon reached the Australians and blew up several blockhouses, but they were rapidly disemboweled and annihilated by depth-torpedoes. At that moment, as the Australians were accelerating their movement, a column of their veteran blockhouses, by way of reputedly impracticable and unguarded paths, reached the summit of the hills overlooking the tunnels and the course of the Zambezi, and covered the Mozambiquan flanks with a hurricane of iron.

The Mozambiquan engineer, fearing that he might be cut off, beat a precipitate retreat without being able to bring the torpedoes placed in front of the tunnel into play. 45,000 dead and 490 mobile fortresses destroyed or captured was the bill for that first encounter.

Noon. The passes of Monomotapa and the city of Zumbo are in the power of the enemy. The submarine division of the Zambezi has also suffered a defeat. An Australian corps, having traveled upriver at top sped in thirty-five submarine case-boats with powerful electrical engines, took the Mozambiquan submarines by surprise as they were taking on air. The casualty figures are unknown. The Australian corps, reinforced by twenty case-boats brought by aerostats, have departed for the grand canal of Loanga to rejoin the upper Zambezi and reach the Lakes.

27 April. The second Australian army has disembarked. The great port of Mozambicoville is entirely blockaded by land and sea. The Australians want to take possession of it and occupy it strongly before marching on the interior.

The Mozambiquan army, having lost the Zambezi line, is concentrating at Mazayamba in order to protect Lake Nyanza against the first Australian army. A second corps is forming up at Lucenda, at the southern end of Lake Tanganyika.

30 April. The siege of Mozambicoville is proceeding with vigor. Two suburbs have been destroyed by enemy torpedoes, but our rocket-torpedoes have blown up a position on the besiegers' right wing along with an armored battery. The enemy perforators, having begun drilling twelve kilometers from the walls, have already reached our ramparts. The garrison of the Southern fort, surprised last night, has perished in its entirety. Honor to those brave men, crushed beneath their bunkers!

The other forts built on the rock have nothing to fear from perforators, but they are suffering greatly from the enemy's asphyxiant shells.

31 April. The perforators have succeeded in skirting a rocky massif and penetrating, through a weak stratum of friable terrain, into the elegant quarter of Mozambicoville. The district in burning over their heads, but the main body of the enemy forces is preparing for the assault.

The chemist Eugene, the governor of Mozambicoville, has recommended that the inhabitants to lock themselves in their homes tonight and to seal all the openings carefully. Something new is expected.

A powerful magnetic current directed at the southern front having totally paralyzed the defenders of the forts and bastions, the Australians captured that portion of the wall without firing a shot, at ten p.m., taking 18,000 prisoners. They were about to launch themselves into the city when the governor found a mean of blowing up their electricity reservoir. Our troops, who immediately launched an attack on the hill were the reservoir was situated, found the entire division occupying it prey to the most violent attack of epilepsy.

Forty-five mobile fortresses fell into our power; the cannons were turned on the enemy, but, as asphyxiating shells converged on the expeditionary troops as well as the epileptic Australians, we were obliged to beat a retreat, bringing our prizes with us and reoccupying the southern bastions.

1 May. The entire army has been obliged to don helmets fitted with chin-bands, and tampons soaked in chemical solution over the mouth, in order not to suffer the deleterious emanations of as asphyxiating fog that the governor and his general staff of chemists have succeeded in producing. The Australian cannonade has become very weak, our fog-rockets crushing the enemy positions.

29

2 May. 35,000 inhabitants not having obeyed the governor's instructions relative to the absolute sealing of houses are very ill and nearly all doomed. The Australians have been severely tested; their losses due to the fog are estimated at 40,000 men. Unfortunately, new reinforcements have disembarked, and Commandant Clifton has supplied all his troops with protective chemical tampons.

4 May. Great aerial and submarine battle to the south of Lake Nyanza.

The Mozambiquan aerial squadron took the offensive. Burning to avenge the Fatherland's reverses, it fell upon the Australian army in the process of extracting war taxes from the rich cities of Nyanza.

The Australian air fleet covering the railway fortress and infantry engaged combat resolutely. The Australians had numbers in their favor, but the gutta-percha armor of the Mozambiquan balloons offered considerable resistance to shells. The victory remained indecisive; after three hours of terrible cannonades and broadsides, the two fleets, their munitions exhausted, withdrew.

During the combat four hundred meters below the balloons, the submarine fleets met beneath the surface. The Mozambiquan submarine monitors *Shark* and *Silurus* sank twelve enemy vessels in succession; unfortunately, the *Silurus* having had her electric propeller broken by a torpedo, was surrounded by four enemy monitors. When the submarine refused to surrender, the Australians sent the *Silurus* to the bottom and drowned her heroic crew.

5 May. Destruction by the Australians of all the factories of the great manufacturing districts of Nyanza. The great manufacturing cities of Australia are delighted; they had requested the destructions in order to obliterate dangerous competition.

6 May. In modern warfare neutrals sometimes have the opportunity to witness superb aerial combats, when they least expect it. Thus, when six Mozambiquan balloons, giving chase to Australian corsair aerostats, caught up with them during the night over Seville, in Spain, the battle was fierce.

Finally, thanks to the terrible Mozambiquan rocket-torpedoes, the corsair balloons perished with all hands. Two churches, twenty-five houses and approximately three hundred inhabitants of Seville suffered grievous damage in the battle; compensation will naturally be paid at the end of the war.

7 May. Mozambicoville taken by the Australians. The Mozambiquan general staff was blown up with a part of the fortifications, two hundred mobile blockhouses and thirty thousand troops, owing to the incompetence of a chemist officer in the middle of a chemical operation while storing a murderous gas in cylinders, on which the governor was counting heavily. The Australians have taken possession of the ruins.

8 May. Attack on the entrenched camp of Mazayamba.

The greatest battle of the war: 800,000 Australians against 625,000 Mozambiquans; the terrestrial and railway infantry maneuvered in profound and exceedingly mobile masses against the Mozambiquan troops supported by solid retrenchments, opened at intervals in order to give passage to the railway fortresses. The reservoir-rifles of the Mozambiquan infantry covered the terrain with a storm of iron and lead; the Australians swept by that machine-gun fire fell in thousands. Unfortunately, their masses seemed more inexhaustible than the reservoir-rifles of the valiant African soldiers.

The Australian engineers worked wonders. They succeeded in bringing their veteran locomotives and mobile blockhouses, armed with enormous cannons loaded with superdynamite, through the machine-gun fire and over a thousand obstacles. Behind the mobile blockhouses the infantry frayed a passage all the way to the Mozambiquan lines.

The bullet-pumping rifles and machine-guns of the Australian railway infantry then demonstrated their superiority, at short range, over any engines whatsoever.

At two p.m., the Mozambiquan army, reduced to 180,000 men, beat a retreat to the fortified locations of Lake Tanganyika; the aerial squadron and the mobile fortresses, retreating slowly, covered the retreat gloriously.

9 May. Foreign powers having offered their mediation, the ambassador of the Congo, Monsieur le Duc de Brazza, has brought the response of the Australians to Livingstonia.

Australia is making exorbitant demands: an indemnity of twenty-five billions, plus an obligation for the Mozambiquan nation to furnish exclusively to Australia raw materials, manufactured goods and objects of consumption that she cannot produce herself, the suppression of all duties on Mozambiquan merchandise exported to Australia, etc.

The Mozambiquan National Assembly has rejected the enemy's demands.

10 May. Counter-offensive by the Mozambiquans. The Australians, confident of their victory, having not expected contact with the enemy, have been taken by surprise in the midst of an asphyxiating fog and driven out of the positions occupied two days earlier. Victory has shifted, essentially. The ex-victors have lost 900 mobile fortresses and 290,000 men in four hours. The Blackrifles, the Mozambiquan negro regiments, have fought heroically alongside white and mulatto regiments.

11 May. The Australians are beating a retreat. The submarine corps that had traveled up the Zambezi, surrounded in one of the reservoirs of the river dried up by means of the sluice-gates, has been obliged to surrender after a fierce combat.

12 May. Mozambiquan torpedo corps brought by the aerial squadron have succeeded in getting ahead of the retreating enemy columns. At Topambas, flying torpedoes and electric rockets destroyed more than three hundred locomotives of war, along with their crews.

19 May. The Australians are counting on retrenching in Mozambicoville and holding it, until a peace is signed or reinforcements arrive. A corps of two hundred thousand Mozambiquans has embarked for Australia on the large transport vessels of the submarine fleet and cargo aerostats.

30 May. Bombardment and asphyxia of Melbourne. The Australians sue for peace. Signature of an armistice.

2 June. A peace congress is about to meet to negotiate the conditions of the peace.

Albert Robida: *War in the Twentieth Century* (1887)

I. Mobilization

The first half of the year 1945 had been particularly tranquil, however. Apart from the usual routine—which is to say, a little three-month civil war in the Danubian Empire, an American attack on our coast repelled by our submarine fleet, and a Chinese expedition pulverized on the rocks of Corsica, Europe had lived in the most complete calm.

On the 25 June 1945, my friend Fabius Molinas, of Toulouse, a charming fellow with an estimable private income, was lounging blissfully, with a cigarette in his lips, the windows overlooking the garden wide open in order to let in the perfume of the flowers and the Pyrenean breezes. Fabius was fatigued; for two days he had been packing his trunks for the bathing season, which he intended to spend on the beaches of the Norwegian coast.

Entirely preoccupied with his preparations, Molinas had scarcely had time to listen to the telephonic news, so he was surprised to learn on the twenty-fifth, by the midday Telephone, that a *casus belli* had arisen two days before and that the adequately rosy political horizon had suddenly become intensely black.

What seemed particularly grave was that the conflict was of a purely financial order, a question of customs duties that touched all interests to the quick. Business is business; nowadays, among civilized people, commercial treaties are imposed with cannon fire.

Well, thought Molinas, *as long as it doesn't disturb my season at the seaside!*

As he finished his cigarette, the telephonograph spoke:

"Order of mobilization. Monsieur Molinas, Fabius, is drafted as Cannoneer second class in the eighteenth Territorial Aeronauts, sixth squadron. At five p.m. today he will report to the airship *Épervier*, three thousand two hundred meters above Pontoise."

"Damnation!" cried Molinas, leaping to his feet. "That'll take an hour—I only just have time. I won't be going bathing this year!"

Accustomed to sudden departures, Molinas rapidly telephoned a few adieux and collected various papers; then, opening his drawers he found all his equipment in order.

Forty-five minutes later, Molinas, jammed into his leggings and buttoned up in his reefer jacket, with his greatcoat over his shoulder, his continuous-fire revolver and saber at his sides, and his reserve oxygen-tank slung around his neck, arrived at the Paris tube with numerous companions.

A special train hurled them toward Paris. At 4:10 he disembarked, slightly dazed, at the Central Tube Station. Airships were waiting for the troops, and, at five o'clock exactly, the squadron of Aeronauts destined for the *Épervier* set foot on the platform of the balloon.

The Commandant of the *Épervier* gathered his men and announced to them in a few words vibrant with patriotism that war was to be declared at midnight precisely. The crew members installed themselves in haste. From time to time, the Commandant took out his watch. Suddenly, at a signal from below, the lieutenant pressed a button, the electric propeller went into action, and the *Épervier* launched forward, carrying my friend Molinas toward glory.

At daybreak, a nauseating odor woke Molinas in his hammock; he went up on to the deck of the *Épervier*, which was flying through a dense fog.

The squadron was moving past a division of flying vaporizers in the process of covering the frontier with a dense fog designed to dissimulate the operations.

II. The Mobile Blockhouses

Fabius, leaning out of the guard-room of the *Épervier*, was dreaming; still dazed by the rapidity of events, he thought he was on his way to the seaside resort.

Have I brought my bathing costumes? Damnation! It's only swimsuits made to measure that have the grace...

A canon shot close to his ear brought him brutally back to a sense of reality. Fabius opened his eyes; six hundred meters away, a corps of blockhouses appeared, stopped in their march by the fog. The engineer's whistle summoned at the *Épervier*'s men to their posts. The squadron spread out rapidly, the forms of balloons passed by, going to take the enemy corps from the flank and behind, as, regardless of the risk, it gave its electric engines full power to force a passage. The *Épervier* and five other airships were engaging in close-range combat at the head.

Fabius, the second feeder on the port side, passed the cartridges to the loader without seeing anything of the battle. Suddenly, a machine-gun burst penetrating the embrasure put the commander of the gun out of action, along with all his assistants except Fabius. Without hesitation, he leap to the loaded gun, took aim with the greatest composure, and fired.

A formidable explosion followed his cannon-shot, and the blockhouse at which he had aimed blew up.

The fog gradually dissipated, and the battle appeared in all its horror. A dozen blockhouses had already been destroyed, others were defending themselves more feebly—but the smoking debris of two airships lay on the ground.

Having sustained serious damage, the airship *Épervier* dropped steeply upon a group of blockhouses whose decimated crews were obliged to lay down their weapons.

It's all over: Only a few blockhouses have managed to escape and take refuge in a forest, where the airships are forced to leave them. The crews of the *Épervier* and a few crippled airships are divided among the captured blockhouses, which are launched forward.

Fabius, having been promoted to sub-engineer in recognition of his good conduct, is given command of the lead blockhouse.

Full speed ahead!

At nine a.m. the blockhouse, traveling as if pursued, penetrates without difficulty into the earthworks of strong position guarded by a female brigade of enemy territorials, summoned to relieve the army of the first and second lines, comprising all men between seventeen and fifty years of age. A terrible surprise for those inexperienced warriors! In the blink of an eye they are disarmed, and the town captured.

Alas, the occupation of the town would not be of long duration. They had been unable to cut the telephonic wire in time; the alerted enemy made preparations to destroy the audacious little corps that had ventured so far.

In the middle of the night an enemy battalion, led by blockhouses to within a few kilometers of the town, penetrated one of its outlying districts without being seen. One by one, men clad in chemists' uniforms, with aprons over their tunics and leather helmets enclosing their heads and necks, slipped through the streets. Silently, they began to set up strange and mysterious instruments on the terrace of a garden, screwing pieces together and attaching tubes. Within ten minutes, a chemical campaign battery was mounted; the men lowered the padded chin-guards of their helmets, took up their battle positions, and waited for their commander to give the order.

"Fire!"

One by one, four asphyxiant bombs described brief parabolas through the air.

III. The Surprised Town

Fabius' companions were camped around bivouac fires. A sentry, having perceived suspect shadows, was about to raise the alarm when the first bomb rose up in a green-tined cloud. A loud cry, a puff of smoke...

Three more bombs followed; then a great silence fell.

The bivouac fires were extinct; everyone was dead, including the unfortunate inhabitants still in the town, suddenly asphyxiated in their homes. That was one of the accidents of war, to which, since the most recent conquests of science, all minds have become accustomed.

By a providential hazard, at the moment of the explosion, Fabius, who was hungry and thirsty, having gone down into the cellars to make a requisition, had just gone into a cellar that was carefully sealed and devoid of any communication with the exterior air. The only one of his company to escape asphyxiation, he remained unconscious for thirty-six hours, without drinking or eating anything.

In the meantime, the general commanding his army corps learned of the recapture of the town by the enemy, and launched a few aerial torpedoes, of the 1944 long-range model.

The torpedists lying in ambush in the cirrus and nimbus clouds at an altitude of three thousand meters allowed the first shades of evening to descend over the town and then, activating their propellers, precipitated from the heights of the sky and, having reached a convenient range, launched their terrible torpedoes.

Suddenly, the town, wrenched from its foundations, swelled up, cracked and leapt into the air.

Fortunately, Molinas, still unconscious, traversed space, along with a certain number of small objects, rapidly enough to escape the jet of flame, and emerged abruptly from his faint, slightly browned, and carried, so to speak, by a column of smoke.

He hung on feverishly to an object that his hand encountered; it was a weathervane that had been hurled into the air with him.

The upward momentum had ceased, and Molinas sensed that he was beginning to fall. That was an anxious moment.

Thirty seconds later, he was gripped by an abrupt sensation of cold.

IV. The Offensive Medical Corps

After remaining underwater for a few seconds, unconscious again, Molinas ended up coming round, still dazed and bewildered, in the process of swimming on the surface of a river. He headed straight for the bank, where he would be able to hide in a clump of reeds.

In the evening, some enemy chemists decided to give themselves the pleasure of taking a bath. Molinas came out of the river, took possession of the uniform of one of them, and joined a patrol that was going back into a domed fort. A sub-officer put him on sentry duty in a large hall in which members of the Offensive Medical Corps, composed of chemical engineers, physicians and apothecaries, were discussing the latest measures to take in order to make a dozen mines loaded with concentrated miasmas and microbes of malign fever, glanders, dysentery, measles, stabbing toothache and other maladies to explode under the feet of the French army.

The mines were prepared; caissons were about to transport the zinc shells loaded with the necessary miasmas and canisters of microbes...

But Fabius, thanks to his comprehension of the language, has understood everything. A sublime resolution ablaze in his heart, he devotes himself to the salvation of the army. Rapidly, he raises his repeating rifle and fires his entire provision of bullets into the large reservoir of miasmas and chemical products...

Terrible, frightful, the explosion that follows the rifle shots of the heroic Molinas!

Everything blows up: the reservoir, the caissons, the shells! The deflagration of all those concentrated and compressed miasmas occurs with enormous violence; thick columns of swirling, rolling vapors flood out through all the exits, spreading over the plain and dissolving in the atmosphere, carrying with them unspeakable odors and innumerable ferments of disease.

Everything has collapsed in the conference room. Generals, officers, chemical engineers, physicians and soldiers have all fallen down suddenly, and are writhing on the ground, prey to all the maladies unleashed by Molinas' action. Epidemics fall upon the enemy army and transport their ravages over a radius of three leagues in three minutes.

Thanks to the tampon in his chemist's helmet. Fabius, who had decided to sacrifice his life, got away with a nasty toothache.

Fortunately, the French army escaped the contagion. A microbial engineer in the French Offensive Medical Corps, on sentry duty at the extreme advance posts, understood the distant rumblings of the explosion the accident that had overtaken the enemy, and telephoned the general, who sent forward all the available chemical batteries to cover the army's front with an insulating fog.

Thus rid of the enemy that was threatening his left, the general, shielded by the fog, abandoned the contaminated region with an abrupt about-turn, and fell back upon the enemy corps maneuvering to his right.

Molinas, still prey to his raging toothache, then rejoined the army and made his report to the general.

Heaped with felicitations by the general, embraced by the entire general staff, decorated and mentioned in dispatches, Molinas finally sensed his dolors calming down.

He retained nevertheless an unfortunate tendency to odontalgia, and was obliged not long afterwards to get an entire set of false teeth.

Let us say immediately that the enemy hospitals had to treat 179,549 civilian and military casualties, and that, from the mixture of all the miasmas, a remarkable and absolutely new malady was born. Cultivated by the physicians of Europe entire, it is now known by the name of Molinous fever, after its inventor, and the place where it first came into existence has remained exceedingly unhealthy.

V. Siege Operations, Pumpers and Mediums

In recompense for his admirable conduct, Fabius Molinas was appointed a sub-lieutenant of pumping machine-gunners. That corps, of recent formation, is a kind of extremely mobile artillery which can be transported very rapidly to any location and instantly cover positions inaccessible to ordinary artillery with a violent fire.

To begin with, Molinas had four pumps under his orders, each maneuvered by five men. In the first battle, fiercely disputed, Molinas, huddled with his pumpers in the ruins of a house, withstood four successive attacks, his men being replaced three times; he alone emerged unscathed from the field of carnage. That same evening he was promoted to lieutenant.

The region in which the army was operating was sown with lines of torpedoes linked by wires, mines, and cleverly dissimulated domed forts. They only marched with precaution, electricians and mediums to the fore in order to defuse the mines and blow up the enemy torpedoes. The Aeronautical Division being occupied elsewhere, there was no possibility of dynamiting the domed forts from above. It was necessary to proceed by means of regular sieges.

The heavy artillery, by means of a series of fortunate shots, having succeeded in smashing or jamming the mechanism that moved the cupolas, the assault columns were launched forward and descended through the breaches in the dome.

Having taken the domes of the first line, the army was preparing to lay siege to a large fortified town. After having simulated a fake attack at another point, the general sent forward a reserve squadron of mediums under the cover of a dark night. Put at his disposal by the Ministry of Science, the mediums in question—the most powerful magnetizers and suggestionists in Paris, according to the scientists—marched slowly toward the enemy lines, emitting torrents of fluid by means of energetic passes.

A moment of terrible anxiety! Are the enemy guards going to fire, or will they, subjugated by the fluid, allow the mediums to pass?

A profound silence continues to reign; the mediums are still going forward; they have passed thought the lines. A column of troops follows them. Firstly, the column finds a few sentries and little guard-posts in catalepsy, and then the entire garrison of a redoubt lying on the ground, stiffened by the magnetic trance.

The general, informed by telephone, moves his troops, racing to occupy the redoubt conquered without a shot being fired.

The mediums have collapsed, exhausted; a full two hours of rest is absolutely necessary to them.

Grave danger! The enemy might flood the redoubt with asphyxiating gas before it can be put in a defensive state—but the enemy has no suspicions, and the cannons remain mute.

Finally, at the first light of dawn, the mediums, having recovered their energy, resume their passes. After terrible efforts of will, and after having lost the hypnotizers to disturbances of the brain, the chief medium succeeds by means of suggestion to bring the commander of the southern fortifications the town to capitulate.

VI. The Battery of the Fearless Chemists

All was not yet finished. The mediums, after a well-earned rest, turned their efforts toward the corps in position. Thy commenced their operations that same evening; unfortunately, in their haste to advance, they neglected to defuse the torpedoes with which the terrain turned out to be sown, and the entire squadron was pulverized by the explosion of a mine that the magnetic passes caused to explode beneath their feet.

It was necessary to revert to regular operations. During the night, under a rain of projectiles of all kinds, the general set up a large chemical siege battery.

A spectacle of sublime horror: the air ablaze with red, green, violet, yellow and blue flamboyance, traversed by sudden fulgurations and great jets of flame, criss-crossed by thousands of shells, canisters and chemical carboys bursting with projections of gas and smokes of every hue!

The enemy chemists are also at work; there is an epic duel between the two corps. That same day they reveal two batteries that pepper ours with paralyzing gas bombs. Our men, paralyzed or afflicted with a mortal catalepsy, fall on their guns. The response is given to them by miasma shells producing frightful attacks of epilepsy. But the asphyxiating shells rain down like hail on our lines, as well as canisters containing the microbes of chemical mange, a superb find by an illustrious enemy scientist.

Our chemists were suffering horribly when one of our engineers finally invented carboys of a corrosive dew (awarded the Medal of the Académie des Sciences for the production of atmospheric vitriol) which destroyed the enemy batteries in a single night.

In the meantime, it was discovered that the enemy submarine fleet was preparing to quit its home port for an unknown destination, either with the intention of ravaging our ports or to operate a disembarkation at some point on our shores. A scout who had ventured into enemy waters had been able to count the magnificent submarine monitors of the fleet, the armored high-speed destroyers and the torpedo-boats moving through the waves with a remarkable velocity.

The French fleet, also numerous and no less beautiful, was at sea, carrying the submarine infantry along with a disembarkation corps The Engineer Admiral's plan was to fall upon the enemy fleet as it passed, destroy it, and then attack the enemy ports.

Fabius Molinas received order to join the French fleet; by reason of his brilliant services, he had been detached to the navy in the capacity of an Engineer Torpedist, and strongly recommended to the Admiral, who entrusted him with the command of the *Cyanure de Potassium*, a submarine torpedo-boat of an entirely new model.

Fabius went immediately to his port of embarkation and took up his command. The *Cyanure de Potassium*, of very restricted dimensions, only carrying six men, was one of those small and slender pisciform torpedo-boats designed for rapid strikes, and also for difficult explorations: one of the terrible myrmidons of the sea that glide just under the surface and come up from below in order to plant their torpedoes in the hulls of huge monitors.

VII. The Submarine Torpedo-Boat Cyanure de Potassium

"You're a landlubber," the Admiral had said to Molinas, when he confided the torpedo-boat to him. "Show me that you conserve all your qualities in the water."

"Damnation! You'll see that, and so will the enemy!" Molinas had replied, modestly.

Almost shaving the sea-bed, hiding among the rocks covered with weed, the *Cyanure de Potassium* pressed ahead at full speed. In two days, she reached enemy waters and almost ran her nose into the lines of torpedoes defending the coast.

In seventy-two hours, during which his men did not have a moment's rest, Molinas succeeded in unfastening the torpedoes of three chaplets, each more than twenty leagues long. Taking care not to cut any wires, in order to allow the enemy to think that the defenses remained intact, he emptied all the torpedoes without any accident.

One last chaplet remained of torpedoes anchored at the extremity of the haven when the enemy fleet charged its electrical accumulators. The *Cyanure de Potassium* succeeded in approaching unperceived. This time, Molinas did not remove the torpedoes; he had another plan. He cut the enemy wires and reattached the chaplet of torpedoes to his electric battery. Then, hidden in a hole in the rocks, breathing through an air

44

tube, the *Cyanure* waited for the moment when the enemy fleet presented itself at the pass in order to go out to sea.

"Go!" said Molinas to his electrician.

The torpedoes exploded; seven monitors were dispersed in fragments in the air, with a gigantic jet of foam; five or six others were thrown on to the coast, badly damaged.

A few monitors of the advance guard had passed through; the brave *Cyanure de Potassium*, quitting her shelter, launched forward and deposited her torpedo in the flank of a huge bombard.

That was her final exploit; the fore section of the bombard, falling on the *Cyanure*, broke her torpedo tube and badly damaged her propellers. At the precise moment that the *Cyanure* was thus disarmed, Molinas perceived all the enemy scouts and torpedo-boats racing toward him furiously.

Let's use cunning! Molinas said to himself—and instead of fleeing toward the open sea, he headed for the coast in order to lodge there, hiding among the rocks.

The *Cyanure* slid into the rocks, bounding into the wider gaps—but behind him, getting closer all the time, the enemy torpedo-boats were also bounding. At nightfall, the *Cyanure* ran aground close to the mouth of a river.

Two enemy scouts, traveling too fast, also ran aground and sustained damage. Taking advantage of the confusion, Molinas had his men put on their diving suits, in order to try one last move. He was just in time—the enemy divers were already attacking the *Cyanure*'s hull with axe-blows.

There was a flight across the sea-bed into the unknown. The enemy divers, after a moment's hesitation, followed Molinas and his men, who slid between the viscous rocks, stopping from time to time in order to send the pursuers a bullet from their compressed-air carbines. By turning into a creek, Molinas succeeded in gaining a little advance in the water of the river.

For nine days they marched thus, sometimes on the bank and sometimes in the river when they passed through towns, pursued by cavalry launched on their trail, lost and picked up again, when one day Molinas hear the muffled sound of cannon fire—water is a good conductor of sound. There had to be a battle twenty-five leagues away, so they were going to meet up with the French army again"

"Forward, damn it!"

Another three days of forced march. They redoubled their prudence and passed through several enemy army corps without any difficulty. Finally, Molinas recognized the uniforms, and during the fusillade at a good moment during an engagement on the banks of the river, he and his divers appeared to the astonished soldiers.

"Who are these men" asked the general occupied in telephoning orders.

When Molinas had explained his presence, the general said "Bravo! But before you go to the field hospital, I need you again."

"I'm ready!" Molinas replied.

"You'll have to go back into the water!"

"I'll go!" said Molinas.

"You're going to go downriver with your men. A league from here you'll find the first enemy lines. Go through them! Further on, the enemy has his big blockhouse locomotives in a battery. You'll pass under their fire…and further on still, you'll find the telephone wires maintaining communication between the enemy's left wing, which I'll pin down by means of a forceful diversion, and the right wing, which I intend to crush. Cut those wires, and then come back, under the fire of the locomotives, and come to give me a report of the expedition. Go!"

Molinas has already gone.

VIII. Airborne Commando no. 39

Having carried out his mission successfully, Molinas reappeared with two more wounds. He immediately went to the field hospital, and shortly afterwards was evacuated to a French hospital. Three weeks later, as he was finishing his convalescence, he received an order to join the aerial squadron in order to take command of *Airborne Commando no. 39*.

Following the instructions he received from the Chief Engineer, he went, by way of a long detour, to the enemy's northern provinces, making abrupt descents here and there to disorganize services, cut wires, impose war taxes on towns, and dynamite enemy fortresses whenever he could.

Airborne Commando no. 39, under Molina's orders, caused an unusual trouble in enemy territory with its rapid incursions its sudden descents and its unexpected attacks. Enemy airships wasted their time in futile flights to one place while he was inflicting ravages fifty leagues further on.

Finally, the enemy, spitting feathers, sent an entire fleet in his pursuit, with hosts of little independent torpedo-craft. Identified by a scout, the *Airborne Commando* was overtaken and surrounded by innumerable torpedo-craft of various sizes, manned by between two and six men.

Molinas understood that only audacity could save him. He attacked himself, risking everything to a charge directly at the torpedo-craft, and continued straight on, ahead of the squadron.

"Damnation!" he said to himself. "If there's nothing more to be done here, I'll go surprise their colonies!"

And, favored by a gale, he headed due south, only followed by a few stubborn torpedo-craft, whose pilots had guessed his plan and were striving to increase speed. Molinas did not allow them to overtake him or take him by surprise; matching wits with them, he succeeded in disabling the torpedo-craft one by one.

In a desperate scrap with the last of them, however *Commando no. 39* was hit in the propeller and its rudder was broken. The enemy colonies were saved.

That damage forced Molinas to descend and land in a wooded area on the bank of a river, which, on taking a bearing, he found to be the White Nile, a few hundred leagues from Belgian Africa, the Empire of the Lakes, the French kingdom of the Congo and the American colonies.

Molinas was working on the repairs to *Commando no. 39* when savage animals, attracted by the odor of fresh flesh, suddenly arrived to inconvenience the workers considerably. A disagreeable encounter! A family of lions, a rhinoceros and his spouse, a few varied snakes and an entire tribe of alligators!

"Too much game!" Molinas exclaimed, beating a retreat toward the rear.

The propeller, temporarily dismantled, no longer being able to function, *Commando no. 39* was condemned to immobility. And the invasion continued, lions and crocodiles redoubling their indiscretion.

"Take your pick according to taste—you have an embarrassment of choice!" said the lieutenant, who had a lugubrious sense of humor, to Molinas. "Would you prefer the stomach of a lion or the belly of a crocodile?"

"Get away!" cried Molinas. "As I said, all that's nothing but game! Don't we still have our provision of sulfuric acid? To the bunkers!"

With great difficulty, they succeeded in getting a carboy of acid up on to the rear platform, as well as a hand pump, and the defense was organized. Molina commenced by giving the stupid rhinoceros, which was threatening to damage the *Commando*, a taste of torpedo. The violent pastille blew him into fifty pieces, which appeared to surprise his lady wife enormously.

"Would you like one too, my dear Madame?" asked Molinas, graciously.

As the lions, serpents and crocodiles advanced toward the refuge of Molinas and his men, the pump came into play. A jet of sulfuric acid projected sometimes into the face of a lordly lion and sometimes into the gaping maw of an alligator, produced a considerable effect on the assailants.

What leaps! What twists! What roars!

"Gently, pumpers!" said Molinas. "Everyone shall have some!"

The well-manipulated pump continued the irrigation with sulfuric acid while two men hastily reassembled the propeller...

And suddenly, the *Commando*, with its improvised rudder, rose up into the air. Lions, serpents and crocodiles, burned, roasted and browned, leapt overboard and cashed on to the rocks.

IX. Aerial Battles

Commando 39 rejoined the aerial fleet above the Mediterranean. As time was pressing, the Engineer Admiral, after having congratulated Molinas, immediately sent him to the advance guard.

According to its instructions, the advance guard was supposed to signal the enemy fleet without engaging it in combat. Nevertheless, during the second night of the flight, the *Commando*, soaring at a great height in a mass of cloud, took a large enemy bombard by surprise, by falling upon it.

After taking his prize to the aerial arsenal at Antibes, Molinas set off again at top speed. The enemy fleet had been spotted, and one of the great aerial battles of the century was about to be engaged. The *Commando* took its place in the battle line at the extremity of the left wing, and Molinas, with his hand on the electric witches, searched with his eyes for an enemy worthy of him.

What a battle! What collisions! What ravages! What plunges from the heights of the Heavens into the depths of the sea! What heroism on both sides!

Long indecisive, victory was inclining in our direction when the sky, menacing for some time, unleashed a frightful tempest. Caught in the turbulence, the two fleets, still fighting, were carried beyond Gibraltar, above the Atlantic in fury.

For three days the surviving airships were carried on the wings of the storm. Glimpses were caught between two clouds, shots were fired, and the combatants lost sight of one another.

Suddenly, the wind dropped, and, not far between the blue of the sky and the green of the sea, the coast of America appeared.

"Mexico!" said Molinas, after taking a bearing.

He looked behind him. Only one enemy aircraft was still visible. The two airships, severely tried by the battle and the tempest, were steering very poorly. Both absolutely had to descend to the ground to repair their damage, but before then, they both wanted to fight.

Molinas aimed his gun himself, and luck sent the first projectile straight into the enemy's hull.

The cannons roared uninterruptedly, the two airships spun, swerved, rose up and dived again, in order to catch one another out in some false move. The combat had taken them over a large town, whose inhabitants were following the ups and downs of the conflict anxiously. Already, a few projectiles had hit the town; there were grave accidents to deplore; three houses had blown up.

Finally, a better-directed shell went right through the enemy airship, with became ungovernable and slowly sank downwards. Then, abandoning all precaution, she sent a dozen projectiles one after another at Commando 39. An immense cry of horror went up from the ground; the two airships, spinning in a cloud of smoke, appeared to be falling directly on to the town.

A frightful fall! A terrible crash! With a thunderous noise, the enemy airship fell perpendicularly on to a monument and disappeared into the rubble, while the *Commando*, slowing in its fall and describing a curve, penetrated relatively gently, prow first, into a block of elegant houses.

Everything splintered. The perforated roof opened up; the prow of the *Commando*, after passing through three ceilings and breaking all the partition walls, finally came to rest on the ground floor of a beautiful building, in a delightful apartment, on furniture on to which Molinas, covered in glory and contusions, tumbled unconscious.

The demoiselle of the house, a charming señorita of the Mexican aristocracy, lay in a faint beside Molinas, who was on the brink of death. She was the first to recover consciousness. Help was organized. Dolores, the young Mexican, did not want to leave to anyone else the case of the hero who had broken into her bedroom...and probably also into her heart.

A fortnight later, when Molinas, having become the lion of the town, was almost convalescent, Dolores' father, in a black coat, came to propose to Fabius that he enter his family, as he had entered his house.

The commander of *Commando 39* was free. The telephonograph announced to the six continents of the world that a glorious peace had just been sighed.

And that is how my friend Fabius Molinas, cured and married, took the road to France again triumphantly, a short while thereafter, on the *Commando 39*, repaired, reprovisioned and joyfully decked with flags.

A. ROBIDA

L'Ingénieur Von Satanas

LA RENAISSANCE DU LIVRE

Albert Robida: *THE ENGINEER VON SATANAS*

Prologue

That all these things happened was the fault of the venerable Abbé Gottlieb, prior of the Augustine convent at Freiburg im Brisgau in 13 or thereabouts.

He was a saintly man, but he was old—very old—gentle and timid, almost child-like, half deaf and three-quarters blind.

One day, he received a visit from a young rogue of a student who claimed that he had enough of deceptive science and the errors of society, and wanted to become a monk, in order no longer to occupy himself with anything but the salvation of his soul, by means of meditation and prayer.

"Accept me as a novice in your convent, Father," he groaned, in a cavernous, hypocritically tearful voice. "I have many since to expiate. It's only here, in the refuge of the Augustine convent, sanctified by your virtues, sheltered from all temptations, that I can dream of cleansing my soul appropriately—with the aid of your advice and your examples, Father."

Alas, the venerable abbé did not see, in the physiognomy of the rogue, a certain truly disquieting sarcastic smile, nor his green eyes, nor, on his forehead, two black patches underlining two protuberances that resembled flattened horns.

He did not see anything! He consented to receive the novice Schwartz, and everything was settled. The old world had ended and a new world began.[4]

At any rate, as soon as the novice Schwartz was introduced, the existence of the convent seemed singularly troubled. The Augustine monks, so meek and so pious, who provided the edification of the town, as they did in all the Germans' burgraviats, margraviats, duchies and grand duchies, suddenly became anxious, nervous, susceptible and quick to disputation. The Augustine's beautiful chapel no longer saw a full attendance every day at all the offices. The idle monks only arrived one at a time, slowly. Often, they even left Father Gottlieb all alone in the chapel, in his abbatial pulpit, and the latter was frequently obliged to ring the bell for matins himself.

The cloister where the monks had once strolled two by two, gravely, talking about edifying matters, resounded with arguments and vociferations, when it was not with laughter and songs.

Only the monk Schwartz consoled the poor prior somewhat; in him alone was piety and austerity still manifest, and all the virtues by which the good Augustines of Freiburg had once been distinguished. In chapel, when the other monks were asleep on their benches, his was the voice that was heard accompanying the quavering of the old abbé: a strange, resounding voice, with rumblings and rollings like an organ, and sudden boomings that made the windows shake.

At the sound of that voice the sleeping monks woke up, to quarrel more bitterly. Schwartz sniggered, the old abbé wept, and the convent became a veritable Hell.

What is more, that rage of disputes spread outside the walls of the convent, in starts and surges, when Schwartz's voice, singing in the chapel, burst forth with bellowings that

---

[4] A monument to the probably-fictitious Berthold Schwarz, or Schwartz, was erected in Freiburg in 1853, thus laying claim to the legendary inventor on behalf of the town.

made the whose edifice vibrate and caused the steeple to oscillate. Domestic troubles, squabbles between burgers and the lower classes, brawls and scuffles over everything—the entire town and the surrounding areas went crazy, in a perpetual fury of fighting, and the duke, who was ruining himself with armor and arbalests, marched back and forth over his lands, showing his teeth and seeking a quarrel with his neighbors.

At the convent, the monk Schwartz deployed a prodigious activity. He seemed to be everywhere at once, circulating in the corridors and the cloister, always sniggering, with a kind of grating sound that made the two points of his long red beard stick out; and he sang in the chapel, where his mere appearance caused something akin to a shiver of fear to pass through the old colonnettes, and something like the pulse of a tocsin through the bell-tower.

He received numerous visits, from lords with nobly rebarbative faces, messengers with shady expressions and students of famished appearance, and he spent long hours of the day and night in his cell, occupied with mysterious labors.

Brother Schwartz's cell made the other monks anxious; they ran away from it in terror. Sulfurous vapors and nauseating fumes escaped from it continually, and sometimes even flashes like lightning and long rapid flames—not to mention the muffled growls that had caused the monks to flee from the neighboring cells.

Inside, it was a genuine den of alchemy. There was no crucifix or holy images on the walls, but retorts and flasks of all kinds, furnaces, basins, mortars, bottles, incomprehensible documents nailed to the wall, old books and dog-eared parchments.

And Schwartz worked, pulverized, crushed and kneaded, always stirring, scuttling and sniggering...

The visits multiplied. Did not a day arrive when the Duke himself arrived at the convent, with three or four individuals who had their faces buried up to the nose in their cloaks?

Thicker smoke spread from the monk Schwartz's cell, swirling around the galleries and the cloister.

Schwartz's face became more and more disquieting; his eyes launched fulgurations, his beard danced and writhed as hoarse and creaky sniggers passed through this throat.

Finally, there was massive popular excitement one day in the vicinity of the convent, and an upheaval in the Augustines' abode.

Here comes the Grand Duke again, with a numerous retinue, with mounted lords, leaders of troops and captains decked in shiny armor. They have been summoned by the monk Schwartz for a final experiment.

The monks are convinced the Brother Schwartz has found the means, at the peril of his soul, to manufacture gold, and has offered the secret to the Duke, in exchange for honors, in addition to some solid fief.

The noble lords crowd behind the prince in the corridors of the convent, while the latter is content to stick his head around the door of the laboratory cell in order to cast a suspicious glance around it.

A strange sight, that cell and the things inside! That big barrel, carefully covered, must be full of the product of the monk's industry, and the smaller casks glimpsed to either side in the smoke. The monk has obviously not been lying to them. It is the triumph!

Brother Schwartz sniggers and rubs his hands. Yes, it is the triumph—you shall see, noble lords!

He whispers for a long time into the ear of the Duke, whose eyes grow wide and sparkle with satisfaction. He gives each of the lords a piece of parchment on which he has scrawled his formula, along with a cask full of a specimen, which he engages them to take home immediately and put it in a safe place.

Brother Schwartz is still sniggering and taking long strides around his cell and the corridor; at every step the gangling monk seems to expand and get taller; phosphorescent gleams pass through his eyes. In front of him the proud burgraves and mercenary leaders feel little frissons running through their bones.

The monk asks them to step away. He is going to carry out one last experiment; they will see well enough from the far side of the garden.

Now they are huddled, slightly anxiously, under the abbé's trees, noses in the air, looking toward the gallery to which the cells open.

They do not have to wait long...

Suddenly, there are sinister rumblings, jets of flame, a frightful suffocating odor...and then a mighty explosion resounds, which throws them all to the ground, terrified. A tongue of flame roses up, dancing, into the sky, as high as the steeple of the chapel, which oscillates and leans over, and beneath the flame, whirlwinds of bitter smoke spurt forth...

Half of the convent is lying on the ground, thick walls broken, arches smashed, with a quantity of poor monks crushed and crippled.

Of the monk Schwartz not the slightest trace, not the most wretched morsel, was found. Some people, who had good eyes, claimed to have clearly distinguished him in mid-air, in the fiery tongues of the explosion, capering madly, immeasurably grown and still sniggering, with enormous horns on his forehead and a long tail.

The Duke, the noble lords and the captains, undamaged, merely frightened, ran away swiftly to their homes, in order to put away the casks of the specimen offered by Schwartz in safe places, along with the formula for renewing the provision at will.

A marvelous gift, more precious than potable gold! It is soon perceived in the world that Schwartz's discovery has not fallen into the hands of negligent idlers.

And that is only a beginning, that coarse little powder, simple and easy to use—exactly what was needed, in times of obscurity, for rude and primitive men habituated, most of all, to striking hard in battles. Meek searchers and excellent chemists would subsequently improve it greatly!

The monk Schwartz

Second Prologue
1909: The Solemn Inauguration of the Palace of Peace
in The Hague

One Congress succeeds another for the inauguration of the superb and grandiose Palace of Peace erected at the expense on the American billionaire Carnegie[5] to the glory of modern civilization, triumphant over the somber ideas of the past.

There is a Congress of scientists and pacifist philosophers, the flower of all the Academies, all illustrious, all venerable or in the process of becoming so, and all venerated, the champions of peaceful and fecund progress, which is working for the wellbeing of peoples, transforming the world, and is about to bring about an Edenic era, a renascent Golden Age for all the races of the Earth.

And finally, there is a diplomatic Congress: ministers and statesmen, decorated with all possible orders, perhaps less venerable in appearance, but full of good will, won over to great and noble pacifist ideas, sent by their respective governments to draw up appropriate international conventions codifying the new rights of peoples and imposing obligatory arbitration to regulate peacefully all the questions, all the dif-

---

[5] The Steel magnate Andrew Carnegie (1835-1919) financed the building of the "Palace of Peace" (which now houses the International Court of Justice) in The Hague. There was no conference there in 1909—it was not officially inaugurated until 1913—so the one described in the story is purely symbolic. The second Hague Peace Conference of 1907 had produced a number of conventions relating to the arbitration of national disputes and rules of war relating to bombardment, the laying of mines, etc., many of which were violated during the war of 1914-18. Chemical and biological warfare were not fully incorporated into the network of conventions until the Geneva Protocol of 1925.

ficulties and all the differences that might emerge between nations in the future...

What a magnificent prospect is opening before pacified humankind—a marvelous vision! All the old quarrels extinct, mildness and benevolence universal! The triumph of science, man dominant over matter, domesticating the blind forces of nature, subjugating the elements in order to put them in the service of creative, redemptive and regenerative Progress! Wellbeing, fecundity, expansion and happiness everywhere!

That is what they were saying, those benevolent scientists in spectacles, while congratulating one another and offering felicitations to the present generations for living in such a beautiful, gentle and glorious epoch! A fusion of peoples, a universal embrace!

And the diplomats nodded in assent, as they signed protocols and conventions.

Conclusively finished, the ages of brutality and Medieval barbarity! All chains fallen, the old fortresses crumbling, frontiers being effaced, the earth is opening up and offering itself, entire, to human genius. Modern man is carving and slicing across the continents, going to search in the entails of the globe for hidden riches that will gives impetus to industries and carrying wellbeing and abundance everywhere. He is exploring the abysms of the seas, capturing and directing natural energies, correcting torrents and straightening cataracts, utilizing the lightning of the heavens for all kinds of tasks—and now he is launching himself into the clouds with his airplanes and his dirigibles, and flying at full tilt through the immensities of the azure, in the immediate vicinity of God!

What joy! How sweet it is to live in such beautiful times, and finally to see the realization of the dreams of all the seekers of the ideal, all the illustrious thinkers of yore!

For six weeks, every evening, the emotional speeches of philosophers and scientists, and the elegant harangues of Statesmen, transmitted by the telegraph and reproduced in all languages by the newspapers of the entire world, have been carrying the good news everywhere.

The Congress, having completed its work, is holding one last session before the great banquet that, naturally, will mark its closure before the separation. The International Convention has just been signed by the diplomats and *chargés d'affaires* of all the powers. On this solemn day, History is inscribing on its tablets the definitive triumph of ideas of enlightenment and progress over the powers of darkness and violence.

From now on, no more wars, no more conquests, no more peoples trampled, right coming before might—or, rather, might respectfully bowing down before right. Humanity can breathe freely. No more armed conflicts between peoples, between brothers gone astray. Obligatory arbitration! It is agreed by a solemn convention concluded between all the government that all differences—if any can still emerge—will be submitted to obligatory arbitration.

Fortunate twentieth century, destined to profit from the harsh experience of hose preceding it!

Everything is settled. It is signed. General congratulations in all languages; the members of the Congress throw themselves into one another's arms and embrace—and in the benches to which a select public has just been admitted, people are weeping with joy.

After the session, the most notable personalities of the Congress, philosophers and scientists, jurists and diplomats, remain to chat in the great Salon of the Presidency. One sees them separating, carrying away the joyful certainty of having opened for the world a marvelous era of fecund and civilizing peace.

Bless you, Torches of Progress, luminaries of Science—you who have prepared the way for the universal embrace!

Everyone is talking at the same time; only one of the Congress members—a tall, then man, stiff and bald—is saying nothing, contenting himself with twisting his russet beard. A philosopher with long white hair, greatly moved by the splendid perspectives opening on such a rose-tinted future, almost falls into his arms, while wiping away gentle tears.

"Well, dear colleague in pacifist philosophy, it is to Science that humanity will owe this happiness, to the peaceful conquests of Science, to its discoveries, its triumphs over matter! At the closing banquet of the Congress we shall drink to Science, queen of the world, to past discoveries, to those that tomorrow is preparing, and will give to us, to the sublime discoveries that human genius is multiplying every day!"

"Hurrah for Science!" says the colleague. "Look, my good sir, in the matter of discoveries, I have here, in my pocket, a design for a new engine—marvelous, I guarantee! Admirable, this engine, I tell you in confidence, for a submarine! Oh, Monsieur, the submarine—what a magnificent agent of progress! This engine would also suit the airplane, the superb bird that suppresses all frontiers and brings people together. I have one of those too, on this piece of paper—a new model of aircraft, larger—armored, even...this model has all the necessary qualities for great voyages: rapidity, power, and the possibility of carrying a considerable load! A precious machine, sir, if one wanted to bombard a city or a fortress...I'm joking, naturally; my aircraft will never carry anything but married couples on their honeymoon...

"It's like these little designs for an improved torpedo. Admire the ingenuity of a discovery completely useless henceforth! I'm keeping it as a curiosity... Oh, this...this is something else—a sketch for an asphyxiating shell. Bizarre, isn't it? But interesting, as an idea? It's beautiful, science, even applied to the search for such useless things. I also have a little plan for an improved zeppelin, a marvel that I've concocted to amuse myself...it would be very nice to realize it and very useful for peaceful voyages around the world...for the benefit of people who are afraid of sea-sickness...

"These little sketches are for research of another kind. This one is a portable gas apparatus for use in campaigns, and this one is for diffusing toxic vapors...original ideas! That reminds me that in my moments of leisure, I've succeeded in isolating the most dangerous microbes at the maximum of virulence...and notice, sir, that it would be sufficient to drop one little bomb—a bombette—furnished with those tiny creatures on a city to cause a serious epidemic. It's very curious…it's certain that our ignorant and barbaric ancestors would never have dreamed of that…

"And I still have a number of other pretty little inventions, thoroughly studied and carefully put aside, for the love of science…"

The diplomats of the Congress had formed a circle; they were listening, very interested by all the ingenious things of which use would obviously never be made.

"Who is that gentleman, then? Remind me of his name, I beg you," one of his colleagues asked the slightly alarmed pacifist philosopher.

"You don't know him? It's the great engineer Satanas, a worldwide celebrity, who dearly wants to put all his science and all his genius as a seeker at the service of our ideas, for the peace and happiness of humankind."

"Admirable!"

The great engineer Satanas, who was following them with his gaze, was still twisting his beard and smiling at them amicably while giving a few explanations to the interested diplomats.

But we know him, that engineer of genius. He is not the alchemist with the face of a Medieval sorcerer, he is the famous scientist, very modern and so well known, illustrious and celebrated: engineer, inventor, constructor, chemist, physicist, Nobel prize laureate, member of all the Instituts, correspondent of all the Academies of Science in the world…it's curious, however, how much he resembles the monk Schwartz, of Freiburg im Brisgau!

"The gas! The gas!"

Part One: The War of Science

I. Various strange details of my return to Europe and momentous arrival in an unknown land.

It was in April 1914 that the Hutchinstone expedition, admirably equipped, set forth on its great voyage of polar exploration. I, Paul Jacquemin, was the expedition's naturalist. We felt full of confidence and hope. All the scientific notabilities on the world had addressed flattering telegrams to us. They were counting on us, anticipating discoveries of immense interest. Glorious perspectives...

Unfortunately, our boat perished, crushed in a collapse of the ice-sheet, in August of that year, just as we were entering the truly interesting zone of the polar regions. Those of us who did not follow the wreckage of the ship under the accursed ice-cap were able, after various vicissitudes, to set foot on a rocky islet almost constantly surrounded by ice, solely frequented by polar bears and penguins,[6] and the poor Hutchinstone expedition was doomed to live for I don't know how many years in lamentable distress, cut off from all communication with the rest of the world, lost, forgotten and desperate!

However, a few months ago, the Ocean, our jailer, brought to our icy rock the debris of wrecked ships in considerable quantity: an extraordinary windfall, a stroke of luck of which it was necessary to take advantage. Quickly, we set to work, so effectively that we reassembled the least dislocated elements of that debris.

We embarked supplies of bear-meat and frozen cod, and a provision of penguin eggs; and, quivering with joy, we piled

---

[6] Robida was not the only armchair traveler of his era to be unaware of the fact that there are no penguins in the Arctic.

into our wreck. Then, with improvised sails, we set forth for good old Europe!

It was a difficult and hazardous voyage, and also very slow. Our sailors were old and disabled, we had no nautical charts, and very little of anything else.

Once we were in the open sea, we expected to be rapidly encountered and picked up by some ship, fishing for cod or whatever, but to our great astonishment, we saw nothing on the deserted ocean but numerous wrecks in a worse state than our own, floating just beneath the surface. What surprised us even more, as we approached what we estimated to be the Scandinavian coast or the north of Scotland, was that there were no lighthouses in the distance to show us the way—not one kindly light to warm our hearts and indicate a hospitable port, before we had finished consuming our supplies of bear-meat.

We were sailing in search of land, groping our way, if I might put it like that, when, I don't know how, in the middle of the night but in the most beautiful moonlight, as I was on watch, my wide eyes scanning the horizon, a frightful explosion sent us all, passengers and ship, in little pieces, to the bottom.

After the shock, when I came back to the surface and recovered consciousness, along with a little strength, I found that I was the sole survivor of the survivors of the Hutchinstone expedition, hanging on to a fragment of broken mast, face to face with a young man I did not know, who seemed just as frightened as me.

I had never seen him before; he was not a member of the Hutchinstone expedition. Where had he spring from? How did he come to be there, astride my fragment of mast? That was a truly extraordinary surprise.

"How do you come to be here?" I exclaimed, as soon as I could speak. "I don't know you..."

"I was here before you," he replied. "This mast is mine. I saw your boat blow up, and even received the pieces on my head. As for me, I was blown up the day before yesterday. I've been floating in this deplorable state for forty-eight hours."

My amazement was redoubled.

When our emotion had calmed down slightly, we introduced ourselves. I was coming from the North Pole, he had arrived after a long haul from a small island in the Pacific Ocean, and we had met up between two explosions in an unknown sea, without having perceived a single sailing ship or steamer during our long journey.

That solitude of the oceans and seas frequented by so many ships, at the intersection of so many shipping lanes, amazed me. It even made cold shivers run down my back—a few more of them, since I was already shivering from that unexpected complete bath. I came back to our accident—or, rather, accidents, since there was also the young sailor's.

"It's utterly incomprehensible," I said to him. "What blew us up? A floating mine? A torpedo?"

"I don't know," the young man replied. "But there isn't much traffic around. For days on end I've seen suspicious objects floating among the wreckage and carcasses of ships. I try to keep my mast away from them, for fear of another explosion."

"What does it all mean?"

"I don't know—but look over there, at that sort of buoy that the wind seems to be pushing in our direction. Look out! Let's try to push it away gently if it comes too close. I don't trust it!"

A little frisson passed through me, and my teeth started chattering. "The water's cold," I said, to explain my emotion.

"Yes," said the young man. "That's the worst part of the situation—I'm frozen. But perhaps we'll be lucky enough to see land before nightfall, or encounter a bit of wreckage more comfortable than our bit of mast. It's quite possible, for since the morning of the day before yesterday, I've already passed an empty barrel, a yard-arm, and half a launch—which I had to let go, because it was obviously about to sink. It was a good find, though, that launch, because I was able to pick up this crate of food you can see over there, solidly moored to that bit of topsail. Do you want a bit of sausage and a swig of whisky?"

I accepted enthusiastically, and thanked the providential young man. Then, warmed up by the whisky, I thought about my poor companions on the expedition, who were asleep in the cabin at the moment of the explosion, dreaming about the return to old Europe, their families and friends, and the tranquil life that awaited them there. Where were they now? Rolled by the waves I don't know how many fathoms deep, alas. Alas!

To escape that vision I recommenced my questions.

"But what does it all mean? We ought to be able to see fifty ships on the horizons: steamers, commercial three-masters, big trawlers, fishing boats…but nothing! Nothing but wrecks. Or mines, which is worse. Has there been some cataclysm, some upheaval, in this region north of Europe? Young man, since 1914 I haven't seen anyone, not a single human being, except for my unfortunate companions, drowned just now, and I haven't read a single newspaper. That makes fifteen years, since, if there's no error in my calculations, it's now 1929…"

"You don't know anything, then? You don't know? I'm only a little better informed myself. Wait until we're a little more tranquil, and I'll tell you what I know. For the moment, let's look out for squalls!"

We had drawn closer together. Both sitting stride our fragment of mast, attached to the topmast by a coil of rope, tossed around by an incessant movement, we scanned the horizon anxiously as we rose to the crests of the waves, to descend again thereafter into the dark green hollows, the sinister valleys of the Ocean, where I thought I glimpsed strange dismantled carcasses, formless and disquieting masses, rolling beneath the surface.

He was right, the young man; more than once, in the course of a long and mortal day, we had to avoid, and with a great deal of difficulty, buoys of malevolent appearance, the impact of which might have pulverized us, or bits of wreckage hurled at us at great speed by the brutal and malevolent waves.

The swell increased, the sea became darker and more difficult, and I closed my eyes in discouragement. Soaked and half-drowned, stunned by the shock of the waves that broke over our heads, what would become of us when night fell?

The young man passed me the whisky again.

"Buck up!" he shouted to me. "Hang on, look over there! There's a wreck of a boat that seems to me to be in fairly good condition. It's gaining on us—if we can grab hold of it as it goes past, we could be almost dry before long, and I think we might sleep tonight!"

He was adroit, the young man, and less rheumatic than me. He was able to get hold of the wreck when the waves brought it closer to us, and succeeded in hauling me aboard, after the crate of food had been securely tied down in the most solid part of the boat.

What satisfaction! We were almost dry in that wreck, except when a wave bigger than the rest broke over us.

Night could come; we would try to pass it as least badly as possible.

"Lovely sunset," said the young man.

I didn't care about the sunset! Exhausted, I could do no more; I was already closing my eyes, without distinguishing anything but vague red and yellow gleams in a westerly direction.

"Quite beautiful," the young man went on. "But no sign of wind. Let's hold on!"

The night wasn't too bad. We took turns to sleep—or rather, when my turn came to watch, I contented myself with drowsing, opening an eye, with difficulty, every half hour, when the cold woke me up.

Dawn deigned to appear; while I slept, broad daylight arrived; hunger extracted me from my dolorous dreams, and the young man completed my awakening by giving me a thick slice of ham, almost shoving it into my mouth.

"Have we arrived?" I said.

"Not yet," he replied, "but let's eat anyway."

We ate. No land in sight. The day passed. We ate again. I saw, anxiously, that the food supplies were visibly depleted.

Nightfall again. This time, I watched the sun set.

"Lovely!" the young man repeated.

"Sinister," I said. "Those red and black stripes don't suggest anything good to me!" Indeed, the inkpot soon overflowed into the sky; the weather was decidedly turning bad. There was no thought of sleep that night. What shocks! And what creakings in every plank of our boat! What furious assaults the waves delivered! We thought more than once that our last moment had arrived.

The squall caught us from behind and we sped. We must have covered a lot of distance! All night we flew vertiginously, in a whirlwind of foam.

Toward morning, without expecting it, having not perceived in the horror of the darkness any shore or beacon, we were hurled on to the coast, tumbling on to sand, fortunately friable, in the midst of the debris of our shattered craft.

I was lying down, or rather embedded, in the sand, half-stunned, and I saw my young stranger rubbing his shoulders and feeling his limbs, fifteen meters away.

"Nothing broken?" I shouted, when I had got my breath back.

"I don't think so. No, I'm all right, I can stand up. You?"

"Me too," I said, hauling myself painfully to my feet.

Oof! We were dripping like sponges, bruised and frozen; the air was keen, the dawn hardly casting a few wan gleams over the gray, flat landscape.

Where are we? Norway? England? No rocky cliffs, nor mountains framing our beach, so it's not Norway.

Anyway, we'll go and see. Saved! Finally, saved! What joy!

I could have kissed the sand of that beach that had collected us, all in all, rather gently, when we might have been crushed on some rock.

"Let's walk to warm ourselves up, and try to find help in some village."

And we set forth, walking straight ahead, at hazard, since we couldn't see anything: not a single steeple, or house, or farm. The coast was nothing but sand dunes, green or yellow undulations, with no clumps of trees.

We walked for more than an hour. Still nothing, and no one. There were no inhabitants on that shore, then, whose yellow silhouette we could now distinguish, in the daylight, from the somber sea?

Ah, here's something: traces of human labor, lines dug in the sand, with embankments to the side, retained by fastenings. It's old and half-demolished. *Ouch!* I step on a round iron object buried in the sand, and nearly lose my footing.

I clear away the sand and try to pick the object up. Damn! It's a shell. There must have been firing exercises around here, so we're in a civilized land.

We go on. Ruins now: a mass of red tiles in an extraordinary chaos of tangled woodwork, on heaps of pulverized bricks. There were once houses here: a group of habitations, a kind of hamlet.

Then there's a little rivulet…or a canal rather, for there are the remains of stone banks in places, and the iron debris of a bridge, beside more heaps of bricks and wooden beams.

What, then? What's happened? An earthquake? A cyclone? It's very strange! I rummage in the debris, looking for a clue. Oh! Over there, in that group of houses, a church! There are the vestiges of the altar, a capital, and a fragment of a Gothic balustrade...

And all that smashed to smithereens. Decidedly, a cyclone must have devastated this corner of old Europe. But those shells? We're still searching. I pick up bizarre fragments of metal. My anxiety and disturbance increase. In his turn, my companion stumbles over round objects. A shell...two shells...three whole shells...and then others, many others, in fragments of various sizes.

Damn! Damn! Damn! War has passed this way. These ruins seem more recent than the first. We've been unlucky!

I scan the horizon in vain; I can't see anything, except bumps in the ground here and there, which might be more ruins.

No noise: a deathly silence around us; no appearance of movement anywhere.

What does all this signify? This frightfully deserted landscape, this devastation, this silence…what? War? Revolution?

We keep on going, cautiously.

Suddenly, as we're climbing over heaps of bricks in a fold dip in the terrain, people hurl themselves upon us, uttering clamors in an unknown language. They knock us down, in spite of our resistance, violently applying cloths to our faces soaked in I don't know what.

We struggle, and we howl, but we're gagged, jostled and thrown into a dark hole, pell-mell with the brutal men, who hasten to shut a kind of door made of thick planks, after having ignited a heap of straw and branches, already prepared inside.

II. Brigands or rescuers?
The asphyxiating cloud.

What is this band of brigands, and what do they want with us? What are they trying to do to us? Bad luck is pursuing me! I'm bruised all over my body, and my gag is making it very difficult for me to breathe.

While I struggle, I notice that our aggressors are gagged too—or, rather, their faces are covered by a sort of hood or mask with goggles, which gives them a repulsive physiognomy. They have two enormous round or square eyes, with a kind of snout, and a bestially menacing expression.

I must look like them, with this mask that they've buckled over my face. There's some chemical ingredient inside the snout that is suffocating me. I cough and cough!

My young companion is doing the same. In spite of his coughing fits, he's distributing kicks at the people who are holding him.

As I try, in spite of everything, to remove my gag, I finally distinguish a few words in the inarticulate cries that the bandits are uttering.

"The gas! The gas!" they're shouting. "Beware, or you're dead!"

More threats! I shout to my companion to give up, in order to avoid our being killed.

Meanwhile, one of the individuals grabs me from behind and howls in my ear: "Leave it on! Are you mad? We told you there's Boche gas. Didn't you see the yellow cloud coming toward us? Boche gas!"

"What's that?"

"Where have you come from, fool? You look like an intelligent man, though. Boche gas! Asphyxiating gas!"

Ah! I begin to understand, and stop resisting. It appears that they don't want my life—on the contrary, they've saved me from an unknown peril. But what? What gas?

"Explain it to me," I say.

I can hear masked me all around me, taking in muffled voices. I catch a few words, in Flemish or Dutch, English too, and French, and even Italian. My interlocutor speaks French with a strong foreign accent. What a cavern of Babel! Where are we, then?

Now that I can see better, their eyes, behind the big spectacles, no longer seem as evil. These people are all dressed nearly the same, in bizarre garments, more or less ragged and muddy, and it seems to me that there are a few women among them.

The man who spoke to me first makes me sit down on a charred wooden beam, and sits down next to me. The others form a circle around us. I can see, now, that their expressions are benevolent.

"Don't worry," the man says to me. Here, you're almost safe. With our masks, and staying well wrapped up in our shelter, nothing will happen to us here—at the most, we'll feel a little stifled, a certain difficulty in breathing. That will pass. But for you, it was just in time. Another five minutes outside, the sheet would have arrived, and you'd be dead. Thank God that we had spare masks with us, as a wise precaution!"

My fear is gradually dissipating, but it gives way to a profound amazement. I renounce trying to comprehend, and let my arms fall. I'm bewildered, nonplussed. It's too much, too much. I gurgle *ohs* and *ahs*, endlessly.

My interlocutor gets impatient.

"Come on, at your age you must be a rational man. How were you imprudent enough…but first, who are you? You're French, it seems to me."

"Yes, yes, I'm French…a peaceful man of science, Monsieur," I reply, sighing. "A man of study and science, cast up on this coast after terrible adventures, by one last shipwreck, after…"

My interlocutor leaps to his feet, suddenly furious.

"Man of science!" he cries. "A scientist! Shh! Don't mention science—you're risking a poor welcome here. Look, the others are growling already! You're a man of science? Me too, unfortunately. I'm not paying you any compliment—oh no! We're colleagues, then; me, I'm a poor devil of a Danish scientist. Doctor of medicine and many other things…very repentant and disillusioned, I assure you. Oh, that slut Science! The harlot! The whore!"

It seems to me that the others, around me, are looking at me with hostile eyes behind their spectacled masks, uttering muffled exclamations, and their fists are clenching.

"The harlot Science! The horrid slut!" the Dane repeats.

"But please," I say, astounded. "Please…why the blasphemy?"

"Eh! You can doubt it, then? Without her, would we be buried in these ruins, in peril of death by asphyxiating gas, with other dangers lying in wait for us in every direction: being reduced to pulp by mines, torpedoes, explosions…devastations coming from the skies, by air-

74

craft…diffusions of epidemic disease by means of miasmas, or grenades of high-virulence microbes…etc, etc…what do I know? Not to mention, my dear Monsieur, the danger of dying of hunger, if we escape violent and rapid death—and that danger isn't the least, as I fear that it's imminent!"

"What are you saying? What jokes are you babbling? Aren't we in a civilized country?"

"Yes, if you can see clearly, since it's full of shells. But you, Monsieur, be more careful what you say...to accuse us of joking! Have you disembarked from the Moon?"

I was seized by a frisson; he seemed sincere in his indignation.

"Where are we, exactly?" I asked.

"In Holland, near Harlem—which is to say, close to the place where the good city of tulips, the lush city of Franz Hals, lived happily and tranquilly before the upheaval..."

I strove to understand.

"Where Harlem was, you say? But...Holland is at war, then? At war against whom, Seigneur?"

"Once again, have you fallen from the Moon?"

"Very nearly!" I cried. "Very nearly! Listen to me, my dear colleague, let me tell you…I've arrived from the North Pole! Yes, the Pole! The Hutchinstone Expedition—you must have heard of it. The Hutchinstone Expedition, departed in May 1914, never came back! Prisoner in the ice for fifteen years! Fifteen years! We were finally returning, the survivors, when, two days ago, an explosion, cause unknown, destroyed our vessel. I'm the last…the only one spared! All the others…swallowed up!"

"The Hutchinstone Expedition to the North Pole! I remember—there was a lot of talk about it once, before the Deluge! I remember...I understand…you don't know, then…you don't know anything! In that case, I have terrible, lugubrious, fabulous things to tell you, my poor Monsieur! But I can't tell you all at once…no, your brain would explode! The sole survivor, you say? And your companion?"

"I don't know him. Encountered at sea on a fragment of mast to which I clung on..."

"Returned from Polynesia," said the young man, who was following our conversation anxiously. "Marcel Blondeau, twenty years old, approximately. Sad adventures, me too; I'll tell you about them briefly. A long time ago, about 1914, when I was about four years old, my parents were coming back to France with me. We too were sunk by a floating mine...yes, already! Only a few survivors were able to reach land, an almost deserted rock. I was saved, but I was an orphan and was raised by kindly savages, scarcely rough-hewn, who had been cannibals forty or fifty years earlier..."

"Good and naïve cannibals," said the doctor, bitterly, "who would never, I'm sure, have invented all these...but do go on!"

"And I was coming back with a few old castaways, driven by nostalgia for old Europe, good old Europe, so beautiful and so sweet! Oh, Monsieur! Their stories, their memories had cradled my childhood on the Polynesian island. We were coming back, and we were blown up again, five days ago. A stray mine again! For the rest, I know a little more than the Monsieur who's come back from the North Pole, but not much. The war...the nations fighting for such a long time, all that is vague and very muddled in my head. I was coming back; I was bringing my arms, to serve the old country, if I could..."

"Pour young man from Polynesia!" said the Dane. "And poor Monsieur from the North Pole! I'll tell you everything, as gently as possible, in a little while, when the Boche gas has gone."

A fit of coughing interrupted him. I started coughing too, and the whole company did likewise; the atmosphere was becoming unbreathable; an odor of sulfur, or bromine— something horrible, I don't know what—filled our cellar. We looked at one another anxiously, without saying anything. Next to me, an individual of the female sex, muddy, like us, was suffocating and clutching her mask with her hands. It was evidently a woman; that was divinable even though she was enveloped in a kind of old infantry coat, threadbare and ripped.

We struggled against the suffocation for three quarters of an hour; then our suffering eased; the fits of coughing became more widely spaced and less violent.

"You said *Boche* gas—what does Boche mean? Is it a new scientific term?"

"No! Boche—the horrible Boche, the anthropomorphous Boche of the Prussified German tribes, the Boches of scientific barbarism, in sum! The new Huns, I'd say, if I weren't certain that, in doing so, I'd be slandering Attila, who didn't have their hypocritical and scholarly ferocity. Well, those asphyxiating gases are Boche, it's the Boches of the Palace of Peace in The Hague, not far from here, who send them to us..."

"Why?" I asked, stupidly.

The Dane shrugged his shoulders. "Not to be agreeable to us! Yes, yes, you've come back from the Pole, that's obvious! Know that the Boche trenches are five kilometers from here. The Palace of Peace, you recall, the great Carnegie foundation for the pacific conferences?"

"I know, I know..."

"No, you don't know. The ex-Palace of Peace, transformed, is both the central redoubt of the Boche positions in that direction, and their great factory of projectiles of all sorts, asphyxiating torpedoes, toxic gases..."

"But how? How? Explain it all to me!"

"Let me get my breath..."

The poor Dane needed a breather. Our semi-asphyxiation, the atmosphere of our cellar, the masks...all of that was hardly calculated to facilitate elocution.

We looked at one another for a while without speaking.

"Oh, great God!" I said finally, when I felt my throat slightly less acrid. "When shall I be in Paris? When shall I recover my pleasant and tranquil apartment in the Boulevard Montparnasse? That, my dear Monsieur, has been my great preoccupation during my fifteen-year sojourn in the Polar regions. On departure, anticipating that the expedition might be forced by circumstances to spend a few winters out there, I entrusted the care of my apartment and my natural history collections—one of which, above all, was particularly dear to me heart, an admirable collection of butterflies, unrivaled...unrivaled, Monsieur!—to my only nephew, a charming young man, tranquil and hard-working, like me, in those days. I made him swear to keep everything in order and await my return, no matter when, however long the delay...and that was fifteen years ago! You understand how much haste I'm in to get to Paris! An unfortunate hitch, this war!"

"Paris!" cried the Dane.

"Paris!" repeated the others, with a kind of snigger.

"Paris! But it's five years now...yes, a little more than five years, since we've had any news of it...five years in which we've known nothing. Before then, we succeeded from time to time in picking up a wireless message, and caught a few fragments of news...but along came another scoundrel of a Boche scientist, to discover a means of disrupting wireless reception absolutely and forever, all over the world, and it was all over. No more communication, no more anything!"

"Yes, we live in absolute blackness," said another, somberly. "Blackness in the head and in the heart, blackness everywhere."

"News!" sniggered a third. "Oh, yes—that's what we miss, as much as bread!"

"Newspapers! A newspaper, what a dream!"

"Families? Did we ever have families? Me, I don't know any more!"

"A house, a nice little apartment! Central heating! Eiderdowns...!"

*III. A fine meeting of human wrecks
and the debris of the Old World.*

"Five years!" I exclaimed, when I had recovered slightly from the shock. "Five years! This war has being going on for five years?"

"Five years, my dear Monsieur from the North Pole? No, not for five years, for many more. How long, alas, how many years has it lasted, the frightful carnage that has devastated the world and is eating away poor humankind? No one, or almost no one, knows anymore!" He interrupted himself with a fit of suffocation that made him clench his fists.

"Shush! Don't get angry—that does no good," said one of his companions. "You're right, this second war, alas, has lasted too long. Let's see, it's now 1929, isn't it? About the eighth or tenth of July, if I'm not mistaken?"

"The tenth. At the Pole I marked every day in my note-book, for want of a calendar."

"Here, in our burrows, we make a notch on a piece of wood every morning, for want of a calendar or a notebook. But one might make a mistake, you know..."

"So," the Dane went on, breathing more easily, "if it's the tenth of July 1929, the second war has been going on since...."

"Second!" I exclaimed.

"Yes, the second."

"The first, which concluded in our victory, began in August 1914," said the young man from Polynesia, advancing his mask before us. "I knew that, myself, out there in that savage island where I was brought up. I learned to read from an old collection of dispatches: French, English, American, Italian, Serb, Rumanian, etc. I would have told you that, Monsieur, on our piece of wreckage, if we'd been able to pay attention to anything but our salvation..."

"Then," I said, "the second war..."

"Has been going on for nearly ten years."

"Oh!"

That was like a sledgehammer blow on the back of my neck. I nearly fell backwards, and, in my distress, I snatched my mask away violently. Immediately, I was punished by veritable spasms of suffocation."

The Dane precipitated himself forward and, in spite of my unconscious efforts, buckled the apparatus over my face again.

"Keep it on! Keep it on for at least another hour or I won't answer for you! You'd be sick—very sick—and we don't have anything with which to care for you. My dear Monsieur from the North Pole, you have a great deal to learn. Hold still, and don't talk anymore! Keep calm—imitate your young friend from Polynesia. He's holding still..."

"He already knew something, while I'm learning everything at once! And my poor apartment on the Boulevard Montparnasse—can you tell me...?"

"We can't tell you anything about that, can we, Messieurs?"

All the masks in the circle around me made signs of negation.

"Excuse those personal preoccupations, Messieurs—I'm blushing about them now. I was thinking about my collection of butterflies, which I haven't seen for such a long time! Tell me, I'll be strong...let's see...that first war ended with our victory, though?"

"Yes, by in a botched peace, with ill-conceived conditions, and poorly-taken measures... Lassitude, enervation, the enormity of the questions, the difficulty of finding good solutions, the neglect of indispensable precautions...and above all--above all!—the work of Boche agents, the incredible folly of international socialist parties propagated by mental contagion, under the triumphant sniggers of the *Social-demokratic kaiserienne*...in brief, instead of radically excising the monster's claws and carefully breaking its teeth, we were content to erode them slightly, with gentleness and delicacy. False capital! Catastrophic forbearance, of which the entire world is now suffering the frightful consequences! Germany replenished her war materiel with feverish haste, multiplying its perfection tenfold...

"Her claws quickly grew back, her teeth were sharpened more furiously. Her aviation, her submarine fleet, her rolling bombards, her hordes of machine-gunners, flamethrowers and poisoners—the entire organism of massacre—was soon ready to function again, and the second world war burst forth.[7] General explosion, universal conflagration, total disruption of the planet. Total, my dear Monsieur—total!"

He stopped, his voiced strangled in his throat.

"Look," he resumed, after a momentary pause, "You won't believe me, if I don't show you right away a picture of the situation: a few human wrecks, the debris of the old world, scattered by the monstrous cataclysm. I'll introduce you to all

---

[7] This reference to a "*deuxième guerre mondiale*" [second world war] is early, but not the first, the phrase having been used even before the 1914-18 war ended.

these Messieurs, the comrades united here by the solidarity of suffering and the desperate struggle for existence. We have the time, unfortunately, before being able to risk ourselves outside..."

The circle had drawn closer.

"Here, one of your compatriots first: Monsieur Miraud, French aviator."

One of the men, perhaps the muddiest and most ragged of them all, bowed and raised his mask for a few seconds—just enough for me to see a bearded face that was trying to smile.

"Oh, an aviator dismounted for a long time," he said, "in this war of moles or burrowing termites, I've forgotten the intoxications of rising into the open sky and hunting the enemy aircraft from cloud to cloud, machine-gun duels at three thousand meters...all that's a long way away."

"Fallen, his wings broken, on to this coast some years ago, Monsieur Miraud is now with us," the Dane went on. "He crawls instead of flying. He's missing his left arm, as you can see—that's rather inconvenient."

"Bah! A matter of getting used to it," said the former aviator.

"Here, now, is Señor Estebano Gomarès, Spanish businessman..."

"At the *disposicion de Usted*," said a stout man, lifting his mask slightly. "I came from Barcelona to Amsterdam on business, after the first war. Imprudence, Señor, fatal imprudence! Forced to stay! Then Spain entered the struggle in her turn...imprisoned by the Boche; then retaken by the French, then tossed around with the Americans, the English...but always impossible to find a way to get back to Barcelona, by land, by sea, any way at all! Fatal imprudence—six years since I heard and mention of Barcelona!"

"Monsieur Demetrius Manoli, businessman, owner of oil wells in Rumania, numerous and once abundant. Enriched and ruined two or three times since the first war, ruined for good by this one."

One of the refugees nodded his head sadly, but all I could see of him was the underside of a rabbit-skin helmet, evidently of his own manufacture.

"Don't be downhearted, Monsieur Manoli—you're no more ruined than the comrades..."

"Monsieur Arbydian, also a businessman, from Andrinople…"

"A Turk?" I said.

"An Armenian, Monsieur!" cried a tall fellow, sharply, whose velvet eyes and black plush beard I was able to perceive momentarily. "Let us distinguish, I beg you...

"There is no more Turkey," the Dane put in, "but there are still Turks, since there are two or three old Turkish regiments with the Boches at the Palace of Peace—Turks Prussified for a long time, who can only pray to Allah in German!"

"But how do you come to be here?"

"I don't know…affair of banking; I was in finance when there were still finances. Anyway, today, still, I'm the sole capitalist among all these gentlemen, for I still have a pierced English coin, which I conserve as a fetish." From the pocket of a waistcoat made of packing felt, which certainly had not emerged from the hands of a tailor, he plucked a string, at the end of which hung a halfpenny bearing the effigy of King George.

"A true curiosity now, and a capital, in order to recommence business if the worldwide torment comes to an end one day, one way or another. Personally, Monsieur, I was surprised in Vienna by the tempest and driven all the way here, I don't know how...soldier enrolled by force by the enemy, prisoner, driver of automobile trucks, explosives worker, ditch-digger, maltreated, starving, tracked a little everywhere, but always escaping, by great good luck, the supreme catastrophe."

"Mr. Howard Gibson, American billionaire, and Mr. Bob Hatfield, American infantry major."

The major, dressed in furry pelts, had both legs wrapped up in old rags, but I could see that he was missing an eye. He laughed at me without saying anything, revealing a big gap in his jaw and an enormous gash across his face.

The American billionaire bowed. I glimpsed the long face of an Uncle Sam who had allowed his beard to grow in complete liberty. The billionaire did not look very cheerful, and beneath an old frayed overcoat, I perceived a wooden leg.

"Billionaire?" said Mr. Gibson, trying to force a smile. "That doesn't prevent me from digging in all my pockets, which are full of holes, in search of a fetish like Mr. Arbydian's."

"A billionaire in America, all the same, and that's something..."

"If I could go there! Any then, what state would I find it in, our America? You don't know, and me neither."

"But what are you doing here?" I asked.

"Ah," said the Dane, "that's a long story. Mr. Gibson made his billions furnishing cannons, shells, tanks, and so on, in the course of the first war. And wanting to make noble use of that fortune made by war, he disembarked in Europe as soon as hostilities ended, with the intention of adding a considerable wing to the Palace of Peace constructed in 1908 by the American Carnegie, and a Museum of the Horrors of War. All his plans were ready, and his collections already assembled..."

"That was a very noble idea!"

"Yes, and Mr. Gibson was passing on to its execution when the second war broke out. He was in The Hague to hurry the work along and to follow, at the same time, the sessions of a great International Pacifist Congress organized by German intellectuals and Social Democrats. You know the...but no, I'm forgetting that you don't know how the second war started...

"This is how it went: the Boches, who hadn't been flattened completely enough, whose war factories hadn't been fundamentally demolished, nor their machines, materiel and chiefs removed, suddenly threw themselves one vile morning on Holland. Aggression by sea, by land and by air! At the same time there were other attacks by the Swiss and elsewhere...but let's not bother with that, and stay in The Hague with Mr. Gibson. He was at the Peace Congress. Interesting session; a sensational speech had been announced by a famous German philosopher, but that day, our German intellectuals weren't in attendance. Suddenly, a *coup de théâtre* even more sensational than the advertised discourse: bombs falling from the sky, Zeppelins, Gothas and Fokkers, a rain of incendiary, asphyxiant and lachrymogenic shells...

"The Congress is badly hit; the session hall collapses. At the same time, we learn about the capture of Flessingue by Boche submarines, the forcing of the Helder, the bombardment of Harlem, the capture of Rotterdam, etc., etc. Personally, Mr. Gibson lost a leg. He found himself stuck in The Hague, a hostage of the Germans, who were able to amputate it, and a substantial part of his fortune at the same time. And Mr. Gibson only escaped from The Hague last year, after a great many tribulations."

Mr. Gibson sighed. The poor billionaire's misfortune had troubled me, but without giving me time to draw breath, the Dane resumed his introductions.

"Maître Saladin. Captain of infantry, previously a notary in a town in Flanders, alas, even more ravaged than him!"

A fit of coughing responded from a mask that inclined. I perceived a man so thin that his garment, a kind of long stiff sack, almost forming a dressing gown, seemed empty—and beneath it, another wooden leg.

A strange captain, and an even stranger notary.

"Monsieur Bustamente, lieutenant in the Peruvian infantry..."

"Peruvian!" I exclaimed. "There are Peruvian infantry in this war!"

"But yes, Monsieur, after we helped Brazil to recover the province of Sao Paolo, proclaimed a German Grand Duchy in

1924, and fought two campaigns on the Panamanian border against Boche guerillas from Mexico..."

"What?"

"Yes, and Monsieur Bustamente is one of the rare officers of a brave Peruvian regiment crushed by mines at the siege of Hamburg in 1926... Well, if you're surprised to see a Peruvian with us, what will you say when I've introduced you to Mr. Archibald Felton, volunteer in the New Zealand Grenadiers, wounded in a mountain skirmish...in Switzerland, during the defense of a pass in the vicinity of Porrentruy! Mr. Felton fell into the hands of the Boches, was able to escape from prison in Germany after three years of the most miserable existence..."

Mute with astonishment, I could only stare at the Peruvian and the New Zealander, while uttering hoarse exclamations in the depths of my mask.

"Don't splutter," the doctor continued. "This is Mohammed Bamakou, born on the banks of the Niger, a sergeant in the Senegalese Rifles; Monsieur Konang. the son of a mandarin from Hué, if you please, an officer in the Annamite Rifles; and finally, to return to Europe, Monsieur Jollimay, a professor at the University of Geneva, a soldier in the Helvetic Mountain Artillery; and Monsieur Vandermolen, from Harlem, a ship-owner whose last vessel sank a long time ago, but who weeps above all for the destruction of his home town of Harlem and the loss of his tulip collection."

Successively, the men thus introduced had raised their masks slightly, and I had been able to distinguish their features. I glimpsed the New Zealander momentarily: a fellow about thirty years old, not at all the tattooed Kanak that I had been expecting. The Senegalese rifleman was a tall fellow of the purest black. The son of the Annamite mandarin I had mistaken for a woman because of his stature, his beardless faced and his small Asiatic eyes. The Swiss artilleryman was a bony fellow of at least forty-five, with long arms and legs, thin features and a benevolent and frank expression.

"This gathering of the most diverse races troubles you a little; that ought to allow you to begin to comprehend the extent to which the worldwide catastrophe has shaken up, mixed up and pulverized its peoples! But I haven't finished the introductions. There are still two ladies, whom I kept till last; they're compatriots of yours."

Indeed, we still had another two companions in our hole. I say two companions because I could see hardly any difference between those ladies and the other refugees. I have mentioned that the garments of both sexes no longer had either form or color. With the masks, all were alike. Only the stature and a certain suppleness in their attitudes could allow their sex to be vaguely divined.

And their footwear! That truly lacked elegance; those ladies, like their companions, were shod in scraps of leather and canvas stitched together with thread or strips of cloth, as one might have seen on the most wretched tziganes in the most miserable land of the Orient.

"Madame Vitalis and Mademoiselle Vitalis," the Dane continued. "Two Parisiennes, one of whom, I believe, has never seen Paris…or very little! Their adventure is worth being narrated to you in detail, but I'm a little out of breath. Know only that in nineteen-something-or-other, Madame Vitalis, whose husband was a young lieutenant in the infantry, went with her daughter, born at the beginning of the first war, to see her husband on the Belgian front, and at the same time to transport woolen socks and sandals to her twelve godsons in the trenches…."

"Pardon?"

"The ladies will explain it to you later[8]… Know, then, that Madame Vitalis arrived, unfortunately, just as a gigantic

---

[8] They don't, but the novel's original readers would have been well aware that it was conventional during the Great War for Frenchwomen to "adopt" individual soldiers in the trenches, to whom they sent gifts of food and clothing, and who were conventionally referred to as their *filleuls* [godsons].

offensive was commencing along the entire front. Caught in the gears, she had to follow all the troop movement with a field hospital: advances, retreats, breakthroughs, charges, attacks and counter-attacks. Completely cut off from Paris, Madame Vitalis finally wound up, still with her daughter, in a village on the Belgian coast, packed off with the wounded.

"She stayed there for some time, while the distant battle carried off her husband, who had become a captain, a commandant and a colonel. She found him again one day, however, in a field hospital, wounded and almost dying. She cared for him, healed him, and lost him again shortly thereafter, forever this time, for one can be sure that he perished in the great attack on the retrenched Krupp camp, near Essen.

"Madame Vitalis and her daughter, after many other tribulations, ended up finding shelter, like us, in the caverns of Harlem, to which we shall go in a few minutes, when the danger has truly passed."

I was astounded, and I lowered my mask in order to press my forehead, for fear that it might burst. Someone told me that the gas mask ought to be maintained, like an extremely precious possession. But how could I stop the tumultuous gallop of my thoughts in my poor head? How could I master my nerves again, and rediscover the strength to question and reason, in order to try to understand? How many fabulous upheavals I had been enabled to glimpse by that strange gathering in a burrow beneath the dunes of Holland, of people of such diverse origins, specimens of races so scantly related, swept there by the frightful torment!

IV. The Doctor lands a few explanatory hammer-blows on my head.

It took me nearly three-quarters on an hour to recover somewhat from so many successive shocks; I felt, in consequence, a veritable mental collapse.

I must have appeared pitiful, wedged between the Dane and the young man from Polynesia. I bowed my head, but my mask could not stifle my sighs completely. I had been dreaming recklessly, and for such a long time, of the intoxication of the return to European soil, to a civilized country!

Huddled in my hole, my eyes closed, all those dreams passed before my mind's eyes again, involuntarily. And I no longer knew...

Come on! Let's see, am I going mad? Or am I dead already?

I was recalled to reality, first of all, by distant detonations, and then by the pangs of my stomach. I was hungry, therefore I was alive.

"What time does one eat lunch here?" I asked my neighbor, the Dane, abruptly, without really knowing what I was saying.

The Dane seemed stupefied. "Lunch?" he said. "You're hungry?"

"Well, we haven't eaten anything since yesterday evening, and it must be two or three o'clock in the afternoon, it seems to me. We've passed through terrible emotions, which have hollowed out..."

"That's a pity, but we don't have anything to offer you. No food at all! We were on a hunting expedition, trying to find some..."

"No one eats lunch any more, and no one eats dinner," said the professor-artilleryman from Geneva. "One eats when one can, when one has the luck to get one's hands on something that can almost serve as nourishment..."

"It's just a habit to acquire," said the Peruvian.

They were jolly, the joys of return! I certainly pulled a terrible face behind my mask, and I uttered a sigh of desolation that ended in a furious growl.

In order to try to forget my hunger, I started to interrogate the Dane again.

"My dear doctor," I said, "you've made the introductions; now I that know these gentlemen and these ladies, I'd be glad also to know to whom I owe my life—for it was definitely you who hurled yourself upon me first, in order to tip me into this burrow sheltered from the gas..."

"I told you, I'm a wretched man of science, a physician, doctor of natural sciences, something of a chemist; my name is Eric Christiansen, of Copenhagen. Among all the enormous fatalities through which we struggle blindly, destiny has rolled me as harshly as my unfortunate associates. My story is no less somber than theirs. In 1920 I was on campaign as a major attached to a regiment of Danish cavalry, first in Jutland—a rude campaign; then, transported to Italy, I took part in the retaking of Dalmatia from the Bolsheviko-Boches, the march on Vienna and the Bohemian campaign. I passed through Rumania, and then defended Constantinople against the Turco-Bulgaro-Austro...I don't know, exactly. I found myself in Poland thereafter, with a Portuguese corps, and then...I don't know any longer...

"Time passed; sometimes we stopped, white and frozen trench against white and frozen trench, during interminable winters. Finally, one day...it was in Silesia...half-frozen and half-burned in an explosion in one of our subterranean forts, three-quarters stunned by the collapse, I found myself a German prisoner. Then there was the prison camp, the forced labor, like all the prisoners, military or civilian, picked up in the lands occupied by the enemy or merely passed through by them. As I was a doctor, they naturally assigned me to making munitions..."

"What? Munitions?"

"Yes—chemical and medical munitions."

"Eh? What?"

"Chemical munitions—you've just sampled a little: a feeble specimen; poison gases. That's already an old game, but medical munitions...I hope you don't make their acquaintance, although it'll be very difficult to avoid it. Anyway, you'll probably see when the occasion arises...let's hope, if it comes to pass, that it will be benign!"

"Thank you," I said, rather anxiously.

"So, I was put to making medical munitions at *Chimische-Essen*, the pendant to the Essen of Steel, in an immense factory comprising a good five hundred armored laboratories, protected by electrified barricades...oh, well protected! At the slightest attempt to get out of the enclosure, inevitable electrocution! Don't worry, the installation had been very carefully organized. Twelve hours work per day, with just enough nourishment not to die completely, and the harshest treatment at any protest, or the slightest appearance of ill will. Horribly dangerous work...I've seen unfortunate wretches, forced to handle all the viruses, collapse over their bottles, poisoned.

"What work it was! The preparation of infectious cultures, studies of ferments and viruses; breeding and pulverizing of all the microbes and bacilli susceptible of transmitting the worst diseases and causing epidemics to break out; dosage of the products of our culture broths, arrived at maturity, in order to load them into miasmatic torpedoes, bombs, canisters, bottles, tubes, pastilles, etc...

"Those medical munitions, those projectiles if every form and nature, some destined to be employed by the artillery, others, apparently more innocent, seeming to emerge from an honest pharmaceutical laboratory, destined to be sown by aviation or carried by rivers and streams, to spread typhus, tuberculosis, glanders, smallpox, anthrax, cholera, yellow fever, or unknown and mysterious epidemics... The entire medical dictionary, in sum, put in bottles in accordance with formulae studied and established by Boche science!"

"Horror of horrors!"

"*Gesta diaboli per Germanos!*" said Jollimay, the artilleryman-professor of history at the University of Geneva.[9]

---

[9] Jollimay's wordplay echoes a classic riposte; a famous 12th century narrative of the first crusade by Guibert de Nogent described it as "*Gesta Dei per Francos*" [The Deeds of God via the Franks], a phrase occasionally borrowed by subsequent French historians to refer to the history of their nation—

"There's no other explanation. Oh, the Germany that we admired naively and stupidly, allowing ourselves to be taken in by its false façade, camouflaged so artfully! What a humiliation it is for us, alas, to remember before the enormous monster the no less enormous candor with which we fell into the trap—along with the entire world, however... Intellectual Germany! Gretchen with the blonde hair picking the petals off the daisy of Science! For us, apart from the Hohenzollerns in the depths of Prussia, apart from a clan of hawks and militaristic Bismarckians, there was nothing but intellectual Germany, the mild, friendly and scientific Germany! And we did not perceive it, loading its cannons behind a protective curtain of suave poets and worthy bespectacled scholars, preparing its satanic arsenal, accumulating its means of aggression, murder and pillage. Blind! Blind!

"Science, like war, was its industry, that Hohenzollern Germany: militaristic and militarizing science, organized with a view to the intensive production of anything that might serve to kill, to destroy, to massacre directly or indirectly... Come to us, chemistry, physics, electricity, radioactivity, bacteriology, etc., etc...and forward march for the King of Prussia!"

"I'm a doctor, alas," the Danish doctor added. "Well, now, I can give people diseases, but I can't cure them. I can't, not any longer! And, then, you remember, Jollimay, when the stock of medical munitions seemed sufficient, we were transferred to chemical munitions... Other abominations, manipulations no less dangerous, for the carboys of sulfur, the gas shells, the phosphorus shells...and the various explosives! The trinitrotoluene and the panclastite, the cresylite, the bromine, nitrogen peroxide....and the various employments of benzenes and kerosenes, and the poisoned mists, and the incendiary fogs, and all the diabolism of previously-unknown compounds, and the entire infernal dictionary of science, all the

---

inevitably calling forth the response that the history in question was more akin to "*Gesta diaboli per homines*" [The deeds of the Devil via humans].

satanism of Cornu retorts,[10] put in requisition and poured over the world by Germany. *Gesta diaboli per Germanos!*"

"May God crush them, all the instruments of that accursed science!" murmured Jollimay.

"He's in the process of doing so," said the doctor, grimly, "and all the rest of us with them: torturers and victims alike, we're all going the same way. I've had plenty of time to reflect on the subject, in all the holes where we vegetate lugubriously. Well, I believe that God has had enough of this planet, which does him no honor, and the creature emerged from his hands, who has decidedly gone to the bad. He's resolved to finish it and liquidate a failed operation. Once, the Bible assures us, he cleared away his work with a universal Deluge, but as God doesn't do things twice, he's renounced the method of water. This time, it's by fire that he's proceeded, by a deluge of iron and fire, and he's confided the work to humans themselves—the humans who find an atrocious satisfaction in deploying all their ferocity, conscientious and perfected, against themselves, in a racial and planetary suicide! The tree of Science, we know only too well now, had been planted by Satan, and Adam got his hands upon it on the very first day!"

"Calm down Doctor," said Jollimay. "You're no longer in the Boche factory..."

"No, no, fortunately, I'm no longer there, and nor are you, Jollimay, since we got out at the same time, escaped—God knows how—on the day when three-quarters of the factory blew up after a deflagration of trinitrotoluene, which then spread layers of poisoned fog, mortal waves of corrosive air, over a radius I daren't estimate! We were locked in our cell underground, but even with the threat, or rather certainty, of an imminent fusillade..."

---

[10] The French physicist Alfred Cornu (1841-1902) had several scientific instruments named after him; they did not include a kind of retort, but the attractiveness of the wordplay inherent in "*cornues de Cornu*" [Cornu retorts] encourages the pretence.

"Suspicion of sabotage of several tons of a new explosive," said the artilleryman Jollimay.

"Justified suspicion," said the doctor, laughing behind his mask, "for we had sabotaged them quite nicely, their gas shells...and others! Infectious bombs whose ferments we had destroyed in advance, bottles of bacilli carefully spoiled, charming little beasties rendered inoffensive..."

I saw his mask stir and shudder for some time under the shocks of silent laughter.

"Our subterranean cell had saved us," he went on. "We only had to push the door, dislocated by the explosion, and risk ourselves outside, prudently, when it seemed to us that the racket had calmed down. What ravages in the factory of death! But what joy for us! It was sufficient for us to pick up coats and helmets to give us the appearance of Boches, and slip away through the fogs with our masks on—no one could recognize us!

"Six months of traveling across unknown country, ravaged lands...and without a map or a compass, relying on luck to get us all the way to the allied lines...and we ended up, after getting turned around, trying all sorts of directions, always running into obstacles, lying flat in certain places, pursued and tracked, finally to end up here, all together, our group having grown somewhat on the way, swelled by the friends you see assembled, fugitives like us, encountered in equally sorry states, escaped like us from various places and tracked like us. We've associated our miseries..."

"In order to try to get out some day, I don't know when, or how," Jollimay declared. "There has to be an end to all this diabolism—there has to be!"

The doctor shook his head sadly. "There are two more of us now," he said, extending his hand to me and the young man from Polynesia.

V. Four wooden legs and a few other snags.

"There's no more danger—we can take off our masks," said the Peruvian lieutenant, who had ventured outside the burrow.

"At last!" I exclaimed, "Help me to undo it—I'm stifling underneath it, with that horrible odor of I don't know what."

"A mixture of hyposulfite, ammonia and various other products—it smells bad but it's indispensable. You'll get used to it, the mask—sometimes it's necessary to keep them on for entire days."

Everyone had unmasked, with a visible satisfaction, and we were finally able really to make the acquaintance of the people who had saved our lives—the young man from Polynesia and me. For three or four hours, in our hole, we had been confronted by creatures of nightmare, phantoms with the faces of fantastic beasts. Once we were rid of our hideous hoods, I found them all benevolent faces, very sad but genuinely sympathetic, and I shook hands all round.

Monsieur Bustamente, the Peruvian lieutenant, was a sun-tanned fellow of thirty-five or forty with hair already going white; Monsieur Gomares, the Spanish businessman, whom I had thought very stout, was, on the contrary, thin,

95

with a wrinkled face and neck. He was a formerly obese individual thinned down by the disagreeable life that he had to lead in the burrows to Holland. Only the various sacks of coarse cloth that served him as clothing gave him a false bulk.

Also formerly obese, Maître Saladin the notary-captain, doubly invalid, having lost one arm and one leg, seemed to have kept in spite of everything a certain joviality, for, seeing my gaze stay with alarm from his leg to his arm, he whispered softly into my ear: "It's not from birth! 310 mortar, a few broken bones at a bargain price and buried under the debris—but don't worry; pulled out three hours after the fact, just when I was beginning to get bored..."

"The Armenian Arbydian and the Rumanian businessman Manoli, both bronzed, one as curly-haired as a negro, the other with his forehead shaded by thick tresses that seemed carved from ebony, allowed the same expression of distress to ooze through their eyelashes, of Orientals disorientated under the cold sky of Holland, whereas the Senegalese rifleman appeared quite calm and relaxed. That Mohammed was a true negro; thick ruddy lips parted to reveal a formidable set of bright white teeth, his broad smile contrasting with the funereal aspect of most of the others. His eyes gazed at the Danish doctor with an expression of tranquil obedience, ready to do anything at the slightest signal.

The Annamite was ageless; I hesitated between forty-five and fifty years. Certain wrinkles at the corners of his moth made me incline toward the latter figure. I thought he looked intelligent and distinguished, with a certain arrogance. Remaking the introduction, the doctor told me that he was the son of a mandarin, and had graduated from the École Centrale de Paris in the class of 1915.

The artilleryman-professor Jollimay, the New Zealander Felton and the aviator Miraud were very thin, and so was the Dutch ship-owner Vandermolen, in contrast to the common run of burgers of his race. Everyone in the burrow had hollow and fatigued features, but those most of all.

The physique of the two Vitalis ladies was no more copious. In the young woman it might have passed for the slimness of youth, but for her mother it was a circumstantial thinness, like that of the Spanish merchant—which is to say, contrary to her nature, due to the deplorable kind of existence that events had forced them all to lead.

But where had my eyes been? In my disturbance, under the sledgehammer blows of the successive revelations, I had not noticed that Madame Vitalis, like the American billionaire, had a wooden leg. As she saluted with her head and upper body during the introduction, with the fine manners of long ago, I heard a dry click, and saw a wooden pillar scraping the ground lightly.

That made three wooden legs in the little troop. That was already a lot, but in his turn, Monsieur Jollimay, the artillery-man-professor from Geneva extended a leg of bizarre appearance. A fourth pillar! On looking harder, I perceived that the Senegalese rifleman was wearing an iron hook at the end of his right sleeve. Then again, the aviator Miraud was missing an arm...

What else? I examined my companions around me. The Spanish businessman had lost an eye. What that really all?

Madame Vitalis, perceiving my gaze obstinately returning, involuntarily, to the wooden stump projecting from her skirt—frayed and ornamented, if one might put it like that, with numerous pieces of cloth in overly various shades—pulled the pillar back inside, blushing.

Poor lady! Coquetry still, in this cellar under the ruins!

Dr. Christiansen noticed the movement. "My dear Madame Vitalis," he said, "don't hide that piece of wood. Doesn't each of us bear the marks of the savage beast's fury? Yours was a shell-burst received in a field hospital bombarded and set ablaze. A war wound—a glorious wound!"

Oh yes, all those unfortunates retained the traces of the teeth and claws of the diabolical beast!

Decidedly, I had returned from the Pole at a bad time, and landed in a sorry place.

Let us hope that we'll find something better further along, and that, notwithstanding the amiability of these good people and their benevolent dispositions in our regard, that we shall remain in this dangerous country for as little time as possible.

The most ravaged of all, in terms of physiology as well as aspect, was the poor Dane, Dr. Christiansen, my savior. I had not expected that funereal, devastated face with hollow cheeks, and haggard eyes profoundly sunk in their orbits: a lamentable face, completed by a drooping moustache and a white beard, a wrinkled forehead and a cranium like yellowed ivory, completely devoid of hair.

"Yes, we can risk ourselves outside," he said. "The layer of gas has been blown away, and will be lost at sea. We're all hungry, and we need to find some food before nightfall. We had come out to search for food supplies for Monsieur's house when we spotted you. Our provisions there are exhausted, and we need to take something back..."

"What?" I asked, slightly anxiously.

"Don't worry. Hunting, fishing and horticulture will, I hope, furnish us with something to give you for dinner tonight. Oh, very frugally—I beg you in advance to excuse us; our resources are exceedingly thin..."

We emerged from the refuge, and I rediscovered the landscape of devastation and ruins that had caused me such surprise after my first steps on European soil: crushed houses, scattered in heaps of stones and bricks, mingled with charred beams and twisted metal; disrupted terrains, enormous fissures whose origin I could not explain.

"Let's see—where are we, exactly?"

"I've told you—in the suburbs of Harlem."

"Harlem is over there, look, to the right" the Dutch ship-owner told me, in bad French, which he mingled with phrases incomprehensible to me, "and over here, you see, Monsieur..." He tapped the ground with is wooden leg. "This was my garden, where my fields of tulips were, my *bloementiunen*...if you had seen them, those rows of flowers, orange, violet, yellow, red…splendid, Monsieur, splendid! I'd paid as much as thousands of florins for certain rare bulbs. And you see, it was here…

"I've been able to save a few precious bulbs, which I cultivate in well-sheltered spots. Look, I keep four bulbs on me, in order to be sure of not losing them; once, I wouldn't have sold them for ten thousand florins, and now, what sadness, one of these days we'll be obliged to make soup with them, in order not to lose everything! Look, here are the ruins of the little windmill that pumped up the water for irrigation. The hole where we were just now was the cellar of my gardener's house; it's still solid, I was right not to skimp on its construction. It's a good refuge, as you've been able to judge…"

"I can't see Harlem," I said.

"Because you're looking for monuments…they're leveled, the *Groot Kerke*, the *Stadthuis*, the Museum…all of them! It's over there, in the direction of those cut trees; yes, that's it—there are lines of trenches made with the debris of the houses of the outlying districts. Behind those is the town…somewhat damaged…"

"We'll be going there shortly," said the doctor. "We live in one of the best houses, and we'll offer you hospitality. Presently, it's our dinner that it's necessary to find…"

"I'm anxious about our salad vegetables," said the son of the mandarin from Hué.

I looked at the vegetation on a bank, bizarrely withered and discolored. It had not been like that before. And the wild plants that had invaded the former squares of the tulip garden and covered the rubble everywhere with their vigorous shoots had lost their color.

"It's the gases that have passed over them," said Monsieur Vandermolen desolately. "Everything's withered."

While our companions dispersed in every direction, the doctor led the ladies, the young man from Polynesia and me toward the entrance to the opening of a trench, which was certainly several years old. We suddenly arrived before immense crevasses carpeted in places by vegetation. Some were very deep and pathways extended over their slopes, all the way to depths filled with yellow pools.

"Mine craters," the doctor relied to my mute interrogation. "There was a siege six years ago, when Harlem was retaken by the Boches. It made well-sheltered gardens; this is ours. We try to grow a few vegetables there. Alas, today's gas has spoiled everything—our poor salad vegetables are lost! Here, look at them..."

Indeed, on one of the slopes there were tufts of verdure that ought to have been lettuces, but seemed reddened and burnt.

The young woman had run into a fissure in the crater. The remains of a tunnel opened there—a black shaft into which I would not have ventured willingly. She soon came out with a large wicker basket, which her mother filled with the least sickly salad vegetables.

"Our potatoes look promising. The gas hasn't done them too much harm. In six weeks, if nothing bad happens, we can start digging them up. The artichokes look beautiful—it's precious, the artichoke; it grows anywhere!"

We went back up with our harvest. Madame Vitalis' wooden leg clicked on the pebbles of the crater. We walked for some time, climbing over heaps of rubble, stumbling into depths and following the guts of trenches.

The young woman made us take a detour; she had discovered two or three partly-broken plum trees sheltered in a hole, and wanted to see if there were any ripe plums. We picked a dozen, which went into the basket to join the vegetables.

VI. Encounters in the dunes.

We found ourselves back in the dunes, which formed true hills near Harlem, over which grand old trees had once waved their foliage in the sea breeze. Poor devastated woods! The majestic trees were now reduced to the state of jagged stumps, or sad slashed and shattered debris, imploring the heavens with their long denuded arms.

As we arrived at the ruins of a windmill that was still standing, on a substructure of stones, half-collapsed beams, with two sails hanging down limply, Mohammed's black head appeared at a small window.

"Good hunting!" he shouted. "I've got three rats today— but all three big and fat!"

So saying, he stuck out his arm, and made the rats, held by the tail, dance.

"Roasted, they're not bad," said Mademoiselle Vitalis.

"You eat rat, Mademoiselle?" sad Marcel Blondeau, his expression alarmed.

"Of course," she said, quite naturally.

While the doctor and the young woman made a tour of the windmill, searching for snails in the cracks, Madame Vitalis took me into her confidence. She talked to me about her husband, the colonel, about her youth in the brilliant Paris of old. She had lived in the same quarter as me, in the vicinity of Notre-Dame-des-Champs. I told her about my apartment; she had had friends in the house, perhaps she had met my nephew! She sighed as she remembered daytime visit's to lady on the second floor, the cups of tea, and the pleasant chats! Melancholy reminiscences, but full of sweetness. She sighed more in thinking about her daughter, a child of the war, brought up in the trenches, and who, poor thing knew nothing about society, and what a ladies' afternoon tea was, in the happy days of old! At eighteen, she had never seen a piano— yes, Monsieur!—except, one day, for a few pieces of rose-wood, with which, alas, they had done the cooking.

"Good!" said Mademoiselle Vitalis, returning with the doctor with the harvest of snails. "There's Maman, bewailing my fate! Of course I don't know anything about scales and pianos, it's a little gap—but I know how to distinguish the whistle of a big shell from that of a trench-mortar, an asphyxiant canister, shrapnel or an aerial torpedo, and that's much more indispensable. In any case, Monsieur, Maman, out of modesty, won't have told you, but she's given me, I assure you, as careful an education as possible. I can read, I can write, I can sew, knit, tailor clothes from no matter what, make shoes and repair them, make faggots and wicker baskets—in sum, I possess all the little pleasing talents of a well-brought-up young woman of our epoch!"

I told Mademoiselle Vitalis that I congratulated her of having successfully cultivated all those leisurely arts, which were now of such great utility, and I was about to ask her whether she added cooking to the list when the mother told me that she had reserved the cooking to herself since they had been living in a group in the house of the Harlem ship-owner.

"A delicate task! Not that these gentlemen are difficult—the times aren't right for gastronomy—but because it's necessary to add to indispensable experience a great deal of ingenuity, in order to succeed in not living entirely on privations, with things that it isn't easy to cook..."

She was dutifully describing a few of her more ingenious dishes when we were hailed by a head that seemed to emerge from the ground some distance away, level with the grass of the dunes.

We stopped. Monsieur Vandermolen immediately responded to the appeal.

"What is it?" asked the doctor.

"Come on," said Monsieur Vandermolen. "Someone's asking you for a consultation. It seems that there's a patient here. Let's go see!"

We made a detour toward the head, which explained something to the doctor. It was the hirsute face of an old mariner, with a white mane under an old discolored cloth cap.

When we came closer we saw that he was in a hole, like the entrance to a cave in the dune, on the other side of a hillock of sand that hid the sea. Another human burrow!

As we arrived, the head sank back into the hole and he doctor followed. Out of curiosity, I went down behind him, while our companions plunged into the long grass.

The hole was narrow and carefully lined with strong wooden beams. There were a dozen steps to descend, and we found ourselves in a deep chamber, illuminated—if one can use the word—by oblique shafts rising up to the dune.

When I had adapted somewhat to the gloom, I saw that the room bore a strong resemblance to a ship's cabin, with bunk beds on one side. A large green plank attaché to one of the walls of the cave-cabin bore the inscription in red letters: *Gredel-Vlissingen.*

"Yes," said the doctor, on seeing my astonishment. "They fished up the cabin of their old boat and reassembled it here, piece by piece..."

"Shipwreck?"

"Sunk! For want of a house, also destroyed, the family lives in here—what remains of the family, at least: one old woman, one young, one old man and four children. Since when? I don't know. They're worthy fisher folk of Flessingue, who washed up here and hollowed out this burrow..."

The family surrounded us; the children still had their masks on, except for a very small one, who was in bed.

"Let's see what's wrong..."

An old woman, bizarrely dressed in the remains of a Zeeland costume, explained to the doctor and Monsieur Vendermolen that the child, too young to understand the necessity of the mask, had struggled for a long time before allowing it to be applied to his face, and then had taken it off too quickly, and seemed very ill.

The doctor examined him, muttering.

"We've lost a lot of children like that—they're afraid of the mask, they don't like it...one can't explain the necessity to them...the gas comes and they succumb."

"Abominable!"

"I knew how to cause maladies," groaned the doctor, "almost all maladies, but I can't, I don't know how, to cure them! I tell these worthy folk that they have to try not to catch anything, that's the best thing. No medicaments—nothing at all! I can find herbs, but that's all. It's a long time since I've been to search the ruins of the pharmacies of Harlem…there's no longer anything there. Let's see, all that I can do…let's see…I still have a few old marshmallow roots, well, he'll drink a tisane, lots of tisane. That's the whole of my prescription. Go on, old chap, tisane for the little one, and confidence, confidence! I'll come back tomorrow."

"Is the child very sick?" I asked the doctor, when we were back in the daylight.

"It's quite serious; he's breathed in a little of the gas; he'll be ill for three weeks, at least. The tisane always does the bronchi good. Marshmallow, borage, a few herbs—that's all I possess in my pharmaceutical arsenal to struggle against no matter what indisposition or malady, and…well, the hygienic conditions in which we're vegetating aren't very good, as you've seen. The most important thing is to avoid starvation…I hope we'll eat this evening. Oh, if you'd arrived last week you'd have had, like us, to forget one meal in two!"

I could not dissimulate a grimace. Hunger had been clawing at me for two hours.

"Aha!" the doctor went on, when we had caught up with our companions. "There'll be rabbit! Our hunters have emptied the snares set in the dunes. How many? Only two? These dune rabbits have become very wary—we'll have to try fishing…"

The Peruvian lieutenant and the Dutchman had rejoined us. They showed us two fine rabbits, with satisfaction, which Monsieur Vandermolen made me feel and weigh in my hand. There had been a third, but it had been spoiled by the gas.

"Well nourished," he said. "There's no shortage of grass—but even so, they're not very plump. It's the worry, Monsieur, the chagrin, the desolation of the poor creatures.

Oh, the dune rabbits I once knew, so full of joy—one saw them in bands, entire tribes, bounding through the long grass and the violet flowers, warming themselves in the sun outside their warrens, watching the boats go by and sniffing the sea breeze! They were pullulating then. Today, you only catch glimpses of them; they only risk themselves furtively; they stay underground, quivering with terror in the depths of their holes..."

He sighed profoundly.

"Poor old dune rabbits! The cannonades that demolished the towns, pulverized the villages and turned all of nature upside-down have addled their brains. They thought it was all for them. 'Humans have become very nasty,' they said to themselves. 'Once they were content to annoy us from time to time with nice little rifles, which, with their little lead pellets, only stung the imprudent, frolicking around the hunters' feet. Now, they attack us with big canons, fire at us with heavy artillery, bomb us from on high with airplanes and send armored fleets to bombard us from the sea. And all the nations of the world join in! Instead of gangs of joyful children running through the long grass, and young Friesians or Zeelanders coiffed in lace, with golden curls over their foreheads and coral necklaces, chatting with their lovers under the beautiful windmills that caught the clouds with their great arms, turning up there in the sky, there are evil encounters everywhere, people of all colors, all armed, all hungry, and all falling upon us! And the Hellish flames that they hurl at us! And the asphyxiating gases that they drop on us. How wretched we are! How can we escape? We dig our warrens deeper, but in vain; their machines collapse everything. Humans, without a doubt, have sworn to exterminate our race! After all, what have we done to Heaven to merit these misfortunes, we poor dune rabbits? Oh, humans have become exceedingly nasty creatures!'"

"Yes," said the doctor, "the poor rabbit of the dunes is quite right; the nastiest beast in the world is the human beast!"

"The superman! The superbrute! The Prussian supergorilla!" cried Monsieur Vandermolen.

The sick child

VII. A city in smithereens.
The warren under the rubble.

We walked for some time with heads bowed, paying close attention in order not to stumble into a hole or step on some grenade. The doctor was muttering into his beard; I heard him murmur, through pursed lips: "*Hou!* Whorish science! Ferocious divinity! Pallas Athene, goddess of somber madness!"

The sun was setting, striping the landscape with long red streaks against a yellow background I perceived strange mounds in that direction, outlined in black against the bloody stripes, desiccated and twisted trees, the distant skeleton of a large murdered windmill, which seemed to be oscillating in the wind, and whose arms were agitating in gestures of desperate protest.

"We're here," said the doctor, stopping his wrathful monologue. "This is our home..."

His hand indicated a few heaps of rubble slightly higher than the rest: the remains of the Villa Vandermolen, already invaded by brambles and nettles, and all kinds of weeds.

"I thought you were taking me to Harlem."

"We're here."

"What!"

"Oh, not in the heart of the city—that's a little further on. You see that lake of sorts from which islets of ruins protrude; that's...no, that was the river...behind it is...no, that was the railway station...you go...no, you *went* straight past that to the *Groot-Markt*, the main square in front of the Town Hall...once... Here, this is the house of our friend Vandermolen, rich ship-owner. He'll tell you how many vessels he owned; he'll tell you their names, their distant routes, and what he knows about the tragic destiny of every one... But he's still the richest of us all, since he's our landlord, and in his munificence, he lodges us without demanding any rent..."

"Come in, then," said Monsieur Vandermolen.

The remains of the Villa Vandermolen

"That was easy to say, but which way? By looking more closely I saw what remained of one of the gateposts, where there had once been a sumptuous grille, for one long upright and a few spirals of wrought iron were still dangling from the hinges.

We did not, however, go that way. Monsieur Vandermolen made us turn right, behind a pile of stones arranged as neatly as possible on top of one another in order to frame—or rather, to shield—the opening of a low vault.

"The main courtyard of the Vandermolen House," the American billionaire said to me. "Before the bombardments, the house must have been rather fine. It's the cellars that we now live in—and we're among the best accommodated in the town, as you'll see."

Before going down I paraded my gaze around. Yes, the house must have been large and well-to-do, and even of noble architecture, to judge by certain items of sculpted debris rolling under our feet: an old sixteenth-century town house, its date revealed by an antique coat of arms, almost intact, in heavy sculpture, still framed by a few bricks.

"The family crest," Monsieur Vandermolen told me. "We've been living here since the times of William the Silent!"[11]

Poor old defunct mansion! Of the façade—or, rather, the four walls—nothing remained but the substructure of the ground floor, jaggedly sliced or dismantled by the catastrophes, on to which substructure the beams of the roof had descended, to pose obliquely, considerably dislocated, but still retained a few skylights and a lovely weather-vane leaning sideways in a melancholy fashion.

There had been a great many breaches in the walls, and large holes in the tiles of the roof—more holes than tiles—but

---

[11] William I, Prince of Orange (1533-1584), leader of the Dutch revolt against the Spanish Hapsburgs, which turned into the Eighty Years War.

it all formed nevertheless a semblance of cover for the house, along with a great many climbing plants, binding the overly fragmented sections together with their vegetation.

I decided to go down. We found ourselves in the old basements of the house, also considerably disturbed. In one large room, almost intact, there was a kind of stove compounded out of pieces of rusty pipe, slotted together by *ad hoc* kitchen-fitters. Monsieur Vandermolen told me that it was the common room, the drawing room, the kitchen and the dining room. All the furniture that could be seen was a long patched-up table, a few more or less rickety chairs, and whitewood crates able to substitute for them. A sideboard fabricated from disparate pieces of wood by well-meaning carpenters devoid, I have to say, of any talent, contained plates and various kitchen utensils.

I felt so horribly tired that I let myself fall on to a chair.

"You're at home here, but you need to see the installation while there's still enough light," Monsieur Vandermolen told me, trying to haul me to my feet.

In fact, night was falling and the house was scarcely illuminated by the twilight coming through two dubious openings that filtered the air currents rather than providing light.

It was necessary to make a tour of the property, visit the various "apartments"—as the doctor said as he pushed me into the obscurity—and admire the ingenuity of the accommodations.

"This is my bedroom," said Monsieur Vandermolen, showing me a redoubt that was six feet square at the most, furnished with one chair and a mattress placed on a student's iron bed-frame, extended at the foot by two planks placed on logs.

I had certainly learned at the Pole to do without luxury, and I could be content with the strictly necessary, but the simplicity of that cell, which appeared to be damp, made me grimace. So the wealthy Monsieur Vandermolen was lodged like that!

But wait and see the rest...

To the right and left of the box reserved for the master of the house there were two other tiny rooms, one for the doctor and the other shared by the Peruvian lieutenant and the artilleryman-professor Jollimay.

"We all have mattresses," said the doctor. "You'll have one too—that's a refinement of comfort that has become rather difficult to find, but we'll find you one. It will doubtless seem a little hard, as flat as a pancake, but it's still better than the planks, or even a bed of brushwood."

The doctor's mattress was posed on a wooden frame of the same manufacture as the dining room sideboard, but the one employed by the Peruvian and Jollimay was supported on the ruins of an old brick oven. Evidently, we were in the former kitchen of the Vandermolen house.

Next—which is to say behind a few heaps of stones—there was the debris of a staircase that no longer went up to anything, a slightly larger room served as a dormitory for several of our companions. Proudly, the rifleman Mohammed showed us a kind of shelf in a corner, on which bizarre weapons were stacked.

"I made all that," he said. "Since the rifles are broken, and there are no more cartridges, there's nothing but bayonets!"

He put into my hands a kind of wooden club with a heavy lump of iron at the end. I perceived half a dozen different kinds of club, artistically fabricated, plus two or three with longer shafts, similar to the maces of the Middle Ages, with heads bristling with huge nails.

Mohamed only had a hook instead of a right hand, but he wielded those weapons in his left hand, and sketched whirling movements with dexterity.

As I was straining under their weight, the negro handed me a much lighter weapon.

"For the ladies!" he said, with a broad laugh that showed all his teeth. "Good for tapping the Boches, when the time comes."

"I made all that"

"But these are prehistoric implements," I said to Dr. Christiansen.

"Well, doesn't everything here seem to you to be prehistoric? Don't we live in caves of a sort, like the men of the earliest times? Caves made by human hands instead of natural cavities—but that's the only difference, as regards habitation. As for lifestyle, aren't we leading the existence of prehistoric troglodytes? And yet, prehistoric people, save for occasional bad moments, certainly lived much more tranquilly than us, the post-historic people, who are tracked everywhere, always under the menace of enormous, strange and complex dangers, ready to fall upon our poor heads everywhere. Oh, how the comparison turns to the advantage of the first humans! Oh, how they'd hate to live with us, the brave people of the prehistoric caverns, who had nothing to dread but bears, or a few other honest predators deprived of malice, almost inoffensive by comparison with the scientific and *kultured* biped of today! Let's study, if you like, their real existence, with the authentic data that we've obtained by digging, and let's compare..."

"Here's the ladies' bedroom, on the upper floor," the Dutchman said, cutting short the doctor's dissertation. "It's a little more comfortable, naturally..."

The "upper floor" was only a few feet above the ground, at the top of a heap of bricks arranged as a stairway. As for comfort, I widened my eyes, but I could see nothing more sumptuous than the other cubby-holes. Yes, though—there was a fragment of broken mirror fixed to the wall, a zinc water-jug and a washing-basin on an old packing-case. Feminine coquetry never loses its rights. I also perceived a flower-pot with a clump of carnations, which added a bright note to the depths of the kind of ventilation-shaft through which a little light filtered. Yes, that was Mademoiselle Vitalis' private garden.

I cast a curious glance over another crate serving as a work-table. Let's take a look at the "ladies' handiwork" of these topsy-turvy times. No, no embroidery, no crochet work,

113

no *petit point* on the work table, but socks of coarse fabric that only form a random assemblage of patches repairs in all colors and all thicknesses, with reinforcements in rabbit-skin here and there, alongside a galosh in the process of fabrication, and then a kind of overcoat in goatskin, to which had been attached, with string, the sleeves of an old jacket made of coarse fabric.

"That's a fur for me," the doctor told me. "The ladies are very ingenious, and admirably clever at making the best of our meager resources, or the finds we make from time to time among the ruins. Thus, we were too poorly furnished for socks last winter, which was particularly harsh, but when we were searching the pharmacy one day for cough medicine, we had the good fortune to stumble on the debris of a cupboard still containing the footwear of an entire family... somewhat worn, but not too badly burned or damaged. What a windfall! That was worth as much as the pharmacy for protection against colds! We pay great attention to shoes, because they get terribly worn walking over all these bits of stone!"

Alas, I looked down at my footwear, made out of seal-skin at the Pole. My fur leggings still had some wear in them; I could count on those—but the shoes weren't up to much.

The doctor understood what I was thinking. "Bah!" he said. "You can find moccasins for the time being, and Mademoiselle Vitalis can patch up your shoes comfortably." He went on: "Ah, the finds! The hunt through the ruins for things once scorned, but precious today, on which one puts one's hand! They're our great joy, sometimes mixed with melancholy when we happen upon little familiar things once of everyday use, the delicacies of the life of old, for forgotten today!"

"Señor," said the Spaniard, who had followed us, "I'd give ten years...no, let's be reasonable, six months...of my life for a bar of chocolate. God chocolate! Oh, *carràmba!*"

"Perhaps we'll find some one day, combing through the rubble of that big grocery in the Rue de Nassau."

"It's already been searched over and over again by everyone. I've searched hard!"

"Who can tell? Didn't we carry out another fruitful dig
last month? That was one of the finds that give me the greatest
pleasure…more even then the footwear! A little bottle of
gumballs, not spoiled at all, and an intact tin containing thirteen sugar lumps! You can taste one—there's some left. Oh, I
need that for the little patient—marshmallow with gumballs..."

"I'll take it to him, Doctor," said Mademoiselle Vitalis.

"That's good, my child—you trot like a goat, you go so
quickly. Above all, don't forget your mask!"

The hunt through the ruins

VIII. The Boutique of Scourges and Abominations.

I had been shown everything in the encampment of my new friends. It was now a matter of installing us, the young Polynesian and me—since, for an indeterminate time, we would have to share our accommodation.

By clearing away a few beams, Monsieur Vandermolen found us a little corner, where two sumptuous beds were laid down, for we had a mattress each that was not too hard. There was only one available blanket, which was for me, a man of mature years; young Marcel Blondeau had to be content with a canvas sack, with his clothing for an eiderdown.

I was still stunned by the day's events, during which my mind had, so to speak, been hammered by so many shocks and extraordinary revelations. My brain was truly seething in my head.

What? I am dreaming? Or am I being deceived, made a laughing-stock? All this is too implausible. It's inadmissible. It's impossible...yes, impossible! Can the world have been changed, overturned, disrupted to this extent? What about civilization, then? What about the general softening of mores? The fraternization of races, the fusion of peoples? That was all people were talking about when I left. And the thinkers, the scientists, radiant humanity? No, I don't understand! I'm lost. Into what cavern have I tumbled? These people are mad, fit for a straitjacket! On the other hand, these ruins, the shells, the toxic gases....come on, come on, it's necessary to clarify all that, this evening, or I'm the one who'll be going completely insane tomorrow morning!

I spotted Dr. Christiansen and Monsieur Vandermolen sitting in a corner of the common room, facing one another, on old packing cases, looking at one another pensively, without saying a word.

The others were occupied in various tasks: the New Zealander and the Peruvian lieutenant were skinning the rabbits captured in the dunes; the rifleman Mohammed was arranging

117

his rats on a spit in order to roast them; the Spaniard was making faggots for the fire; Madame de Vitalis was preparing her saucepans. As for the Swiss artilleryman, Monsieur Jollimay, he had his nose plunged in a little book. As I approached him, he looked up and handed me the volume.

"It's a manual of expert gardening—in Dutch, but I'm beginning to understand it. Do you know anything about gardening? Me, I'm just a simple professor of history, not good for much. We've cleared patches of garden here and there, planted with potatoes, but there's still space. I'd like to sow haricot beans. Is there still time?"

"I don't know," I said, thinking about something else.

I took a chair and went to sit down with the doctor and Monsieur Vandermolen. The young man from Polynesia, who seemed as tormented as me and never left me for a moment, remained standing behind me, attentively.

"Monsieur," I said, putting my hand on the doctor's arm, "we have time to talk tranquilly now. I'm anxious—terribly anxious—finally to have a clear and detailed explanation of al the somber revelations you've sketched out for me. I've been living in a nightmare since my disembarkation this morning, a frightful nightmare...ever since you saved my life in the midst of incidents incomprehensible for me...."

The doctor raised his head, apparently looking at me without seeing me, like a man completely absorbed in his thoughts.

"But first of all," I went on, "please excuse the vivacity of the protestations that I can't help expressing. How can I let your blasphemies against science pass tranquilly? You see me scandalized and indignant. I shiver, the more I think about it. What, you—a man of study, a man of science, a medical man, a physician, you..."

"A man of science...repentant!" exclaimed the doctor, returning to himself.

"Repentant! Get away!" I exclaimed in my turn. "Come on, Doctor, that's a further blasphemy!"

"Although I don't have on my conscience any invention having, to any degree whatsoever, produced or added to the sadness and misery of humankind, I'm making honorable amends, all the same, on behalf of others...imprudent, unconscious, if you wish...whose works and research, without any evil intention, I admit, have nevertheless, in a hundred of our short years, absolutely perturbed the world and precipitated humankind into the formidable cataclysm under which we're struggling. Woe, woe everywhere! A Deluge of frightful evils, a flood of atrocious calamities, a general annihilation of humankind! The author of the evil? Quite simply, that which you proudly call *progress by means of science!* Accursed Science, that slut Science!"

The worthy doctor became animated; his bushy eyebrows were bristling, his long beard jutted forward with every one of those abominable affirmations.

I got carried away too. Neither the Pole nor age had chilled me.

"Monsieur," I said, severely, seizing his hand. "Be sure that I am still full of gratitude to you for having collected and saved a poor shipwreck victim, but there is no longer anything here but two men of science, arguing, contesting...courteously..."

"Do as I have done, repent! As much as you, I once admired, and followed, alas, as a fervent disciple, the masters of that satanic science. Well, remorse is crushing me! With the energy of conviction, I protest against that accursed science; I accuse it formally of being the great culpable, the frightful criminal..."

"You're continuing to blaspheme! On the contrary—calm down, look harder, and see the uninterrupted march of humankind, guided toward progress by beneficent science, that increasingly rapid ascension toward the luminous summits...a magnificent and sublime spectacle! That course of Progress, the scientists of all nations spending their lives in laboratories, dogged in the study of natural forces, clarifying phenomena and laws of nature, extracting from nature all her secrets, in order that grateful peoples might profit from them..."

"Contrition!" said the doctor. "Remorse!"

Poor Monsieur Vandermolen bowed his head, with a defeated expression, but the young man from Polynesia, standing behind him, seemed even more frightened than consternated.

"...And discoveries succeeding one another incessantly, multiplying, ever more important, discoveries leading incessantly to new discoveries. Come on, instead of crying anathema against science, tell me about its new conquests! Since I left Europe, it has moved on, radiant science, it must, continuing its splendid work, have accumulated marvels, realizing yet more, ever more, new dreams, opening ever vaster horizons... I'm waiting—speak, talk, tell, bring me up to date!"

"Indeed, indeed, she has moved on, more and otherwise than you think. She has sprinted, the slut! Let's talk about her marvels, then! Let's talk about that famous 'course of Progress' with which our brains were stuffed on the college benches, cramming us with all dangerous nonsense and forcing us to swallow the entire boutique of Academic poisons! You'll see! You'll see!

"Progress is a pretty word, agreed, but first of all, at what point is it necessary to suspend the forward march toward the promised land? On what plateau of the mountain is it necessary to stop? At what moment does fortunate and fecund progress become dangerous and harmful momentum? At what moment does that sought-after and blessed progress become, with its suspect benefits, a producer of unknown evils and a generator of unprecedented sufferings? How does one perceive, in the intoxication of discovery, the horrors that those discoveries and marvelous inventions are about to unleash? How does one discern the danger, perceive the unintended consequences, the side-effects of our marvels?

"Impossible! One never can...no one thinks about the danger, in any case! Oh, wretched blind men, you don't see it, you can't divine it, but some little discovery, insignificant in itself, or even bringing certain immediate real advantages that are welcomed joyfully, bears within it, without anyone suspecting it, the seed of frightful misfortunes with an imminent term! You ought to weep and tremble...but in the meantime, the Academies hand out crowns, and the scientists congratulate one another...

"However, I know one, at least, who repented: Nobel, an inventor of explosive for good motives, Monsieur, for great works of industrial transformation...the good motive! Yes, it's always the good motive they invoke! And after a while, it turns out that one has worked primarily for the bad. That one, the culpable Nobel, tried to redeem himself by founding prizes of all the arts, literary and scientific...yes, scientific again, decidedly, the poor fellow hadn't fully understood!"

I had tried to interrupt, but he wasn't an easy man to stop. "I protest!" I cried. "Wait for the dawn that your eyes don't yet divine! Wait for the sun! Be certain that from all these discoveries, new enlightenment will surge forth for the good of humankind!"

He sniggered. "The final conflagration of the world. *Mene Tekel Upharsin!* We're there, my good Monsieur. It's the liquidation of humankind! People have talked many times about the bankruptcy of science, impatient for change, discontented by petty inconveniences... Bankruptcy? Oh, may it please Heaven! Alas, pitiless Heaven did not want it." He raised his long arms into the air and repeated: "Bankruptcy? Bankruptcy? Yes, bankruptcy for the real wellbeing of unfortunate humankind!"

I tried to get a few words in: "The immense progress realized thanks to her, in all the orders of human activity: locomotion, steam, electricity, aviation, chemistry..."

"Have only served to furnish humans with new and more ferocious weapons with which to destroy one another, more and more formidable means of instantaneous and devastating aggression. To the pillory with science! Certainly, war has been something sad and horrible at all times, but our science has come, and she has multiplied a hundredfold...what am I saying?...a hundredthousandfold, the horrors and the terrors of war; she has developed, multiplied and generalized the possibilities and the facilities of massacre, at any distance and over the widest range. She has so altered and aggravated the conditions of the struggles of nations, so frightfully spoiled, uglified and hideously soiled the horrors of warfare, that the wars of old seem no more than simple lively scuffles, the battles of old a game of brutal heroism...

"Yes, there they are, the marvels of Science, the benefits of Science, the surprises of Science! Hurrah! Appreciate and admire, humans crushed by Her! There happened to be in this world a nation of prey, a ferociously covetous race, which has divined, which has understood, the advantage to be obtained from these famous marvels, and why has slyly heaped up all the weapons, combining all the new, as-yet-unemployed means that that accursed science was able to furnish...and when the moment came, the eagle-vulture of Prussia flapped its wings, and the entire race, proud of the invincibility, rushed joyfully to the slaughter, to the immense scramble for the land, the property and the riches of neighboring peoples, coveted for ages."

His beard trembled; he had a coughing fit. Jollimay and the others surrounded him, and nodded their heads approvingly.

"The progress of locomotion, railways, the automobile, O marvels! Charming, the circular voyages in luxury trains! Very agreeable, the softly padded automobile that transports you at eighty kilometers an hour through the countryside. Delightful, all that! But that is what has permitted the gathering and rapid transportation of those armies of millions of soldiers, with their immense and scientific weaponry, and superb engines of destruction brought to the peak of perfection and enormity, the fabulous stocks of munitions and necessary food supplies, and the regular circulation between the militarized factories of the rear and the and the armed factories of the front, of the nourishment of men and cannons!

"Without those modern means of locomotion, none of that would be possible, and the most formidable wars would continue to be, as they were in the past, nothing but the collision of one big army—an enormous army of two of three hundred thousand men at the most—and another army of similar strength, with the result that after three or four pitched battles, the decision would be clear and everything would be settled. O good old times of innocence!"

"Yes," said Jollimay, the professor reappearing beneath the artilleryman, "We all thought and said such stupid things once, swallowed in good faith and made others swallow terrible blunders! Where is the time of the Medieval armies of fifteen thousand men, of the poor Middle Ages that we made so Dark? Oh mild calumniated Middle Ages, I make honorable amends! Doubtless those fifteen thousand men could ravage the country over which they battled. Certainly! I agree entirely—but they did not all have thirty thousand arms, and they only ravaged for fifteen thousand men!

"Listen! In the sixteenth century, one of the captains of your king Francois I—I remember having once read about it in a journal—proposed the creation of a national army, constituted at a rate of one man per village…yes, imagine that, a conscription of one man per village: a volunteer to serve for three years and to remain available for disposal, in return for certain advantages, in his hearth, for a few years more. And that good captain would render himself strong enough, with twenty-five thousand men on each frontier, to render France unassailable! What do you think? Those times are far away, alas—a thousand times alas!"

"Yes, indeed! Yes, indeed! Poor Middle Ages, Monsieur Jollimay," said the doctor. "Brave centuries and good men!"

I remained speechless for a moment. That damnable doctor had assailed me with such arguments that I was weakening under so many violent blows. I tried to pull myself together, though, and furnish a few objections to that anathematization of great Science, which was making me suffer cruelly.

"But medicine, Doctor, medicine—think of everything that the research of physiological scientists, chemists and bacteriologists has produced in the course of the last few decades:

discoveries of genius overturning the old ideas of the quacks of the past, and coming marvelously to the aid of humans in their struggle against maladies once incurable and all the scourges that besieged..."

"Let's talk about those discoveries! Excellent intentions, no doubt! One finds a microbe, one cultivates it, one weakens it and forces it to combat itself—that's very nice; one passes for a benefactor of humankind. But from those discoveries, other doctors, and other chemists, obtain advantages with another goal entirely. We have them now, those maladies and those scourges, they're thwarted, and we have those germs and those bacilli at our disposal, but they're also a redoubtable arsenal, and we can draw new munitions from them for battle!

"We can put those microbes in bottles, after having rendered them as virulent as possible, and look! A new artillery created. Look! A medical corps no longer defensive but offensive, to launch against the enemy! Do you want scourges to ravage a city, an enemy capital, a province? To destroy the population of a coveted region or to suppress an inconvenient race, an entire population of men, women and children—even animals, if you wish, for we also have bacteria with their intention—to ruin and poison an entire race, in its constitution and its physiology, to suppress its future and clear it away? If you want shells loaded with these microbial machine-guns, your doctor-chemists will furnish you with all there is of the best and the worst!

"And that's what they have made of the beneficent discovery of the naïve researcher who only thought of curing the maladies of poor human beings. He scarcely suspected that the worst of all our maladies is the malady of science...and it's that one of which we're dying."

"Bah!" said the aviator Miraud, softly. "Your encumbering and invasive science, your progress turning back tranquility, has made the world, that poor ball, so ugly, flatly banal or outrageously hideous, that I almost feel consolation at the thought of its demolition. I don't regret anything...anything, except perhaps, for my arm..."

IX. A soirée at the Vandermolen house.

"To table!" put in the voice of the charming Mademoiselle Vitalis. "To table, Messieurs—that's six times I've called you without your hearing me."

She had slipped her head between mine and that of the enraged doctor, at the moment when both of us, having risen to our feet, features contracted and eyes ablaze, we looked as if we were ready to devour one another, him in the fury of his blasphemous maledictions, and me in the energy of the protestations that he would not let me express, and which I felt literally choking me.

"When the doctor is in one of his black moods," the young woman added, cheerfully, "even dinner doesn't succeed in getting him out of it. It is, however, a good moment of tranquility, after days that are often hard, and if the dinner is good, as it is today, one blossoms…come on, Messieurs, it's necessary to blossom!"

The doctor seemed to swallow, with some difficulty, the flood of maledictions that still wanted to emerge. He closed his mouth, looked at the young woman with wild eyes, took a deep breath, and said: "Oh, yes…oh, yes…but…well…and the little patient in the dunes…it's necessary to take him..."

"His medicine? He has it; I've just taken it to him. They'll give him his marshmallow; he took a gumball in front of me. His mother says he's much better, your visit alone reduced his fever. To thank you, the father gave me two whitings he caught yesterday..."

"That will be a dish for tomorrow," said Madame Vitalis. "Let's go, Messieurs—to table!"

Madame Vitalis was right. I should have had a terrible hunger; so many emotions should have hollowed me out profoundly—and yet, I no longer felt the appetite that had been clawing me a little while ago. It was the fault of that damnable Dr. Christiansen. Anyway, to table all the same!

A good moment of tranquility

The places had been set on an old extending table, resting on three solid sculpted legs, with a fourth meriting les confidence in simple white wood—a table extended even further at one end by planks set on trestles.

There was no luxury in the home of our rich ship-owner, no flowers on the tablecloth of the rich tulip-collector—and, in fact, no tablecloth. And what a miscellany of cutlery and crockery! Let's not talk about it: in that heap of ruins, everything was poverty and dilapidation.

In my capacity as a stranger or a guest, I found myself seated between the doctor and our host, Monsieur Vandermolen. My young companion was installed facing us, between the two ladies…and I saw a very animated conversation engaged between them, rapidly. The young man from Polynesia, instead of displaying the slightest depression, took on the appearance of a man at a salon, disengaged from all care, and I saw him leaning very amiably toward one or the other of his neighbors to say something gracious to the young woman, or something polite to the old one, like a guest at a bourgeois dinner in ordinary times.

Madame Vitalis had made us a vegetable soup that was more succulent than abundant. Afterwards, we had a few snails, a mutton stew without any mutton, and then rabbit fricasseed without any oil, and a salad, likewise without any oil. One could fill up on potatoes, which were eaten instead of bread.

A few gourmets, among them the Senegalese rifleman, Monsieur Jollimay and the Spanish businessman, did full honor to the roasted rats. My appetite began to return. I devoured my portion. The doctor was alarmed, and remarked to me that the dinner was a veritable feast, and that I ought not to expect such plentiful nourishment every day.

And I had been sighing for such a long time at the Pole for white bread and civilization! We had no bread to eat at the Pole, and I had dreamed so much during our return voyage about crusty croissants, tender brioches, etc. etc...

As the doctor remained somber and mute, I tried to make Monsieur Vandermolen talk, and to extract a few items of information to verify what the doctor had said, but it was a waste of time. He talked to me about his vessels, four great steamers torpedoed at Flessingue, two others sunk by mines off Dunkerque. He described his tulip fields in their heyday, and reeled off lists of the names of particularly rare tulips—or ships, I'm not entirely sure. Similarly, I couldn't tell whether he most regretted the ships, the tulips or his family manor, in the ruins of which we were sitting.

As I persisted in lavishing condolences upon him, he showed me, hanging on the wall behind us, opposite the kitchen stove, a little painting grossly framed with white pieces of curtain-road.

"No more than that," he said, "for consolation for the ships, the house and the tulips. Franz Hals, Monsieur, the great Franz Hals…a masterpiece!"

"What! What is it?"

"Franz Hals from the city Museum, Monsieur—a little fragment. The Museum and all the Franz Halses burned, along with the City Hall and the city. Fire of Boche joy! I found in the rubble that last little fragment of a *Banquet of the Civic Guard*.[12] I cut it out of the burned canvas, neatly, cleaned it and framed it. The last masterpiece!"

I got up to take a look. It was, in fact, the head of a handsome officer of the arquebusiers, with a wide collar. One could also see a tankard with a hand and the rutilant nose of a second officer. But the fire had cooked or seared the colors to such an extent that the Franz Hals looked more like a Rembrandt.

So that was all that remained of the magnificent Franz Hals room, the glory of the Harlem Museum?

The Dutchman nodded his head sadly.

---

[12] *The Banquet of the Officers of the St. George Civic Guard* (1616) was one of Franz Hals' most famous paintings, which led to a series of commissions to paint similar scenes.

"Yes, perhaps all that remains of the entire Dutch school, for what has become of our other Museums? Have they not suffered the same fate, gone up in flames in the same fashion? I don't know for sure..."

"Let's talk about this excellent fricassee instead," the French aviator said, from the other side of the table. "You see, Monsieur, that there are still good moments in life! The rabbits of the dunes are nourished on almost-marine grass, which gives them their flavor. Oh, if only we could catch more—but they're so suspicious, the brigands!"

"The rat possesses even more flavor," said Monsieur Jollimay. "I advise you to sample some, since it might be the case that you'll have to, some day. Would you like a thigh?"

I thanked him, but put it off for another time; my stomach still had scruples.

And during the whole of that soirée, no one talked about anything but food, the game that they hoped to catch with the snares, the fish that they hoped to net on the sand at low tide, and the best way of cooking octopus. And the carrots and turnips that were looking so hopeful, and the spinach sown in a certain mine-crater, the salad vegetables that it was necessary not to allow marauders to pick. Or the work of excavation secretly undertaken in a cellar in the Ridderstraat, in order to try to tunnel into the basements of a block of ruins where there ought to have existed, before the catastrophe, a large storeroom of comestibles: tins, jars of jam, cooking oil, other groceries, etc., etc. All those etceteras made the mouth water, as they competed in detailing their hopes for good finds.

I imagine that there must have been conversations of the same genre on the raft of the *Medusa*. At the North Pole, where we had had the meat of bears and seals at our discretion, we talked about *pâté de foie gras*, cream tarts *à la Savarin*, candied apples, jam and pineapple...

Fatigue overwhelmed me. As soon as my hunger was almost satisfied, I felt my head spinning and my eyes closing involuntarily. I could no longer think. Monsieur Vandermolen perceived that, for I almost slumped on his shoulder.

129

"Come on," he said. "Bed, sleep—very good!"

Dr. Christiansen, compatriot of Hamlet, did not add: "Perhaps to dream?" He was still frowning, lost in his bitter and furious sadness.

Two minutes later, I don't know how, I was lying down, fully dressed, on my mattress, and sinking into sleep. The benevolent Dutchman covered me with a blanket and put the gas mask down beside my face, crying recommendations into my ear that I heard rather vaguely, as if they were coming from a very distant voice.

Good sleep! My mattress, I saw the next day, was as flat as a pancake and no softer than a billiard table, but I found it so pleasant! All the lugubrious news, and all the frightful discoveries of the day were absolutely effaced from my mind. I slept, and I found the sleep delightful.

And I dreamed too: gentle, pleasant dreams, which completed the relaxation of my overexcited brain and calmed my nerves.

I was in Paris, at home; I rediscovered my armchair, my work-table and the divan on which I loved to reflect while smoking cigarettes. I found my collection of butterflies, and my nephew too. Then I went to a great banquet held in honor of my return; there were speeches in which people said to most flattering things; ladies covered me with flowers and ministers brought me various decorations. I heard salvos of applause loud enough to make the banquet hall collapse...

Only one thing astonished me: almost all the women had a wooden leg and were missing an arm.

How happy I was; how sweet and beautiful civilized life seemed!

That lasted for hours, and suddenly, just like that, I woke up. There was noise outside...more salvos of applause, no doubt. As I said, it could have cause the hall to crumble, with that truly excessive enthusiasm...I could actually hear stones falling...

It was light, but a dubious, smoky daylight. I didn't recognize my apartment. Where was I, then? In a Rembrandt painting, no doubt about it...yes, exactly that...let's see, was I still dreaming? That smoke, those faces...or rather, those shadows I glimpsed, that bizarre interior...but where was I, then?

Oh! Ah! Oh! I uttered a loud cry and closed my eyes again. Adieu, my sweet dreams: I fell back into the hideous nightmare of reality.

People came running in response to my cry. I heard wooden beams hitting the ground.

There was Madame Vitalis first, then Monsieur Jollimay, then the worthy Senegalese, and finally Dr. Christiansen.

"Well, my poor Monsieur," said Madame Vitalis, "are you ill? You mustn't be, you see..."

"No, no," I said, "I'm not ill...it's not me, it's the planet. Unless I've gone mad. I'd like that! Yes, mad...completely mad...utterly mad...how glad I'd be! Madame, my good friends, I implore you, tell me that I'm insane, demented, unhinged...I demand cold showers and a straitjacket!"

"No, no, it's nothing like that," said Madame Vitalis. "You're not mad, I assure you, but you have to pull yourself together. From time to time, we all have little moments like that, little crises...and then it passes..."

"Slight depression," said the doctor. "That was inevitable: shock to the brain!"

"*Cafard!*" declared Jollimay, in a somber voice.[13]

"Dirty *cafard*—very bad!" agreed the Senegalese.

"Pull yourself together—we've let you sleep late. Do you know that it's nearly midday? There were only five or six shells this morning. They've finished demolishing a few bits of wall not far away, but nothing on top of us, fortunately.

---

[13] The literal meaning of *cafard* is "cockroach," but it had long been used metaphorically is France to refer to fits of depression, and an acute sense of the pointlessness of existence, before the Great War added a further twist of dark emphasis to the term, when applied to the mental troubles experienced by soldiers in the trenches.

Five or six shells—yes, yes, the salvo of applause in my dream, the banqueting hall collapsing!

"It's nothing; we get used to it. The Boches in the Peace Palace don't have that many shells—a shortage of raw materials—and their factory was blasted one day by bomber aircraft. But they'll catch up with the gas; there's no shortage of chemical products. You'll get used to it, I tell you."

"But I don't want to get used to it, my dear Monsieur. I have no intention of staying here forever…I want to go away. I'm made a firm resolution to leave as soon as possible, no matter how—this very day, if I'm not too tired."

Monsieur Jollimay smiled. Monsieur Vandermolen smiled. The others who were grouped around the entrance of my redoubt burst out laughing, as if I had said something enormous.

"Good, good," said the doctor, who wasn't smiling. "We'll talk about that at table—the morning meal is ready. Can you smell frying? Your shipwrecked companion is more reasonable; he's already at the table."

Let's go to the dining room. I can, indeed, smell the frying, and also the appetite, which is beginning to make demands in spite of the troubled mind.

"A good lunch cures the *cafard*," Jollimay says to me.

Let's go treat my *cafard* according to the prescription, as long as the menu isn't too wretched.

Marcel Blondeau greets me cheerfully.

"I announce to you fried artichokes, Monsieur Jacquemin—and very successfully, by Mademoiselle Jeanne!"

These young people present a strength of resistance to emotion that stupefies me. I no longer have that spring, myself; I don't bounce back so quickly… I arrived desperate, arms and legs broken, but him, that little Polynesian, that Marcel Blondeau, who I expected to find more depressed than me, by reason of his youth, appears rested, fresh and rosy, in the process of setting the table and joking with Mademoiselle Vitalis—what am I saying?—flirting with her! He's been well brought up, in Polynesia!

"Mademoiselle, I beg you, let me do it...I can't permit...come on, leave that cooking-pot to me..."

"You'll burn yourself, Monsieur!"

"No, I..."

"There you see—I told you so!"

Marcel swiftly takes his hand off the cooking-pot; he is heroic, and turns his grimace into an amiable smile.

"Better me than you—I have a less delicate epidermis...and then, yesterday I was frozen. A little roasting will do me good."

Oh that youth! Watch it go! One would think that young Marcel, before the beautiful eyes of the young woman, has already forgotten the terrible news, the sledgehammer blows that have just rained down on our heads, and accepted his part in the worldwide catastrophe into the midst of which we've fallen.

Ha ha! It'll take a lot more than eyes and more eyes, blue or black, and smiles, to drag me out of the nightmare, the obsession and the haunting of all these horrors!

But where are we, then? In a tranquil and brilliant Paris? Are we taking afternoon tea with Madame Vitalis in a nice apartment in an elegant quarter?

I am forced to perceive that Marcel is cutting a dash, in spite of his accoutrement as a dilapidated shipwreck victim...a handsome lad, in fact, with a fine nascent moustache, a keen and clear gaze, and an impression of masculine frankness in his expression.

I turn to poor Madame Vitalis. In spite of all her misfortunes and her wooden leg, she doesn't have a lugubrious expression either, and doesn't seem any more depressed. That's the light mind of women! But I know that she has, to maintain her in that fine firmness, in that apparent calm, the concern of the administration of resources and the management of the household, of this clan of unfortunate debris camped on the rubble of the world. That's something.

"The mother of us all!" Vandermolen says to me. "Before her arrival, Monsieur, there was perfect disorder here, organized famine, general hunger six days out of seven, at least! She was able to arrange everything for the best. And that little Mademoiselle Jeanne—we all adore her, Monsieur!" He leans close to me. "I'm getting old; I'll leave her my Franz Hals and my house...."

"His house! Where is it, his house? Just fifty cartloads of gravel, outside of these cellars increased in size by a torpedo crater—which torpedo, in exploding, has furnished a supplement of accommodation that has permitted, as has been pointed out to me, the offering of hospitality to Marcel and me, without inconveniencing anyone overmuch.

"She's exquisite," Miraud says to me, slipping into the conversation.

"Who? Madame Vitalis?"

"Jeanne, Mademoiselle Jeanne. You'll see..."

"We were as hideous as savages, we were sordid, dressed in rags and holes," said Monsieur Vandermolen; these ladies took the needles they'd discovered God knows where, and the clothes that were still usable, and in a few weeks they rendered us this appearance of civilized men—for we've resumed, as you can observe, the manners of civilized people, And Mademoiselle Jeanne repairs marvelously, Monsieur! Admire this frock-coat, which she's rendered presentable and respectable!"

Monsieur Vandermolen's frock-coat! A kind of jacket restored with tan leather at the elbow and a big piece of yellow parchment in the tails, fragments of the binding of a sixteenth-century Bible, on which one can still distinguish a title in red Gothic capitals, almost washed away by the rain. Beautiful work, indeed—a masterpiece!

"And the cooking, too, with her mother..."

"Let's leave those vulgar details," said the aviator Miraud. "The ladies are charming, and possessed of a rare ingenuity. They've acquired all the talents necessary in adversity. I'm not denying the importance of the question of nourishment..."

"Primordial importance!"

"Primordial, if you like—but there's something else, also very important: Mademoiselle Jeanne has a natural disposition for medicine. She saved my life! My life is hers—I owe it to her. Yes, Mademoiselle Jeanne, I owe it to you!"

"She's saved all of our lives," said Vandermolen, "including Dr. Christansen of the slightly seething head. He has a thousand good reasons for his clamors and furies against Science, but it gives him distractions that could be dangerous...if Mademoiselle Jeanne weren't here to keep watch on him. She knows everything, she brings back the slightest course...as well as good salad, roots and excellent plants for tisanes..."

"She saved my life last month," repeated Miraud. "Fluxion of the chest, possibly pneumonic..."

"Bah! Simple cold, slight bout of flu," said Vandermolen.

"No, no, much more serious; I knew that, me!"

I left them to dispute Mademoiselle Vitalis' merits, and after the meal, I followed Dr. Christiansen, who undertook to show me, in the vicinity of our cellar, the dangerous places to avoid and the refuges prepared in case of surprise by gas, pathogenic microbes or something else.

Marcel Blondeau, invited to follow us, declared that he would see all that later, when he had completed some task for which he had begged Mademoiselle Vitalis to utilize his good will.

When we got back he had gone with Miraud and the two ladies to finish clearing a square of land, in a corner of the demolished and nonexistent suburb, now a formless mass of rubble, appropriate for the growing of vegetables.

Oh, I was counting on not tasting those vegetables, and being far away from Harlem before they had even begun to emerge from the soil.

A formless mass of rubble, appropriate for the growing of
vegetables

X. A flirtation in the New Cave Era.

I swore to myself, I had made a form resolution, in spite of all the frightful revelations about the fabulous events that had occurred, that I would go, as quickly as possible, and at any risk, to launch myself into the anguishing unknown and try to reach Paris, no matter how.

Certainly, I felt the keenest sympathy, my heart overflowing with gratitude, for the worthy men who had picked me up and saved me, and particularly for Dr. Christiansen, so discouraged and so discouraging, but I could not resolve myself to accepting as absolutely exact, in every particular, the picture of the situation as it had been presented to me.

Fabulously steeped in black, that picture—there had to be great exaggerations in it, originating from the morbid pessimism into which they all appeared to me to have sunk, in consequence of their sad adventures.

A lugubrious nightmare, a macabre dream, madness!

I decided to attempt something and see for myself. I gave myself a few days to study the terrain, determine my plan and make my preparations—but no more than a few days. No matter how, I would be gone within a week.

Marcel Blondeau will leave with me, of course, and he will be a valuable companion, but I can see that he's clear-sighted and valiant. Two knowledgeable and determined men can get themselves out of trouble more easily in a bad situation, and I can see well enough the enormous obstacles that will rise up before us as soon as we leave.

I joke with the young man about his passion for gardening. Every day he goes to the garden with the ladies, clearing and digging ardently. The aviator Miraud goes too; he seems to have the same passion for the lettuces and cabbages in prospect.

"You'd do much better," I say to Marcel, "to explore the surroundings with me, to discover the best direction to take and try to avoid the dubious paths, the possible ambushes and traps..."

"But Monsieur. I have to do something here, to make my small contribution to the communal food-supply. Think about it! We're not precisely swimming in abundance among these ruins, and I wouldn't want to be a parasite, a trimmer of exceedingly meager portions..."

"Of course, of course—but the preparation of our departure is important and urgent too, since we don't want to be here forever. Haven't you told me that you want to get to Paris, where you still have family, as quickly as possible?"

"Yes, Monsieur, certainly...I think so...but no one's waiting for me..."

"Of course, nor for me either, but I'm desperate to know for certain...in haste to see for myself. Oh, Paris, Paris! How are things out there, really? How will we find it? Anyway, let's make preparations—for an early departure, I hope."

"Yes...yes..."

He appears to me to be quite cold today, the fellow who was burning to get to Paris, to embrace a couple of aunts left in the homeland, and to put himself at the service of the fatherland right away.

This morning, I went out to go exploring. The Vitalis ladies had just left for the suburb with Marcel, Miraud and the Senegalese rifleman. They were going to lend a hand with the clearing of the restored terrain and then go hunting for wildfowl in a ravaged and abandoned park.

While cautiously coming down the hill of the broken windmills, with which I was already familiar, I saw Marcel pass below me, marching with a spade under his arm beside Jeanne Vitalis. They didn't see me and I was able to overhear a few words that made me prick up my ears anxiously.

"You're going to leave us, then, Monsieur Marcel?" said the young woman.

"That's the plan, at least," Marcel replied, "but...it requires reflection...yes, it demands serious reflection. It's necessary to examine the possibilities of the journey..."

"Very difficult, Monsieur Marcel; we're blockaded here. I don't see at all how you can go into that unknown, plunge into that darkness...through obstacles that are said to be insurmountable..."

"But I'm not in a hurry, Mademoiselle," the young man murmured. "We've been welcomed so perfectly here...collected...saved. We've fallen on our feet...everyone is so good to us...you've been so good, Mademoiselle Jeanne! We're very grateful to you, Mademoiselle Jeanne, me particularly..."

The young man's voice was emotional. He was looking at Jeanne Vitalis with moist eyes. One might have thought that the young woman had snatched him from the waves and saved him from the toxic gas all by herself. The boy was exaggerating, truly!

"Well, young Marcel!" called the aviator Miraud from the other side of a mine crater some distance away. "If you amble along like that you'll scarcely have time to dig your patch!"

"All right all right!" said Marcel. "I'm examining the terrain—I haven't been living in the caves of Harlem for two years, like you." He went on in a lower voice: "Anyway, Mademoiselle, I find charm in the region, in spite of all these ruins that nature is in the process of covering and embellishing. And then...and then, you're here. There are presences that render the most frightful and the most dangerous places habitable, and allow one to support the..."

Jeanne Vitalis laughed quietly. "The desert most denuded of comforts, uncertain nourishment, the lack of everything, etc., etc."

"No, no, don't joke. You're here; you accept, courageously, the daily perils, the..."

"Quotidian privations?" suggested the young woman, laughing.

"Certainly: sorrows, dangers and privations! And I'm only thinking about running away...without looking back... No, no! I'm staying, definitely...unless you want to send me away?"

"Oh, of course not! Quite the contrary."

A flirtation in these caverns! A flirtation, in the midst of such terrors, these somber days, in the midst of these horrors! Oh, I didn't expect that. However, I really ought to have noticed that Marcel had immediately shown a particular sympathy for the Vitalis ladies, and that Jeanne Vitalis didn't appear to receive him with an ill grace when he hastened to come running at the slightest difficulty of material organization or renewal of the food supply.

Stones that I caused to roll down the slope interrupted the conversation. Marcel and the young woman hastened their pace. I grabbed Miraud, who was going toward them, by the arm.

Since Marcel Blondeau seemed determined to remain in the refuge of Harlem, I could try to entice the aviator Miraud to set off for Paris with me, in spite of all the risks.

Miraud seemed pensive and melancholy—or, rather, in a bad mood. So much the better. After vegetating for two years in the caves of Harlem, the ex-aviator had to be chewing the bit; it might be possible to convince him to attempt an escape with me.

While we walked, I immediately broached my proposal, but as soon as I spoke, Miraud exclaimed: "Oh, no, no—not me. Take your young man from Polynesia, if you want, your Marcel Blondeau—he's not afraid of fatigue, he'll be a good companion, solid and courageous. Take him, I tell you, but not me!"

He hastened his steps, trying to catch up with the young couple, who, for their part, were advancing more rapidly through the gulfs and mounds formed by the already-aging heaps of rubble.

"No, no, not me," Miraud repeated.

"Why not? If I can judge by my impatience and anxiety, you, a Parisian, must he..."

"No, no, my dear Monsieur, impossible! You want to go, so be it—but the least that can happen to you, after having circled around, bumping into insurmountable obstacles everywhere, is to remain hemmed in, gone to earth, lost in some hole without being able to budge, and die there slowly of starvation, if some shell or cloud of toxic gas doesn't abridge your suffering. Me, I refuse to risk those displeasures. I find life good, perfectly bearable, in our cave in Harlem, sufficiently comfortable, and almost tranquil, with only a few petty dangers close by, dangers to which we're accustomed, and which we've learned from long experience to avoid as much as possible. I'm going to wait here for the end of this long planetary quake. Everything indicates, Monsieur, that we're in the last throes of world collapse, the last spasms of ferocious Boche dementia. On all sides I think, everyone is out of breath, out of explosives, chemical ingredients and virulent microbes. Hope is returning to help us to be patient."

"I'd be a lot more patient in Paris..."

"Paris! Paris! What's become of Paris? A mystery! How are things out there? No one knows..."

"All the more reason to go and see!"

"Go then! I've warned you. Above all, take Monsieur Blondeau!.... Well, Mademoiselle Jeanne, you're running very quickly...you were going quite slowly a little while ago..."

We had caught up with the two young people. Jeanne Vitalis, very pink, replied, laughing, that she was in a hurry to plant out her lettuces, but it seemed to me that Marcel was looking daggers at the aviator.

I left them, to continue my exploration of the devastated plains around Harlem, hollowed out here and there by dips...

And I recommence the next day, and the following days; we all recommence, for the entire colony scatters to work the fields, to search and dig in the chains of hills formed by the debris, where brushwood is already sketching thickets and brush, and to hunt rats, and dune rabbits, and to go fishing...

If it rains, which happens quite often—beware of the bad season!—one puts the sack that one always carries with one over one's head, and one braves the downpour.

The other day, it was fine. Marcel Blondeau went with me; it was his turn to suffer the melancholy and the *cafard*—I don't know why. He didn't say much while we walked; he didn't look at anything, didn't seek the sunlight and went straight past nettle-beds perfectly capable of furnishing a nice plate of spinach, distractedly, in spite of Mademoiselle Vitalis' recommendations.

Suddenly, near a formless heap of stone and plaster that had once been a row of villas, the sound of voices rose from black hole leading to old cellars, which had been indicated to me and where I knew that my companions were trying to grow mushrooms.

Someone was singing. I recognized the voice rising from the excavation: it was Miraud's. Marcel shivered.

Her hair is brown, so brown, so brown!
Her deep, soft eyes are like an azure lake;
In my heart and all my woes night drown
And...

Miraud appeared, blinking in the light. He started when he saw us.

"What's that you're saying?" demanded Marcel Blondeau, in a voice that lacked amenity.

"I'm singing. It's beautiful; the sun is making me vibrate," Miraud replied.

I'm a furtive wanderer of river shores,
Watcher of reflections in green still pools,
A picker of florets from ivy stores
On the old crumbled wall of... of...

"Damn it, I've lost the rhyme!"

"That's not what you were saying," said Marcel. "I heard something else. You were singing another song.

"You think so? I've forgotten…one jumps so easily from one tune to another...

A dispatch from the days of Dagobert,
Tells of a bad attack on the French,
With neither gas nor...

Marcel turned his back. One might have thought that the boy didn't care for the music or the lines—unless it was the singer who was getting on his nerves…for he was visibly nervy.

I tried to attenuate his impoliteness with regard to Miraud.

"Oh, Monsieur Miraud, what courage, to rhyme and sing in the ruins of the world!"

"It's to numb my cares, Monsieur Jacquemin."

Pensively, I caught up with Marcel, who was marching on with long, stiff strides. He seemed to me to be furious, but I was beginning to divine the reason for his mood changes. I understood. Until then, my preoccupations had prevented me from distinguishing things that ought to have leapt to my eyes.

Of course. *Her hair is brown, so brown, so brown!* That's Mademoiselle Vitalis! Charming, the young woman, the exquisite flower of our colony, and good, and gentle, and full of talents, as useful as they were various... No, let's pass over the talents... She's delightful, and it's scarcely astonishing that my young friend Marcel should have fallen madly in love in the space of a fortnight. Yes, yes, I see—he has all the appearances of a fellow prey to the ancient malady. Why didn't I see it immediately? So he's renounced going with me; he no longer wants to leave the ruins of Harlem, an enchanted abode, the cellars of the Vandermolen house, which she illuminates with her presence!

And Miraud? That's obvious too; Mademoiselle Jeanne's lovely eyes have set fire to his heart as well; he's in love with her too... Anyway, how could it be otherwise? They all adore her, each in his fashion. Vandermolen, who no longer has a sou, wants to make her his sole heir. Dr. Christiansen proclaims her his favorite pupil, in medicine and pessimistic philosophy, in spite of the laughter with which the young woman resists all catastrophes. And Jollimay gives her lectures on History or the progress of artillery, and the Annamite, and Gibson, and the Peruvian—all of them, the rifleman Mohammed...and me too, of course! Naturally. All those individuals, depressed by so many misfortunes and sufferings, sense the sweetness of her presence among them, amid this rubble, under the perpetual threat of death. She represents both the dolorous beauty of the past and the little glimmer of hope that filters through the funereal blackness of our caves...

All the same, this evening, here's Marcel taking me to one side and telling me that he's changed his mind and wants to go with me, as soon as possible...

What's got into him now? The aviator Miraud and he are avoiding one another. As soon as one appears in one of the corners of our lodgings, the other moves away and disappears. At meal times, as it's necessary to come together in the part of the cellar that serves as dining room, they make a point of not looking at one another, and stare at the ceiling, frowning.

Fortunately, my noisy arguments with Dr. Christiansen or Monsieur Jollimay prevent the others from noticing. But Jeanne Vitalis remains silent; one no longer hears her young voice striving to cast a little tonic gaiety into our morose conversation.

Amour, amour! Your flames are dangerous; you too bring us redoubtable explosives! Now my two fellows have become rivals. It's becoming disquieting. Are they looking to murder one another? Are they going to bring hatred and discord into our refuge, where all these specimens of such diverse races live in perfect harmony and general sympathy?

What if I convinced one or other of them to go with me? That would pay my saviors back nicely for my debt of gratitude. All things considered, it's Marcel I'd like to take, and as soon as possible. It would be better for him. He's very sad. Undoubtedly, he's taken stock of the situation; he's telling himself that Miraud has been living for longer in the intimacy of the Vitalis ladies, and that there must be a more long-standing, more proven, sympathy between him and the young woman, against which he can scarcely compete.

Well, I declare to Marcel that I'm delighted with his resolution, and that we're going to make our final preparations for the departure. While he was wasting his time gardening or hunting, I've explored the terrain around Harlem methodically, and put all the information together. Monsieur Vandermolen, while regretting and disapproving of our attempt, has indicated the suspect points, the directions to avoid, and the paths to follow in order to avoid running into Boche positions, at least within a certain distance—twenty or twenty-five kilometers. Beyond that is the unknown, the plunge into the mysterious horror that surrounds us and encircles us on all sides.

Twenty-five kilometers of relative security, and afterwards, everything to fear, a thousand possible accidents and catastrophes, and all perils: the enemy, fatigue, hunger…especially hunger. *Brrr!* Let's not get frightened; we'll soon see!

"After twenty-five kilometers, if you run into insurmountable difficulties, as I expect, don't be obstinate—come back to Harlem," said the hospitable Vandermolen, who has drawn me an approximate map of the region and made me a gift of a compass. "We'll be very glad to see you again. Your apartment in the house will remain at your disposal."

It's settled; we're going to risk everything and go; we'll soon find out what there is ahead of us.

Part Two: The Age of Burrows

I. One epidemic more or less.

A week! I gave myself that interval, which I thought very large, to finish the last preparations for our escape, and if I can believe my notebook, if I haven't forgotten to mark a day on the little calendar I've improvised, it's now seventy-three days that I've been living in Harlem, in Monsieur Vandermolen's basements, with all the companions who have become my friends.

And seventy-three very busy days, well furnished with incident, filled with emotions, and with a few new anguishes into the bargain!

We've had a few alarms during those seventy-three days. A shell demolished our chimney, but the American billionaire, who is very dexterous, was able to repair the damage. Five or six layers of deleterious miasmas of various sorts have passed over us.

One night, we nearly all perished. The gases were fabulously lacrymogenic. I wept all the tears in my body; it seems to me that I'll never again be able to shed the smallest one in the chagrins to come. Another time, Madame Vitalis, having adjusted her mask poorly, found herself badly intoxicated, and was in danger for a long week.

Afterwards, we were inconvenienced by infectious shrapnel fired from the first Boche lines, in advance of The Hague. They brought us typhus. There were a great many sick people in the town—by which I mean in the holes, in all the shelters under the heaps of rubble that represent the town of Harlem—and no medicines with which to treat them. The doctor ran around everywhere, but there was a very anxious moment in confrontation with the development of the epidemic.

We avoid going into the town, enclosing ourselves in our cellar, only going out for food supplies in the direction of the dunes. When the weather is good, we gladly spend our days in the midst of excavations of varying profundity, the labyrinth of holes and grassy knolls taking the place of Monsieur Vandermolen's old tulip garden or the ruins of the windmill that one raised water for its irrigation.

Oh, those gardens! They've been terribly watered by shells of all calibers; there were long battles here in the early days of the second war, and in certain places it's necessary to refrain from touching the ground, for many of the combatants are asleep under all these tumuli, more or less disrupted by the projectiles and invaded by weeds that are covering the remains of crosses.

The epidemic seems to have spared us. The doctor isn't sparing himself. He does everything he can, but the struggle is very difficult without medicines. Pastors, a few priests and people of good will are devoting themselves heroically to helping the sick, trying to save those whose organisms offer sufficient resistance to the scourge—and bury those who succumb.

Fortunately, according to the doctor, the epidemic isn't very serious. It's not like a previous epidemic, four years ago, that made terrible ravages in Amsterdam, Harlem and Delft, and probably elsewhere, claiming thousands of victims in those towns alone.

It seems that the scourge is evolving somewhat; it no longer presents the same characteristics; there are modifications and attenuations in the symptoms and the effects. The doctor attributes these favorable changes to various causes: an attenuation of the toxicity of the microbes because of their great diffusion, or the multiplication of other more or less virulent microbes and the struggle established between them; and then a sort of semi-vaccination acquired by the population, hardened by the kind of existence that they've been leading for so long, becoming refractory even to viruses.

Nevertheless, according to the doctor's own estimates, I know that this benign epidemic has already killed three or four hundred people in the drastically reduced population of the town. We learned from one poor fellow escaped from the German trenches at The Hague that typhus is also rife among the brigands, with almost the same diminished gravity as here.

The doctor has no fear for himself; he had typhus in Silesia, and is now immune to it. We see very little of him. In order not to risk bring the scourge to us, he sleeps at the end of the garden, in the remains of a old stable. Our other companions aren't afraid; they've seen many other scourges and maladies; they declare that they too have been fundamentally vaccinated.

One morning however, there was an alarm among us. Marcel Blondeau, very valiant, very active, and, by virtue of the demands of a twenty-year-old's appetite, always disposed to run off into the dunes in search of some nourishment—rabbits, rats, vegetables or fish—felt very ill.

The doctor came to see him, and seemed dissatisfied.

"Fresh organism," he said to me, taking me to one side. "The boy arrived here from a healthy country, free of all our scourges, falling on to ground saturated with horrors, swarming with bacilli, carrying into his veins all the poisons that a frightfully soiled and polluted atmosphere can contain. He can't present the same resistance as the poor Europeans who are still surviving, for the moment, so many opportunities to die, natural and scientific. We're mithridated, so to speak, by habituation to the scourges, accustomed to breathing and vegetating in the midst of all the abominations distilled so abundantly on all sides by the satanism of accursed Science. I have a fear fears for him…and for you too, who arrived with the same freshness from a fortunate and tranquil land, perfectly healthy, for at the Pole, you had nothing at all to fear from everything that we suffer. Oh, why the devil did you quit those pleasant Polar lands?"

149

He caused a cold chill to pass down my back by looking at me an examining me very closely.

"No headache? Let's see, no pink patches on your skin? No...at least, not yet..."

"You're not very reassuring, you know, doctor!"

"That's because I've seen pink patches on our young friend's epidermis which have taken away the last doubts. He has typhus, damn it! Beware of contagion!"

The patient was isolated, very near to the doctor, in the corner of an old automobile garage, almost as comfortable as a coal-hole; and Madame Vitalis took her chair into it in order to keep vigil with the doctor. We had grave fears for several days. The doctor didn't prognosticate, but when we interrogated him we could tell from his reticence that the boy was gravely afflicted.

Madame Vitalis cared for him with a great deal of devotion—or, rather, nursed him, for deprived of any pharmacy, there was nothing much we could do against the disease. Her daughter was perpetually running to the fields and the dunes, hunting for herbs requested by the doctor for miscellaneous anodyne tisanes, since he didn't have anything better to wage war against the malady.

The young woman, who hadn't previously shown any fear of the epidemic, was utterly distressed and demoralized; her eyes were perpetually imploring the doctor, and when he came back from seeing Marcel she bombarded him with anxious questions—but without ever naming the young man.

"And how is our invalid, Doctor? Has he slept? What of your anxieties yesterday evening? You don't fear for our invalid any longer, do you, Doctor?"

I believed, however, that the two young people had quarreled, since Marcel, ravaged by jealousy, had previously shown poor Jeanne an almost hostile coldness, to which she had responded with an affectation of perfect indifference.

And now, what desolation and anxiety! In the end, the resistant strength of youth and the young man's mental vigor reckoned with the attack. Madame Vitalis came back to us, in the common room, with her face almost joyful.

"Well," I demanded, "Is there hope?"

"He's saved! The doctor is rubbing his hands and he's gone into town to visit other patients. By the way, it's said that there's cholera now..."

"Cholera! And you announce that calmly!"

"Yes, cholera—like last year, the malady has begun very quietly, in the Melkbrug district, where there are little canals obstructed by ruins, and stagnant water..."

"Bah!" said the aviator Miraud, who was coming back from the dunes with two rabbits in a sack. "We've seen many others. By taking a few little precautions, we'll get through your cholera."

The American billionaire was in the midst of discussions with Mademoiselle Vitalis regarding the repair of his single shoe—he only had one leg—which resembled a Mohican moccasin in a poor state, more like what we would have called a sock prior to 1914. He shrugged his shoulders with a perfectly indifferent expression. Jeanne Vitalis smiled. She had suddenly recovered her gaiety.

"One epidemic more or less," she said, "is of no importance."

The worthy Senegalese rifleman rolled his eyes and showed all his teeth in a broad silent laugh. "Boche cholera's worn out now," he said. "I don't care about that."

So be it—let's treat these plagues with scorn and think about something else—for example, of getting away from here as soon as possible. "I want to go home, damn it!" I repeat every day it the doctor, who replies with his usual pessimism.

"Home my dear Monsieur? Do you even know whether anything is left of your 'home?' Perhaps your apartment, your house, and your entire quarter are in an even worse state than this superb family home, the patrimonial manor of our friend Vandermolen—which is to say, the heap of broken ruins in which we've organized our precarious existence."

A scarcely agreeable perspective! However, the terrible doctor is a little less somber and bitter at the moment, because he's very busy. He runs to his patients, he agitates, he lavishes petty cares or soothing words on them for want of medicines, or brutalizes them, in accordance with circumstances, in order to rebuilt their morale. While doing that, he spends less time devoting himself to despair, and forgets to roar his wrath and maledictions.

He laughed sarcastically while making me glimpse such awful possibilities for the peaceful apartment that I loved to describe to him in our conversations when, bleak and weary, we went back to our cavern.

Monsieur Jollimay and Maître Saladin laughed too, looking at one another.

"Your peaceful apartment!" said Maître Saladin. "Yes, yes, perhaps—continue to hope, that's not forbidden to you…as it is to me for my study! Where is it, my poor study? In what state? More damaged than I am, my second clerk told me, when I met him in Bavaria in a village we'd just taken. He was able to inform me about my study. He was in the air force, my second clerk; one day, three or four years ago, patrolling on the western front near here he was able to make a detour to fly over the area. He circled and circled, at a low altitude looking for our poor study…impossible to discover it, to recognize the street, or even the neighborhood. The entire region in little pieces, in smithereens! And I had a major affair in progress—the liquidation of an important inheritance: a magnificent Renaissance château in the area, superb estate, woods, farms, etc. But I think the château, converted to a strong position, was bombarded for eighteen months. Oh, my minutes, my poor minutes!"

"Perhaps your second clerk didn't see very clearly, or didn't search very hard," I said to him, in a low voice. "Listen—what if we were to go to see for ourselves, try to get out of here…?"

Maître Saladin shook his head.

II. Excursions and Reconnaissance

I go out every day with a few of my companions in the refuge. I've explored the surroundings with them, usually circulating in the trenches that are dug more or less everywhere, and which replace roads on the surface, long since disappeared under rubble or invading vegetation.

In order to formulate a plan of campaign I study the routes, trying to obtain dome notion of the facilities or difficulties and the eventual perils—in brief, everything that I might find before me in such and such a direction.

The ruins of villages, almost all dating back several years have a less lamentable appearance than that of the own; nature has rehabilitated them more fully, dressed and ornamented them. Sometimes, we pass the cadaver of a farm or a hamlet, collapsed in the course of some frightful drama and one might think that they were cheerful and verdant hillocks where children go to play among the flowers, picking poppies or strawberries. Sometimes we discover a path where one might expect to see young girls emerging from beneath the foliage, singing, and that path leads to some tumulus planted with hundreds of wooden crosses, keeling over, bearing effaced inscriptions, covered in brushwood, under which one also glimpses shells, old rusty helmets, the debris of weapons...

Where are they, those village girls that I imagine pink and pretty underneath their Dutch plaits, in their old brightly colored picturesque costumes? Where are the insouciant children? Yes, where are they all, alas?

I sometimes perceive inhabitants; I see them coming out of holes underneath the ruins, or burrows similar to the one where we were collected after our disembarkation: people with wan faces, clad in raged costumes, advancing prudently, with anxious expressions, their hands clutching old weapons adapted as clubs. They go forth like us, in search of more or less bizarre game; they head toward some square of ground spared in the genera devastation, where they grow vegetables,

154

the precious potatoes, onion, turnips and carrots, awaited by their families or their companions left behind in the refuges, hidden in the woods or under the ruins.

In such encounters we look at one another suspiciously, one calls out from a distance before approaching. I also interrogate, asking questions, in quest of news; I'd so much like to know what is happening elsewhere, beyond our narrow horizon. Of news, there is none. No one knows anything; everyone stays confined in his hole, hiding like a hunted animal, only trying to live and to endure.

And in the city—in what we persist in calling the city—it's the same. People live in families or in groups in old solid cellars, which have so far resisted them bombardments, and have often been consolidated by beams and heaps of rubble or sacks of earth. Some quarters, more maltreated than others, are entirely deserted, while the population has concentrated in better protected places, leaving the excessively ruined ruins to packs of dogs and wild cats, thin, bristling and hungry, always hunting and always tracked themselves by hunters with empty bellies.

The human faculty of adaptation is extraordinary, of people living in these deplorable conditions, always under the threat of worse catastrophes, at peril from shells and bombs, collapses, poisoning by gas, maladies and plagues that the world no longer knew, with the dread of famine as well—ever-imminent famine, always possible with brief delay if everyone, in the quotidian struggle for nourishment, doesn't do his utmost in the perpetual effort to keep going as best they can. And I observe that they seem to consider that wretched day-to-day existence as entirely natural, and don't appear to be astonished or indignant at all. They only think about the danger at the moment it materializes; the rest of the time, I believe, they don't think about anything except the pursuit of their daily bread.

What am I saying, bread? There has been no more bread for a long time, since there are no more wheat-fields and no more agriculture. Bread has been replaced by potatoes, which everyone tries to produce in the gardens that are shared between all the available arms, in all the accessible terrains, vague fields and old public promenades.

It's the triumph of ingenious people, of practical people, and above all of those who possessed, before the great torment, a little knowledge of gardening.

The families of the bourgeois class, in general, the former rich, the people with strong-boxes filed with the title-deeds of income from Estates, of shares that were said to be absolutely safe, have fallen, along with those derisory pieces of paper to the utmost degree of poverty, and are vegetating awkwardly and lamentably in their devastated homes, while the poor devils once devoid of cash are making their way in the new world with more facility. The rich men of today are those who possess a goat or two, or well-protected chickens, precious resources in case of bad days, but over which it is necessary to maintain very careful surveillance, for fear of the envious and hungry marauders.

And those worthy people don't moan about the misfortunes of the times, and don't make a fuss about an emission of asphyxiating gas or one epidemic more or less; they try to keep apart, to protect themselves from and against everything, and to live—to live in spite of the accumulation of impossibilities. I scarcely see anyone except the doctor, who doesn't accept these new conditions of existence, without perpetual protest.

"Well, yes, my dear Monsieur, you're up to date now. You know as much as I do. You find it jolly, our super-civilized existence, eh? Come on, though, stick out that tongue so that I can see it...not bad. And no headache? That's good, you'll avoid the typhus. Anyway, the epidemic is decreasing, petering out! Yes, yes, you see here all Europe in miniature. The same thing everywhere, Monsieur, and the same pleasures!"

"What stupefies me," I say, "is to see these populations, the peasants, the ravaged villages, the mariners of the coast, as well as the inhabitants of that wretched ruined city, showing such a perfect resignation—or, rather, a tranquil acceptance of their dire lot!"

"Can they do otherwise? It's necessary. Flee? Seek to go elsewhere? Where, if you please? In the beginning, yes, there was many an exodus of population, bewildered flights from the unleashed Teutonic hordes, fearful of ravages and barrages, under the hail of explosives and he sheets of gas, extinguishing life everywhere in front of the invading troops. But now, where would they go? Flee through all the dangers? Why? To find oneself somewhere else, further away, no matter where, in exactly the same situation? As futile as it is impossible! Better to stay in one's shelter, and try to endure, with difficulty, scratching the earth to maintain one's life..."

"If that existence is really worth the trouble..."

"Well, well, you're in a black mood—are you becoming a somber pessimist too? I told you so! My good Monsieur, examine the state of Europe, only to think about her—look at the picture! Europe! Do you remember the photographs of the Moon, which showed us a world in demolition, a soil covered in holes, in brittle and crumbling craters? Well, if there are astronomers on the Moon, that's exactly what they must see here now! Undoubtedly, the Moon has passed through the same horrors as us; there will have been some race of prey there, lunatic Boches to devastate everything and turn everything upside-down, to the extent of complete and definitive extinction.

"In our devastated Europe there's no longer anything but trenches. Those trenches, zigzagging across all countries, furrowing, cutting, slicing and crosshatching plains and mountains, have been, for a long time already, the sole fashion of laboring that the poor earth has known European! The fronts—I don't say armies; there are no more armies, but entire peoples under arms—the fronts penetrate one another and become entangled, friends and enemies all mixed up, pell-mell. Gradually, they've formed islets of a sort, more or less vast; regions of resistance and combat, around a center of war factories, in a state to function more or less actively. The old war materiel, with which the carnage commenced, having been used up long ago, they fabricated improvised materiel as best they can; then it was necessary to have recourse to untried methods, to engines of war entirely new, especially chemical and miasmatic. The modern Bellona was Science, that slut Science! Oh, the frightful visage of the scientific Bellona!"

He went on. He had already repeated all that to me; I knew the picture: the devastated and depopulated countries, the surviving populations crammed together or heaped up in regions forming vast entrenched camps of a sort; war everywhere, danger everywhere, from one end of Europe to the other! Cities destroyed, vast chaotic and desert extents, abandoned fields returned to the wild state, or rather, rendered uncultivable...

Frightful explosives, a hundred thousand infernal volcanoes, have ravaged everything at certain particularly disputed and assailed points, where nothing subsists, neither an intact tree nor a standing section of wall—not even the appearance of houses or edifices. The very soil is burned, corroded and cracked.

Aerial squadrons traverse the skies in rapid flights, bombarding with chemical grenades anything that allows itself to be glimpsed. Death comes, precipitated, rising or falling everywhere.

So it's finished; humankind finds itself forced to live underground henceforth, in order to escape the diabolical engines, themselves well-hidden and buried, which sweep the ground everywhere with storms of metal, electric or paralyzing currents, corrosive clouds and asphyxiating sheets, visible or invisible, burning and mercilessly ravaging the lungs that breathe them in.

The populations that escaped, in the first years of the general war, being smashed by explosives, intoxicated by sheets of gas, canisters of mortal vapors, infernal projections of flames, acids or miasmas, have buried themselves in the soil. People live underground, hollowing out the fields as profoundly as they can, the good old once-nourishing earth; one digs through clay, through stone or through rock.

The European of today is a troglodyte almost everywhere; he has gone back all the way to the age of caves, has bored shelters under rock and carved out catacombs. I've seen all that in Harlem. There are strange architectures, "dug-outs" and "rat-runs" the aviator Miraud calls them. I don't know those new terms of the art of building. People huddle together in long dark burrows, with entrances as well-concealed as possible—"camouflaged," as the aviator puts it, once again—and inside, they nourish themselves on privations, vegetate in the pangs of hunger. By night they slip out of the burrows, cautiously, to cultivate some corner of land and plant vegetables on the slops of craters or shell-holes.

This long-distance, blind, scientific warfare, can no longer make any distinction between civilians and belligerents; everyone lives fully exposed to the same dangers, always and everywhere, in the same common infernal furnace, and I distinguish in everyone the submission to the inevitable, the resigned fatalism, that is the new and dismal form of courage.

Thus, all the treasure of civilization, all the capital of beauty heaped up by the golden centuries of the earth, is lost, smashed, crushed, along with the Arts, wealth, with thought itself.

Horror! Terror! Abomination!

III. Strange game, wild dogs and horses.

My young companion in shipwreck, Marcel Blondeau, has entered into full convalescence. The doctor had given him permission to go out and breathe the sea breeze on the dunes. He is delighted. He has gone with Madame Vitalis and Mr. Gibson, the American billionaire. Two wooden legs constitute a guarantee against the dangers of too long a walk.

The young man is overflowing with cheerful spirit. The return of health is making him see everything rose-tinted. War, massacre and famine, bombs and flames, gas and miasmas—

bah! What's all that? One has heart and solid legs again, the sun is shining…and Jeanne Vitalis' smile is blossoming frankly again, whenever their eyes meet.

Madame Vitalis has taken a basket in order to bring back vegetables, if she can. Mr. Gibson is hoping to catch crabs on the sand, or catch a few fish on the way. One hears the two wooden legs going tick-tock over the stones of the ruins, and Marcel Blondeau, impatient, runs on ahead. I have to catch him up in order to give him his mask, which he has forgotten.

When they came back, three hours later, Madame Vitalis pulled a face, because her basket only contained a little greenery destined to be converted into spinach, and Mr. Gibson could only display a single eel of very small dimensions, two octopodes and various shellfish. But the young convalescent came back even more joyful than when he set out, and more alert. He had seen the clouds racing across the sky again, under the great breath of the breeze, and the sea sparkling green and yellow under the sun, and the fringes of foam of the yellow sand, and the verdure of the dunes dotted with flowers of every hue.

He brought back a bouquet. Oh, flowers! No one even spared them a glance; my companions gave a better welcome to the fake spinach and the eel. Marcel Blondeau was desolate.

"Bah!" said the doctor, to console him. "Do you think that a bunch of the rosiest and freshest roses, with the accompaniment of pearls of dew, would have had any great effect on the castaways of the *Medusa*? You don't suppose so? Well, as I've already told you, we're on the raft of the *Medusa*."

Poor Marcel was welcomed more kindly when he offered his bouquet to Mademoiselle Vitalis. The young woman gladly breathed in the perfume of the flowers, which smelled most of all of the open air and the briny mists of the sea. But Marcel had something else to offer: two dozen little strawberries, which he had discovered in a sheltered hollow, doubtless an old shell-hole, behind Monsieur Vandermolen's old gardens. It was Jeanne, again, who divided them between us all.

A few days later, our society was able to rejoice in two windfalls of greater importance. Firstly, it was Mohammed Bamakou, the Senegalese, who came back from a long-distance hunting expedition with the cadaver of an enormous dog over his shoulder and two geese in a sack. As he was beating the country in quest of some sort of game in the direction of the old polders reconquered by the sea since the destruction of the dykes and drainage mills, he had become game himself, attacked by a pack of hungry roaming dogs, living—as I had already had occasion to observe—by hunting.

"Fortunately," Mohammed told us, showing us the saber-bayonet passed through his belt and the iron hook on his right hand, "I thrust into the dog-pack left-handed, and struck down from above with the right."

He had got out of it fairly lightly, with only a few nips, and had brought back one of his assailants.

"The biggest one," he added, with a legitimate pride. "The fattest one too—good to eat!"

My companions palpated the prey and congratulated Mohammed. The Senegalese went to skin his dog right away, and two haunches were salted in order to conserve them as provisions for the winter, since Madame Vitalis was not over-stretched with regard to food supplies for the present.

"But what about these two geese, did they attack you too, Mohammed?" asked Monsieur Jollimay, when the Senegalese showed off his other catch.

Mohamed smiled. "These are wild geese that I trapped, wild geese passing through the dunes."

"Ha ha!" went some of our companions. "Very fat, your wild geese. Mohammed always has good luck hunting!"

"Be careful, Mohammed," said the doctor. "Hunt as much as you want, but no marauding!"

"Only pilfering," said the Annamite smiling at Mohammed's protestations.

The second find that fell into our laps was even bigger. Game again—but the game was a horse.

Horses galloping across deserted and uncultivated fields had already been pointed out to me, in the distance—horses that had reverted to the free and wild state of distant ages, living in groups of three or four, and living rather poorly, because they seemed rather skeletal to me. The Peruvian Lieutenant Bustamente, the New Zealander Clifton and the aviator Miraud had been promising for some time to try to capture one. To that effect they had fabricated lassos and practiced their use in the dunes, without telling anyone about their intention to consider the Dutch countryside as an Argentine pampas.

That day they had gone out hunting rats, taking their lassos just in case.

They came back late in the evening. We were beginning to get anxious about them, because we had head cannon fire in the distance, toward Leyden. Nothing fell on Harlem, though. Doubtless the Boche in The Hague were firing at the lines of Utrecht and Amsterdam, or receiving a few shells themselves.

Finally, night having fallen, utterly black, with no stars in the sky, without the slightest tiny light anywhere, we saw—or, rather, heard—our rat-hunters coming back. They were cheerful, because we could hear muffled laughter and heavy footsteps that were making stones roll. Slightly intrigued, a few of us went up into the courtyard to meet them.

"There you are," said Monsieur Vandermolen. "How many rats?"

"Only one, but it's a big one," Miraud replied.

In a soft voice, to the tune of a funeral march, and bumping into rubble, he sang:

> *Behold the work of the hideous Boche.*
> *Hideous his soul, hideous his sin.*
> *His Kaiser vomited from the trash,*
> *His princes born of the Devil's kin...*

A great black shadow appeared between two heaps of debris, drawn by the Peruvian lieutenant and driven from behind by the other two, with blows inflicted by sticks. The moon would have been useful, but it did not show its face.

Our companions' prey was showing a marked reluctance to come into our abode, but, unceremoniously abused, it was obliged to abandon any idea of resistance.

> *Hypocrite pastors, satanic men of science*
> *Reiters and panders all, slouching to the feast,*
> *Meek poets singing German impenitence*
> *At joyful carnage, slavering like beasts...*

"Artillery horse," said Miraud, recovering his ordinary voice. "A bit thin, but it can be fattened up. Damnation, it gave us a hard time!"

"Where did you find it?" asked the doctor.

"Over there, a long way out between the lines, toward the Palace of Peace. We lay in ambush for three or four hours in holes, at the bottom of a slope with yellowing verdure—

which, we supposed, ought to be appreciated by the wild cavalry. In the end, as we were beginning to despair, five horses arrived, trotting toward the provender. That was the delicate moment—we feared being spotted in our hiding place. Then, as soon as the horses had their muzzles in the grass, we fell on them. Devilish cavalcade, pursuit, they got the bit in their teeth, and so did we…you can see the gallop from here, and the Boches could have spotted us…anyway, I'll pass over the details; we haven't come back empty-handed, but that's because this big old nag was limping. With a lasso, Monsieur—we caught him with a lasso, like gauchos!"

"To the stable, quickly!" said the Peruvian, "And above all, tie our prey up solidly, he's run us ragged, and it's necessary not to let him get away."

In anticipation of a successful hunt, they had prepared a little stable of sorts some time before, in an old laundry in the basement. It was sufficiently comfortable for a wild horse, and a solidly barricaded door guaranteed it against any escape attempt.

The animal was attached to the iron bars of a small window, a rick of hay brought back from the hunters was put in its trough, and it was left tranquilly to its meditations.

"Artillery horse, a big Pomeranian—a fine animal in his day, for sure," the aviator went on, sitting down. "He's slightly lame, but it's trivial. He must have stumbled in some shell-hole."

"But what the devil do you intend to do with your Pomeranian?" I asked.

"First of all," replied the three hunters, all speaking together, "we're going to pamper him, lavish him with caresses, feed him up—fatten him up, if you prefer—that's indispensable."

"And then?"

"Then keep him carefully in the larder for the winter. Think about it—an entire horse; that represents a good provision of meat, and we'll be very glad to find that in December or January, when food becomes scarce."

"Poor beast!" I said.

"Yes, pity us," said the doctor. "There's yet another lamentable consequence of the frightful cataclysm: the disappearance of the best animal species. That infernal science has precipitated humankind into an ocean of misfortunes, and not only humankind, but also the inferior friends of humankind, the good and worthy beasts that have put all their confidence in humans—a wretched placement! The horse, the ox, the dog, the sheep, docile servants or slaves of humankind...they have nothing to expiate; they don't have any part in our criminal follies! And where have we led them? To a general massacre, to complete destruction! Where are they? Second-class canon-fodder, which no one thought of sparing, poor beasts thrown into incomprehensible terror, amid the thunder and the flames, under rains of metal falling from the clouds, succumbing under overwhelming fatigues imposed by the dementia of the pitiless master, and rotting in the fields, in ravines, in shell-holes...all of them, crushed, exterminated, eaten, except for a few specimens that escaped the carnage, escaped across the empty fields, wandering miserably among the ruins, in terror and stupor..."

"Yes, there are some," said Miraud, "which must have their own ideas about the devastation of humankind...*humans*, the dispensers of caresses, work and nourishment, the masters of everything, the God gone suddenly insane!"

"The ox, the sheep, unknown now, abolished, destroyed. Fabulous animals! The horse and the dog almost as rare!"

"A precious capture, that horse! That gives us a respectable number of assured meals for the impending winter. The winter is the hard season, when hunger and sadness reign in our cellars and dugouts. In spite of all the foresight, all the economy possible in the good months of summer and autumn, rationing is necessary...so, a precious capture, that horse! Smoked horse, you know, is very good, and that conserves it. Oh, if we'd had it last winter, when the potatoes and the artichokes ran out and it was necessary to buckle our belts very tightly!"

A precious capture, that horse!

"Truly? Nothing to buy, then?"

Everyone looked at me, as if astonished by my naivety. Madame Vitalis burst out laughing, frankly.

I ought to have known, however, that there had been no more question of money for a long time among the Troglodytes among whom I was going to live—and it must be the same in all the desolate regions of unfortunate Europe, no one having anything to buy or to sell. Everyone had to strive to produce and extract from the soil by his own industry what was sufficient for his alimentation. A problem bristling with difficulties—and it was with great difficulty that anyone was able to extract anything from that old earth, spoiled and massacred everywhere as well. It was still necessary to protect it—and sometimes to defend it. A frightful and perpetual worry for wan humankind!

All commerce between humans was now reduced to a few meager exchanges of foodstuffs, or wretched items of any sort.

What use could money be in the new conditions of life? That money, so coveted once for all that it could buy, was no more now than base metal, less useful than iron and utterly disdained, which is worse than being scorned. Gibson, the ex-billionaire, told me that he might still pick up a brand new *louis d'or* or a pound sterling, if he happened to stumble over one in the street, but only as a simple curiosity of an extinct age, to keep alongside his old check book!

IV. Warming discussions for rainy days.

We're living an existence that I find very miserable, for want of habitude. Our comrades are better adapted to it, having been accustomed to it for such a long time, and they have known worse distress and more frightful situations, before arriving at one they genuinely considered to be a haven of refuge.

The good Madame Vitalis has conserved a residue of affectation in our burrow; she wants to show that she was a woman of the world when there was a world. She cares for our burrow; she has fabricated a feather duster, with which she dusts our heap of bricks and stones continually.

Jeanne Vitalis, who cannot have any memory of better days, is very much sat ease in our miserable encampment; she is cheerful, always laughing, especially now that Marcel Blondeau has recovered his health, disposed to find everything perfect and agreeable in our cellar, in the town around us, and perhaps in the entire world, provided that Marcel is no longer sad and that he continues to aid her in her little tasks in the various gardens cultivated here and there, or to ask her advice about the fabrication of rat-traps and rabbit-snares.

The billionaire Howard Gibson also accepts things very well, and doesn't weep over his vanished millions any more than his missing leg. The man has the blood of a rude squatter, a wood-runner of the Far West, and he doesn't make any kind of chorus with the complaints and furies of Dr. Christiansen. He is full of valor and takes each day as it comes.

When the sun shines, that works. We go out, we devote ourselves to movement. I try to be of some use in the association, in order not to live here as a costly parasite. But what can I do? How can I play my part in the labor and its profits?

In my capacity as a naturalist, I know mushrooms. I beat the dunes in search of *Boletus edulis* and other edible cryptogams. I garden a little, but I find that I dig ineptly and that it's better for everyone if I stick to giving advice, which the practical and experienced men follow when they judge it acceptable. That's a little humiliating.

But what becomes of me during the long rainy days, when it seems almost impossible to emerge from our cellars, when the downpour stings, when the paths over the rubble become slippery and one paddles through the ravines, running the risk of getting stuck in the mud and drowning? It's already bad enough in the summer; what will it be like in the winter, when Pluviose, Nivose and Ventose[14] come to persecute us?

On days of heavy downpours we have to stay at the bottom of our hole. Mr. Gibson has fabricated a chessboard and plays with Mohammed or Madame Vitalis. The Armenian businessman, the Rumanian and the Spaniard talk about business and commerce, and tell one another about fine deals they once made.

These people of various nationalities and mentalities, get along very well and almost understand one another. They've created a kind of dialect particular to our burrow, which, with effort, I'm beginning to grasp. But I let them chatter away and I prefer to talk to the two Frenchwomen, Miraud the aviator or Maître Saladin the captain-notary when Dr. Christiansen and Monsieur Jollimay don't start an argument when the first raindrops fall, designed to be continued more or less excitedly until the downpour ends.

Monsieur Jollimay almost gives us lectures in history when he fulminates against the imperialisms that have upset the world in the course of the centuries, but at least he fulminates without exploding, in a slow, sad voice, while the doctor, in his rages against science—the servant of imperialisms and the purveyor of engines of death—shouts and vociferates,

---

[14] The three winter months of the new secularized calendar introduced after the 1789 Revolution.

gesticulates and thumps his fist, to the great peril of our furniture, except when he gurgles muted imprecations in the depths of his throat, when his voice fails him.

"Imperialism, Empire: abominable words that ought to be despised and cursed by all human beings and banished from dictionaries. Despotism weighing upon the submissive and conquered countries, the organized exploitation of peoples to the profit of one man, one family or one patriciate. Always and everywhere, in the history of the world, those empires cemented with blood, crumbling after a time over mountains of ruins, always those hegemonies provoking just revolts, always the insensate dreams of universal domination of a man, a caste or a race, end in slaughter, producing frightful misfortunes, hurricanes, whirlwinds and cataracts of dolor over the world! Follow me, Doctor, let's take the Oriental Empires of old, and we'll see..."

"No!" exclaims the doctor. "Let's leave Nebuchadnezzar and Assurbanipal in the Hell where they're suffering their punishment, I hope. They're very petty sires and paltry malefactors by comparison with the satanic Hohenzollerns of today! But who, if you please, has forged and prepared the formidable unknown weapons and perfected them ferociously the while, for the frightful organizers of the universal carnage of today? Who, if not Science?"

"...The folly of domination," Jollimay goes on, without paying any attention, "the imperialism of despots, their rage of domination and hegemony, producing and propagating the dementia of blind and deluded people..."

"...The furious delirium of a race of prey!" shouts the doctor. "Filthy Prussia, eldest daughter of the Church of Satan, vomit of the Devil! We're living in full Demonocracy, Monsieur!"

"Agreed!"

"Yes, a people of prey aspiring to booty! But it's the idea of the invincibility of these new weapons forged by Science that decides the movement and brings peoples to make themselves the instruments of despots when, by study, cunning and duplicity, everything has been prepared for the vast rapines and universal looting!"

"The monstrous appetites of a few ferocious brutes, a caste of feudal lords hungry for wealth and advantages, theoreticians of productive massacre, overlords of great industry and finance avid for billions and power...to table for the feast! To table! Growls and howls of joy, gods and demons of Germanic Hells, Odin, Thor, Wotan and all the rest, and Mephistopheles, and the witches, vampires and ghouls of the Sabbats of the Brocken! You see that: he collective soul of an entire people sold to the Devil at a stroke, fifty million Fausts joyfully signing the pact with Satan that will deliver them all the wealth of the world, universal empire and total power over the Prussified planet!"

"What revelations of humankind!" cries the doctor, hoarsely. "What extraordinary observations, what stupefying data on the real depths of the human soul! The true limits of human nature were unknown, the extreme frontiers of humanity, the limits of human strength and faculties, for evil as well as for good... we didn't know how far human ferocity could extend...or descend...but we know now. The diabolicoarabic horrors of Germanism have marked the point, never before attained! Do we know the supreme limits of heroism?"

"That's true," says Jollimay. "Let's ask at Verdun, the banks of the Yser, the Marne or the Somme, the plains of Picardy or Champagne... And the high-water level of love and hatred, the limits of endurance, of patience and devotion, of rascality and ignominy, of all the sentiments and all the passions, of all the exacerbated faculties... And the extreme point of madness? Look at Russia..."

"Oh!" clamors the doctor, taking his head in his hands as if he wants to tear it away. "Oh...! Madness! madness! madness! Quickly, the straitjacket for Humankind! What years we have lived! There were times, in the immense terror of that seething fulguration of explosives and gas, grinding the living and the dead into the ground in all directions, sweeping the atmosphere with great gusts of fire and making the planet

171

shudder to its utmost depths, there were times when I felt my brain jumping and colliding with the walls of my skull, and I held my head, ready to fly away; the general, universal madness gripped me...I searched, in the lightning and the fire setting the sky and all the heights ablaze, I searched for the Exterminating Angel of the End of the World... And I saw him, the Exterminating Angel of the End of the World... Yes, I saw him...the Exterminating Angel of the End of the World, sent by God, finally revolted by the delirium of his creature. I saw him greeted in the clouds by an immense barrage of gunfire!"

But the clouds have passed over, the downpour has stopped. One after another, we quit our cavern to climb back up into the daylight. The doctor and Jollimay don't notice it; they continue their discussion. From outside, I can still hear the two voices, alternating in the depths of our burrow.

"...Science, accomplice for the work of iron and fire...science preparing the bloodbath of the Hohenzollerns...

"And do you know, Monsieur, how many, in the course of the last century—that century of enlightenment and mildness, of refined civilization and increasing rapid progress—how many Europeans in the flower of their age, in the full bloom of their youth, have been devoured in wars, the struggles of various imperialisms? Thirty-five millions, Monsieur, thirty-five, if not forty! European scholarship can be proud of its crushing superiority, for in the same lapse of a single century, warrior massacres hardly caused one or two million people to perish in Africa, a land of savage tribes, a land of ignorant barbarity...scarcely one or two millions..."

"And then, for them, for those worthy cannibals, it was to eat them!" cries Miraud, looking back toward the disputants.

Scaling the slippery banks, the aviator starts declaiming dully into his beard, "Request: *Death in the Heavens*...a novelty unknown to our ancestors, limited and earthbound...

Humankind, ferocious insect, scales the skies,
Surpasses in the azure the eagle of the snowy peaks,

172

And goes forth bearing death as he sublimely flies,
To splatter blood on clouds and God's pink cheeks!

V. The supreme conference at the Palace of Peace.

It was all very well to have a horse, entire and alive, in the larder, but while waiting to sacrifice it to the appetite of the community, it was necessary to feed it, to stuff it with oats and hay to fatten it up.

The difficulties materialized when the question of the indispensable ration of oats came up. How were we to procure that daily ration, that provender, in sufficient quantity? A council was held, and an expedition to lay in supplies was decided. It was necessary to go quite a long way into the grassy meadows of the interior, to have any hope of discovering, for want of oats, enough forage and fresh verdure, not withered, burned or poisoned by emissions of toxic gases.

Early one morning we set off in a troop, well equipped with a very varied collection of weapons and furnished with our masks, which Madame and Mademoiselle Vitalis had checked carefully, or sown up the seams. The ladies remained at the house to carry out domestic tasks, for they had to carry out a thorough cleaning of our burrow and repair a pile of worn-out clothes.

The billionaire Gibson and Maître Saladin, by reason of their wooden legs, stayed to form a garrison with Marcel Blondeau, always active in helping the ladies in case of need, and to see to the gardens in the dunes, as well as the rabbit-snares. The valiant Jollimay, in spite of his wooden leg, had insisted on taking part in the expedition.

The weather was fine; the sun rose behind the hills of sand where the opulent villas of Dutch Nabobs returned from Java, Sumatra and Borneo had once displayed their sumptuous and picturesque white and red facades, beneath the verdure of their parks, refreshed by the benevolent sea breezes.

Where are they, the opulent excessively decorated villas? Blown away by the breath of heavy cannons, pulverized by the

173

squalls of huge shells or aerial torpedoes. Where are the Nabobs? Perhaps crouched in the depths of some cellar, miraculously uncollapsed, in some hole contrived among the ruins of their shattered manors, striving to eke out as best they can a dangerous, precarious and malnourished existence, just like us in Monsieur Vandermolen's house, for want of being able to go forth under kinder skies.

Monsieur Vandermolen guided us. He often sighed, the poor man, at the memory of the splendors of old; he groaned in passing through certain ruined parks, in front of certain façades shredded by projectiles or certain portals that no longer led to anything but dismal heaps of stonework and tiles.

"Here, Monsieur, I dined at least once a fortnight in the home of my friend Zuremberg... Very rich, my friend Zuremberg, huge fortune brought back from Batavia, plantations of tea, coffee, etc... What dinners, Monsieur! What menus! Can you imagine...?"

"No details please! No menus! Don't say anything!"

"You're wrong—they still make my mouth water. And to think that we've only been able to bring for our expedition a few boiled potatoes and beets, with no salt! Let me at least console myself be remembering truffled capons, salmis of woodcock...and look, here's Monsieur Floris' house—a former planter in Sumatra. Huge fortune, heaps of millions. We had delightful gatherings! Charming woman, Madame Floris! Magnificent dresses from the great Parisian couturiers, Monsieur! Miraculous liqueurs, the curacaos of the Rajahs! Exquisite teas. Cigars such as the gods of Olympus certainly didn't smoke!"

"Let's not talk about that, I beg you," said the Spaniard Gomares and Lieutenant Bustamente, in unison with artilleryman-professor Jollimay, whom I had already caught resignedly smoking elder-pith or some other pseudo-tobacco of a similar ilk.

Monsieur Vandermolen sighed again, but he consented to stop talking about the dinners of yore.

We marched for three or four hours, sometimes in the tunnels of old trenches, sometimes in bare country, through ancient polders, flooded again, where we waded in Indian file over grassy undulations. To begin with we had veered northwards to avoid the marshes, and then turned eastwards, and I perceived thereafter that we were setting a course frankly southwards, in the direction of Leyden and The Hague, to which the Germans—or, rather, the Germano-Turco-Bulgaro-etc.—had been driven back when Dordecht and Rotterdam had been recaptured, Rotterdam, Amsterdam and Harlem blockading the Hague, and blockaded themselves by the enemy forces entrenched toward Nimegen all along the Waal, the southern branch of the Rhine, perhaps linked with those of Antwerp, or those blockading Antwerp...no one knew, exactly...not to mention the little islets, friends or enemies, lost in the unknown in the middle of devastated territories: a complicated geography, very difficult to sort out for lack of reliable information.

We arrived on hills raised about forty meters above sea level, veritable Alps by the standards of flat Holland. We were not sorry to take a breather, well sheltered by bushes, and rest our legs while having our miserable lunch.

A pretty part of the country! I couldn't help thinking sadly about hunting in the olden days, in the distant times before the deluge...

Monsieur Vandermolen had brought a telescope recovered from the ruins of his house; I borrowed it from him in order to examine the vast spaces we were overlooking, enemy territory or contested deserts, cut by dark lines and speckled with white and yellow patches.

"Way over there is The Hague," Monsieur Vandermolen said. "Can you make it out?"

"Yes quite clearly."

"And can you see, in that direction, those big ruins? Are you there?"

"Yes, I can see. One might think it was an enormous redoubt with several lines of trenches in front..."

The Palace of Peace, transformed into a den of war and death

"The Palace of Peace," said the doctor. "The Boches have their heavy artillery in there, their biggest guns, the giant cannon and all the improved satanic engines... What hurricanes of fire, what fulgurant cyclones, they unleashed in the early days! The Palace of Peace was flamboyant, like a volcano in continuous eruption, among whirlwinds of multicolored smoke. Hell opening up! It's calm now; the enormous guns are silent, doubtless for want of projectiles; the monstrous engines are mute, the red mouths no longer spitting out their tons of poisoned explosives!"

As if to give the lie to the doctor, who was waving a furious fist at the Palace of Peace, transformed into a frightful den of war and death, there was a sudden flash in the distance, and in spite of the distance, a frightful detonation made the ground shake around us. The Palace of Peace, or what was left of it, was covered by a cloud of yellow smoke, which overflowed, swirling in a heavy cumulus, and then rose up into the sky in green, red or violet spirals.

I had ducked down involuntarily, and was almost lying down behind our brushwood. There were further flashes and further shocks, which made the foliage shiver—and me too, I confess. I counted five explosions, and then silence fell again, but the thick clouds of smoke, rolling into one another, floated for a long time over the International Palace of Peace, where the speeches of the pacifist Congresses of old had sung so eloquently to us of the joys of peace between men who had become tender lambs again, and announced so exactly the return of the Golden Age to Earth.

What remained of those promises, those bucolics, those garlands of roses swayed by the brutal breath of heavy artillery, those delights announced by the meek prophets and utopians in god faith, among whom had slid a good number of reptilian hypnotists and "*social-demokrat*" secret agents of Panprussianism and the insatiable vulture of the Hohenzollerns?

What remained of the Palace itself, the imposing architecture of which I remembered vaguely, beneath its colossal ruins, armored shields for the steel monsters of Krupp, the great engineer and stage-setter of the bloody feasts of the old German god Odin, resuscitated by the Hohenzollerns?

"Five!" said the doctor, after the last shock. "But those shells aren't for us. Listen—follow the rumble in the distance. That must be over Amsterdam or Rotterdam."

Scarcely had the roar of the fifth shell died away in a swirl that the wind bore away, than a detonation resounded in the distance, jostling the low clouds on the horizon, traversed by the projectile... A dull sound, a ululation, a growing thunderous din, like an approaching railway train...explosion!

And then a cloud of thick red smoke, with jets of bright flame, in the green and yellow turbulence of the Palace of Peace.

"The Peace Conference!" said the doctor.

"Amsterdam's response," said Monsieur Vandermolen. "Take a look with the telescope..."

There were three responses; three jets of flames rose high into the sky—and that was all. Rings of variously colored smoke remained suspended for some time, paling, and ended up disappearing. The terrified silence of the countryside was no longer troubled.

"Bromine, trinitrotoluene, peroxide, aminol, etc.," said the doctor. "I know that; I've ground it, alas, when I was a captive in the laboratory, cast into the slavery of the Boche factories. Fortunately, I spoiled their monstrous chemistry as much as possible. Oh, if you had heard the concert in those days, to make brains explode, to make the vaults of heaven collapse! But nowadays the lack of raw materials has forced economies, a dearth of explosives everywhere...they're trying to make up for it with miasmas, gases, infectious bombs and bacterial shells, but for how long? What we heard just now, Monsieur, is the death-rattle of the expiring scientific Bellona, the supreme convulsions, the coughs of the final agony of the

monsters of steel spitting out their last tons of explosives before kicking the bucket…Satan uttering his last howl..."

"And that, Doctor," I exclaimed, "will be the end of it?"

"The end, no—but it's the imminent exhaustion of
stocks, complete penury everywhere, the absolute lack of munitions."

"Well, what then?"

"Well, there will still be the other weapons, the old
weapons, those of pre-scientific humankind. Everything that
can smash, slice and perforate, the blade and the club, the bow
and the sword: the sword of the truly valiant! When it's well
established that no one has any more cannons, machine-guns,
explosives, mines or torpedoes, when everyone in both camps
is certain that they no longer have anything to fear from asphyxiating gases, stupefying vapors, deleterious chemicals or
perfidious electrocutions, there will be the savage and hectic
charge of all those who have survived the scientific hecatombs, the supreme assault, to finish it off!"

I was about to protest, to show, on the contrary, peace
gradually renascent, in the general exhaustion, on the ruins of
worn out and demolished engines of war, among the horrified
and breathless survivors, when furious clamors cut off my
speech, and a horde ragged and hirsute individuals surged out
of a trench cutting through the brushwood, brandishing strange
weapons.

VI. A horde of prehistoric warriors.

What an emotion when I think about it! But for the doctor and Monsieur Vandermolen, who had abruptly thrown
themselves forward, their arms raised, we would at least have
been knocked down and pinned to the ground by those fanat-
ics!

And what a sudden apparition of the most distant past,
after the fulgurant recent visions of the most advanced civilization, turned to ferocious *kultur* and finishing in the mon-

strous terrors of scientific barbarity, that abrupt return to primitive ages was!

But the doctor and Monsieur Vandermolen shouted
things I did not understand in Dutch, protesting and arguing
with the most furious members of the menacing horde, and
fortunately, the weapons were lowered, the faces relaxed.

Deeply disturbed, in the shock of surprise, we had fallen
back and assumed defensive postures. As everything seemed
to be settling down, I uttered a sigh of relief.

"Friends, they're friends!" cried the doctor. "Don't worry—worthy people like us, who live in the ruins over
there...departed in quest of nourishment, vegetables or game
of some sort, and who, having mistaken us at a distance for
Boche marauders, crept up on us, crawling from hole to hole,
in the sweet hope of reducing us to little pieces. Fortunately,

we recognized one another in time. It's settled—we won't be killing one another; these gentlemen are good friends!"

I considered with wide eyes those "gentlemen" of such unreassuring appearance and such strange clothing.

With what extraordinary weapons they had wanted to exterminate us a little while ago! Out there, in the expiring citadel of the Palace of Peace, the latest perfections and refinements of technology and science, here, the instruments of war of resuscitated prehistoric peoples. He was right, the doctor—as ever...

There really was a return to primitive might, for the last phases of the struggle, for the final act of the formidable tragedy. I recalled a painting by Cormon at one of the Salons of old, depicting the return from a bear-hunt in prehistoric times:[15] the rude tribesmen, hirsute and muscular, brandishing stone axes and clubs, returning to the family caves with the felled game.

I rediscovered all of that, minus the bear. The newcomers numbered about twenty, young and old men, mostly thin but robust, with solid arms, suntanned, with beards as bushy as those in Cormon's painting, covered rather than dressed in rags more reminiscent of those of prehistory than the civilized costumes once worn in this region of neat and tidy Dutch villages of white, pink or pale green houses, pulverized today.

For the most part, they were wearing cassocks of a sort, of coarse cloth; some of them had torsos covered in goatskins, worn over what might have been the remains of overcoats, secured by rope belts, from which cutlasses dangled.

Leather or canvas socks, extremely worn, and sandals, or rather moccasins, on their feet, and bonnets of furry hide, completed the costumes of the horde.

---

[15] *Retour d'une chasse à l'ours. Âge de la polie Pierre* by "Fernand Cormon" (Fernand Piestre, 1845-1924), exhibited at the Salon of 1885, now in the Musée d'Orsay, part of a series of prehistoric paintings commissioned by the Parisian natural history museum.

They all grouped around us in order to gaze at us curiously with their anxious and wild eyes. They were leaning on large clubs garnished with iron spikes, spears or crude axes with long handles. Two or three of them were even clutching large bows in their muscular fists, shiny and polished, and wearing quivers on their backs furnished with long arrows.

In what times were we living, really? The age of caves? Yes, doubtless, on seeing those fellows, but alas, the age of concrete and armored caves, the lairs not of large wild beasts armed simply and honestly with teeth and claws, but of fabulous monsters of steel spitting hellish flames and toxic gases.

Reminiscences flooded by troubled brain. I thought about another painting, by Puvis de Chavannes this time: *Doux pays*.[16] A pastoral eclogue, a noble dream of poetry, truly dolorous to remember in this era of frightful horrors. O mildness of time times gone by, expired, abolished forever, times that will never return, which never can return! O sweetness of the past! Extinct splendors!

And the memory also passed through my head of a motto inscribed on the bell-tower of a Belgian town, Alost, between Termonde and Antwerp: *Neither hope nor dread*.[17]

In what condition is it now, the bell-tower of Alost? Neither hope nor dread, a desperate motto engraved in the stone in the sixteenth century, an era of calamities: wars, sacks and plagues, doubtless terrible, but which passed, leaving the tons still standing and their populations in a state to resume their lives.

---

[16] *Le Doux pays* [The Ideal Country] by Pierre Puvis de Chavannes (1824-1898) depicts a group of women and children in a placid setting by the shore of an intensely blue sea. It was exhibited at the Salon of 1882 and is now in the Musée Bonnat at Bayonne.

[17] The actual inscription in question reads *Nec spe nec metu*, but the original, the motto of Philippe II, is in French, and it is almost always quoted in that language by French writers referring to the tower of Alost, as Robida does here.

Wars and plagues, sacking and burnings of old, of the times when men only had their arms for evil endeavors as for others, what are you by comparison with our cyclones of fire, of universal cataclysmic destruction?

It is us, the unfortunate people of today, who bear in our hearts that motto of somber depression! *Neither hope*: where and how could we find the slightest ray of hope? Hope, the divine cradler of souls, gone forever... *Nor dread*: the excess of our misfortunes and suffering has given us resignation to the worst, and absolute consent to the inevitable.

But I perceive that I am becoming as funereal as the doctor. It's the sudden appearance of the prehistoric horde that has caused me to take that plunge into the black. No, no, unfortunate Belgians of Alost and elsewhere, hope regardless! And this impression of the recommencement of the world ought, on the contrary, to comfort us, to warm our hearts. Are we not about to see the end of the Scientific Era and the dawn of a better epoch?

"All's well, then," said Dr. Christiansen, at the end of his palaver. "These rude warriors bristling with pikes and cutlasses are friends, the worthy men of Noordwik..."

"That little village you can see over there," added Monsieur Vandermolen. "They're inoffensive fishermen and agriculturalists..."

"I can't see anything at all over there."

"Yes! Can you make out that reddish line in the green of the dune? That's the scattered bricks of which the village was constituted. The more visible square to the right was the church, or the tower, at least. The people live under that undulation, in those holes hollowed out in the earth and consolidated with bits of wood."

"Good, good...they won't scalp us, as I feared at first sight; I'm very glad of that..."

Monsieur Vandermolen, who served as our interpreter, set about explaining the objective of our expedition to our new friends.

The one who seemed to be their leader was a man at least six feet tall, with broad bony shoulders, and long muscular arms terminating in formidable fists—a kind of thin Hercules, doubtless undernourished—with a long yellow beard, clad in animal skins and armed with a long club with iron spikes. He was smiling at us now, and I liked him better like that than when he was running toward us with his teeth clenched, raising his grim weapon against us.

"It appears that he's the burgemeester of Noordwik," the doctor told me. "He commands about forty men like this."

"He's replaced the old burgemeester, whom I knew," added Monsieur Vandermolen. "He was a worthy and peaceful farmer…"

"And now, as of old among the people of the caves, the chief is the strong man," the doctor continued. "He's the robust warrior who imposes his direction on the others. And there you are! Our miserable humanity will soon have completed the cycle and returned to the point of departure. So much the better! May the evolution conclude as rapidly as possible!"

"It appears that we won't find forage in these parts; all the vegetation has been reddened and poisoned by the recent emissions of gas. The chief thinks that it will be necessary for us to go past his village, and circle behind Leyden in the direction of Utrecht; and there, in meadows that haven't been inundated, we'll certainly be able to cut a good provision of grass and hay. Let's go—*en route* with these gentlemen! We'll pay a visit to their caves in passing. To see people, new faces, will be an event for the families vegetating in those shelters…"

The cove of the old mines

VII. The cove of the old mines. A new recruit.

Our new friends took the lead in order to show us the way. One by one, in Indian file, they went down the hill through the holes and the brushwood. No danger was perceptible on the horizon; the Palace of Peace would not want to waste a precious shell on a few human ants glimpsed through binoculars twenty-five kilometers away. Nevertheless, our prehistoric—or, rather, post-historic—warriors marched bent over, hiding behind the undulations of the ground or clumps of meager vegetation. It was evident that for a long time, with permanent danger, the unexpected and menace on every side, the habit had taken hold.

Soon we were zigzagging along the slopes in the remains of half-collapsed trenches, and were forced to march more slowly. Obstacles cutting off our route and obliging us to make detours, we had to move cautiously along the rim of some of the enormous holes that I knew so well now, the craters of bombs or mines, filled with salty water, having become dangerous pools or wells, into which it was necessary not to fall. Sometimes that muddy water filled the bottom of the trenches and we had to wade knee-deep in it.

With those obstacles and detours, the road to Noordwik as much longer than I had thought. We could hear the sound of waves breaking gently on the sand nearby, and the trench suddenly ended in a cove, invisible until then.

Through breaches in the abandoned dykes, the sea had crossed the line of the dunes at many points. The furious assault of the waves at high tide, in the bad seasons, enabled it to take a further leap forward every time into the polders, and the reconquest of the Zuider Zee.

Here the sea filled a rather large cleft in the shore; in the calm weather, it was gently caressing it with little tranquil and regular waves, which seemed to be amusing themselves sketching out a few fringes of foam in the manner of Japanese artists.

I admired it, and then I immediately thought that crabs, if I could find any, would be well-received in the kitchen by the Vitalis ladies.

So, very happy to be able to read on fine sand, gentle on the feet, I descended rapidly to the border of the foam and stated hunting, while my companions picked up shellfish as they walked.

I couldn't help thinking, bitterly, that we had the appearance, on that strand, of bourgeois holidaymakers at the seaside, as in the good old days. Oh yes, the seaside! How far away those times of distraction there! The pleasant beaches with the bourgeois families chatting in front of the beach-huts or the striped tents, the ladies in white bathrobes, the children in swimsuits fishing for shrimp in rock-pools or paddling in the sunshine, the casinos with their concerts and balls...

Beaches fashionable before the deluge—Scheveningen and Zandwort—were not far away. Alas, what strange bathers were on those beaches today? For years, what infernal concerts, what satanic music on all sides! What frightful balls were held there, where death held the great Maestro's baton, with which to conduct the orchestra!

Come on—I've forgotten the crabs! It's necessary to live, though, and to bring back some nourishment from our excursion. I resume the hunt. Then I perceive huge rusty masses in the water, all covered with algae and encrusted with shellfish, run aground in the sand. What are they? Buoys, presumably. I move closer, and start collecting shellfish, with which I fill my pockets.

But some of our comrades come running, uttering loud cries. They try to attract me attention with broad gestures.

Eh? What's the matter?"

"Stop! Don't touch anything!" the doctor shouts at me, while our prehistoric men continue gesticulating.

"What's the matter? These shellfish are very good—I know them…"

"Fool!" shouts the doctor, out of breath. "Leave it! Don't touch!"

"What is it, then?"

"Mines! Mines! Unexploded mines—understand?"

"Dangerous!" proffers Monsieur Vandermolen, trotting away in order to distance himself. "Dangerous! Explosives!"

The shock nearly caused me to fall on one of the detestable engines, but the chief of the tribe arrived just in time to catch me.

"How the devil did these infernal machines get here?" I exclaimed. "There must be fifteen of them...."

"It's the currents that bring them," said Monsieur Vandermolen, still keeping his distance prudently. "The Boches have sowed so many of them at sea—floating mines, or positional mines that the sea has ended up carrying away— that they're spread all over the Oceans..."

"That's true," I said. "We know something about that..."

"Three-quarters of the mines end up exploding on some rock, but there are plenty more, as you can see! These have been in this cove for a long time, the burgemeester tells me, and he'd really like to be rid of them..."

"All the more so," added the doctor, "Because, if the Boches in the Palace of Peace, short of explosives, knew of the existence of this little provision, they'd try to get their hands on them..."

"Let's go, let's go," said Monsieur Vandermolen, eager to get out of that troubling neighborhood. "We mustn't be too late back..."

The domicile of the prehistoric men wasn't far away. After having gone around the cove with the inconvenient mines, we took a small trench, which, after a few turnings, brought us out in front of a series of holes plunging into the dune, well hidden in the vegetation.

Children leapt outside the holes on hearing the whistles with which the newcomers signaled their approach. Women and men appeared.

All of them were costumed like the warriors of the tribe. In the troglodytes of Harlem one still found a little of the city-dweller of old, but here, far from the town, among these wor-

188

thy seamen or peasants, they had been using rope for belts for a long time, and had had to be ingenious in making garments, first weaving wool from a few sheep, then tailoring the sails of their boats, and then using the skins of beasts they had eaten: sheep, goats, rabbits... And now, all of them, men, women and children alike, constituted a tribe almost similar to those of the primitive caves.

These people could be perfectly happy in their shelters, in spite of all the dangers of wild nature, against which they knew how to arm themselves and struggle. Over time, moreover, their situation would improve. The future opened, immense and marvelous, before these people of the youth of the world.

But we, alas, who know—how can we support out misery our broken hearts, our crushed spirit, tortured by the memory of better times that will never return, and all the fears that weigh upon us?

The former village once grouped its houses at the base of the dune, around one of those old squat churches built as a pendant of a big windmill amid the greenery, as in the old paintings of the Dutch school, which give such an impression of pleasant and peaceful life, in the atmosphere of a beautiful summer evening...

In front of the village was a beach of yellow sand on which the fishermen had once moored their boats within a framework of dykes made of stakes and cross-pieces. None of that existed any longer. The church, the houses, the surrounding farms and the dykes had all been destroyed, crush and ravaged. The sea and the squalls had completed the ruination of the ruins, and carried away most of the debris. I could scarcely distinguish the location of the unfortunate village when the primitive burgemeester tried to indicate it to me.

I went into a few of the burrows, similar in all respects to those I had already visited in the course of our excursions. The earthworks were maintained by wooden beams, the debris of boats, tree trunks, branches and wickerwork. There were items of furniture saved from the demolished village, and in the depths of the refuges, even a few items of faience, Delft plates, shining softly in the obscurity, sad and dear relics more treasured than ever, wreckage of the tranquil happiness of old, of which these poor folk were trying to conserve the memory. The burrow only seemed sadder in consequence.

In one, under clusters of onions drying on walls of planks, and packets of arrows exactly similar to those once seen in ethnographic museums, with the quivers of tattooed savages, I saw a dainty little blue Delft pot containing a bouquet of dune flowers. A young woman in an exceedingly ragged skirt made of sail-canvas and a worn sheepskin bodice, was mending the sleeve of a leather jacket, doubtless that of one of the robust men of the tribe, a father or perhaps a fiancé—and I immediately imagined an idyll of the cave age.

I noticed that her hair, although a trifle ruffled, was not without a certain coquetry. Eternal femininity still persisted; that caused a vague suggestion of hope to pass through me.

Suddenly, as I had doubtless thought aloud, someone spoke to me in French. Two men were coming back to the troglodyte village; they had been hunting along the shore and were bringing back two wild geese killed with arrows.

One was a Picard from the vicinity of Noyon, a former bowman in his native land, the other a Belgian from Ypres, once a skilled archer, often winning competitions, run aground among these Dutch fishermen after many vicissitudes and bloody adventures.

They utilized their archery skills here now, for want of cartridges or powder, their rifles no longer being able to serve as anything but handles for bayonets.

I questioned the two men about the events that had cast them up here and trapped them in this little corner of the Dutch dunes. Still the same story: deluge of fire, iron and gas; violent drives northwards or southwards, crushed under machines or explosives, slavery in the Boche mines or factories, and to finish, miraculous escapes under fire, through the networks of electrified wire...

The burgemeester

Everything they told me about the circumstances only served to confirm the fantastic stories of the doctor and the others; even so, I kept asking questions, hoping for some information about the state of things in France, in the country that held me by the heart, beyond our restricted horizon. It was so close, and yet so far away!

But who is that man who has just joined our group? Prominent cheekbones and hooded eyes, an entirely Asiatic face. He's very small of stature beside the tall Dutchmen. He has an arm in a sling—or, rather, attacked to his breast by bits of cord, and he's limping. He's clad in shiny leather, badly scorched. His only weapon is a long cutlass in his belt.

As I draw him to the attention of the doctor, he advances and says to us in French: "Permit me to introduce myself…Yamato…"

"You're not Dutch," I say, naively.

"Yamato Yradonou, of Yeddo, aviator-bombardier of the ninth Japanese army, operating in northern Germany, siege of the lines of Berlin and Danzig…"

A surge of surprise and a flash of joy for me…news, at last!

All that I could say was: "Oh! oh! oh!" as I shook the hand of the man from Japan.

"Not so hard," he said. "I'm still slightly injured."

"Excuse me," I said, "but I'm so glad! Finally, we're going to have news!"

VIII. Imprecise information and not-very-fresh news.

"It's just that we haven't much time to get back home," said the placid Monsieur Vandermolen. "It's getting late."

"Bah! A few minutes more! Let's chat first with Monsieur Yamoto. If the news is good we'll walk all the better afterwards."

We formed a tightly-knit group in front of the entrances to the burrows. The entire tribe was outside, the men to one side, slightly to the rear, the women, slightly more curious, clustering around us, the late-comers climbing up the bank or the woodwork, some carrying babies in their arms or on their backs, wrapped up to the neck in sheepskins.

"Finally, news!" I exclaimed, still shaking the Japanese aviator's hand, albeit with a little more care.

"You're wounded?" asked Dr. Christiansen.

"Yes, yes," I said, with egotistical haste. "Monsieur Yamato is wounded, that's obvious. But let him speak first. Fresh news from the rest of the world—you can guess how keen we are to hear it—how keen we all are."

"Oh, fresh, fresh!" said the Japanese, smiling. "That's saying a lot, Monsieur, given that I arrived here, falling from the sky...how long ago?...sixteen, seventeen or eighteen...? How long, exactly, burgemeester?"

Monsieur Vandermolen having repeated the question, the prehistoric burgemeester went to a large beam supporting the entrance to one of the raves.

"The Mairie...the the Hôtel de Ville," the French aviator told me, having taken hold of the hand of his Japanese colleague in his turn.

The stake was engraved from top to bottom with notches of various sizes, figures and letters, carved with a knife.

"Calendar and register of Civil Estates," the Japanese told me, still smiling.

The burgemeester examine the variously-sized notches, counted and recounted, and then came back to us.

"Not eighteen, nineteen and a half," Monsieur Vandermolen translated for me.

"It's not important, to the day," I said.

"Nineteen and a half, but not days, months! It's nineteen and a half months since Monsieur Yamato arrived here...

I had suddenly gone considerably colder. The news was going to lack freshness.

"Yes, time passes, all the same," said Yamato Yradonou. "It's nineteen months and a half, then, since I had my accident... Well, it's quite simple; we were manning apparatus 38 of fighter squadron no. 27 of the ninth Japanese army, a biplane armored in four places. Operations before the entrenched camp at Brandenburg had been going on for two and a half days, all going well, good results, the enemy driven back, crushed, defenses demolished, towns in pieces, disappeared, evaporated. We'd taken their big explosives depot, and we were using its provisions ourselves, which we were serving to them in nicely cooked little dishes. Would you care for some trinitrotoluene, superclastite, gases and deleterious vapors? There you see, Messieurs les Boches! Stuff yourselves, eat your fill, since you like it so much!

"To us, squadron 27, only two almost usable aircraft remained, nos. 26 and 38, mine, against a dozen Boches, who scarcely dared show themselves any longer. Shortage of fuel, presumably..."

"Good, good," I said. "But outside the entrenched camp of Berlin...let's talk a little about France. How is Paris doing?"

"Paris? Hang on, let's see...1922, 1923...yes, before Brandenburg, we were operating near Dresden, then retreated to Leipzig, and then the big counter-offensive by the Bulgaro-Turks, to which we gave a warm reception with an Anglo-French corps, and drove back to the lines at Berlin. For the latest news of Paris that makes something like six years..."

"Tell us anyway..."

"All was well...that's all I know."

I let myself fall on to a heap of sticks, discouraged.

"To get back to my accident," Yamato went on, "it's quite simple. We were carrying our reconnaissance in the direction of Aix-la-Chapelle. Caught by storm, error in direction, engine breakdown, steep descent, disastrous crash behind the Boche lines! Three killed outright, one only three-quarters killed—that was me. So I find myself on the ground, badly demolished, and I set off straight ahead. Not funny! I have no idea where I am and among whom. Hungry and no food. Less and less funny. Not even the possibility, with my broken paws, of trapping a rabbit or picking a lettuce, or even of opening my belly, in the fashion of my ancestors of the good old days, if no other resource remains. Forward march! Two days like that! Not much ground covered. I'm about to turn up my toes, as they say. Forward march! And I suddenly happen upon these Messieurs, who receive me with the points of their improvised halberds. Salvation, or the contrary? It's salvation! I'm collected, cared for, lodged, and I live with these worthy folk for nineteen months and a half. They're totally kind, and I like them a lot!"

Monsieur Yamato's speech plunges me back into the black.

How I envied the beautiful insouciance and resilience of that Far Eastern aviator!

Monsieur Vandermolen, who was getting impatient, reminded us that we had a long way to go to find the forage and get back to Harlem. He was in a hurry to get back to his slippers and the dining room.

"Let's go! Let's go!" he said, while my comrades distributed handshakes to the good troglodytes of Noordwik. The clapped the robust shoulders of the burgemeester, weighed the warriors' clubs in their hands, and arranged a rendezvous for the day of the big push, when the Boches of the Palace of Peace have definitely expended their last explosives.

It was necessary, however, to leave, when Dr. Christiansen had made a tour of the caves to see a few poor old men in the process of ending their existence in such strange circumstances. The burgemeester gave us a few men to serve as guides for a short distance, in order to put us on the right path.

Yamato Yradonou suddenly decided to go with us.

"I'll go with you," he said. "I'm sorry to quit these worthy folk and their rude burgemeester, who makes such a fine warrior in the mode of the most distant antiquity, but I can't stay here forever, sheltered in these burrows in the dune. I'll go with you—that will be new, other adventures, perhaps a step toward the ninth Japanese army..."

I shook his hand, delighted with that new companion.

We strode forth.

The village

Dunes, polders, marshes, more marshes, more polders, more dunes—and green intervals filled with disorderly brushwood and clumps of wild flowers, from which flocks of little birds rose up, which mocked the follies of men; and desolate spaces strewn with scattered stones or bricks, with dubious pools covered with weeds...

A glance in passing at the ruins of villages, traversed with prudence, or the cadavers of big windmills, finishing their collapse, tragic skeletons that still raise long beams toward the sky, like desperate arms that the wind stirs with plaintive groans. Encounters with a few hunters, always with the same aspect as the prehistoric warriors.

The afternoon advances, the sun declines toward the horizon. Finally, here are the desired grasslands. To work! Rapidly, we cut as much as possible, making large bundles, as much as we can carry. It's excellent forage; our horse will feast on it; he'll get fat, and when winter comes he'll...but no, I expect to be far away, not eating him.

Off we go, in Indian file behind Monsieur Vandermolen, who tries to find his way through the maze of the marshes.

Our caravan makes a picturesque line of hunchbacked silhouettes, outlined against the setting sun, which is setting too rapidly, alas, much too rapidly for us to be able to be certain of still being on the right route.

We climb banks only to tumble down into the sand, climb back up, go round almost-invisible holes, or fall into them. Look out! Let's not break anything—let's take precautions!

Those precautions cost us time; the sun finishes putting itself to bed and disappears, and now we're almost in pitch darkness. Monsieur Vandermolen, already anxious, becomes as somber as the night. He makes the cruel admission that we're completely lost.

None of us can see anything except the vague outline of the person in front of him. It's almost necessary to hold hands in order not to get separated. It's definitely impossible to go any further. A hole—we need a hole, in which there isn't any water, in order to camp: a shelter, no matter what, in which we can lie down to sleep…without any supper, because our provisions, like our reserves of strength, are exhausted.

But we can't find one. However, here's some firm ground without too many cracks; let's advance slowly, and search...

IX. The aviator Miraud. I take a prisoner.

It's Miraud the aviator who is marching in front of me. I only know that because while moving forward, he sings in order that I don't lose track of the file.

Songs in that funereal décor of ruins, which the night will populate with phantoms—how out of place!

We have been close for some time, poor Miraud and I. Deep down, he held a grudge against me at first for having brought into the association that overly sympathetic coxcomb, that rival who has stolen the heart of Jeanne Vitalis from him, but as he needs to talk in order to distract himself from his troubles, he has taken me for a confidant, for covert admissions, without naming anyone.

And between complaints about the candid cruelty of the sweetest young women, or the unusual luck of certain young coxcombs who have only to appear to conquer, he recounts to me his memories of old, of the brilliant and joyful Paris before the torment, of his cruises in the clouds, his machine-gun combats at fifteen hundred or two thousand meters, and the final bad encounter at the corner of a cumulus cloud...

"…Which won me the pleasure of making your acquaintance, my dear Monsieur…"

Poor Miraud, on an aerial patrol, had run cross a squadron of large armored German airplanes, which had sent his apparatus, his pilot and himself, pierced like a colander by machine-gun bullets, straight down to crash into the ground, fortunately behind the allied lines.

And there, as he put it, he had nearly had to swallow his last rhyme. But that had been sorted out, save for the arm; they had taped up the colander, and the one-armed poet was now lining up black rhymes instead of rosy rhymes, the singer translating into grim verses the wrathful outbursts of Dr. Christiansen.

Extraordinary transformations of everything in this upside-down world! Where are our Montmartrean cabarets, singers and students, poets and painters? And you, old Chat Noir of the distant times of my youth, how, through this nightmare, will I be able to think about you?

Miraud has woken up; the perspective of the imminent great assault, the collision, perhaps supreme, with thrusts of pikes, axes or clubs, has reanimated him and made him vibrate. He's nervous; his gaze has been keener and more decisive for a few days; I've noticed that. He has allowed himself to be overly influenced by the funereal ideas of Dr. Christiansen; he's detaching himself now that he's glimpsed a glimmer of hope.

As we stride over the dune he murmurs:

Let's unstuff, let's unstuff, let's unstuff all the skulls!

I interrogate him about that refrain, which seems singular to me. It isn't slang, no—merely a metaphor that's slightly bold but perfectly clear. Let's unstuff all the heads of everything heaped up therein of false ideas, hollow nonsense and harmful chimeras, utopias or illusions that are doubtless generous but so replete with dangers. Let's get rid of the stuffing completely, and we'll see thereafter![18]

Let's unstuff them completely, to hell with big words,

---

[18] I have translated *débourrons* [let's unstuff] in a brutally literal fashion, because it suits the narrator's decoding, which appears to be correct, but it could also be construed as "let's scalp," or even, "let's bash the brains out." Another listener might well have interpreted it in that fashion and construed subsequent embellishments in the same light.

Empty of all sense, misleaders of herds,
To the puffed up masters we prefer fools;
Let's unstuff, let's unstuff, let's unstuff all the skulls!

He had couplets about philosophical unstuffing, political unstuffing and scientific unstuffing. I didn't want to follow him as far as that; I supposed that he, like the doctor, wanted to unstuff the skulls of the remaining humans of everything that the doctor called the "deleterious rubbish of knowledge," in the hope, by rejecting the whole lot, the good with the bad, of putting an end to infamous science.

We were advancing with difficulty, utterly exhausted. I was holding on to the end of Miraud's bundle of foliage, and was almost being towed, I'm ashamed to say. Truly, I wouldn't have been sorry finally to encounter a shelter where we might try to sleep, in order to forget hunger and fatigue.

"Pass it along to the guide," Miraud said to the bundle of forage preceding him. "No need to search for a tourist hotel— we don't need comfort or electricity; the bottom of a ditch, grass or sand—that's all!

If ever Dame Fortune
Smiles on my desire,
I'd buy myself the moon
And stars by the quire.

"Mark me well, we're going to get lost in the dark, and the column will break up...

Quickly by airplane
I'd reach my port
I'd take my refrain
And my kindly thought

And my family too
High into the sky
In the infinite blue

As I wave goodbye!

He stopped abruptly, and his bundle of forage hit me in the face. The entire column did likewise. Was it finally the shelter so much desired?

The Japanese Yamato went to the head of the column, his nose in the air, striving to pierce the obscurity with his feline eyes.

We put our bundles of forage on the ground and sat down on them.

Monsieur Vandermolen was anxious. Yamato took a few steps forward and came back.

"Look out," he whispered in Vandermolen's ear. "I can see something—a big black menacing machine—in front of us. Ruins? Château? Village? Old abandoned battery? I don't know. Perhaps there are people there; we need to go carefully. I'll go see—follow slowly...

After taking a few more steps, I too could make out the bizarre silhouette toward which we were marching. It was strange enough as an outline against the blue-black of the sky. Doubtless a ruin, but the ruin of what?

I joined the Japanese, in order to advance on reconnaissance, lying face down on the rough, stony ground, with a mixture of brambles and nettles, semi-brushwood full of thorns, where I left bits of the skin of my hands behind, not to mention a few shreds of my trousers.

Soon, the two of us, Yamoto and I, were getting very close to the ruin, redoubling our prudence before that troubling somber mass, when a ray of moonlight slid between two clouds and made it even more gigantic and stranger still.

Yamoto nudged me with his elbow.

"Machine!" he whispered.

Machine? In fact, I could make out something like the debris of colossal wheels, and above it, what I had thought at first was a wall, I now realized was a kind of iron carapace, holed and dislocated in places.

But what kind of machine was it?

What kind of machine was it?

"Tank!" said the Japanese. "Rolling bombard, demolished."

As no noise was coming from the dune, and it did not seem to be hiding any danger in its flanks, our companions had advanced.

"All seems tranquil to me," said the doctor. "There's the desired shelter for the night. Let's see..."

Yamato had already introduced himself into the place, and was searching the shadow.

"You can come," he said. "We'll sleep very well in here."

Close up, the machine seemed even more forbidding than it had in the vagueness of the night. It was visible now, with the ray of moonlight gliding over the rusty iron. We had to scale a mass of twisted metal, dislocated armor plating, the enormous remains of fabulous wheels, which made me think about steam-rollers for flattening macadam, all heaped up, forming a substructure around a deformed and monstrous breached carapace, pierced by cracks and riddled with holes.

Hoisting myself up, in spite of my fatigue, as far as a black hole, I bumped heads with Yamato, who had just finished exploring the interior.

"We'll be fine," he said. "The bundles of forage will make soft beds. Tomorrow we'll be fresh and rested."

The bundles of forage were passed up to the Japanese, who laid them out inside the machine, and we formed a short human ladder in order to go and join him. *Oof!* I sank delightedly into the hay, with a sigh, for, once the legs were tranquilized, the stomach began nagging in its turn, and unfortunately, we had nothing for it.

I tried to think about other things than the untimely demands of appetite.

"But after all, what is it, this war machine?" I asked one of my comrades in misfortune, lying beside me, similarly racked by hunger.

"I told you," Yamoto replied. "It's a big allied tank, the cadaver of an armored automobile bombard, demolished in the course of some attack by large-caliber shells."

"And it was already a ruin a long time ago," added Monsieur Vandermolen. "Everything is rusty, and vigorous vegetation has slid in everywhere, invading everything. These tanks are formidable machines, much improved after the first war. This ruin of an ambulant fortress must have been here since an attack on the retrenched camp of The Hague five or six years ago. I recall the frightful debauch of explosives of every sort that completed the devastation of the entire region. The Boche in The Hague still had plenty of munitions in those days!"

I was about to ask more questions when I sensed something moving in the heap of scrap iron, under my bed of fodder. But what was it, exactly? I sat up, somewhat anxious. Something gripped my leg, and I uttered a cry, to which a growl responded. My comrades were also sitting up on their couches of hay.

What is it? Paw or hand? Slightly emboldened, I grope in my turn, and I grip an arm. I pull; the growling accentuates and a large bearded head appears through the grass, jabbering rapidly in an imploring tone. I don't understand very well—there's Dutch, German, French, and words in an unknown language.

"What is this intrusion?"

My companions got up and pulled the individual from the hiding-place where he had secreted himself when we arrived, between broken iron traverses and a long tube that appears to me to be a torpedo-launcher. In a hurry to lie down, I had thrown my bundle of forage on top of it without looking very hard, and I shivered retrospectively at the thought that I might just as easily have been lying on top of a torpedo or some dangerous chemical bomb.

"Bulgar! Don't hurt me! Prisoner!" said the intruder.

"Good—a Bulgar!" said Jollimay and Bustamente, shoving the man roughly into a corner. "What are you doing here?"

The doctor having succeeded, with some difficulty in lighting a taper, we were able to see the face of our prisoner. He was an individual of about forty or forty-five, with a thin, even emaciated, face with an unkempt beard and a shock of hair.

Monsieur Vandermolen interrogated him in German. The man replied humbly, and showed that he had no weapon, Our comrades searched the entire bombard to make sure that it did not contain any other occupants. No one. Very frightened, the man swore that he was alone.

But what a mass of twisted iron, the debris of unknown machinery, the feeble light of the taper caused to appear, among fragments of projectiles, bolts, tubes, fragments of mechanisms and plates of armor.

"The latest marvel of science—admire!" said the doctor, bitterly, kicking away some kind of machine-gun corroded by rust.

The interrogation of the man continued. The doctor translated his replies for me. He was a Bulgar escaped from the Palace of Peace, who had been living hidden in this bombard for ten days. According to him, everyone in the Boche camp in The Hague was dying of starvation—and the unfortunate inhabitants even more so. Better still, they were entirely out of explosives, shells and chemical products to make gases. No more munitions! Nothing to eat for the men, and even less for the cannons and all the bulimic engines of war, worn out for the most part, corroded by the infernal storms of gas, red hot or corrosive liquids that they breathed, vomited or poured out over their perimeter of devastation.

The situation out there was frightful. The monstrous factory of massacre was in its death throes. People were killing one another by night in order to snatch a few shreds of nourishment. It was the end. The Bulgar had been able to flee in the company of a few other starvelings, lost on the way.

As he talked a great deal about famine, that reminded us of our appetite. The man understood. He asked permission to get up, and pulled out a heavy sack hooked on to an iron road behind a sheet of armor.

Provisions! Two rabbits and a first-rate rat, almost as fast as the rabbits. A magnificent windfall! At a stroke, our fatigue was forgotten. We got up very quickly; brushwood was piled up under a corner of the bombard, with bits of dry wood, and a flame shone.

Our cooking didn't take long. The rifleman skinned the two rabbits and the rat and spitted them on iron rods. We all found branches and blew on the fire in order to make the roast go more quickly.

We showed the Bulgar a little more respect.

"Go on, sit down—you'll have your share."

The rabbits, browned rather than cooked, were soon dispatched. That was a pleasure. I also had a small slice of rat; it's a delicate dish that we all appreciate now.

After that almost lavish meal, we would be able to lie down and sleep!

The Bulgar lay down in the hay beside me, finding that better than underneath in his hidey-hole.

X. An agitated night in the ruins of a tank.

A profound silence is established in our ruined bombard in the depths of that pitch darkness, only disturbed by a few vague sounds of respiration, the rustle of brushwood, and a snore that rises, and abruptly ceases.

I contemplate the slightly brighter sky through the breaches and holes with which the armor is riddled. Thought leaks away from my weary brain; I don't know exactly where I am. Is that the heavens I perceive up there, through the holes in the carapace above my head? They heavens, with theirs stars, seen through the vaults of Hell? Yes, more like Hell, that's where we are...

And I stir, I turn over, I struggle...

Then, a shock...

I have an abrupt sensation of a fall on to sharply-pointed rocks. I must have fallen off my bundle of fodder on to the iron debris, which is wounding me. I roll over slightly; I try to get up…impossible. I remain on my side, and sink into an exhausted sleep.

Now I'm dreaming…

Mountains glaciers, precipices, the bristling crowns of gigantic fir trees, twisting and writhing monstrous, menacing arms…that must be the idea of my fall on to jagged rocks just now…

The mountains rise up. It's the Himalaya. Thunder rumbles…thunder or explosions? And the mountains talk, the Himalaya frowning its eyebrows of white rock, cries furiously: "Come on, you out there, you, the Alps! You, the Caucasus and Carpathians! You have no more volcanoes, then, to finish off these enraged pygmies, these frenetic myrmidons? Shrug your shoulders—a good earthquake to crush the race, summon the fire of heaven to the rescue…"

"Silence, Brother," replies the terrified Mont Blanc. "It's those pygmies who have blown the volcanoes up! The fire of heaven? It's theirs, they have it, they're making use of it to demolish my peaks and blow up my summits. Shut up, I beg you—I'm scared!"

I don't know what the Himalaya might have said— someone pushes me again, and the metal on which I'm lying is scratching my sides. The Himalaya disappears; I open my eyes; I can only see blackness, but I can hear bizarre sounds outside in the dark. What is it? Howling in the countryside…

I remember now; we're a long way from the Himalaya, lying in the ruins of a wheeled bombard. Let's sleep, then…

Someone pushes me again. It's the intolerable Bulgar who grabs me by the arm.

"Let me sleep, satanic Balkan Boche! I need my eight hours of sleep."

"Wolf! Wolf! *Wolves!*" he shouts in my ear.

"What? Wolves?"

Wolves!

"What?" The comrades have heard the word, vaguely, and are trying to wake up.

"Wolves," I say to them. "This damned Bulgar doesn't want to let us sleep."

"Wolves!" cries the doctor, bounding from his straw at the expense of my tibias. "It's serious, then! Packs of wolves—I've heard talk of them. A bad encounter! Get up! Barricade ourselves in, quickly!"

The howling was getting closer. Mohammed, the Senegalese, got down outside our fortress to reconnoiter, and leapt back up again.

"They're coming," he said. "They're all around us."

Already we were foraging at hazard under our bedding, pulling out iron rods and fragment of armor plate, the debris of a door, various lumps of iron and piling them up in the breach through which we had got into the tank.

The Bulgar was more familiar than we were with the resources of the rolling blockhouse, his domicile for a week, and he passed us the materials for our barricade. Fortunately, there was no other practicable breach for the four-footed assailants. The other holes not being accessible, we only had to face up to a frontal assault.

We were just in time; as we finished blocking the breach, the wolves leapt to the assault, howling. That woke me up completely. Until then it had seemed that my extravagant dream was continuing, but I saw the embers of their eyes gleaming, I heard their raucous breath and the grinding of their ferocious teeth. They too were hungry!

If they seemed furious, we were even more so, because of our troubled night—and out prehistoric weapons were about to make them see it! Above our barricade, through the scrap iron, we were already thrusting judiciously at the menacing snouts, or into the pack, or at the spines of those that were trying to get through the holes.

That first attack lasted a good quarter of an hour; then the assailants retreated. We heard them circling our refuge, scratching and growling, wearing away their claws on the armor plate.

"The enemy is on the run," I said to the doctor as the growling and the panting gradually eased. "I think that with a watchman at the barricade, we can resume our interrupted sleep."

"All right," he said. "Try. Me, I'll stand guard—someone can replace me when I've had enough."

It took us a good quarter of an hour to go back to sleep; the battle had started our blood flowing vigorously. But finally, little by little, we all departed again for the land of dreams—a happy land, the sweet land of the past, on which we tried every evening to focus our thoughts, with the hope of going there to find a few hours of repose, forgetful of somber realities.

Personally, I strove to think about my apartment on the Boulevard Montparnasse, my study, my soft bed, my breakfast in the morning, with cream, chocolate, gilded crusty croissants—and I had been savoring the delights of all that for hours, it seemed, when the Bulgar gave me a hard punch.

"Wolf! Wolves!" he cried.

I heard the howling without understanding. I had forgotten the enemy. Fortunately, my comrades, behind the barricade, resumed thrusting at the assailants, more furious and panting harder than the first time. While still half asleep, I did the same as the others, jabbing through the holes at the enemy.

That lasted ten minutes. Again the wolves renounced the assault and resumed circling the tank, howling, or trying to climb up to the higher breaches.

Then they disappeared, and I lay down again.

"Who'll take guard?" asked the doctor.

Mohammed offered. I didn't dispute the post, and stretched myself out beside the Bulgar.

…Howling again, pressure again our barricade. Someone comes toward me. I get up, groping, and I go, almost in a dream, to make spear-thrusts, almost at random. The attack weakens; the wolves resume circling. They're crunching something, jostling one another and growling. I hear the sound of their jaws and I shiver. One of ours, perhaps?

"They're eating their wounded, for want of anything else," the doctor tells me. "Will you take the watch?"

I make no response to the invitation. Tranquillized, I'm already asleep again.

Thus, seven or eight times before morning, it's necessary to wake up, to get up, numbly, cold, yawning and groaning, and endure the assault of the wolves, striking and thrusting at random through the augmented and consolidated barricade—which holds firm.

"Oh, if I only had two or three grenades!" roared the artilleryman Jollimay, finally driven into a rage by all the sudden awakenings.

With daylight, we all wake up, this time for good, harassed, stiff and bent, but definitively rid of our enemies, disappeared at dawn.

When we emerge from the tank to stretch our limbs, we find three carcasses torn apart, scattered bones and bits of bloody skin—all that remains of our victims.

No booty of war. Mohammed and Jollimay grumble. They had hoped to find a few cadavers of wolves to take back for the larder.

In the damp morning mist, our ruined fortress stands out in an impressive and dramatic fashion, dominating a vast and sinister landscape of devastation, where everything is ravage and ruin: the ground cracked and broken, full of asperities, holes and scars, with white or red traces of evaporated farms or villages, disappeared forever; the water of streams with changed courses spread out in stagnant pools in the craters; the trees decapitated, crippled amputated and dislocated, but obstinate in living regardless, putting out new branches and garnishing their miserable broken stumps with foliage.

The tank is grounded on a kind of mound, its rusty mass looming up ponderously on the debris of its enormous wheels, brandishing twisted metal, seemingly still threatening the entire horizon through the black holes of its breaches and battlements.

But I'm not allowed to linger in the contemplation of our fortress; I'm summoned to take up my burden of forage. It's necessary to get back without wasting time. Monsieur Vandermolen takes the head of the caravan; he has got his bearings and knows approximately where we are.

En route, then, to try to arrive early.

XI. The return to the cavern.
The misfortunes of a henhouse.

We had been advancing for about half an hour when the doctor, who was walking alongside me, pointed out shadows to our right, moving through the brushwood some distance away, bounding behind the undulations of the dune.

"The wolves," he told me. "They're following us. Bah! In daylight, they don't scare us."

Old memories came back to me as we marched. My grandmother once told me that in her childhood, after the great Napoleonic wars, wolves had been seen to reappear in her province: the ancient forgotten terror of villages in forests...

Here they are again, brought back by the frightful upheaval, emerging in famished packs from what distant forest, what wild Balkans, what steppes?

Under our bundles of hay, wary eyes watching the wolves, the doctor and I philosophize as we stride along.

"I knew one worthy fellow," the doctor said, "who contended that the Earth was, in reality, the Purgatory of which our religion speaks: Purgatory, the place of deportation, into which we're precipitated at birth in order to expiate sins committed on another planet, and where we're condemned to live a more or less long existence, in accordance with the blackness of our faults, venerable centenarians being, in consequences, those most heavily charged with grave sins. And in sustaining that, he thought himself frightfully bitter and pessimistic, the poor fellow!

"How wrong he was! Our Earth is much better than that, I'm sure, better than a simple and gentle little Purgatory! It's quite simply Hell, the realm of Satan. Everyone, whoever we are—you, me, the others—if we've had the misfortune to be born on this sorry ball, it's because we've merited it thoroughly, by crimes of all sorts, committed elsewhere, in perfectly deplorable anterior existences, which have obliged the great judge to exercise severity on our souls and our bodies..."

"That seems quite probable to me, alas! Yes, we must have been frightful rogues elsewhere..."

"That'll teach us! Let's expiate, since we must, expiate and redeem! I swear, from now on, to conduct myself in the most edifying fashion, throughout the time I still have to live. That's what you say, isn't it, for a moderately pleasant existence? I swear to show myself, as much as possible, kind, good, helpful, even devoted when I can, in order to merit a reduction in punishment...and if my soul has to come back, as is probable, to animate a substitute body somewhere, please, Lord, let it not be on this accursed Earth! Let it be elsewhere; there's no lack of room in your universe...send me to some little planet, far, far away from here—as far as you like! O Lord, to obtain that mercy, what would I not do? Penitence, fasting, disgrace and unpleasantness, I can accept it all, even solicit it... Here, my dear Monsieur, put your load of forage on mine—I can easy carry two!"

A little more, in his desire for mortification to augment his merit and his chances, and the doctor would have invited me to climb on to his back. I didn't want to abuse his good will, and I even kept my bundle of forage.

We kept going. Toward the middle of the day, when noon was sounding in our stomachs, we recognized familiar landscapes. Harlem and home couldn't be far away. A little more courage, one more stage, and we'd be home.

We went through the remains of a village that we'd visited before. There the doctor found an opportunity to devote himself a little to the relief of the miseries of the world. A few invalids in a few huts were signaled to him. He ran to them.

213

He bled one old woman, set a fisherman's broken arm, massaged rheumatisms, distributed a dozen gumballs to children with colds, and searched for simples to make tisanes. That was all he could do.

In the meantime, we rested. Monsieur Jollimay, with is wooden leg, needed to catch his breath, and we dined on snails we'd picked up along the way.

The doctor rejoined us exultantly. He had been given four beets for his honoraria—in spite of all his protestations and refusals, I ought to say, but, after all, the beets were very welcome; we ate two of them, reserving the others for the evening salad.

The wolves had abandoned us; we didn't see them again. We warned the people of the village to look out for their children.

We're almost home; here is familiar territory, our own dunes, with the holes and craters cultivated by our hands, or those of the people in neighboring caverns.

I'm not sorry to reach port, or our legs can do no more, and if the doctor keeps going on, I think I'll end up climbing on to his back—but we've been spotted; people are coming to meet us, Here comes someone waving their arms at us.

Howard Gibson, the American billionaire and Madame Vitalis tumble down the slope, followed by Mademoiselle Vitalis and Maître Saladin, the captain-notary. The three wooden legs of the captain, the American and Madame Vitalis are going tick-tock on the pebbles.

"How anxious we were yesterday!" cries Madame Vitalis. "We were waiting for you all night..."

"We were too far away and too tired," I said. "We had to camp in a tranquil spot...relatively tranquil...but here we are, with a good provision of forage, as you see. We're going to fatten up our horse...."

"And is all well at the villa?" Monsieur Vandermolen asked

"Yes, yes," said the two women, in an evasive tone.

"Imprudents!" cried the doctor. "You don't have your masks with you! What if there was...?"

"Oh, yes...er, no...the thing is, we thought there was no more danger..."

"You don't know," said the American. "During your expedition, prisoners have been taken—or, rather, deserters fleeing the Boche lines at the Palace of Peace have turned up. It's true, it's right! Out there, they've run out of the munitions of their infernal chemistry! We have the details...there are a couple of chemists among the deserters. Nothing's happening any longer out there; the ammunition dumps are completely empty: no more explosives, and nothing with which to manufacture them, nor anything for the toxic gases."

"Is that absolutely certain?"

"There's been penury there for a long time, since an accident, it appears," said Mademoiselle Vitalis.

"Oh," said Maître Saladin, "say a catastrophe, a delightful catastrophe! I got the details of the order and the progress...explosions of carboys of asphyxiants in a laboratory, fire spreading from depot to depot, a series of increasingly powerful explosions, the big factory blown up, with all the storage bunkers. The best of all is that the entire general staff of chemists perished along with the laboratory! Nothing to be done, impossible to approach! Eruptions of deleterious gas at every moment, clouds of asphyxiating vapors, geysers of corrosive liquid hurling death in all directions..."

"No more chemists!" the American added.

"Good riddance!" said the doctor.

"No more acids, no more explosives, nor raw materials for mines, no more sulfur, niter, bromine, manganese, benzol, no more iron, no more tin, copper, nickel, no more coal, no more...no more anything...in sum, no more materiel. Engines, machines, cannons—all worn out, finished, and replacement as impossible as the renewal of stocks of munitions. Finished, this war of machines in which humans were only a derisory accessory, destined to be flattened more or less rapidly—the factory war has ended up destroying the factory itself!"

"They're eking out the scrapings from the bottom of the barrel. What do they have left? A few old torpedoes, a few charges from fished-up mines, a few canisters of viruses and bacilli. They're the monster's last spasms!"

We arrived home. What a joy to drop the bundles of forage and sit down properly, while awaiting the dinner we'd certainly earned.

However, it appeared that Madame Vitalis was a trifle melancholy, and she seemed rather embarrassed. Jeanne Vitalis and Marcel Blondeau were plucking the salad without breathing a word, with worry lines on their forehead, which was entirely foreign to their habit, the young people usually exhibiting an insouciance that bordered on cheerfulness.

"What's wrong?" asked Monsieur Vandermolen, anxiously. "Is the goat all right? And the horse?"

"Very well, very well, but..."

"But?"

"Well...it's the chickens."

"What's wrong with the chickens?"

"They're...there aren't any, any more. They've been eaten."

"What? You've eaten the chickens!"

"In our absence!" said Miraud, dolorously. "That's not polite..."

"No, not us—the rats! Last night...an invasion of enormous rats!"

"The henhouse wasn't properly closed, then?"

"Yes, but there were holes. We heard noises, without suspecting the disaster at first! The rats were killing the hens and the cock. In the end, as the din went on, we arrived...too late, alas! None were left, except for the white hen besieged at the top of the ladder. Monsieur Blondeau fell on the rats, hitting them with a stick. He was heroic—he killed seven or eight!"

"Nine," said young Marcel.

The rats were killing the hens

"He's closed the door in order to massacre the miserable rats, but he had to open it so that we could help him, or the rats would have devoured him too. Enormous rats—look, look at the plate over there."

Mohammed got up to run to the henhouse.

"Damn! Damn! Quickly, traps, we need to make traps. I have to kill them all, the rats. It's your fault—you didn't want to eat them…very good, though!"

"Fortunately, all is not lost. They didn't have time to eat the slaughtered hens—that will give us provisions for a few meals."

The catastrophe of the henhouse saddened our dinner somewhat, although we were all glad to be back after our fatiguing expedition and our nocturnal battle against the wolves. Two of the murdered chickens fortified the dinner and made it more sumptuous than we had hoped; our appetite did honor to the victims. They had very tender flesh—but, alas, there was no hope of any more eggs.

Madame and Mademoiselle Vitalis shivered when we recounted our adventures. Marcel Blondeau regretted not having been with us in our rusty fortress for the battle against the wolves. I'm quite certain that he was insincere, and preferred having stayed behind to help Madame and Mademoiselle Vitalis look after the house and the garden.

Youth, youth! In the ruins of the world you persist! Is it really worth the trouble, though?

Good—now I'm falling back into the black again; Dr. Christiansen has infected me with his pessimism.

There are two more of us now: the Japanese aviator Yamato Yradonou, our new friend, and the Bulgar from the tank. Yamato will share the aviator Miraud's room; they can tell one another about their experiences of combat in the sky. It's necessary to find a corner for the Bulgar, our prisoner. What are we going to do with that intruder?

218

XII. The revenge of the pike, the bow and the club.

Mange! We all have the mange! Catastrophe! It's the wretched Bulgar who's brought the mites from the German lines.

For days now we've all been scratching and looking at one another anxiously. The doctor was scratching too, preoccupied and thinking about other things, but one evening, I extracted him from his somber reflections to ask him for a consultation.

"You see, Doctor, horrible itching, unbearable pruritus. I'm scratching, we're all scratching, everyone here is scratching. What is it?"

The doctor's only response was to scratch himself—then he slapped his forehead.

"Where's my head?" he cried. "Of course, it's the mange! It was well worth the trouble of escaping the wolves in the ruins of our bombard to bring that back! Malediction!"

"It's nothing serious, Doctor, since it's only mange, as I thought. Cure us!"

"Cure you? Cure us? That would have been easy once, but today...with what, if you please? I don't have anything for that...let me think... In the meantime, don't breathe a word to anyone; leave them ignorant of that displeasure for another day or two..."

Mange! That's not going to extract me from the depression into which my attack of pessimism has thrown me. Why did I have to come back from the Pole, where we'd organized a supportable, even tranquil, little life, devoid of emotions and torments, with various kinds of hunting for distraction? One is never content! Life there was possible, after all, in a nice cozy cavern, well equipped; the bears furnished us with food and clothing, we had an abundance of aquatic game, birds and fish, with good companions to keep the fire going. I was able to sort out my observations, and even to occupy my mind; I was planning to write a great natural history in fifteen or twenty volumes...

How far away all that is now, since I've rediscovered Europe, with its present pleasures, the flood of horror brought by what they called Science and Progress, Civilization and other follies collapsed forever, illusions drowned in rivers of blood.

It's the doctor who was in the right when I tried to combat his ideas about that and refused to accept his conclusions. Where has that hateful Science led us, which put so many resources and discoveries in the service of a race of prey? That Science, which furnished them with the frightful arsenal from which they gleefully drew their infernal weapons: gas, flames, vapors, acids, viruses and bacilli, all their maleficent chemistry! And iron to fabricate the plowshare with which the labor peoples! Yes, the engine is everything, and the value of the human being, its slave, is nothing, or almost nothing.

Into what bloody gulf has it precipitated us, that famous Progress of which we were so proud, when we puffed ourselves up with admiration for ourselves, the Progress that suddenly permitted the rapid and complete demolition, the sudden collapse, of an illusory civilization, which, in reality, was nothing but degeneracy, and a mortal malady...

I spent a bad night scratching myself, turning back and forth in my fury.

Will we ever get out of the abyss in which we're struggling? Shall I ever see Paris again? What would I find there? What would I do, what would become of me? Shall we ever see less somber days again, less hideous times? Do we even have a future? I don't want to stay here forever, though, exchanging somber ideas with the doctor! It's necessary to go, to go—but how? I'm still looking, always, for the how, rolling more or less absurd projects round my head, which maintain my insomnia...

When morning comes I rush to the doctor, scratching frantically. I'm not the only one; the others arrive, all just as anxious. They know, and are scratching themselves in the knowledge of the cause. We can talk.

"Well, Doctor, have you found it?"

"For the little inconvenience?" says the doctor. "It's quite simple very easy. I'll tell you: a little special ointment or black soap, or lotions of essence of turpentine or fuel-oil. In two days, it's gone. Except that, to reckon with this accursed mange we have no ointment, no black soap, no turpentine, no fuel-oil, and I can't see where I'm going to find any..."

Such desolation is painted on our faces, and Marcel Blondeau groans so dolorously as he looks at Jeanne Vitalis, as red as a poppy, that the good doctor is moved.

"Wait, though, before lamenting," he said. "I don't have anything at the moment, but I'll search. There's a means. Let's go into the town, four or five of us, with spades and pick-axes, to the ruined shops. Let's dig in the ruins of the pharmacy...or the paint-merchant...yes, that would be better, the paint merchant's hasn't been excavated so thoroughly, because there's nothing worth eating there. There's more chance of finding something for us..."

"Right away!" I cried. "Let's go! Quickly!"

Marcel already had a pick in his hand, and Jeanne Vitalis ran to fetch a spade.

"Yes, that's right—run!" said Madame Vitalis. "Find something!"

The hope of soon being rid of the wretched acarid, the minuscule enemy that has just added its unbearable assaults to all our troubles, makes me forget my other preoccupations.

Everyone wants to go on the expedition; five minutes later we leave, all full of ardor.

People we encounter in the town, in much greater numbers than in previous weeks, grouped in discussion, stop us as we go by, to confirm what everyone already knows about the total exhaustion of resources, and above all of munitions, in the Boche lines. Wretches escaped from The Hague or neighboring ruins are still arriving, their accounts can't leave the slightest shadow of doubt.

Finally! We're going to see something new!

But I confess that I was thinking first and foremost about our new enemy, the acarid!

We worked for two days on our excavations, feverishly and furiously, turning over and scattering all the heaps of rubble, without discovering the slightest thing that might serve to massacre that brigand of a mite. Finally, as we were despairing, the doctor laid his hands on I don't know what horrible hardened mixtures, which resembled paint, in the debris of crushed tins and drums. He brought everything back, carefully, and took possession of Madame Vitalis' stove, to the detriment of our cooking, in order to devote himself to a nauseating chemistry that was almost as bad, in mephitic terms, as the Boche gases.

I heard the young people moaning in low ones in the corners.

"Marcel, I beg you, don't look at me with horror," stammered Mademoiselle Vitalis, still crimson and trying to hide in the shadows of our cave.

"Jeanne, Jeanne, will you love me in spite of these…oh, I'd much rather have a good wound!"

"No, no, Marcel, don't say that!"

But there's no need to go into the ridiculous details of our cure. Three days later, the infinitesimal and tenacious enemy was vanquished; we were all cured! We uttered sighs of relief. Mademoiselle Vitalis no longer blushed when she looked at Marcel Blondeau, who gave the impression of having to retain himself in order not to dance and sing. He embarrassed our savior with excessively warm expressions of his immense gratitude, shook the hands of Jeanne and Madame Vitalis, expanded in effusions and came back to congratulate the ladies, to congratulate everyone...

The acarid having been annihilated, crushed in its lairs, my thoughts returned to the other enemy, the frightful monster at bay in its trenches and fortresses, having reached the end of its means of destruction.

Information arrives with increasing certainty. The people buried for such a long time in their holes and their cellars, are emerging and going from ruin to ruin, spreading the good news. They no longer hide during the daylight hours, only risking themselves outside with a thousand precautions, or only after nightfall.

I'm surprised to see so many people emerging from all the holes in a country that I had thought deserted. Children are running over the dunes in the sunlight, without masks: poor children born in misery, famine and suffering in the depths of cellars, where they had lived as little troglodytes, far more unfortunate than their ancestors of the age of caves, who had only had to fear natural forces and ferocious beasts, and not all the horrors and perfected ferocities of the scientific age.

All the men of the surrounding burrows, the Batavian tribes of the ruined villages, are coming into the ruins of Harlem to hold councils and seek allies for the great battle that they're preparing.

I admire the beautiful clubs and the rude pieces of pointed iron, forged, reshaped and naively equipped with handles by people who are reinventing the lance, the pike, the guisarme, the vouge, the halberd, the mace, the battle-ax—all the old hand-weapons of distant ages—and who will be happy to make use of them in the great final charge at the enemy of the human race.

The bow will also be at the feast, manipulated by men who haven't forgotten the Fleming and Picard traditions of shooting at birds. There are archers desirous of sending their arrows at the abhorred Boches, at the scholarly barbarians who have crushed them with huge shells, bombs, torpedoes loaded with superdynamite, panclastite, trinitrotoluene, phosphorus, poisoned them with their emissions of asphyxiating, suffocating or corrosive gases, and buried or electrocuted them under the eruptions of electric volcanoes…

Finally!

And their thirst for vengeance grips me. It really is going to be the end of *Gesta diaboli per Germanos!*

Emissaries are being sent toward the allied lines, toward Amsterdam, to try to find out how things stand there, and to reach an understanding in order to coordinate the movements.

The country is silent, except when Amsterdam launches a few shells—for it still has a small provision—at the Palace of Peace, which no longer responds.

I'm no longer thinking of leaving before the big push, the imminent mass attack that our prehistoric warriors are preparing. I shall be there. We shall all be there!

We're furbishing weapons in the cellar, as people are doing everywhere. My comrades are rubbing their hands together, joyfully. Yes, one can see people smiling now, and brandishing their primitive weapons at the thought of the use they're going to make of them, and that perhaps the end of the frightful nightmare is nigh—and the hour of vengeance too.

Mohammed shows his teeth; his smile is a rictus. He has sharpened the tip and blade of a magnificent saber-bayonet, passed through his belt like a dagger, and all day long he polishes spears or hooked vogues with multiple points for our friends or for the amateurs of the neighboring caverns.

The military men of our little association, the wreckage of various armies who have ended up here, brought together by the hazard of catastrophes—the Peruvian lieutenant, the Japanese aviator, Monsieur Jollimay, the Swiss rifleman, Maître Saladin, the captain-notary, and the New Zealander—are organizing those neighbors, with the valid men of the town, into a single company, which has very rapidly become a sizeable battalion, and training them for the supreme hand-to-hand battle with prehistoric clubs. They practice running, combat and skirmishing, in preparation for the great charge, devoid of pity and mercy, that is to liberate the world—"or what still remains of it and is worthy of being conserved," says the doctor, ever pessimistic.

Marcel Blondeau is showing a frenetic ardor. He goes out, running around incessantly, carrying out distant reconnaissance in the direction of the Boche positions. He recruits warriors with solid fists from the surrounding area, awaiting the great day with impatience.

Jeanne Vitalis is as excited as he is, and when we depart for the battle, she will be there. She is already able to put one arrow in two into the black at fifty paces. It's an appreciable talent, added to all those she possesses already. She is going to avenge her mother's wooden leg—poor Madame Vitalis, who is shivering in advance, and would like to prepare, with the doctor, the provisions of lint that we're certainly going to need before long, when we come to blows. But to make lint one needs cotton, and we don't have any, or so very little!

XIII. A wretch who wants to reinvent gunpowder.

And I too shall go to the great battle—me, a man who is so peaceful, even pacifist! I would once have treated as a madman anyone who had told me that I would one day march to combat full of ardor and fury, ax in hand, like a warrior of prehistoric times—but that is what I am going to do.

I feel myself, I look at my arms, I even pick myself to make sure that I'm not dreaming again. No, I'm awake; it's really me who is brandishing this heavy ax and wearing an enormous cutlass, which Mohammed has carefully sharpened for me, passed through a rope belt.

Through the main square of Harlem—what remains, at least, of the old Groot Markt, so prettily formed by beautiful brick houses and monuments: the Saint Bavo cathedral, the Town Hall with the Franz Hals Museum, and the old meat market with the gigantic Renaissance gable—file a strangely equipped troop of thin but robust men, warriors dressed in badly-worn cassocks of coarse fabric and animal skins, showing glimpses of suntanned chests and muscular arms, all marching with and energetic and decisive stride, carrying various weapons over their shoulders: enormous pikes, clubs, long-handled axes, sparkling scythe-blades attacked to the ends of solid handles.

They all have cutlasses in their belts, or sabers of all forms. Alongside one infantry saber that must have seen service in the army of 1810 or 1830, I perceive a huge rapier from the time of William the Silent, and a bizarrely-sheathed steel blade, the work of some contemporary blacksmith.

A strangely equipped troop of men

Oh, old Franz Hals, painter of the bourgeois guards of the heyday of Harlem, the feasts of pikemen and arquebusiers of the good old days, what would you say if you saw the descendants of your models of yore, the primitive horde that is traversing the main square today and going to line up before the masses of red and white stone, the scattered rubble of the monuments that were the adornment of the destroyed city?

You would not find among their descendants the expansive rubicund faces of the brave bourgeois soldiers of the sixteenth and seventeenth centuries, any more than the well-tailored doublets and the magnificent collars. But you might admire the energetic heads refined by misfortune and long suffering, the attitude of resolution of all these men and all those who are coming to join them, arriving one by one or in small groups from all the streets, or ruins of streets opening on to the great market square, and the paths circling or cutting through the mountain of crumbled stones.

And there are warriors arriving in little troops, armed with pikes or scythes, sometimes in groups of archers carrying quivers on their back garnished with a provision of long arrows.

Some on them have come from a long way away, contingents furnished by the villages of the interior, peasants from farms lost in the polders or coastal fishermen. I recognize our friends from Noordwik, led by the formidable burgemeester, carrying the huge ax of a tribal chieftain of the age of caves. Yamato the Japanese aviator goes to clap him on the shoulder joyfully, happy to see the Batavian Hercules again, who laughs into his coarse beard and must be expressing to him, if I understand correctly, his loud desire to come to blows as soon as possible, his haste to rush to the assault on the Boche fortress of the Palace of Peace.

People come together, fold discussions, bring news from more distant regions, where people are also emerging from caverns and burrows under the ruins. Men go to examine the bands and groups that are arriving.

227

The tribes of distant centuries

Every band has its war-chief, who makes them carry out various drill movements, bearing no resemblance to the military maneuvers of old, the days, so near and yet do far away, before the cataclysm.

What we have before our eyes really are the tribes of distant centuries, united by common danger, exercising with primitive weapons, the honest weapons used by the men of old to repel some invasion.

They seem ready, all of them, and disposed to march to battle with the will to win, the resolution to finish off and smash the common enemy, the scourge of humanity, the execrable scientific barbarian who was run out of his diabolical inventions and munitions.

The great day is nigh. Is the dawn of a new and better era about to shine over the ruins of the old world?

Dr. Christiansen and I are looking at one another, very emotional, our hearts beating hopefully, when Monsieur Vandermolen comes over, bringing the doctor a man from Harlem who has a big bulging sack under his arm.

"What's that?" asks the doctor, when the man opens his sack.

"Saltpeter," replied Monsieur Vandermolen.

"Saltpeter? What for?"

"To make gunpowder, of course," says Monsieur Vandermolen, "With carbon and..."

The doctor jumps. His eyebrows frown, his lips purse and his beard juts out, his eyes flamboyant with such indignation that I interpose myself anxiously between him and the man from Harlem.

"So!" cries the doctor. "So, wretch, you want to reinvent gunpowder! What! You infamous scoundrel, you miserable dolt! We have the fortunate, the marvelous, the miraculous luck that all the powder-kegs are empty, that all the explosives are used up, exhausted, finished, that all the satanic horrors that have ravaged the world and reduced the planet to this state of devastation, woe and misery are abolished, and you want to remake them, reproduce them…you want to start all over again! Nothing can and nothing ever will change! What are you saying? What are you saying? You're proposing to re-commence the work of the monk Schwartz, whose soul has gone to the devil!"

His expression contrite, Monsieur Vandermolen bowed his head in shame. The man with the saltpeter dropped his sack.

Dr. Christiansen turned his back on them furiously and kicked the sack. He grabbed me by the arm and dragged me away.

"Oh, it's like that, is it?" he said to me. "Well, so be it! Let's go! Let's plunge back one last time into the abomina-tions of that accursed Science! Let's go! Listen to me—I ha-ven't told you everything. I too am, have been, one of those detestable and abominable scientists who have led us to where we are, gradually, step by step, with their pretentious follies, their pursuit of the false progress demanded by the stupid and the imprudent, their rage for false ameliorations transforming the god old ways of life of fortunate centuries, and who ren-dered possible the frightful adventure, general destruction and universal carnage...that slut Science who has crucified poor unfortunate humanity, the vampire Science, the chimera in spectacles, devourer of man, scavenger of cadavers...that whore science can only be killed by science! Let's go, let's force the serpent vomited forth by Hell to bite itself, in order that it does of its own venom!"

The doctor planted himself in front of me; he looked at me with wild eyes, his voice trembling, clenching his fists as if he were about to strangle me.

"I think as you do, Doctor!" I said, swiftly. "You're right, absolutely right! I too have retreated from the deceitful mirages of false progress, the destroyer of all beauty, the cor-rupter and demoralizer, and by virtue of that fact, the universal instrument of death. I've recovered from the blissful human admiration of that Science, which I curse as you do now that I've been able to see and judge the depths of the abyss! You've forced me to open my eyes and comprehend! Yes, that

Science is nothing, in the final analysis, but the servant of the ferocious and insatiable Moloch to whom she furnishes, more and more abundantly, rations of victims to crush and devour!"

"Yes, yes…Moloch…the last idol, the monstrous idol it's necessary to cast down…!" The doctor struck me on the shoulder with his fist, as if it were me that he wanted to strike and cast down.

After a momentary pause he went on: "Listen. I didn't tell you everything when I told you about my miseries in the great German war factory, I didn't tell you everything! A slave of the factory, condemned to forced labor in their laboratories, I labored…but I also thought, I reflected, I sought…I sought for my own account, and I found! Do you understand? I found…at least, I almost found…yes, yes, it needed so little! And the proof of my success, I was able to obtain it. The proof! The proof…

"You know the explosion that liberated me, that permitted me to escape—well, it was me who provoked it, me who produced it, sooner than I expected by means of…imagine my joy! From the depths of the cell where I was imprisoned, I was able to explode the cartridges in the cartridge-cases of the Landsturmers of the post, then the crates and carboys of explosives in the factory, and then the great depot…."

He could see in my face that I doubted those assertions; he grabbed me by the collar and shook me violently.

"Yes, yes! I repeat to you, I found it, I found it. I have nothing here to demonstrate it by experiment, the proof…I'd need…but you'll see, you'll see…since it's necessary. A few final studies, a verification of the procedure, and it will go. Do you understand? Do you understand?"

"No, Doctor. No. Explain it to me…"

"In brief, this is it: I have…yes, I have the means, with a simple little instrument on the table of my study, or even in my pocket, to cause the explosion, at a distance of x—that remains to be determined—to cause the explosion, I say, of the cartridges in the cartridges cases and the rifles of the enemy soldiers, the shells in the caissons, the depots of munitions or explosive products, the mines, the ammunition-stores of ships, the torpedoes in the bunkers, the powder-kegs, the arsenals...in sum, everything. Everything! To make, at will anything at all capable of explosion, inside or behind no matter what, suddenly enter into deflagration and explode! Do you see now? Do you understand? At will. Whatever, and whenever and wherever I want!

"What?" I said, a trifle bewildered. "What?"

"Simple!" I was led to my discovery by the study of Hertzian rays—I'll explain all that to you later. You're going to help me; I'm almost at the end, I only need to determine certain points, regulate the mechanisms. Out there, in the German factory, I reached the final experiments. It was difficult; I had to hide...I wasn't entirely certain of my discovery yet, I tried somewhat at hazard, hesitantly, but it worked, since the explosion as produced more rapidly than I thought, and in conditions that I can easily rediscover, with a little more research. It's necessary, then, for me to take up my work again, to go a little further. I lack many things, but when I find a laboratory, it won't take long. After a few trials, certain difficulties regulated, I'll soon have it perfected. And then...then, you'll see!"

"So," I said, "you've become one of the instruments of that accursed Science again?"

"Since it's necessary! Since, as you can clearly see, humans who haven't understood anything, haven't learned anything, want to start again, and will start again. Oh, they want to bring back explosives, powders, mines and torpedoes! Well, I'm going to blow them up in their hands, and make the usage of all that impossible, forever! Do you understand? No more powder, black or gray, no more terrifying explosives to devastate one's neighbor, no possible artillery! Definitively vanquished, the monster cannon, no more bombards, no more mines, no more anything—I'll blow it all up, and I'll even cause all explosive matter, no matter where, to blow up by itself, automatically... That will hinder the industries that use explosives, it will render impossible or difficult certain large-scale works—too bad! We'll go back to tools alone, to the only means of old. Antiquity didn't make use of explosives, I think, and it still left great works! So, humans will be forced to revert forever to the old natural weapons! Since humans are determined to remain the arch-tiger of humans, I'll erode their claws and teeth as far as possible..."

I had understood, and I shook the doctor's hand vigorously.

"Come on," he said. "In the meantime, let's train ourselves with these old weapons for the final assault!"

XIV. The death-throes of the scientific Bellona.

They were all in full swing, the friends of our refuge, the burrow under the ruins of the Vandermolen house, those soldiers of such diverse races, who had fought the common enemy so far from their fatherlands, and those civilians caught up in the torment and washed up here, all of them felt hope gradually reborn in the depths of their hearts.

The somber motto of the bell-tower of Alost, so discouraged in its resignation, *Neither hope not dread*, no longer came back unintentionally to chill the blood in my veins and overwhelm my energy. Yes, I have hope now; Dr. Christiansen has hope; we all have hope.

The professor-artilleryman, Monsieur Jollimay, and the doctor no longer engage in those duets of bitter pessimism in the long evenings, in which the historical arguments of the former alternated with the anti-scientific imprecations of the latter, furnishing us with lugubrious dreams and nightmares for the long nights.

"The history of the world is about to commence an entirely new volume," says Jollimay.

"Blank pages!" says the doctor. "But watch out—I'd like to be able to burn all the old books, too full of dangerous lessons!"

The aviator Miraud no longer has those fits of humor, or black humor, which sudden caused him to pass from an expansive and torrential loquacity—just like a Montmartrean from Toulouse—to the most complete mutism for hours and days on end. He's started to sing again. In the morning, from his bedroom next to mine, he wakes us up with refrains, murmured at first, and then resumes in a voice that grows gradually louder. He repeats himself, he begins again, he modifies...

Here come all the toxic shells.
The strangling, choking wave,
All the torpedoes and chemical wells
That Hell hurls at the brave!
That Hell hurls at the brave.

Can you smell in every field,
The clouds of poisoned gases,
Making us keep our faces sealed
Lest they kill our lads and lasses?
Masks on, chaps,
Adjust your straps…

I can scarcely sleep, thinking about what's in preparation, and I call out from my bed: "What's that you're saying, Monsieur Miraud?"

"That's poetry," replies Mohammed, my neighbor on the other side.

"I'm rhyming," says Miraud. "It's coming back to me. I'm thinking about Montmartre again, you know. One arm less

234

doesn't hinder me as much as I thought for holding a lyre! It's gone, but the rhymes come all the same. What you hear there is the *Marseillaise of Protest*, sadly written in our holes, under the projectiles, with the gases and mephitic vapors raining down from the Boche trenches. You ought to remember it, Monsieur, because I sang it to you the day you arrived, under the wave of gas. My self-esteem as a poet is cruelly offended by your inconceivable forgetfulness. Anyway, let's pass over the dolorous humiliation. Today, I'm rhyming something else, the *Marseillaise of Vengeance*—you'll see, the revenge of the innocent army, courageous and loyal, over the ignoble engines of chemical warfare...and then something else, which you'll have the politeness to learn by heart, the *War Cry of the Troglodytes*, for the imminent day of the attack...

Mr. Gibson the American billionaire is making plans. If the shock for which we're waiting really is the last, if calm finally is to be reborn after the frightful cyclone of devastation, he invites us all to spend some time with him in America, in his vast estates in Illinois, which can't have evaporated like the dozens of millions he brought to New York.

He's no longer thinking of adding a wing to the Palace of Peace, in order to constitute a museum of the horrors of war. That museum of the horrors of war is the whole of Europe, in its length and breadth, no matter where; one only has to look around.

Monsieur Gomares, the worthy Spanish businessman, Monsieur Arbydian, the Armenian businessman and Demetrius Manoli, industrialist and financier, huddle together in the evenings in our subterranean kitchen in order to converse mysteriously.

God forgive me, they're talking about the immense upsurge of business that will be provoked by the reconstitution—or, rather, the reconstruction—of society.

Harlem and the surrounding villages are increasingly animated. Armed bands are arriving from all directions, detachments of men sometimes coming from a long way away, carrying, in addition to their weapons—pikes, clubs and cutlasses—packages and luggage for encampment and nourishment, and all of them, like those here, are entirely disposed, with an appetite for combat and a range of vengeance.

The organization is feverish; leaders are being appointed. Scouts have advanced very close to the Boche positions and have set up observation-posts to keep watch on the enemy.

The Boche retrenchments remain silent; the canons are mute. The batteries that thundered for such a long time and so furiously all around the Palace of Peace, collapsed and turned upside-down, transformed by the interminable battle into an extraordinarily strong and complicated citadel, and improbable labyrinth of covered trenches or uncovered tunnels, sheltered galleries for masked and armored batteries, reservoirs or engines of toxic gases, caverns for giant bombards, fixed or mobile…all of it remains mute and inactive.

A heavy silence weighs upon the factory of death; the satanic engines, having vomited their last breath, are like the impotent cadavers of steel monsters, ferocious Leviathans slain in their turn, finally crushed!

When is the battle? I'm getting impatient; our prehistoric warriors are nervous. Everyone wants to get it over with. It's Dr. Christiansen who moderates that impatience.

"We need every chance," he says. "Let me work a little longer…be patient, calm down. Just think, what a catastrophe it would be is, with our primitive weapons, we're going to run into loaded rifles? What if the enemy has conserved cartridges as a supreme resource, or a few shells? No, no, let me work!"

Emissaries have been able to reach the lines of Amsterdam. We're assured of the cooperation of the people there, who will launch their own mass attack on the day and at the hour that the leaders fix. And they've been able to furnish the good doctor, in spite of a little difficulty, with the various things he requested in order to bring his great project to a conclusion.

Enclosed in a redoubt that has been fitted out as an improvised laboratory, he's working, his eyes shining with a fever of anxiety that causes tremors to pass through his hands, and in his voice when anyone questions him about his results.

Will he discover—or, rather, rediscover—the secret he has already held, in the hazard of trials and triturations, the secret of the sovereign antidote that will cure humankind forever of the infernal chemistry of powders and explosives?

"Well, Doctor?"

Dr. Christiansen emerges from his laboratory, his features convulsed but joyful, We all throw ourselves upon him.

"Well, I finally have it! I hope...I have it...I'm sure of it...I've found it again...I've reconstituted my machinery. We can prepare for the attack. If the enemy has the slightest quantity of explosives, the smallest munitions store, I'll blow it up in his hands! I'm going to the Council of Chiefs to make the final preparations. And immediately thereafter, the assault with hand weapons. Their rifles will be nothing more than bayonet-handles; we'll see the work of our pikes, our clubs, our axes and cutlasses!"

"One more explosive," I say.

"No, an exploder—the supreme exploder!"

"Bravo, Doctor! Hope! Confidence! Hurrah!"

"Banzai!" cries the Japanese. "Forward march!"

"I'm certain," the doctor goes on, "but as proof, today, I'm going to make the mines washed up on the coast at Noordwik explode—you know, the ones that gave you such a fright because of your imprudence."

We shake the doctor's hand joyfully, and we leap upon our weapons in order to caress the shiny and well-sharpened blades. Yes! They're going to do good work!

"And forward the *Marseillaise of Vengeance!*" Miraud shouts to us. "For the deliverance and the great clearance!"

Marcel Blondeau almost dances for joy, and, under the pretext of helping her, squeezes Jeanne Vitalis' hands as she checks her arrows, as emotional as he is. She doesn't want to quit Marcel; she will fight by his side.

They appear to me to be symbolic, those two children. Among all of us, old and worn out, lamentable survivors of a generation rushed by the enormity of the fatalities that have descended upon their shoulders, they represent the future in revolt, the future that is detaching itself from the frightful past, the race that will grow and hope—or rather, resume hoping—that will survive the frightful crisis in which it saw the annihilation of the entire heritage of centuries, so slowly accumulated.

And Madame Vitalis, who has understood, kisses both of them feverishly.

There is a great stir all day around Harlem, the concentration into numerous troops, making the final preparations for the march toward The Hague, to occupy the advance positions in front of the Palace of Peace—of complete and definitive peace, this time.

In the afternoon, there are formidable explosions in the direction of Noordwik; they are the old mines run aground in the sand blowing up, and with them, old shells buried in the vicinity, in the dunes.

Other explosions are heard in the distance, at sea; they are surely drifting mines, tossed by the waves. Dr. Christiansen has succeeded—succeeded completely! The era of explosives is definitively closed.

And now, to arms! The big push is tomorrow!

I, the peaceful man, pacific until today, caress the point and the blade of the scythe of sorts that has been fabricated for me, and I clench my teeth...I'm waiting for tomorrow impatiently; I'm slightly nervous but I'm not afraid. On the contrary, I already feel completely stirred by joy, by the intoxication of the battle for the human race, finally liberated from devouring Science...

From tomorrow onwards, a new world will begin, which I can already glimpse...

In the years on end during which all study has been suspended, all education abolished, the connecting thread to the centuries abused by fatal Science has been cut; it's necessary not to fall back into the gulf...

She doesn't want to quit Marcel;
she will fight by his side.

The Tree of Science has been felled; it's necessary that it doesn't grow again, to rip it up, root and branch!

Oh, holy ignorance of recovered infancy, I bless you...

Adrien Bertrand: *The Rain that surprised Candide in his Garden*

Preface

We owe apologies to Monsieur de Voltaire; he even asked that Candide should be left to look after his garden, and that no maladroit amateur should continue the story of his hero's adventures.

"O Muses!" said the patriarch of Ferney, at the end of *La Princesse de Babylone*, "prevent reckless continuers from spoiling with their fables the verities of which I have informed mortals in this true story, as they have dared to falsify *Candide, L'Ingénu* and the chaste adventures of the chaste Jeanne."

In fact, we have had no more respect for the great Voltaire than he had for the powers and the ideas of his century. We have been obliged to recount an event that took Candide by surprise in 1914, and report at length a conversation that he had at that time with various individuals.

Voltaire's desire was poorly heeded. Three operas and a pantomime have been made of *La Princesse de Babylone!* Marmontel and a few other malefactors of his species have based comedies on *L'Ingénu!* As for *Candide*, barely two years after it was printed, it was falsified by the publication of a "second part," a literary hoax attributed to a certain Thorel de Campigneulles, a former guardsman and treasurer of France of the generality of Lyon.[19] The latest imitation of *Candide*, due to an excellent writer of our epoch, Abel

---

[19] Charles Thorel de Campigneulles (1737-1809) published *Candide, ou l'Optimisme* in 1761. He had previously written several other *contes philosophiques* in the Voltairean mode.

Hermant, dates from this year.[20] And that will not be the last, if we can judge by our own attempt; others will follow.

Between those extreme there are so many sequels, imitation, refutations of *Candide* and works inspired by him that it is impossible to count them. They range from philosophical dissertation to comic opera![21] Their study would be fine material for a doctoral thesis. Sub-Lieutenant Vaissette, former pupil of the École Normale Supérieure and the Institut Thiers, was about to devote himself to that work when he was killed, in the course of the Great War at the dawn of the victory.[22]

It seems to us that all the imitators of Candide, our predecessors, are culpable; what interest was there in showing us the lover of Mademoiselle Cunégonde in Demark or the two Indies,[23] when M. de Voltaire had taken him, between Eldorado and Constantinople, everywhere that he thought necessary and sufficient?

---

[20] Abel Hermant's short story "Le Nouveau Candide" appeared in *La Vie Parisienne* in 1915

[21] The author inserts two references, the first to "*Remerciement de Candide à M. de Voltaire*, Halle & Amsterdam 1760, octavo 35pp, attributed to Louis Olivier de Marconnay, counselor of legation and principal registrar of the Department of Foreign Affairs in Prussia" and the second to "*Candide, grand opera-bouffe en cinq actes et sept tableaux* by Desiré Pilette, Paris, Dentu 1861, octavo, 123pp."

[22] The author inserts a reference here to his own quasi-autobiographical novel "*L'Appel du sol, roman*, by Adrien Bertrand. Paris: Calmann-Levy, 1916, octavo, 302pp," in which Vaissette is the central character, his *alter ego*.

[23] The author inserts two more references, to "*Candide au Danemarc, ou l'Optimisme des honnêtes gens*, Geneva, 1769, octavo of 8 plus 200pp" and "*Candide Anglais ou aventures tragic-comiques d'Amb. Gwinett avant et dans ses voyages aux deux Indes*, Frankfurt & Leipzig, 1771, 2 vols. octavo, 184 & 132pp."

We alone find grace in our own eyes! That is not merely an indulgent weakness on the part of the author; it is because our time has been so fertile in accidents, which have surpassed anything that Voltaire imagined, and of which it appeared indispensable to us to see the traces that they have left, all the way to the inoffensive Ottoman farmhouse of the naïve Westphalian.

The French Revolution has passed, along with the European upheavals of the eighteenth century, those of the nineteenth and even those of the twentieth, which is seeing the revolution of young Turkey, a sad parody of ours, but no one has thought to tell us whether Candide was informed of those cataclysms. We would, however, not be sorry to know what the pupil of Pangloss and Martin—the brainchild, to say all, of Monsieur de Voltaire—thought of Robespierre, Talleyrand, the Emperor, and even Prince von Bismarck and Monsieur Thiers.

It has been given to us to know the reflections that current events have suggested not only to Candide but also to various other individuals as celebrated as him. Those events surpass in horror and range all previous events. That is why we thought it our duty to consign the following conversation to print.

Monsieur de Voltaire, the sovereign of French prose, will pardon us for our awkwardness, by reason of our good intention and our good will. Nor will Anatole France, his heir and our master, think that we are in the wrong.[24]

---

[24] Anatole France—who was still alive in 1915—is included in the apology because the author borrows the character of Jérôme Coignard from the satirical historical novel *La Rôtisserie de la Reine Pédauque* (1893; tr. as *At the Sign of the Reine Pédauque*) and its companion-volume *Les Opinions de M. Jérôme Coignard* (1893; tr. as *The Opinions of Jerome Coignard*). Coignard becomes the mentor of the initially-hapless protagonist of the earlier novel, whom he renames Jacques Tournebroche [i.e., Jack Turnspit] and both of them

I. In Candide's Garden

Candide was living alone in his little farmhouse.

It was on the shores of the Sea of Marmora, not far from the Bosphorus, a few leagues from Brousse, which hides its white houses, its fountains, its minarets and its terraces beneath climbing roses and the shade of mulberry-trees. He had lived there happily since he had been able to discover the virtues of work, inner peace, and the joys of the heart and the mind; since he had decided no longer to ask of life what it is not capable of giving us, and his skepticism prevented him from seeking the best of all possible worlds; since he had found an infinity of beautiful adventures in the cultivation of his vegetables, the equilibrium of his thoughts and the love of Cunégonde, his wife, whose beauty was for him an illusion voluntarily conserved, and who cooked him delicate dishes and excellent pastries.

The Old Woman had died first, then faithful Cacambo, who went to town to sell the aubergines, the pistachios and the lemons that they harvested. Pangloss and Martin had followed them, converted to Candide's mildness, the one without regret for not having taught at Leipzig or some Westphalian university, the other estimating that existence, although not being the greatest benefit there is, was at least bearable. A little later, Cunégonde had joined them under the mounds of a lawn irrigated by a spring and shaded by high blue cypresses.

Candide could only console himself for all those losses by going to dream on the graves in the depths of his orchard, while surrounding himself, in accordance with the custom of Muslim countries, with several young and beautiful maidservants and cultivating his enclosure better than ever.

He told himself that twenty centuries before, beyond the waves into which he saw the sun sink every evening, further away than Lemnos, Skyros and the Cyclades, on the other

---

assist the alchemist M. d'Astarac in his scholarly but futile alchemical researches.

shore of the Archipelago, a man had possessed, like him, a modest garden. He had gathered a few friends there, and the divine Epicurus had expounded his doctrine; by virtue of the charm of his mind, the vigor of his thought and the grace of the Hellenic Muses, the meek Athenian's doctrine was what the adventures of his life had caused Candide to adopt. Thus, the charming philosopher of genius, like the naïve and simple man, encountered happiness, one by divine inspiration and the other by human experience, in a small garden.[25]

In his turn, on a warm Oriental evening, Candide went to sleep in the peace of the tomb. His companions perfumed his body and buried him next to his friends, under a cedar, at the foot of a myrtle bush and under a carpet of asphodels. But the next day, by the first rays of the sun coming over the orange groves and the village mosque, they saw Candide, smiling and rejuvenated, contemplating his red tomatoes and his golden grapes. As they had learned, from the wisdom of Islam, to resign themselves to not being able to understand, they were not astonished, and life pursued its course.

That was because Candide was immortal.

II. Candide Encounters a Philosopher

The most beautiful months of summer were manifesting their glory, and the heat would have been difficult to bear but for the neighborhood of the waves of the Propontide[26] and the springs that sang at the feet of the laurels, the bamboos and the plant-trees.

Toward the evening of one magnificent day the wind rose; it blew from Europe violently, stripping the leaves from the melons, causing the peaches and nectarines to fall like hail,

---

[25] Anatole France had followed up his volumes featuring Jérôme Coignard with a more earnest account of *Le Jardin d'Épicure* (1895; tr. as *The Garden of Epicurus*).

[26] The Greek name for the Sea of Marmora.

and scything through the aubergine plot. A yellow and livid sun announced rain.

Anxiously, Candide went through the olive grove to the end of his field, which sloped toward the stream of a valley. That area was planted with vines; it was a matter of checking the condition of the grape harvest; at that time of year abundant rain risked drowning it.

As Candide's gaze alternated between the menacing sky and the already-heavy grape-clusters, he perceived a strange individual coming toward him. The other was clad in a long robe, in the manner of the muezzins and muftis—or, rather, of Syrians and Persians. When the person came closer, Candide discovered that he was a priest. For a moment, he was afraid, dreading that it might be a Jesuit.

He had often heard laudatory mention of the work of the Jesuits in Asia Minor, but he retained a bad memory of them because if his adventures in Paraguay and those of his brother-in-law, the Baron de Thunder-ten-Tronckh, he feared that his tranquility might be troubled. For a long time, he had only known the worries caused by droughts or, as this evening, sudden tempests.

He reassured himself, however; a fine collar under a worn and modest robe showed him that he was dealing with some good priest who had strayed in this direction. The other possessed, in spite of his open soutane, which lacked buttons and was secured by several pieces of string, a great air of dignity; the benevolence legible in his eyes was indescribable.

The abbé lifted his soutane with one hand, allowing a glimpse of his thick white woolen stockings, panting because of the temperature and the corpulence of a jovial and complacent midriff. He advanced over the labored ground with difficulty, between the vines.

"Don't disturb yourself!" he called to Candide as soon as he could make himself heard. "Excuse me, but the wind is fierce and the rain is already starting to fall. I thought of asking you for shelter for a little while."

"Be welcome, Monsieur l'Abbé," said Candide, "And come into to the house with me.

"Also, Monsieur," the abbé went on, "I'm very pleased to meet you. I've wanted to see you for a long time, and even though you're the son in spirit of that rogue of genius Arouet, we have a thousand ideas in common. I'm a priest, and a submissive son of our holy mother the Church, but also of Saint Thomas Aquinas, Saint Augustine, the meek Saint Francis of Assisi, and above all of the Gospel—so I am, therefore, very glad to meet you, Monsieur Candide."

"You're very honest," the latter replied.

"My name is Jérôme Coignard," said the abbé.

"Monsieur l'Abbé Coignard!" exclaimed Candide. Is it really you I see? Weren't you assassinated more than a century ago by an accursed Jew on the road to Lyon? Is it really you that I see, Monsieur Coignard, and will my roof, which sheltered Pangloss and Martin, the wisest of men, and shelters your servant, the moist philosophical of all, have the honor of sheltering the eloquent and savant theologian who possessed as much scorn for his fellows as forbearance in their regard, who was truly humane in his actions—his poor human actions—but who tried, by means of his discourse and his thoughts, to raise himself up as far as the divinity and show himself to be truly divine, in imitation of Plato? Are you not dead, Monsieur l'Abbé Coignard? Is it really you that I've met in the midst of these grapes whose juice is so dear; is it really you that I see?"

"I've certainly been killed," replied Monsieur Coignard, "and I died in a Christian fashion—but to tell the truth, like you, I received immortality, and you see me confused by it. In consequence, here we both are, meeting in your orchard."

In fact, Abbé Jérôme Coignard had not had to wait long for the blissful resurrection. While his body reposed in a Burgundian cemetery, on a hillside, in the midst of the grapes that produced the best vintages in the world, his soul had presented itself at the threshold of Paradise. Saint Peter had not made any difficulty about admitting him, for he was irreproachable in his doctrine, his repentance and his confidence in the grace of God. There had been no hesitation at the divine tribunal; his morals and his conduct, often reprehensible, were those of all mortals, the brother in misery of whom he had not failed to be, by virtue of his sins; but his faith and his good will had distinguished him among them all. And as he had written: "Blessed are the merciful, for they shall obtain mercy," and as the Master had said: "Blessed are the meek, for they shall inherit the earth," it had been given to him to see his body, like those of Lazarus and the daughter of Jairus, resuscitated from death.

Since then, having forgotten Zozime the Panopolitan and all the follies of Spagyric philosophy, Abbé Coignard had lived in Benedictine abbeys, most often on Monte Cassino, and sometimes also in a certain convent in the Orient, sunlit and cool, and filled with precious manuscripts. At this precise moment he was undertaking a studious retreat there, and it was while walking in the country that he had strayed as far as the farmhouse that had been indicated to him by the local people as Candide's. He still read, with a rejuvenated passion, Dr. Boethius, who flourished, as scholarly as a doctor of the Sorbonne, in the dusk of Latinity; St. John Chrysostom, who led his troubled existence in all the countries of Asia and Turkey, whose eloquence perfumed like honey the supreme moments of Hellenism; and, above all, Cicero, to whom no orator had ever got close, who was the finest artisan of the manipulation of the most beautiful language ever forged by humans, who manifested so much grandeur and so many weaknesses, but who loved justice enough to die for it.

The reading of those cherished writers only furnished Abbé Coignard with a distraction, but he also worked on writing his history of the great revolutions that have agitated peoples. The idea of it had come to him in Rome. It was from there that he had witnessed the French Revolution, which had not astonished him. In fact, he had expected it, and seen it coming. In the Eternal City, moreover, he had encountered Abbé Capmartin de Chaupy, who had just discovered the country house that Horace possessed in the Sabine, and who had written three octavo volumes about that discovery.[27] That excellent archeologist also expected the Revolution, and had told Abbé Coignard, for he had noticed that it was predicted in Horace, and he had shown him the passages that had clearly announced it.

At any rate, the sequence of events that went from the Constituent Assembly to the Consulate struck the indulgent philosopher so forcefully that he had set about relating them. He wanted to find their origins. That was what had caused him to undertake his famous work on tempests, *De tempestatibus*, that word being taken in an allegorical and moral sense, signifying the storms that disrupt the course of the human chronicle. The principal ones seemed to be the ending of the Roman Republic by Marius and Octavius, the invasion of the German barbarians, the Renaissance and the Lutheran and Calvinist heresies.

From those past events, considered in their development, their relationships and their ends, related without wishing to put them at the service of the quarrels of the present time, but with the sole concern of philosophy and truth, one could doubtless extract some information regarding their consequences, which would form the unfathomable future.

It was thus that Jérôme Coignard penetrated Candide's farmhouse.

III. The Storm

It was raining.

Winds were blowing from the four corners of the horizon, seemingly converging precisely on the farmhouse. The downpour stripped the yellow and crimson roses of summer that decorated the flower-beds and scaled the walls of the house. Fruits that were still green fell from the orange trees.

---

[27] Bertrand Capmartin de Chaupy (1720-1798). The three volumes in question were published in 1767-69.

Clumps of reeds were flattened like ripe wheat over which the scythe has passed. The Alep pines resounded with the rattle of their needles.

"The earth and the heavens have gone mad!" said Candide. The instinct of property, menaced by the heavens, awoke in him.

"We need a good log fire," said Abbé Coignard.

Vine-branches were already burning in the fireplace; they illuminated the faience walls, which were decorated with the precepts of the Koran, the Bible and various philosophers. The abbé dried his big shoes.

"It's insane, insane," Candide repeated. "In the middle of summer, in the heart of the Orient..."

"Think what it must be like in Westphalia," said the Abbé, to console him.

But that did not console Candide, who was thinking about his lost harvests. Standing at the window, he watched the rain and hail fall.

"Here come some more strangers," he said. "I'll go open the door for them."

Abbé Coignard stood up in order to present his civilities. Candide opened the door. Immediately, three unfortunate individuals, streaming with water, hurtled into the room. They were in a lamentable state, filthy and bewildered. Rain was dripping from their clothes, their hair and their noses. On the mosaic around their feet a little lake formed. Under the layer of mud that covered them, neither their faces nor their garments could be distinguished.

"We had taken refuge under the great cedar in the grounds," said one of them, "but it has just been struck by lightning."

"Malediction!" exclaimed Candide.

"You weren't hurt?" asked the abbé, charitably.

His interlocutor was as round and jovial as he was. "Bah!" he replied, laughing. "It's just one more adventure after a hundred others." Then, remembering that he had not yet introduced himself, he said, with British stiffness: "My name is Pickwick."

He dipped his head, in order to offer the abbé a reverential bow, his silk hat in his hand, and his gold-rimmed spectacles slid down his nose. His white twill culottes squeezed his buttocks to bursting point, and two trickles of water ran down the tails of his blue frock-coat.

"I'll introduce you to my traveling companion," he said. "You'll know the name: it's His Grace the ingenious hidalgo Don Quixote de la Mancha."

"Don Quixote! Mr. Pickwick!" exclaimed Candide and the abbé, in astonishment, with one voice.

Don Quixote bowed, breaking his tall silhouette in two. He was, in fact, wearing his strange armor, covered in damp earth: leggings, thigh-pads, tassets, breastplate, shoulder-pads and armbands, all more corroded by rust than ever; but he was bare-headed, for the morion that ornamented his head, as you will remembered, was made of cardboard, and it had dissolved in the rain. The green ribbons that had attached the morion to his high collar were dangled with wisps of his hair and the whole fell down over his eyes and his big hooked nose. In spite of that, Don Quixote conserved a certain Castilian nobility.

"Are we in a castle," the knight errant asked, "like those presented by my imagination, or in a hostelry, like those into which reality made me penetrate?"

"You're in my farmhouse," Candide told him, "and you're welcome here."

"We had decided," Mr. Pickwick exclaimed, "in order to complete our adventures, to make a tour of the world together, but to do it without making any fuss, for experience has served us. Fundamentally, we resemble one another, and are almost the same person, full of idealism and faith, as nearly identical as a paladin from the luminous banks of the Tagus and a free citizen of the foggy banks of the Thames can be."

"You'll be mistaken for Sancho Panza," Candid remarked, naively.

"He's dead, and so is his donkey," replied Mr. Pickwick, good-humoredly.

"And also Rosinante," added Don Quixote.

"But who is this young man-at-arms traveling with you?" asked Abbé Coignard. "To judge by the salad covering his head, he's some squire of Seigneur Don Quixote."

"No," declared Mr. Pickwick. "We encountered him under the cedar, where he had taken refuge, like us. He's a French traveler, who told us that he's come to this region to distract himself, and in order to visit the tomb of Achilles and Candide's orchard."

He went to fetch the stranger, who was modestly distancing himself from such important people and poking the fire.

The rain continued to rage.

Mr. Pickwick introduced him: "Monsieur le sous-lieutenant Vaissette, bachelor of philosophy." He added: "We've been chatting together about archeology, morality and military art. He's a true scholar!"

"He's a true soldier!" declared Don Quixote, soberly. And he smiled at Vaissette, who was embarrassed by these introductions, with a warm fraternal bounty.

"Excuse me, Monsieur, said Abbé Coignard, "but that salad ornamenting your head led me to believe that you were some sixteenth-century adventurer."

"I'm a humble professor," replied Vaissette, "Who teaches sleepy youngsters in a southern lycée, boring them with the theories that you rendered so limpid and charming to your disciples; but if your grace is lacking, Monsieur l'Abbé, still it has nourished my mind—and if I wear this salad, it's because I was, before being killed in an attack, one of the soldiers of the Armies of the Republic. You're doubtless not unaware that war has burst out between France, Prussia and a few other nations."

"We're not unaware of it," said Candide, who did not care about that, only being concerned with the storm over his garden.

Meanwhile, the tempest was increasing. Thunder broke window-panes; gusts of wind penetrated the room. Smoke, chased from the fireplace by the wind, blinded them. Swirls of water invaded the pathways in the grounds. The branches of trees and bushes were borne away by waves. The sea could be heard roaring.

"I know what it is," said Candide. "It's an earthquake. I've seen one before, in Lisbon."

"Well, you didn't die of it," said the abbé, philosophically.

"No," Candide replied, "but I was so amply spanked on that occasion that I still remember it, and that was when I doubted the perfection of the world for the first time." Then he cried: "Mercy! Now the water's rising. We're going to be inundated, and doubtless engulfed."

Abbé Coignard wanted to take account of the progress of the inundation. The door was threatening to give way. He went to the threshold.

"Seigneur!" he shouted. "There are two unfortunates at the bottom of the perron, enduring the tempest stoically..."

But the others paid no attention. Egotistically, they were warming themselves around the hearth.

"They're mad, they're mad!" the abbé went on. "They're not trying to come in. God knows, though, they're soaked! It's as if the rain were going to strip them naked. Strange people...one is half-naked, with a spear and a big helmet surmounted by a big crest; one might think that he had come down from the fronton of some Hellenic temple. The other is wearing a black robe and square bonnet, like some physician or advocate. I assure you that they're mad!"

The abbé opened the door abruptly. "Come in, Messieurs!" he shouted.

The man in the robe approached. "Is this not," he asked, in an embarrassed fashion, "the farmhouse of Candide, Westphalian gentleman become French by the will of Monsieur Voltaire? Are you not Abbé Jérôme Coignard? Have we not already seen Mr. Pickwick, Don Quixote and Monsieur Vaissette come in here?"

"Indeed," said the abbé. "But come in quickly—you're going to freeze to death and I'll catch a chill."

The cleric withdrew swiftly and returned at a run to his companion. He seemed frightened.

"Come in, then!" shouted the abbé.

"Come in!" howled Candide "And shut the door!"

"It's just…," shouted the wretched individual.

"What?" said the abbé.

"I'm a Boche," he confessed.

"I'm Greek," added the other.

"Ah!" said he abbé, perplexed. He was about to close the door, but then said: "God forgive you. Come in anyway."

The poor fellows did not make him ask again. They irrupted into the room.

"I'm Achilles, son of Thetis and Peleus," said the Greek.

"And I'm Dr. Faust," declared the German.

IV. Why the Tempest is Growling

"Make yourselves comfortable, Messieurs," said the abbé, in such an amiable voice that everyone felt at ease.

Candide had courageously reconciled himself to the ruination of his farm. His calm and good humor were coming back. At his invitation, they went into another room; pine-logs were burning in the fireplace; mimosas and palms were flourishing in amphoras; a slight odor of myrrh perfumed the air; thick rugs from Smyrna and Persia covered the floor; divans offered their softness to the travelers; on the low tables, incrusted with nacre and gold there were boxes of snuff, cigarettes and narghilas; a negro was pouring an excellent fuming mocha into cups.

"This will make mock of the tempest," said Candide.

At a sign from him a tall fellow dressed in white, beardless and wrinkled like a old woman, introduced young women, the sight of whom was an enchantment.

"They're my maidservants," the master of the house explained.

Everyone kept his reflections to himself, although Jérôme Coignard said: "I can see why you're not bored."

Each of the maidservants attacked one of the strangers; they had soon rid them of their wet clothes and helped them put on beautiful silk garments. It was necessary to see how graceful Monsieur Coignard was in a little pink jacket, Mr. Pickwick in a yellow turban and Don Quixote in ample green culottes!

"Here we are," said the abbé, "dressed like pachas or mamamouchis!"

The forgot about the storm; while drinking the hot coffee they ate little pink pastries, jam, pistachios, roasted almonds, cherries and candied violets.

"Have you noticed, Messieurs," said the abbé, "that there are seven of us: Candide, Don Quixote, Mr. Pickwick, Achilles, Dr. Faust, Monsieur Vaissette and me?"

"We could form a club and elect a president," proposed the gallant Englishman.

"Seven," the abbé went on, "like the sages of Greece. But while the names of the latter have been forgotten, so completely that no one could name them for me without consulting a dictionary, it seems to me that our names remain in human memory; we're a little like the adornment of each people, and whatever our origin might be, we're reconciled in the eternal domain of Letters!"

"We're of countries and all times," affirmed Dr. Faust delightedly, having not said a word thus far.

A more violent thunderclap made the Sages jump. Candide began to sing:

It's raining, shepherdess!
Bring in your white sheep...

"I seem to have heard that song before," said the abbé. "It was, if I'm not mistaken, shortly after 1789. It was addressed to Queen Marie Antoinette, who had played the shepherdess in the Petit Trianon."

"And she paid no heed to the rain," said Vaissette. "This storm is even more terrible, though—but we don't realize it."

"Do you think it is more terrible?" Candide asked.

"It seemed so to me in Europe," Vaissette affirmed.

"Shall we ever see again," said the abbé, "the Conventional poet who wrote that song, Fabre d'Églantine, of the spring-like name? Shall we see proud Danton, cold Robespierre, ferocious Marat, the incorruptible and accursed Saint-Just, who haunted dreams of patriotism, fraternity and blood? Shall we see Brunswick, Pitt and Coburg? Shall we see Kellermannn, Hoche, Kléber, Narceau and the brown locks of young Bonaparte?"

"I scarcely bother with politics," said Vaissette. "I only know that the great men of these times are named Lloyd George, Monsieur Briand and Marshal Hindenburg."

"Right!" agreed Don Quixote.

Now the lightning flashes are becoming so numerous that their eyes are fatigued; the cyclone is threatening to knock the house down, the hail is falling like an avalanche, scything down branches; the torrents are carrying trees away and hurling them like battering rams against the farmhouse.

Everyone feels anxious.

Now the din increases and the walls shake. This unchaining of the earth, the sea and the sky seems to be coming from the shores of the Hellespont and the Dardanelles.

"Ah!" cried Vaissette suddenly. "I understand the cause of the tempest!"

"Well?" interrogates Candide.

"Can you hear that noise?" asks the sub-lieutenant.

"Yes," say the philosophers, in unison.

"That noise," Vaissette declares, "is cannon fire!"

V. War

"War—who would have believed it?" said Candide, overwhelmed. "The sound of cannon horrifies me. I haven't heard it since the great battle that set the King of France at odds with the King of Prussia—the battle that marked the beginning of my catastrophic adventures."

The noise reminded Don Quixote of Lepanto, Monsieur Coignard of the worst days of the Terror. Vaissette was obliged to explain the events that he had witnessed, of which Candide and the abbé were completely unaware, and were only partly known to Mr. Pickwick and Don Quixote, and of which Achilles and Dr. Faust were ashamed. The sub-lieutenant told them about the overturning of the Old World, the fury of a tempest that unfurled all the way from the ancient ports of China to the young American shores, all the races running from the four points of the horizon to slaughter one another on the poor soil of France, the crisis that was the most tragic in human history, the pity that was the saddest in the annals of humankind.

The seven philosophers were invaded by amazement and dolor. Night fell, The rain was falling steadily now.

"Let's stay here together," Candide proposed, "if you find my modest hospitality sufficient. Let's stay here for a few days, until the sun affirms its sovereign authority again."

"We won't have any lack of curious conversation," the abbé remarked. "We'll be able to rise above the facts, into the domain of general ideas." He added: "War is the greatest crime that a sovereign can accomplish, and the greatest stupidity that a republic can commit."

"It's a long misery," Vaissette affirmed, "even when it's a duty—which is to say, when the maternal earth imposes on our love, in order for us to defend her sacred frontiers, the future of generations to come, and her ideal inherited from the series of centuries past."

"It's a crisis of madness of our poor humanity," said Dr. Faust. "A bloody phase in its quest for happiness."

257

Achilles had no idea that war was such a complicated affair; in his estimation it was another hunting party, perhaps more dangerous, but certainly more glorious, and just as simple.

Candide remarked: "If everyone were content to cultivate his farmland..."

"It would be necessary," remarked Mr. Pickwick, pragmatically, "to defend his crops against brigands and pirates. I have no desire to sow in order for a thief to harvest my field. Here, my interest and my British dignity are at stake."

Don Quixote concluded: "Dignity did you say, my dear Pickwick? Duty, declares Monsieur Vaissette, ensign of the French infantry. Personally, I say honor. The three words have the same meaning. It's for honor that I undertook the exploits of my chivalry—and that high ideal has conserved no more dazzling symbol than my charge against the windmills!"

VI. Barracks and Armies

"Crime, stupidity or madness—I can't get away from that," insisted the good Abbé Coignard.

"I can see," Vaissette replied to him, "that antimilitarism is going to become fashionable. It will no longer be elegant, after the war, to prevail upon its great deeds. The French have a false modesty regarding its virtues; they aren't like the Greeks, who love to sing its glory; Achilles and I don't resemble one another much. People will deny us, and we'll deny ourselves."

Don Quixote said, gravely: "That bitter word has been reported to me. As a mutilated man was passing by, a woman said: 'There goes one of our glorious wounded.' 'Yes Madame,' the invalid replied, with a resigned smile, 'glorious wounded today, but mere cripple tomorrow.' Was that man right, even in the moral domain? Three centuries ago, I recall that pamphleteers mocked my friend Cervantes because he only had one arm. He'd lost his hand in an attack on a Turkish galley."

"That's why we ought to react now," the philosophical officer, "if it's true that the souls of the dead create the spiritual atmosphere of the world."

The Knight of La Mancha pronounced, nobly: "The most terrible thing of all is that your generation has died in the flower of its youth solely to assure Europe of more equitable frontiers. It's also necessary to hope that people will draw some education from the drama, so that such an atrocious war will not be entirely futile in their life and in their consciousness."

That was, alas, doubted by Monsieur Coignard, whose scorn for humankind equaled that of the cynics, in spite of the charity that his Christianity put into his heart. He declared, in all candor: "I can't perceive the good that a earthquake, or any cataclysm of that sort, does—but on the other hand, I can see the ruins it causes."

"What relationship is there between an earthquake and what we're talking about?" said Achilles.

"For the few noble souls that war exalts," said Dr. Faust, "and whose virtue it causes to shine, for the thousands of humble and passive individuals that it awakens to the consciousness of duty and sacrifice, what a bleak lesson in violence, ugliness and crime it will have given, I don't only say to the future, but to the past! Will the world emerge better from this ordeal? I dare not reply."

"Perhaps, all the same, thanks to the suffering," the abbé conceded.

"It doesn't matter!" said Don Quixote, violently. "The light of a few souls will have been projected in broad daylight. What does it matter if they shine over a worse century? The just have always been few in number, in the time of the Galilean as in ours—what does that prove against justice?"

"Let's hope," said Vaissette, "that pity won't be forgotten so soon. When it becomes fashionable in society to laugh at it or treat it as folly, it will be necessary for some people to conserve its dolorous pride!"

"I fear that turn of your mind," said Monsieur Coignard. "A patriot quickly becomes a chauvinist. You love your motherland, and the sacrifices she imposes; that's fine—but you approve as certainly of war, and you tolerate barracks; that's less praiseworthy."

Thus, the abbé gave proof of an irrefutable logic, and a philosophical audacity that he pushed to its limits. But Vaissette had a sufficiently subtle intelligence to grant seemingly contradictory postulates, in order to show that he was not guilty of any misjudgment in being simultaneously patriotic and an enemy of war, and being, at the same time, desirous of safeguarding the military spirit and contemptuous of barracks."

"Do you like, Monsieur l'Abbé," he asked, "plague, tuberculosis and cholera?"

"God forbid!" replied the abbé. "I remember, in that regard..."

Vaissette did not let him continue. "I don't like war any more than you do," he said. "I observe that it exists, like all those maladies, that's all. You'll grant me that it's as old as humankind and that it's natural to it, by virtue of its extreme malignity."

"I'll even grant you," the abbé said, "that it will last as long as humankind, which will always be as wicked." Looking into himself and divining, beyond the sadness of our times, the dawn of new days, he added: "It's true that, while remaining wicked, it would suffice for humankind, in order not to fight any longer, to be a little less stupid..."

He had not realized that he had expressed that thought aloud, that it was only a meditation; nevertheless, it was heard and welcomed by a murmur of approval.

Vaissette went on: "I don't think much of physicians, who are often charlatans, and whose science is almost as uncertain as in the era of Doctors Tant-Pis and Diafoirus.[28] Physicians are like you, Monsieur l'Abbé; they worship a god in whom they don't believe."

"I don't want to get into a theological discussion here," said Monsieur Coignard, "but know that I'm irreproachable with regard to doctrine and faith."

"Well," said Vaissette, "Skeptical or credulous, whether they're ignorant or deceitful, and however impotent they are, I judge them useful to humankind, so long as the plague and the other miseries I mentioned exist. Similarly, as long as there are people who are pillagers, uncivilized, friends of vice, rapine and brigandage, forgetful of sworn oaths and scornful of the weak, as long as wars are susceptible of breaking out, like other epidemics, I'll remain a partisan of barracks and armies, because I don't know of any better means to defend ourselves. I know their defects, however, as well as you do."

The abbé countered: "A doctor in theology and professor of eloquence, secretary by turns of a kind Huguenot gentleman, an archbishop and an opera dancer, on occasion an actor, a lackey, a popular writer, I've tried many métiers and experienced many vicissitudes, but, less naïve than Candide, I've never enlisted. I've never been a soldier."

"I have," said Vaissette, "and I'm speaking from experience. I even departed for my garrison town with the best intentions, for, a socialist and already an antimilitarist, I believed nonetheless in the necessity of arming the entire nation. It was the armed nation, ill-equipped and in clogs, that defeated Brunswick's troops at Valmy, whose soldiers knew the mysteries of the goose-step even then. It was the armed nation that triumphed, by a strange turnabout, over Napoléon in 1813; the German burgers, more accustomed to drinking their beer and smoking their pipes than wielding weapons, stood up against the Emperor's professional armies as our heroes of the year II

---

[28] Docteur Tant-Pis [i.e., Dr. Too Bad] features in Jean La Fontaine's fable "Les Médecins"; Diafoirus is featured in Molière's *Le Malade imaginaire*.

had risen up against the military professionals of the King of Prussia and the Emperor of Austria; clad in the same sky-blue frock-coats that they wore on Sundays to go to the temple, in the villages of Saxony, or to church in the Bavarian towns, they triumphed over Napoléon's soldiers.

"I believed, therefore, in the irresistible strength of a people defending their land and their liberty; such was, for me, the education of our revolutionary victories, and the sad lesson of 1813. Since then, the miracle of the Marne has confirmed that doctrine. That's why I departed for the regiment full of good will; after a week, I was thinking of deserting!

"I didn't leave the barracks for a month; that privilege is forbidden to recruits, who don't know how to wear their trench-coat, their kepi and their bayonet in a military fashion. I was stifling, as in prison. I was excited the day when, designated for a work detail, I went into the town and saw the housewives in the streets, and men dressed other than in smocks and denims. In the canteen I saw myself in a mirror: shaven-headed, I had a face like a bandit and the expression of a man condemned to death. I was no longer anything but serial number 777.

"The sergeant was scornful of me because I swept the room poorly. Not a soul with whom to talk. Around me, men simple to the point of imbecility, rendered even more stupid by their reclusion and the labors of their new existence. One did not see the officers at all, in a manner of speaking. While I waxed the floors of corridors with potatoes, while I made the iron staircases of the building shone with fuel-oil, I was unable to understand that it was for the salvation of the fatherland.

"We were sent to pick up the droppings behind the horses and mules, with our hands, in order to train us. The stables were, however, ornamented with spades and forks, provided by the government of the Republic, but which we were forbidden to touch, which always drove my reason to despair. My corporal, who hated me, ordered me to all the worst chores. Life was untenable.

"The period of brutalization was followed by the period of revolt; in brief, I decided to escape from my company, and to get away without any fuss. And I don't know what impotence to react, what habituation to servitude, what absorption my individuality by the immensity, what weakness of my will and my thought it was that prevented me from deserting."

"You had courage," said the abbé.

"I resigned myself to it," said Vaissette. "That's the great secret, in barracks in peacetime and in armies in wartime. I resigned myself; without trying to understand, I became ingenious, from then on, in avoiding punishments by means of a thousand ruses. In order to have my equipment complete, I stole the brushes, assembly screws, underpants and cravats from my comrades that they had stolen from me. I lived in fear of responsibilities and terror of my superiors, so the regiment, with its façade of rectitude, honesty and deep-seated courage, appeared to me as a school of deceit, theft and cowardice."

"I don't believe," said the abbé, "that I've ever heard it tried so violently. You're a dangerous friend for the army."

"Afterwards," Vaissette continued, "I realized that those conditions originated from permanent equivocation; I was in the army in a time of peace, and the army, designed for war, only manifests its virtues in wartime. I also realized the grandeur of that submission, that acceptance of servitude. An unfortunate event always comes along to oppose a pretty pleasure, advancement or permission that ne thinks one has the right to expect; it's necessary to accept it. That's the school of renunciation; I followed it. Soon, having become a corporal in my turn, I experienced the sentiment of being useful to the fatherland in supervising the tidiness of my barrack-room and the instruction of my platoon. The fatherland lives on the obscure effort of all the corporals and brigadiers; without them, Miltiades and Hannibal would not have won any victories—and without their victories, what would the Hellenic or Punic fatherlands have been?"

"Athens has only survived," said Abbé Coignard, "because of the artists who wrote *Antigone* and constructed the

263

Propylea, while Carthage owed its renown to its navigators and merchants who founded trading posts all over the Mediterranean, and even the coasts of the glaucous Ocean. The military leaders did nothing for their people except acquire a certain dubious glory and occasionally to bloody them by leading their sons toward triumph or disaster."

"You know as well as I do," replied Vaissette, "that it's behind the shield of the breasts of soldiers that artists can make eternal works surge forth from their pens or chisels and merchants can accumulate gold behind their counters. If Miltiades had been defeated at Marathon, the Acropolis would have remained a hill covered, not with marble temples but, with thyme, rosemary and wild flowers, like Hymetta. When Hannibal was defeated by Scipio, it spelt the imminent end of the rich city of African merchants.

"That's why I incline before the necessity of constructing barracks, as well, alas, as hospitals and prisons, and before the obligation of maintaining armies. Otherwise, within a century, our nation would know enslavement, and soon, the language of Racine and Voltaire would no longer be anything but the delight of a few scholars, as the forgotten language of Homer and Plato is presently your joy, Monsieur l'Abbé, and mine to some extent too."

VII. Doctor Faust Confesses his Anguish

"Like all of you," declared Doctor Faust, "I felt an immense love for humanity; that is, I believe, the feature in which we all resemble one another. I leave you to imagine the bruising left in my heart by the war, which is a crime against justice and the sweetness of the world, and my sadness is augmented by that fact that I represent to some extent, in the realm of Letters, the people who bear the responsibility for the crime."

Faust spoke slowly, lost in his metaphysical reveries, and genuinely dolorous. He inspired the pity of the circle of philosophers that surrounded him. He was wearing a long black robe, over which his white beard hung down. He was as stiff as Don Quixote, and no one would have recognized in him the famous lover of Marguerite. Chagrin had eaten him away. Alone among his companions he looked like a centenarian, and one might have wondered whether he was truly immortal. What a difference there was between that old man, disappointed in all his dreams, deceived in all his efforts, and the handsome knight, rejuvenated by the beverage that the witch had given him, departing for the conquest of the universe!

Faust went on: "I loved human beings; that is why, escaping from my books and science, which were sterile, I wanted to plunge myself into life, in order to attain fecund realities. I sought justice; I sought the truth!"

"I haven't always understood your actions," said Don Quixote. "So many things, in your singular existence, remained obscure for me. But my Spanish province of La Mancha is so distant from the banks of the Rhine! That distance explains many of the differences between our minds. You too have surely not grasped the meaning of my worst follies. At any rate, you have been a true friend of humanity."

"We have each loved it in our own fashion," Faust replied, "and in accordance with our own temperament. In your fashion there is more nobility, panache and light; there is more realism, obstinacy and good humor in Mr. Pickwick, more inimitable grace, elegance and Christian bounty in Abbé Coignard. I confess that mine, veiled by northern mists, remain obscure and forbidding. It has often seemed to me that the truth resided in the restlessness of a mind tormented by metaphysics; I have confused the profundity of an idea with its obscurity, and I have sometimes attempted to attain that verity in darkness!" He went on: "Abbé Coignard and I scarcely have the same philosophy or the same theology..."

"Undoubtedly!" exclaimed Abbé Coignard, sharply. "But believe nonetheless in all my esteem and admiration. As regards theology, we have, I proclaim, nothing in common; only our good faith unites us. For I'm a Catholic and, in the final analysis, all the arguments of reason, which is as dear to me as it is to Monsieur Descartes, yielded abruptly before faith and dogma; I incline before the *Credo quia absurdum* that Saint Augustine never actually proclaimed.[29] You, Monsieur, a heretic as much as Luther, an atheist at times, have no rule, no doctrine, no rampart.

"In your restlessness you have gone so far as to seek the truth in alchemy, devoting yourself to the quest for the philosopher's stone. Take note that all that is of a nature to interest me, for I once knew a half-mad alchemist, who didn't find the philosopher's stone either, nor the means of fabricating true diamonds, nor the truth. You were reading Paracelsus, Basilius Valentis and the *Opus mago-cabbalisticum et theosophicum* in the days when, in the Astaracian library, surrounded by the manuscripts of Synesius and Olympiodorus, I was translating that of Zozine the Panopolitan. But while my curiosity once asked magic and the cabala for mental diversion, yours demanded the truth from them. You didn't find it, and that's what led you to make your pact with the Devil. That's one sin that I haven't committed."

"The pact that I signed with Mephistopheles," said Dr. Faust, proves what a thirst for the ideal, the absolute and the infinite I carried within me. All the means in my power having been exhausted, Satan offered me satisfaction. Oh, how I summarized within myself, at that moment, the anguish of humankind! I had cursed everything that I had seen to be empty: our miserable science, the illusions of our dreams, wealth, the juice of the vine, the kisses of women, hope, faith and patience."

"Patience and resignation are the first glimmers that lead toward the truth," said Vaissette.

"And so I arrived," said Faust, "at crying to Mephistopheles: 'Show me a fruit that does not fall before it is ripe, and

---

[29] *Credo quia absurdum* means "I believe it because it is absurd." It was actually credited, apocryphally, to Tertullian.

trees that become verdant again every day!'[30] It was then that we concluded our bargain. Satan had to take me among human beings. My enlarged heart knew all joys and all dolors. I descended into all abysses, I went up to all summits, I confused my existence with that of the human race. On the other hand, if, in that voyage, I finally encountered the absolute for which I was searching; if I said to the fugitive moment: 'Suspend your flight!' the Demon has the victory and could carry me away.

"I was victorious, alas! I never demanded, alas, that the passing moment should pause. Even in the arms of Marguerite, alas, I realized that my joys were incomplete: desire rendered me unhappy, for I wanted sensuality; sensuality rendered me sad, because I regretted desire. I never sated my soul, alas. I never extinguished my thirst for infinity, alas. A sad victory, was my victory over Mephistopheles, a poor triumph, that of humanity. But where are the wellsprings that cannot dry up…?"

"They're in my little garden," said Candide, simply.

Dr. Faust was absorbed in his meditation. The philosophers imitated him, and each them reviewed his life. But Achilles found the time long.

Faust went on: "You can imagine my anguish in the presence of this tempest. Did humankind not find itself sufficiently unhappy, then? What is the folly of the Sabbat that I witnessed in the Hartz Mountains, what is the delirium of Walpurgis Night, the fête of all the witches and the demons, compared with the unleashing of this storm?

"I once saluted war with joy; I felt that it was necessary, then, to the march of human progress; that was when the French Revolution broke out. And with Goethe, I quivered with hope on the eve of Valmy. I hoped that that last errors of

---

[30] Author's reference: "*Faust*, study scene." The reference is to the third of the three scenes set in Faust's study in Part I of Goethe's *Faust*; it is, of course, specifically Goethe's Faust who is taking shelter in Candide's house.

the Middle Ages, over which the Renaissance hadn't triumphed, would go down in the torment; I anticipated the rising of the sun. And Wagner, whose great silhouette looms up beside Goethe's, proclaimed in the *Twilight of the Gods* and in *Parsifal* the decadence of the old divinities of Germany, the collapse of their Valhalla, the defeat of Odin, the Valkyries, the giants and the Aesir, the somber cults of the North, before the evangelical light that rose from Judea, bring with it the sweetness of better days...

"Everything is to begin again! It isn't my voice, nor that of Goethe, Wagner and Kant, that has spread through our harsh valleys of Thuringia and the sad, gray, flat plains of Pomerania and Brandenburg. It's not our speech that resounded in the pulpits of our studious universities. In the course of the eternal struggle between darkness and the light, all the forces of darkness were concentrated in pensive Germany. The students, who lost themselves in the fog of their pipes and their metaphysical conceptions; the burgers, who came together to empty barrels of beer and sing choruses; the housewives, who made children and cakes unrelentingly, have been touched by a wind of dementia. Mephistopheles has taken his revenge on me; he has triumphed, in the guise of Hegel and Bismarck!"

"But he's fighting in the guise of Emperor Wilhelm II," said Don Quixote.

"Germany," said Faust, "requires a new Jena."

"The misfortune," remarked Vaissette, "is that the innocent are paying for the guilty."

"That's life," affirmed the abbé, gently.

"And there are no more citrus trees or roses in my garden," added Candide.

VIII. Patriotism and the Fear of the Gendarme

"Monsieur l'Abbé," asked Vaissette, "How do you explain that France, the France of Valmy and Verdun, manifested so little patriotism in 1870?"

"I don't understand your question, my friend," replied Jérôme Coignard. "Defeat doesn't prove that the defeated were less ardent in their patriotism than the victors."

"That's something I won't dispute with you," the young philosopher replied. "It would take us too far. I believe, on the contrary, that victory is not to the side that is able to suffer for a quarter of an hour more, as a Japanese general once said, but to the one that has desired it with the most implacable will and the most stubborn patriotism. But let's pass on. I meant that in 1870, a magnificent generation of men between eighteen and forty years of age, lamented the misfortunes of France without taking up arms."

"Conscription only existed in Prussia," the abbé said. "In France, we only possessed a professional army."

"But how is it," Vaissette persisted, "that our intellectuals and our peasants, who rushed to the defense of the fatherland in 1914, allowed it to be amputated forty-four years earlier without involving themselves to the last man? I don't say it about me, who, who wasn't born, or about you, who had been dead more than a century, but patriotism has strange fits and starts."

"Undoubtedly," said the abbé, "my descendants and your forefathers sensed the futility of all resistance. They would only have added tombs to tombs. Their struggle and death would have been vain."

"It's never vain to fight and die for justice!" declared Don Quixote, who had heard the last words.

"Yes, but what is justice?" asked the abbé, whose skepticism was universal and cheerful. "You know very well that it varies from one side of the Pyrenees to the other. Were the causes of France and justice identical in 1870?"

Vaissette intervened, and, as always, spoke from his heart and in all conscience. "I would have adopted your general doubt before the war," he said, "but in the course of that long servitude, I learned to possess a few certainties. I'll grant you that justice is uncertain and troubled, but one ought to give oneself to it, when one believes that one has discovered it for oneself. In any case—I'll get back to the subject—our parents did not lose themselves in that confusion. The fatherland was about to succumb; they should all have enrolled; duty is simple."

"Their sacrifice would not have served France," replied Abbé Jérôme Coignard. "It was preferable to wait until later." Looking at Vaissette over his spectacles he added: "They reserved that proof and that glory for your generation."

"Of course," murmured Vaissette. "It's always easier, whatever people say, to sacrifice one's son rather than oneself." He added: "Of course, I'm not talking about mothers and lovers, who are also, in every fashion, the sacrificed. I'm talking about men. Abraham and Agamemnon didn't make a lot of fuss about it. We're giving our fathers a rude lesson in patriotism."

Abbé Coignard, perhaps surpassing his own thought but glad to launch a quip, declared: "Doubtless patriotism, like honesty, is merely fear of the gendarme."

"What do you mean?" Vaissette asked.

"Let me tell you my theory, said the abbé. He installed himself comfortably in his wickerwork armchair, drank a sugared lemonade, and declared by way of an aside: "I prefer the modest white wine of the Lord's vines," and went on:

"Although the law and its apparatus are, by virtue of their iniquity, one of the shames of society, although the laws and the magistrates are equally frightful, that is because the law is man-made, and only the naïve Jean-Jacques and dreamers of his species have ever doubted he extremity of human wickedness. However, I deem those laws necessary, however lame, and those magistrates too, however rotten; without them, thefts, crimes and rapes would be far too numerous, given the malignity of human nature. Without the fear of the gendarme, there would be no one in the world but scoundrels.

"Now, it is that same fear of the constabulary that makes patriots. The law, in 1870, did not establish general conscription; the mass of the citizenry was not engaged. In 1914, the citizens obeyed the mobilization under penalty of being arrested as deserters. But those who had surpassed forty-six years of age, and who could have departed nevertheless, did not depart, and were estimated nevertheless to be good Frenchmen.

"I'll give you an example. I know a serious man, who has taken as a profession—like you, Vaissette—the teaching of philosophy. You'll admit to me that his presence in the interior is not indispensable to the existence of the nation. He has no son; the war does not afflict him either in his fortune, or in his person, or in his children. He's forty-seven years old and as strong as a Turk. Few men in the trenches are as robust as he is. He is content to make patriotic dissertations to his daughters and, in Autumn, to go rabbit-hunting, which is more demanding physically than hunting Prussians. One year fewer, and he would have to go. He has not gone; Pandore[31] does not oblige him to!

"That is why I said to you, my friend, that the terror of the agents of the police is the commencement of sagacity and the love of the nation. The case of my professor is that of thousands of citizens of his age, just as able to bear arms, who have not undertaken to do so. It is that of many young men, excused by a fortunate hazard, doubtless not very solid, but nevertheless as solid as the majority of our soldiers, and who expend their activity, not in enrolling and fighting, but in work singularly more exhausting: making money, taking the place of those who are fighting, playing comedy, giving speeches and matinee performances in honor of writers wounded or killed by the enemy."

"You're severe toward that rabble, Monsieur l'Abbé," said Vaissette, "but I admit that we very often said the same in the course of our reveries in the trenches; and I would have experienced a sentiment of revolt, if the war hadn't taught us to accept everything with resignation, and not to believe any more than you do in the justice of things of this world. There

---

[31] Pandore became a contemptuous argot term for a policeman after the use of the name in a popular song written by Gustave Nadaud in 1852.

are men who offer themselves as victims and are killed; there are others who remain in the depots or who escape at all their medical examinations; it's fatal, just as it's inevitable that there are poor and rich, sick and healthy individuals, geniuses and imbeciles—which are equally unjust."

The master of Jacques Tournebroche, benevolent and subtle, freed from the errors of his century and many of the centuries that preceded and will follow his own, continued in these terms:

"I have no doubt that men, following their natural instincts take great pleasure in being soldiers. They are borne by their inclinations toward marauding, murder and false glory, and to the brutalization that is the prerogative of barracks; I once defined a man as an animal with a musket. But if he likes to be a soldier, it's in order to parade in peacetime. The métier doesn't agree with him in wartime; it's decidedly too dangerous! Personally, I can't criticize those who are untouched by a fervent patriotism and don't join up. My horror of arms is such that I would do the same."

"Criticize them, Monsieur l'Abbé!" cried Vaissette. "Criticize them! If everyone had reasoned like you, it would have been all over for France—which would have been an irreparable disaster for humanity. I want to be finished with your paradoxes. Some young people have, indeed, escaped the popular conscription, but what does their opprobrium count by comparison with the generation that has sacrificed itself entirely? Some men, robust in spite of approaching fifty, have stayed at home, but what is that weakness in the presence of the devotion of the old men who have gone of their own will and have given everything, including their lives? Alongside the former and the latter, younger than their age, there are those who bear their years; would we have required that decrepit army of valetudinarians? Their place was not really in the firing line, and that is why they had the wisdom not to go there.

"You have stigmatized a few individual cases, Monsieur l'Abbé, which are indeed shameful, but you cannot generalize them without injustice. The law, in imposing the sacrifice of blood on thirty classes, was only observing the will of those classes and the whole nation. We forged that servitude ourselves, in our determination to defend our soil. The gendarme has only ensured the play of our free decision. When the aggressor came, we stood up."

Having paused thoughtfully for a few moments, Vaissette continued:

"Doubtless I know better than anyone what our misery was, and the sadness of those lambs that were led to the slaughter. I'm making use, you see, of an evangelical figure of speech. The uniform I wear, once horizon blue, now yellow, reminds me of the ennui of the trenches, the dismal days that passed, the rain, the anguish and the sweat of the eve of an attack…I remember all that. But I also remember the irresistible surge of the waves running toward death. It was so beautiful that I wept at commanding such men. It's necessary not to have been a real soldier not to retain the memory of the assault. Shame on anyone who denies it. I don't know what miracle or movement transformed us; we carried in our souls a Christ running toward Golgotha. Oh, I don't know whether what was driving us was patriotism or fear of the gendarme, but I know that, deaf and blind in the unleashed tempest, while the heavens were exploding over our heads and the earth was being torn apart under our feet, we experienced the horror of a sacred frisson!"

IX. "War is divine," proclaims Achilles

"I've finally heard the words I was waiting for," said Achilles. "I was lost in your discourses, as subtle as those of Odysseus. War is divine in essence, like justice and religion!"

"A Greek is certainly qualified to sustain that thesis," declare the Abbé. "There's always been a little of the boastful soldier so well described by Plautus in him. If he daren't bite, at least he's able to bark."

273

"My name has remained the personification of bravery in all languages," the hero of the ancient poet went on. "When I was a child, you know, a centaur nourished me on the marrow of lions. Would you dare to compare me with Ulysses, all of whose courage resided in his advice and speech, or Ajax, son of Telamon, who calmed his furies by slaughtering sheep that he had mistaken for warriors?"

"That's the kind of thing that can happen!" observed Don Quixote, without insisting.

"Would you dare to compare me with that unfortunate Agamemnon, or that other Ajax, son of Oileus, the proudest of the Greeks, who, rebellious against destiny, threatened the heavens in vain? I alone, the cherished hero of Homer, remain immortal. I am the symbol of valor in battles and the very soul of combats. Joseph de Maistre glorified war, declaring it an expiation and a kind of purification of humankind. He was wrong; one ought to glorify it by proclaiming it the grandeur and the beauty of the world. It is a virtue, not a punishment. War has taught humans everything; it has rendered their coarse minds subtle; it is the mother of the family, the city, of government and the arts; it is the daughter of religion and justice!"

"The poor fellow is more demented than you ever were," Mr. Pickwick whispered to Don Quixote.

Achilles continued: "To begin with, people fought to defend their hearth and the altar of their household gods, and the first epic was born of battle; can you deny, after that, that the origin of war is divine and that even poetry has its source therein? War is the crucible in which nations are purified, the bloody Fountain of Youth in which they are rejuvenated, the touchstone that puts nations to the proof. By means of war, sick and weak peoples are destroyed. By means of war, the most worthy and most powerful States dominate. Whatever your paradoxes and sophisms might mean, of which I don't understand a word, recognize that the right of force is the most ancient, the most solid and the most durable.

"One could believe that we were listening to Hegel, Fichte or General von Bernhardi!" exclaimed Faust, alarmed.[32]

But Achilles, unleashed, could no longer be stopped. He went on: "War was present at the genesis of the world, since the murder of Abel by Cain. And even before then, was there not the struggle of the Titans and the Gods? The Ancients thought a goddess sufficient to incarnate wisdom, Minerva, and another to incarnate love, Venus, but they required two divinities, whether they were Greek or Latin, to incarnate war: Ares and Pallas, Bellona and Mars."

Candide interrupted. "Such is the way that you see war," he said, "when I see it as nothing but pillage, theft, murder and brigandage—and, in sum, crime and madness? Whence comes that difference?"

"Does it not come," Abbé Coignard replied to him, "from the fact that you have made war, as Vaissette has, whereas Achilles, in spite of his renown, never has? There is no greater strategist and more valorous warrior than one who rests tranquilly in his armchair, in his dressing-gown, shod in carpet-slippers 'where spring and flowers bloom'"

"I haven't made war?" repeated the son of Thetis and Peleus, bewildered.

"Or very little, you must agree, Achilles of the light feet," said the abbé. "If I can believe Homer in his *Iliad*, and my dear Statius, in his *Achilleid*, your role, at the beginning of the Trojan war, was primarily, while disguised as a woman under the name of Pyrrha, to amuse yourself at the court of Lycomedes with the king's daughters; you were secreted on the Isle of Skyros! The ingenious Ulysses could only discover you among that chorus of nymphs by disguising himself as a

---

[32] The Prussian general Friedrich von Bernhardi (1849-1930), a best-selling author in the years before the Great War, regarded war as divine, recommended a policy of ruthless aggression and the total disregard of all treaties and conventions. He made the earlier militant nationalism of G. W. F. Hegel and Johann Gottlieb Fichte seem rather tame.

merchant of jewels and weapons; they admired the jewels while you, your boiling blood having spoken, seized the spear and sword."

"It was then," said Achilles, ashamed, "that the enemy knew my wrath. "Ask the dead Trojans, the ravaged fields, the smoking towns..."

"You success was very brief," the abbé continued, implacably. "Because, the tyrant Agamemnon having stolen a captive, you retired to your tent, and for ten years you consented to remain tranquil while the siege unfurled its ups and downs. Admit that that's a strange method of going on campaign!"

Achilles, crestfallen, said nothing.

"What distinguished you, Achilles," said Candide, naively, "from Caesar, Napoléon and other great captains, is that they are celebrated for their exploits, while you are only known from Homer's poem."

"You're making very light of my legendary intrepidity," replied the vanquisher of Hector.

Candide went on, imperturbably: "Caesar, whose legions followed the sturdy horse, conquered Gaul and subjugated the Empire. The world was his domain. He perished on the eve of accomplishing a grandiose dream, which could only be conceived by a poet and rhetor like him: to set forth against the Parthians in order to conquer the East, then, heading northwards, to vanquish the Dacians, the Suevi and the Germans, astonished to see him arriving from the direction of the dawn, thus to return to his province of Gaul, to conclude his career where he had begun it. As for Napoléon, from Arcole to the Pyramids and Austerlitz to Moscow, Europe and Africa saw his legendary frock-coat pass in a cloud of glory.

"Is it necessary to talk about other warriors whose victories have been reported to us by history? And to crown these bloody battles, you see Sergeant Vaissette, unknown to literature, a humble hero in the midst of millions of others whose names will not remain, who was one of the obscure soldiers of the Marne, the Yser and Verdun and died on the Somme in

1916, in the course of the most implacable of all the wars that have ravaged the world.

"Caesar, Napoléon, Vaissette, seekers of glory, conquerors or defenders of the sacred ground that was your fatherland, your deeds are traced in furrows on the fields of history! You have done nothing, Achilles, and scholarly annals do not know you. Your exploits are of the order of Don Quixote's follies. You do not exist in yourself, but only through the *Iliad*."

The seething Achilles did not explode in fury, because he was not entirely sure whether Candide was flattering him or mocking him; in that, he proved that he really was of the race of those braggarts and professionals of battle, striking in appearance but limited in their words and prudent in their actions.

Martin's pupil went on: "Nothing, moreover, is as boring as Homer. I remember on that subject the theory once sustained in Venice by Seigneur Pococurante: for him, as for any sincere person, the poem had no interest. 'The continual repetition of combats that all resemble one another,' the Venetian senator declared, coldly, ' the gods that always act but never do anything decisive; Helen, who is the subject of the war but is scarcely an actress in the drama; Troy, which is besieged but cannot be taken—all that causes me the most mortal boredom.' At first I was scandalized by such impertinence; then, having become wiser, while I was hoeing my aubergines, I said to myself that Pococurante was right. That is why, Achilles, the tale of your imaginary exploits is only conserved, among our books, by tradition. Who else, then, possesses the courage of his opinion, as I do?"

Abbé Coignard laughed like a Homeric hero, all of his ample midriff dancing. "I'll grant you," he said, "even though the genius of that old author is eternal, that his works are unskillful and soporific, and are only placed alongside Sophocles or Horace, perfumed by the rarest odor of antiquity, out of habit. Just as, with regard to the moderns, Descartes and Bossuet are placed alongside Fénelon and Racine—but who reads them?"

"No one," said Vaissette, unless they are on the syllabus for an examination or a degree." I understand that those authors, whose influence was considerable, are studied if one teaches theology, like Abbé Coignard, or philosophy, like me, but what are they doing in the city of Letters? My dear master, Monsieur Lanson,[33] in spite of his independence and clear mind, only left them there because Monsieur La Harpe had found them there. It's time to expel therefrom those who have no other concern that to cultivate the arts as Candide cultivates his garden—that was the last concern of Calvin or Pascal! But we're getting away from the war, proclaimed divine by Achilles."

"I no longer insist," said the Greek, courageously, "since I see that I'm alone in my opinion."

"That's all right, then," concluded the abbé, taking a pinch of fine tobacco perfumed with rose-water from a snuff-box, which he then held out to Candide. "I'll tell you something I remember, which once struck me vividly. It's a matter of the strange admission made to me by a captain who fought in the War of Succession and had served the king for eighteen years under Monsieur le Maréchal de Villars. I confess that it was late at night and that many empty bottles justified his eloquence while excusing his frankness, along with the thick pipe-smoke and the presence of his mistress, who, being too warm, was only wearing her chemise—which was, to tell the truth, short and transparent.

"'Monsieur l'Abbé,' that captain confided to me, 'war consists uniquely of stealing chickens and pigs from serfs. Soldiers on campaign have no other occupation than that.'[34]

"That confidence," Monsieur Coignard continued, "did not fail to furnish me with matter for reflection. But give me

[33] The historian and literary critic Gustave Lanson (1857-1934) was teaching at the Sorbonne when the author (and hence Vaissette) knew him.

[34] Author's reference: "*La Rotisserie de la Reine Pédauque*, p. 297."

more of that Oriental tobacco, Candide, my son; our greatest bishops never had the like. It's worthy of the nose of a philosopher, or even a theologian."

"That's because its leaves, the object of my diligent care, grew at the far end of my farm," replied Candide, "near a stream enveloped by tall plants of a propitious humidity. What will becomes of them, alas, Monsieur l'Abbé? Oh, now, for the first time in five hundred years, I'm regretting my establishment in this region. Our arguments and the misdeeds of the storm are making me reflect. I recall the land of Dorado, where there was no Palais de Justice and no parliament, and where the only soldiers were twenty beautiful young women! It does not much resemble Westphalia, I assure you, nor France, nor even this fortunate corner of the Orient, a land of contemplation, dreams and prayer, where I've been able to find peace and dispose my kitchen garden, which the tempest is in the process of destroying."

X. In which there is Competition in Erudition

"The armies," replied Jérôme Coignard, "for which I experience such a great hatred, are obviously not as amiable as the battalion of maidens that you mention. The unfortunate thing is that if you conserve armies because of the wars you dread, it's precisely the existence of those armies that render new conflicts possible!"

He continued: "I detest war and its apparatus not only for its ferocity and cortege of mourning, but also for the ignorance of men-at-arms, their stupidity, their hatred of independence and their routine."

Achilles, the seething Achilles, wanted to make one last protest, but he sensed that no one would support him—not even Don Quixote—so he kept silent.

"It's true that they don't know anything much," conceded Vaissette. "At the beginning of this war they were ignorant of the employment of heavy cannon and trenches. And as for the German reiters, the destroyers of Louvain and Reims, let's not insist on their rancor and scorn for arts and letters."

Dr. Faust intervened. "A hundred and fifty years ago," he said, "I solemnly pronounced in Auerbach's Keller: 'The German is an animal of prey, who sleeps when he is not hunting or eating like a beast'"[35]

That condemnation having been pronounced, the friend of Goethe fell silent.

"The fact is," declared Candide, "that I haven't retained an excellent memory of my sojourn among the Prussian armies. To begin with, I received four thousand lashes one day, a punishment the reason for which I'm unaware, but the memory of which I still retain from the nape of my neck to my buttocks, and I no longer believe the stupidities of Doctor Pangloss, who would have been bound to affirm that the reason was sufficient and that everything was for the best. As for the battle that was fought between our army and that of the King of France, I can scarcely remember it, having hidden throughout its duration."

"My dear Horace has confessed to acting no differently at the battle of Philippi, where he commanded a legion," said the abbé. "Military courage is not a prerogative of Epicurean philosophers."

"All that I know," Candide went on, "is that villages were burned and everyone was massacred, while each of the princes had a *Te Deum* sung in his camp. And yet, none of the soldiers had known the reason for the battle. Scarcely one of them remained who was not wounded at least slightly. And Mademoiselle Cunégonde, who later became my wife, was violated by a great Bulgar, whom I shall never forgive for such a trampling, if I might put it like that, of my rights. And as she struggled, not knowing that such is the custom of war,

---

[35] Author's reference: "*Faust*, Auerbach's tavern scene." The famous tavern in question is the first place to which Mephistopheles takes Faust in their travels in Part I of Goethe's epic. It is now a restaurant, with a Mephisto Bar.

he stabbed her in the abdomen and left her for dead; and the Baron Thunder-ten-Tronckh, the greatest of the Barons of Germany, was killed, and his wife the Baroness cut into pieces; and the schloss of my youth, the witness of my first amours, which consisted of picking up the handkerchief of Mademoiselle Cunégonde behind a screen, the schloss, which was the most beautiful and agreeable of the schlosses of Westphalia and the world, was so completely demolished that not a stone remained of it, nor a tree in the park, nor a duck in the poultry-yard. Judge from that what I think of war and soldiers!"

"I'll quote to you," said Abbé Coignard, "a passage from your friend Monsieur de Voltaire, who concluded as you did. He wrote it in his first philosophical letter on the English and it's a Quaker who is speaking, 'We never go to war, said the Quaker. It's not that we fear death…but it's because we're neither wolves, nor tigers, nor dogs, but human beings and Christians. Our God, who has ordered us to love our enemies and suffer without a murmur, undoubtedly doesn't want us to go to sea in order to murder our brethren because murderers dressed in red with bonnets two feet high enroll citizens by making a noise which two sticks in a stretched donkey-skin; and when, after battles are won, all London is lit up by illuminations, the sky ablaze with rockets, and their air resounds with the noise of hymns, bells, organs and cannons, we mourn in silence the murders that cause that public delight…!'"

Abbé Coignard thought, in his tender and equitable heart, that he shared the opinion of that heretic Quaker, and terminated by saying: "Jesus said: *Diligite inimicos vestros.*"[36]

"It seems to me," said one voice, "that someone has just directly incriminated by an allusion the attitude in this war of the United Kingdom and the government of His Britannic Majesty." It was Mr. Pickwick, who had just got to his feet.

---

[36] "Love your enemy"—from the Vulgate Bible's version of *Luke* 6:27.

But the abbé did not take the trouble of proving to him that it was nothing of the sort, that letter being nearly two centuries anterior to the intervention of Great Britain in the conflict of 1914.

A silence having marked a pause, the abbé declared: "I shall conclude and summarize the depths of my thought. He coughed, wiped the lenses of his spectacles, and went on:

"I shall repeat to you what I once declare to my disciple Jacques Tournebroche, who has reported in two modest volumes my modest instructions—or, rather, my opinions: 'I will not hide it from you, my son,' I said to him, 'that military service appears to me to be the most frightful plague of civilized nations. It is admirable that war and hunting, of which the mere thought ought to overwhelm us with shame and remorse in recalling the wretched necessities of our nature and inveterate wickedness, can, on the contrary, serve to make people proud, that Christian peoples continue to honor the métier of butchers and executioners when it runs in families, and that, finally, one measures in the most polite peoples the illustriousness of citizens by the quantity of murders and carnage that they carry, so to speak, in their veins...'"[37]

Candide interrupted. Memory was his principal quality, as with all serious minds.

"You're quoting, Monsieur. I shall cite in my turn, on the same subject of service and military nobility, the philosopher Martin. I've remembered his speech word for word, as Tournebroche remembered yours. 'Everywhere,' he said to me, 'the powerful treat the weak as flocks, whose wool and flesh one sells. A million regimented murderers, running from one end of Europe to the others, carry out murder and brigandage with discipline to earn their daily bread, because they have no métier more honest.'[38]

---

[37] Author's reference: "*Opinions of Monsieur Jérôme Coignard*, chs, X and XI, 'The Army.'"
[38] Author's reference: "*Candide*, ch. XX, 'What Happened at Sea to Candide and Martin.'"

"What is more," Candide continued, "you remind me in discussion of my dear philosopher Martin, so strongly that I could believe that I could believe that you were one and the same person if I did not know that your existences are completely different, and if I did not see every day the myrtle bush under which his body reposes. What astonishes me, however, is that our conclusions are identical and similarly opposed to the optimism of Dr. Pangloss, who almost caused me to believe, in spite of my disgraces, that everything is always for the best. It is therefore right to say that extremes connect, for Martin was a Heresiarch, something of a Socinian and considerably Manichean, while you, Monsieur l'Abbé, an excellent Catholic, a priest whose orthodoxy is stainless, and who condemn all heresies, those of Lelio Socin[39] and Mani along with the Jansenists or those dangerous Huguenots."

"Now we're in the heart of theology!" declared the abbé, delightedly. "But it's dangerous terrain; let's stick to that of war and peace."

"Let it pass," said Don Quixote, "for I too have always been a something of a theologian, knowing Latin like a the possessor of a baccalaureate and making speeches like a graduate—so much so that Sancho Panza often said to me that I resembled a churchman as one egg resembles another, and that I was more suited to being a preacher than a knight errant. Once, in the course of my adventures, I pronounced a great speech, before a select assembly, on Letters and Arms. *Cedant armae togae*,[40] Cicero said. I rose up against that stupid maxim; I affirmed the preeminence of arms, uniquely because they serve to maintain peace. I was thus a pacifist in the time of my madness. Imagine what I am now! And, quoting in my turn, I'll cite you a fragment of my speech. 'The end and goal of

---

[39] The Italian humanist Lelio Sozzini (1525-1562); his nephew Fausto is generally given more credit for the formulation of Socinianism.

[40] Arms give way to togas (i.e., military means give way to political ones).

Letters is to encourage the observation of good laws. That end is assuredly great and generous, and worthy of praise, but not as much as that of Arms, the end and objective of which is peace—which is to say, the greatest good that humans can desire in this life. The best greeting, the greatest master of the earth and Heaven informed his beloved disciples was to say when they went into someone's house: *may peace be with you.* And on many other occasions he said to them: *I am giving you my peace, I am leaving you my peace, let my peace by with you,* as the most precious gift that such a hand can give and leave. Now, that peace is the veritable end of war, and war in the same thing as arms.'[41] You see, Monsieur l'Abbé, that I too am a pacifist theologian."

And the abbé, by way of conclusion, murmured a verse from Ecclesiastes: *Melior est sapientia quam arma bellica.*"[42]

The night was advancing, however, and they were already anticipating the dawn. Immortals have no need of sleep. The storm was beginning to calm down.

"It will be necessary to resume our journey," said Mr. Pickwick to Don Quixote.

Why not stay here?" said Candide, hospitably. "Travel is only good for youth. For us, it's no more than a vanity.

"Don't you know, then, Monsieur Candide," asked the Abbé, "the letter in which the philosopher Seneca explains to Lucilius that voyages have never cured the trouble that one carries in one's heart? And don't you know this passage from the *Imitation*:[43] 'What can you see elsewhere that you cannot see where you are? You have before you the heavens, the earth and the elements; are not all the things of the world composed of them?'"

---

[41] Author's reference: "*Don Quixote*, part one, ch. XXXVII."

[42] *Ecclesiastes* 9:18: "Wisdom is better than weapons of war"—but the verse concludes ""But one sinner destroys much good."

[43] i.e. *De Imitatione Christi* [The Imitation of Christ] (c1425) by Thomas à Kempis

"We need have no hesitation," said Vaissette, "in employing erudition and citations. Citation is very agreeable, for one often finds ready forged, to express one's thought, formulae more adept than those one could invent at hazard in the course of conversation. Besides which, the authority one is quoting adds to the verity of the remark. That is why, joining my supplications to those of Candide and the Abbé, and in order not to be behindhand in knowledge, I will give you in my turn, Mr. Pickwick, a word from Pascal. Imagine the solitary, wandering among the arbors of Port-Royal, giving this advice to the impetuous poet Racine: 'All the unhappiness of men,' he wrote in his *Pensées*, 'comes from just one thing, which is not being able to remain at rest in a room.'"

XI. The Philosophers Announce a New Order

Meanwhile, the storm seemed to be diminishing and the rain was diminishing in its intensity over the garden; in the very bosom of the deluge, there was a presentiment of the return of the sun.

Two young women came into the room where the philosophers were sitting. They had come from Constantinople and were carrying various newspapers. The storm had been raging for several years, but the Immortals were not conscious of time and had no suspicion of that.

Candide asked the messengers for a few explanations. They were rude and not very obliging. They were employed to deliver the post for lack of men, who had all been requisitioned to fight the storm. For that reason, all the harems in Turkey had been depopulated of brown Arab women and white Circassians.

"It's noticeable," declared the abbé, "in the slightest details that the grace and beauty of the world have perished in the torment."

They started leafing through the papers.

"They're stupid," Vaissette assured them, "but people read them anyway. The style and intelligence of the poor fellows who practice the métier of journalism doesn't gain anything from contact with such great events."

The philosophers, moving from deduction to deduction, understood that the storm was easing because there was no corner of the world left to devastate.

Born in the Balkans on the banks of the blue Danube cherished by waltzers, descending under the pressure of the wind to the wild plains of Germany, the hurricane had been unleashed over the whole of Europe, moving closer and closer to France, her unfortunate orchards of Artois and Picardy, her Champenois vines, the fields of Flanders, the woods of Argonne, all her lands of classic invasion, and then to England, her gray smoky cities, lush countryside and errant steamships...

"The lovely British coasts that Dickens and David Copperfield loved," said the melancholy Mr. Pickwick, "have been bombarded."

The storm had devastated fertile Belgium, felled the cypresses of the Italian lakes, ravaged the Balkans, growled over all the fiefs of the Commander of the Faithful, and had lost itself in the infinite Russian steppes. It had blown over Africa, bloodied from north to south, the coral islands of the Oceanian archipelagoes and the flowery cherry-orchards of Japan. It had shaken the walls of old China and its palaces with violet porcelain roofs, astonishing the sage mandarins indignant at its fury. Finally, beyond the oceans, it had fallen upon America the shelter of peace, the refuge of liberty, the land of justice, and its waves had splashed the republics of the New World, breaking against the Rocky Mountains and the Andes.

"There are mothers weeping for their sons in the fabulous modern villas of Australia," said Abbé Coignard. "They are raising their eyes to the heavens, in which the stars that shine in those latitudes are not those their children are contemplating while dying in our climes. There are lovers weeping for their spouses or fiancés all the way to the Sicilian mountains and valleys of which Theocritus sang..."

"In Baghdad," Candide read, "the capital of the Caliphs, Baghdad of the palaces ornamented with marble stables, whose minarets protrude from vaults of palm trees, an English military post has been established at the foot off the mausoleum of the sultana Zobeide, the favorite of Haroun-al-Raschid..."

"Are you criticizing those courageous Tommies?" demanded Mr. Pickwick.

"Certainly not," replied Candide. "I'm even glad to see them camped there. But Baghdad, and I suffer in consequence, will henceforth evoke for us the memory of battles and heroic deeds, when it ought to be the capital of that indolent and perfumed Arabia traversed by caravans of camels, bathed by the Tigris, encumbered by boatmen singing in their rounded gourd-like boats. The Caliphs of the Arabian Nights received ambassadors there in a palace of prodigious splendor; twenty-two thousand carpets hid its floor-tiles, twenty-eight thousand tapestries hide its walls; artificial birds with ingenious mechanisms agitated and sang in aviaries, and lions were heard roaring as they pounced on their guardians..."

"I regret, in fact, that those beautiful things are no longer to be seen," declared Mr. Pickwick. With one hand graciously placed beneath the tails of his blue coat, rubicund and full of amenity, smiling behind his large spectacles, his midriff inflated by dignity and covered in beautiful gold chains, with his twill trousers sticking to bright gaiters, he spoke, as he had in the golden days of the Pickwick Club.

"Followed by four disciples—or, rather, four good friends—I set forth one fine day in the year 1831, like Don Quixote in 1605, to conquer the world. A conquest as peaceful as could be: a simply a matter of seeing and annotating everything. I scarcely left the environs of London, but that permitted me to form an idea of the world.

"Later, installed in a comfortable cottage surrounded by lawns, served by devoted domestics who looked after my table, beat my carpets and polished my sideboards, I recalled my adventures to mind. What had they not given me to contemplate!

"In the course of those few weeks, I had learned more than during my entire life, spent behind the counter of some ironmongery where I had enriched myself. Unjust courts convicted me when I was innocent; faithful friends crushed me, when, as an unfortunate, I appeared before the judge; Companions surfeited with renown but nevertheless resistant to all avatars; electoral mores to disgust the drafters of all charters and constitutions; debauched puritans, drunken Christians and Pharisean hypocrites; scholarly society as dogmatic as solemn in their science, uncritical and stupid; female poets and German spies—nothing was lacking! So I hesitated to go with Don Quixote when he came to look for me in my house in the country.

"I have seen everything, even maneuvers and small wars, in the course of which cannons thundered, the charges of the red uniforms succeeded one another, a mine blew up, trenches were taken by storm, while the commanding General Budler,[44] in his rutilant uniform, galloped, howled, spurred his horse, red-faced and congested, his voice hoarse, agitating like a madman, without any sergeant understanding his orders and without anyone knowing the reason for his delirium. Meanwhile, the spectators vanished, ate sandwiches or acclaimed His Majesty's army. It's necessary to admit that that is something else entirely and that there is not much in common between the idea one has of battle and the one we are seeing."

"Let us hope," Candide said, "that the experience will be useful to us."

"Let us hope so," affirmed Mr. Pickwick. "I shall return to Dulwich, where everything in my garden and my house was beautiful, neat and solid, where order reigned. There is some

---

[44] This reference is enigmatic. If the name is a misprint it cannot refer to the American general Smedley Butler, of whose belated involvement in the Great War the author could not have been aware.

risk that the storm might have done some damage there, but I shall console myself, being practical by nature; one can't make a ham omelet without killing a pig and breaking eggs. No one is more pacifist than I am, but that avalanche was required to create a new order of things."

"That's the key phrase," affirmed Vaissette, "and that's the philosophy of our times."

"It's possible," agreed the abbé. "The clamor of humanity has affirmed, in its dolor, the rights of liberty and justice."

"Liberty, justice, honor, peace!" proclaimed Don Quixote. "Great words empty of meaning, at which the world has learned to smile, of which it has just discovered, in blood, the virtues. It's for those words that Vaissette and millions of young men have died: so, will they acquire their complete significance and force of action? I was treated as a madman, and it's true that my chivalry was a derisory and grotesque folly, but it had a meaning nevertheless; and it was for those great words that I fought against the windmills, that I was showered with blows in the hostelries that seemed to me to be enchanted castles, that I set forced laborers free, that I did penance in the desert of the Sierra Morena, weeping with love for a Dulcinea that I had never seen, that I fought frightful battles with skins of red wine, that I withstood imprisonment in a cage, like an animal—and I don't regret any of it. I don't even regret this storm, since it has given reason to law and liberty."

"I wouldn't regret anything either," said Abbé Coignard, "if this new order that you've announced were to be established. I'd like to believe so, in spite of my skepticism. Otherwise, it will be too sad. Centuries of strife, Don Quixote, and of suffering, in order to arrive at the greatest dolor of humankind and the greatest crime in history! I'm suffering too much. Too much blood has been shed; its torrent has drowned everything. Religious and civil wars, social wars and all social revolutions are useful; their fecund sadness renders the world a little better, a little freer. But what profit will people obtain from this slaughter? Let me weep."

"Don't weep, Monsieur l'Abbé," said Vaissette. "Intelligence has triumphed in this storm. To die for our cause, for France, was to die in order to leave the generations of the future what you desire: consciousness of great necessary virtues, the progress of humankind, the sweetness of life."

Vaissette and Abbé Coignard shook hands solemnly.

"Perhaps it's the end of the insensate paradox, *si vis pacem, para bellum*," said Monsieur Coignard. "Shall we have discovered the truth, which is simple, of knowing that if one wants peace, it's necessary to prepare for peace?"

"I might," said Don Quixote, "be able to witness the end of militarism, as I witnessed the end of chivalry."

"Will war have exploded by virtue of becoming too large?" the abbé wondered. "like the frog in the fable that wanted to inflate itself so as to resemble an ox, has it become so overinflated that it has perished of it?"

He added: "Let's not despair of the future."

"As Mr. Pickwick said," Vaissette affirmed, "we've witnessed the collapse of a world."

"Yes, yes, here comes a new order!" repeated the amiable Englishman.

"May the next world," declared Candide, "in spite of what Pangloss said, be better than this one!"

Everyone fell silent. After a pause, Abbé Coignard murmured: "By the grace of God!"

XII. Future Harvests

Jérôme Coignard left the room and opened the door which gave access, via a perron, to the garden. It was no longer raining. A new day had decided to dawn. It manifested itself confusedly, hesitantly and timidly, and the young azure was stained by bloody streaks. The storm had raged for several years,[45] but to our philosophers, those long atrocious months

---

[45] The author is, of course, guessing; he had no idea when he wrote this story in 1915, or when he died in 1917, how long

had only lasted for the space of one night, in the enchantment of an ingenious conversation.

"The tempest has eased," said the abbé.

The philosophers came to surround him.

"What devastation!" murmured Candide.

His park, his vegetable garden, his vines and his orchard were no longer anything but a desert. Not one shrub, not one pathway, not one thicket, not one tree; no more borders, no more grapes. The ripped earth and the leveled plots were arid fallow land, with not so much as a clump of couch-grass, where tall plane trees, and orange and lemon groves had once grown, along with quincunxes of peach-trees and the green stocks of vines, the slim and twisted trunks of almonds and olives, aubergines and melons, myrtles and box-trees, laurels and privet, arbutus and palms heavy with dates, carpets of violets and anemones, trees from which pistachios and vanilla were suspended, the cedars beloved by the turtle-doves, the clumps of bamboo and cypress...

Sadly, the philosophers considered the devastated garden.

"If you had seen my farm before!" Candide said, simply. He sighed. He had tears in his eyes.

"Let's all stay here," said Don Quixote, generously, "to repair the disaster."

"To work!" cried Mr. Pickwick.

They went down the steps of the perron, energetic and full of ardor, in quest of a spade and a rake.

"The field remains," Vaissette affirmed, "even though the crops have been scythed down. We'll give birth to other harvests."

"And we'll strive to protect them against further tempests," affirmed Dr. Faust.

Achilles, full of good will, was already disturbing the soil alongside Mr. Pickwick.

---

the war would last. This chapter is, therefore pure optimism—but that was, after all, *Candide*'s subtitle.

"I'll be able to plant and prune the rose-bushes and the vines," said Abbé Coignard.

They all went down into the garden.

"Oh, the harvests of tomorrow!" murmured Vaissette.

His soul appeased, Candide added: "Let's get to work!"

Louis Baudry de Saunier: *How Paris was destroyed in six hours on Easter Sunday, 20 April 1924*

A Translation of an Issue of
the German daily newspaper *Berliner Tageblatt*,
25 June 1924

HOW PARIS WAS DESTROYED IN SIX HOURS
ON 20 APRIL 1924

The detailed account and the complete story
of the incredible event, related yesterday
IN THE PRESENCE OF HIS MAJESTY
THE EMPEROR AND KING
WILHELM II
in the Hall of Mirrors at Versailles

As reported by the celebrated Otto Walter

FINALLY WE HAVE HER!
FRANCE IS OUR PROPERTY!

Since the immortal night of 20 April 1924, which gave
the Chosen Race the dominion of the entire world, our readers
have found every morning, in their *Berliner Tageblatt*, that cry
of glory: "Finally we have her! France is our property!" From
daybreak to sunset, let all Germany repeat it until the voice
gives out. Let that cry become our national gargle![46]

---

[46] Here and in numerous other places the author inserts a foot-
note offering the last sentence in the "original" German, but I

293

Finally, we have her! France is our property! Today, while she is writhing under our invincible boot, let us sing in the face of the world that she is the most beautiful of beauties, that no soil richer, no climate milder and no prey tastier than Gaul can ever fall to patient and tenacious Germany!

Finally, we have her! But let us calm the lyricism of our joy! Let us not leave any longer unappeased the hunger for the story of the glorious events that all our readers are feeling. Let us pass on quickly to the splendid reality of yesterday's event; here it is:

Three days ago, our hero of genius, His Excellency General Hans von Stick, was informed of the desire that the Emperor had just manifested to learn from his own moth the details of German prowess, forever memorable in the succession of the centuries, that crushed Paris in a single night and caused France to fall into our helmet.

His majesty intended that the Lecture should be solemn, but limited to a hundred selected guests. He deigned to order that the reading, every line of which will make the heart of even the humblest of our peasants beat faster, should be given in the Hall of Mirrors at Versailles.

To that memorable room was owed, the Emperor said, aloud, both honor, since it was in the Hall of Mirrors in 1871 that the German Empire had been proclaimed, and disinfection, since the petty piece of paper known as the Treaty of Versailles had been signed there on 28 June 1919.

Three days after the imperial desire was manifested, the Hall of Mirrors was ready. The slide-projection apparatus that was to illuminate the lecture of our hero of genius, Hans von Stick, stood on the marquetry-work parquet of the Sun King. And the entire court, swollen with gladness, awaited the arrival of His Majesty.

By permission of His Excellency the High Chamberlain W. von Schmitterdorff, the very humble representative of the

---

have considered that ironic courtesy to be superfluous in a translation of a "translation."

Berliner Tageblatt was authorized to witness the grandiose lecture with two stenographers. That signal generosity permits us to give our readers a complete account of that incomparable ceremony. We are convinced that more than one of them will pin it up on his bedroom wall.

AN INFORMAL MAJESTY

His Majesty the Emperor had deigned to order that yesterday's ceremony would commence at two o'clock.

At five minutes to two the first horseman of the escort preceding the imperial automobile emerged on to the esplanade of Louis XIV's château. The great fountains were playing, the mirrors of the basins reflected the sun, and the air was embalmed with joy.

With the charming simplicity that heightens his August Character and Lucid Intelligence, and the affability that befits a Democratic Emperor, His Majesty came into the Hall of Mirrors, sat down in the midst of his court on a throne with golden feet, and soon permitted the members of the audience to raise their heads, which they had bowed down before him since he came in.

Our hero of genius, standing next to the slide projector, bowed profoundly in his turn. Immediately, however, a chamberlain approach him and, breaking the solemn silence, proclaimed that His Majesty deigned to order the glorious Destroyer of Paris to speak in his presence.

A little pale to begin with, but quickly overcoming his emotion, His Excellency General von Stick expressed himself as follows:

THE STORY OF AN IMMORTAL HERO

Your Majesty,

The story of the immortal exploits that German genius accomplished on the ever-memorable night of 20 April 1924 ought to emerge from a mouth more eloquent than mine. I am a soldier and an engineer. I am neither a Pindar nor a Dante—those incontestable Germans of old—to sing your glory as it merits. I am scarcely a Leonardo da Vinci—another of our illustrious ancestors—and I apologize for the scientific dryness of my report.

In order better to comprehend, from deduction to deduction, the events of 20 April 1924, it is necessary to go back six years, to 1918.

In the month of November of that year, the Allies thought that they had defeated Germany! Their eyes were truly closed by nutshells, for they ought to have seen, inscribed in the history of the world in red letters, these words: *Germany is never defeated!*

In reality, when the armistice of 1918 was signed, Germany was performing an action of both great humanity and great strategy. She was imposing on the Allies the cessation of the war that they had declared against her. She was weary of the torrents of blood that they had unleashed. She finally forced them to take pity on humankind. Thus she demonstrated once more to Neutrals who judged without prejudice her mildness and her bounty. Enough tears, she said, thereby. Enough deaths! Enough windows! Enough poor little orphans!

But at the same time, the armistice permitted Germany to collect herself, to seek to discover by what rapid course, by what sudden realization, which would fill the World with amazement and admiration, she would be able to reclaim from events her due—which is to say, the empire of the entire Earth.

For our Race must, no matter what the cost, pursue the supreme goals that Destiny has imposed upon it. Being the Salt of the Earth, it is necessary for us to cover the Earth with Salt!

THE COUNCIL OF SEVEN

Majesty,

I shall merely remind you that an imperial decree, made from Holland in 1919, to which you had had the sublime wisdom to withdraw, in order better to judge the chessboard from a distance, had instituted an Imperial Council of seven individuals charged with examining the means by which Germany would finally obtain recognition from the entire world of her divine mission. Your Majesty was kind enough to take into consideration the doggedness with which I had always done my duty as an engineer at the Krupp factories before the war, and the good fortune, of which my humble talent is scarcely worthy, of constituting on the Champagne front the squadron of aviators that compiled the most impressive lists of kills throughout the war. Your Majesty deigned to order me to join that committee.

Germany has neither both hands in the same glove nor both feet in the same boot. When she has decided, she realizes immediately, while her adversaries are still searching for an appearance of reason not to realize tomorrow what a hundred good reasons commanded them to realize yesterday.

Five days after the signature of the decree, the seven members of the Imperial Committee met in Stuttgart, under the pretext of studying the requisition of eight hundred thousand dairy cows that France was still claiming from us last spring, as you will recall, two months before her death.

The three senior military personnel and the three eminent diplomats that constituted that Imperial Committee, and myself, were soon in accord in ridding the problem of all the parasitic ideas by which people then had the custom of obscuring it. We gradually made it appear in all is nudity, in its skeleton, and we soon came to this conclusion:

In order imminently to possess the entire world, what must Germany do? Possess France!

In fact, confronted with France, suddenly vanquished, what would England do? England has Ireland attached to her flank, like a jaguar, with its fangs in her flesh; she senses that her wealth is in grave peril in India, that her social health is battling with fever. How would she dare even to dispute our victory when, with her troops unmobilized and her fleets scattered over all the seas, she saw us suddenly installed everywhere along the French coasts of the Channel, the Atlantic and the Mediterranean?

As for Italy, she has never detested us very much. Spain is our friend. Bulgaria would like nothing better than to love us. Turkey is submissive. Holland, Finland and Sweden are still drunk on our breath. Russia will swallow Poland tomorrow and come to place her lips on our mouth!

Who, then, in Europe, would permit themselves not to cry "Bravo!" if we were suddenly to crush France?

Who, then, in America, in Asia, would put a sword across our path? The United States has declared with reason that God has not given men the blessed hours of the day and the night to cut one another's throats, but to sell one another a great deal of cotton and a great deal of lard. From one end of the planet to the other the cry would ring out: "Enough war! Enough war!" And Japan, a fatalistic as Arabia, would say to a Germany that was mistress of Europe: "The gods have been good to you, doubtless because you deserve it!"

(The emotion is so great that one expects the singing of "Deutchscland über alles" to burst forth somewhere in the room, but His Majesty keeps his eyes fixed on the lecturer like two blades, and his great face imposes silence on everyone.)

Such was the first stage of the reasoning of the Imperial Committee. To take France today is to take the world tomorrow.

The second stage was this: It is necessary to take France swiftly, or our entire future will crumble. In fact, if attacked, she will defend herself, and we have seen how she is able to defend herself. Attacked, she will be supported by obliging allies; then there is a recommencement of the interminable war; that is the destruction of our ideal of human war, or extremely brief war.

In consequence, we decided that if we were ever to see France in the bottom of our helmet, it was necessary—please forgive me, Your Majesty—to win the game in a single hand: quickly, ultra-quickly, or everything would be spoiled! So, only a surprise coup, only a lightning strike, one of those manifestations of extravagant audacity that only a German brain can conceive, only a few hours of cold and reasoned madness, would permit us to gamble "all or nothing" for France!

But the third stage of our reasoning immediately ran into an evident obstacle: France could not, in her entirety, be captured by Germany in a matter of hours. Let us not emerge from the domains of the practical and the realizable. Let us not allow the breath of patriotism to blow us beyond common sense.

What could we do?

Certain insects—the cockchafer, for example—in order to make sure of a prey, do not risk themselves in combat; they throw themselves on it suddenly, sink their sting into a nerve-center that they know well, and it is all over! The prey is paralyzed! They butcher it thereafter without danger, in their own time, as it pleases them to digest it.

In the same way, the toreador who wishes to fell a bull does not bother to declare war on it, to cry out to it: "Pay attention! I'm drawing my weapon; prepare your horns!" Nothing so stupid! He seems to play with the beast, deceives it, and then plunges his sword straight into the spinal cord. The bull is dead, and the mules drag him away.

Well, we thought, does not France too, have a nerve center, which it is sufficient to crush in one night in order that the next day she will be paralyzed and dead? Let us consult a map! Here are the arteries and the veins, here are all the canals, all the roads, all the telegraph wires, which come together at the same point: Paris! Let us open a history book! Paris is taken, the entire nineteenth century demonstrates, and France is taken!

Certainly, if Paris is taken, a few groups of stubborn soldiers will try to form up behind the Loire. A fortnight later those bands will have disappeared; on that miserable little army it will be sufficient for us to sneeze.

(*The Emperor smiles. The court laughs.*)

There was the solution, grandiose and devastating! Paris, the nerve center, the heart, the alimentary center of France, seems to have been placed close to our frontier by God in order that Germany might one day annihilate it with ease. The inexplicable shame of General von Kluck, in August 1914, was to fail to take Paris, to have put off for ten years the glorious idea of a fresh and joyful war, in sacrifice to I don't know what Napoleonic principle!

(*The Emperor moves his fingers feverishly. The court stamps its feet.*)

The first meeting of the Imperial Committee ended, therefore, with this conclusion:

To conquer the world, it is necessary to take France. To take France, it is necessary to pulverize Paris. To pulverize Paris, it is necessary to bring off a coup of almost insane audacity, in a matter of hours, before the French have time even to try to defend themselves, before anyone can come to their aid.

After which, we could say to the other powers: "What have you to add, Ladies? Come on! Give us your reverence."

OUR FUTURE IS IN THE AIR

As it is not in the German character to wait for porcelain fruits to ripen, the second meeting of the Imperial Committee took place two days later, this time in Mannheim. We had judged it politic not to hold two meetings in the same city on the matter of the eight hundred thousand cows; a wise German never forgets that there might always be a pair of eyes in the wall, looking to see how he makes his sauerkraut...

Each of the committee members revealed his idea. My colleagues held on to the old methods of surprise by the main army, but they admitted themselves that they did not even merit being attempted. Certainly, in spite of the appearance of disarmament that we had accepted to put on at the behest of the Allies, we secretly possessed a considerable army, fully imbibed with the spirit of revenge. Without that, what would we have done the day after the glorious night of Easter, when, Paris having been annihilated, it was sufficient for our battalions to advance across the plains of France with weapons holstered and a flower in the mouth to conquer all of Europe? I need not tell the eminent men of war who are honoring me with their attention about the sacred hiding places from which we could bring forth instantaneously, over the entire territory of the Reich, cannons, shells, rifles, machine-guns, grenades, tanks and floods of gas and flames!

But to discuss such proposals, to recommence a war on land, of blockades and trenches, was to misunderstand the very spirit of the decision of the first meeting of the Imperial Council: to act in a matter of hours.

It was then—and Your Majesty will absolve me is I seem to be glorifying my feeble person here, although my praises are addressed to our good God who inspired my brain—that that I asked my colleagues to huddle around me next to the table...

In a low voice, fearing that too loud a tone might compromise the future of the Fatherland, I sketched out in broad lines the project that was shining in my head like an incandescent filament in a glass bulb.

"Aviation," I explained to them, "will makes masters of the entire world the first people who are able to see everything, absolutely everything, of what it carries beneath its wings: the end of wars on land; the end of wars at sea; the end of war itself! For the day will come when via the air, death will come so terribly, so sure of its hecatombs, that humans, if any remain, will reach accord in order never to summon it again. Before that definitive progress is achieved, before science has killed Holy War, let us profit from the miracles of aeronautics; let us, thanks to them, claim the world!

"France is tergiversating, understanding one day, and then seeming not to understand the next. She would like a formidable army of the air, because she knows, deep down, that salvation is there in its entirety, that it is henceforth nowhere else but there; but she jibs at paying the necessary price and making the effort of will that it imposes.

"Let us take advantage of her stupid faith in a future that will work out of its own accord. In four for five years, let us gain over our enemies and advantage in air power that will discourage them from ever catching up with us! Let us possess an unmatchable fleet! Let all of Germany have no hope in anything but aeronautics! And if people in high places will listen to my experience, one night, Paris will disappear from reality. The following day, the horrified and dazzled world will say: "What! Is it possible? Babylon is no more? What supernatural power, then, does the Vanquished of 1918 have, which, in a few hours, has been able to vanquish the Earth?"

I sensed my colleagues trembling beneath my arguments. The Holy Spirit of Revenge descended into them.

I had the prudence only to reveal to them the general lines of my plan, so that no indiscretion could harm it. For greater safety, I naturally mingled a few false details with the exposition of my project, appropriate to throw an overly ardent curiosity off the track. And I waited.

THE BLIND CANNOT SEE LIGHTNING

A few days later, the eminent individuals making up our Imperial Council had me appointed Minister of Aerial Transport, with unlimited powers. My mission was henceforth to seek the eternal glory of the Fatherland in the air. When I went into my office for the first time, I swore to myself to shoot myself with a pistol in five years time at the latest if, by that time, I had not sent Parisians the aerial transports they deserved.

At the beginning of 1921, Majesty, if someone had explained to the French that Germany, anemic and extenuated, would be able, three years later, to reveal herself as the Mistress of the World, and that she would owe her universal empire to the little mechanical birds that furrow the sky, they would immediately have declared that no buffoonery more amusing had ever been served to them in a boulevard theater, and that the ideas of the air were simply "fiction."

God has permitted that our enemies never believe in reasoning that it is disagreeable for them to hear. If the French had pulled themselves together in time, if they had organized large air fleets, they would have remained the most envied, the richest and the most respected people on Earth, and we would have remained for another century in the dolorous servitude into which the Treaty of Versailles had thrown us. There is no shame, when one has emerged stronger and greater from a terrifying abyss, in recognizing that one nearly lost one's life there!

But let us repeat, God has permitted that France would not have the revelation of the supreme power that aeronautical power could give to a people. Her stupidity and our clear sight has permitted us to scratch out her name from the list of nations.

These general considerations are the ways that are now leading us a little closer to the fact itself: the destruction of Paris.

Far from priding myself on that incomparable event, I intend to draw a lesson from it for our people, to demonstrate how the stupid Welches,[47] their eyes glued to the ground and

---

[47] Author's note: "The German nickname for the French." (In the same way that the French, throughout the Great War, called the Germans "Boches.")

the stream of the Rhine, were stubborn in preparing for their own death; how right the Cassandras had been, crying to them in 1918 that Paris could be destroyed in a day by German aircraft; how easy such an operation would become, on condition that someone to in our homeland cared to meditate it, and to organize it methodically. After so many centuries of hopes, struggles and sanctifying sufferings, Providence sent to virtuous and laborious Germany the doves of universal domination!

Aeronautics? It soars above all human beings! Our steely gaze had pierced the clouds in 1897. In that year, on the fourth of October, one a day of rain and squalls, on the other side of the old frontier, in France, a machine heavier than air, which he called an "*avion*," a Frenchman had left the ground: Clément Ader! The French had shrugged their shoulders, but the Germans had frowned.[48]

Ten years later, almost to the day, on the twenty-seventh of October 1904, again on French soil, Henri Farman carried out a flight of 770 meters in a biplane. The advertisement became precise! The Sign of the Times was designed in the firmament!

In 1908, when the American Wilbur Wright, perfecting Clément Ader's idea, accomplished at Le Mans, again in France, the series of flights that attracted all of Parisian High

---

[48] The inventor Clément Ader claimed to have made his first flight in his *Avion II* in 1892; hardly anyone believed him but he did obtain funding from the Ministry of War for further experiments; he arranged with the War Ministry for a secret trial for his steam-powered *Avion III*—which resembled a giant bat—on 12 October 1897. Unfortunately, it was caught by a gust of wind and blown off the circular track on which Ader was attempting to build up sufficient speed to take off. The Ministry's observers, unimpressed, withdrew funding; the Ministry eventually released the report on the trial in 1910, after it has been conclusively demonstrated by more fortunate pioneers that heavier-than-air flight was, indeed, practicable.

Society to the Camp d'Auvours, the die was cast for us. Germany, no matter what the cost, had to assure herself of supremacy in the air, because the people who were only masters of the land of all the continents only had a fifth of the world's surface in their possession as yet; because the people who were only masters of the water of all the oceans, only had an illusory domain in their hands as yet; awaiting the time when the people who would be masters of the air would obtain sovereignty over all the continents, all the oceans and all the skies. That people alone would be the masters of all humankind, because the air is everywhere that humans can live!

Stupid France! All the progress of nascent aviation—all of it—took place on your soil! On the fifteenth of September 1908 Wilbur Wright carried out at Le Mans the first flight with two passengers. Your children did not understand that the passengers could immediately cede their place to two 75-kilogram bombs! Heil to our God! The Santos-Dumonts, the Voisins, the Blériots, the Delagranges, the Farmans, the Esnault-Pelteries, the Bréguet-Saulniers, the Nieuports, the Renaults and the Moranes clarified the question for the Deutschland!

On the sixth of March 1908 the Michelin brothers created the Prix du Puy-de-Dôme, which consisted of transporting a passenger in an airplane from Paris to the summit of a 1,445-meter mountain; the proof constituted a feat that the most competent experts judged it unrealizable within twenty years. Three years later, almost to the day once again, on the seventh of March 1911, the prize was won, in five hours!

On the twenty-second of August 1911, the same Michelins created the Prix de l'Aéro-Cible: to place projectiles from a height of two hundred meters within a circle with a radius of ten meters. If a layman thought about the enormous speed of the airplane from which the projectiles are dropped, and the extremely small area of the target drawn on the ground, he would think, rightly, that success could only be achieved by a particularly adroit marksman, equipped with very complicated, much improved apparatus, with many years experience in that extraordinary kind of shooting. Now, less than a year later, on the twentieth of August 1912, Messieurs Gaubert and Scott put into that target, which, from a height of two hundred meters, looks as big as a pancake, twelve projectiles out of fifteen! In 1913, Lieutenant Varcin placed thirteen out of fifteen and, furthermore, declared that few exercises in the world are as easy as carrying out extremely accurate fire from an airplane! I shall shortly have the great honor, Majesty, of demonstrating that to the court.

Progress in the science of the air, therefore, defied all human anticipation in its unexpectedness and rapidity—that is the truth! If God, for the accomplishment of his impenetrable designs, had not decided that France would one day perish by way of the air, the French would have grasped the scope—which has no limits in time, in space or in power—of the aerial marvels that all unfurled before their eyes and in their homeland between 1897 and 1914!

Their parliamentarians squabbled, their senior civil servants shrugged their shoulders, and the French laughed, as crickets sing and dancers dance.

Then, on the eve of the events of 1914, while England was still trying to take off and could not oppose to us any substantial aerial force, Germany, by means of her Zeppelins, her Taubs and her Gothas got a head start in the sky over all the nations of the world. On the second of August 1914, France had the ridicule of aligning against us a hundred and twenty aircraft, produced by fourteen different manufacturers, divided into twenty-one squadrons, some of which were composed of five or even six types, aircraft that all flew at different heights, at dissimilar speeds, possessing neither sighting-devices, nor bomb-launchers, nor bombs, nor machine-guns!

At that moment, however, Divine Bounty seemed to want to give the French one final warning, in order that faith in the victorious airplane might be embedded in their memory forever, very profoundly! When our immortal armies marched on Paris—defended by nine aircraft!—on the third of September 1914, one of those aircraft reported in haste to General

Gallieni the enormous news that General von Kluck had veered toward the south-east! Only an aircraft could have discovered that the German army had thus left its flank open to attack!

That attack was launched from Paris, and that was the Battle of the Marne!

But the French did not understand yet, and God kept their head in the fog thereafter. After an enlightenment in 1918, during Foch's battles, the clouds closed again, and France, today, has died of incomprehension. Our God be praised!

(At this moment the Emperor rises to his feet and the orator falls silent. His Majesty turns to the court and pronounces these words slowly, which will roll over all the territory of the Empire like echoing thunder: "Yes, our God be praised! The French have killed immortal France!" A sovereign clamor rises from the throats assembled around the Emperor, who quietly resumes his place on the throne.)

LET US GIVE THANKS TO THE ALLIES

God, in sum, had tested us severely in 1918 in order that we might sense his predilection. His punishment was a blessing. God showed us that he had blinded our enemies and that we would find our victory in the sky. *Victoriam in coelo!*

But he demanded that we should merit that victory. In order to win it, we would have to bind our loins with the *cilice*[49] of obstinate hard labor, and cover our head with the hood of dissimulation.

Without hard labor and dissimulation, it was impossible that the trophy of the air would ever belong to us, since, in

---

[49] A *cilice* is an instrument of self-torture once employed by devout Catholic clergymen to mortify their flesh, taking the form of a belt or bracelet studded with internal spikes—a technological refinement of the traditional hair shirt.

order to test us, the Eternal had installed Allied monitors inside our very workshops.

But also, in order to lead us more surely to triumph, he had installed at all times in our solid German heads the cunning of a thousand smiles!

Incomparable virtue, O Cunning, supernatural power which succeeds in thwarting the best-establish rights, you have soared over our entire history like a mysterious Genius! In the report that I am presenting today to the Master of the World, your hand appears in every event! You alone rendered infallible the plan whose details are about to unfold.

In 1918, at the time of the armistice, the German air force was rich and powerful. But in 1920, progress in that field being frightfully rapid, having aged, it no longer consisted of any but obsolete apparatus.

The Allied Commissions rendered us the unappreciable service of constraining us to destroy those antiquities or surrender them. If we had been the only judges of our decisions, we might perhaps have hesitated to reform all that equipment of backward warfare; the Entente was kind enough to demand that we renew our aerial armaments as early as 1921, in order that it would be entirely in conformity with the most recent progress.

Inestimable intervention, O Cunning!

COMMERCIAL AERONAUTICS CONSTITUTES MILITARY AERONAUTICS

Yes, joyfully we signed up to the end of our military aeronautics, because, in all verity, "military" aeronautics does not exist, and never will! No State can or ever will be able to maintain aerial armies in times of peace, because progress in such an industry transforms the apparatus within a year, with an absolutism that no public budget would be able to support.

In addition, no aerial army, in peace time, is capable of providing its pilots with continuous exercise, the daily training that is the sole determinant of their value.

Undoubtedly, every government possesses ultra-rapid hunter aircraft, which form the police forces of the air and are crewed by career combatants. But the bulk of aerial armies, of the armies that determine victory, is constituted, and will remain so, by commercial and passenger apparatus.

From whatever angle one envisages such a solution, one cannot help admiring its marvels: the aeronautics of commerce and transportation enrich the country and, while enriching herself, she easily subsidizes the costly demands of progress. The Ministry of War thus has in its hand a weapon of immense power, which costs no more than the price of munitions, and which it can mobilize in a matter of hours—for a decisive surprise attack, for example.

We were the very first to understand that, and that is why the years from 1918 to 1924 appeared to us less cruel than Europe supposed. We did not moan, because we had the certainty of our dazzling future!

The mastery of the air in commerce thus procures, for a people sufficiently clear-sighted and sufficiently hard-working to obtain it, the mastery of the air in war; one can no more separate those two terms than one can separate an effect and a cause, or conceive an upstream without a downstream, a recto page without a verso, the right-hand side of a blade without the left-hand side. Transport aircraft and bomber aircraft are two faces, scarcely dissimilar, of the same coin.

TO WORK!

As soon as I arrived in power, I therefore spread through the public, by all means possible, an obsession with commercial aeronautics. The government lent me the most enthusiastic collaboration in that crusade, creating numerous lines of aerial transport, subsidizing all the companies that showed audacity in the length of journeys or the magnitude of the weights transported. It ordered the banks to support every establishment that was contributing, proximally or at a distance, to the progress of aeronautics.

New postal services by air were installed with every passing week, making practical tariffs inferior to those that remained imposed on the old modes of transporting correspondence. I divided cities into sectors that were visited every morning by beaters charged with recruiting an ever-increasing clientele for our aerial services among manufacturers and traders. They demonstrated to them the advantages of rapidity and punctuality offered by the new methods; a large number of businessmen came to consider automobiles and express trains as obsolete, for themselves and for their merchandise.

All the newspapers in the Empire were constrained to keep their readers breathless for news in regard to these questions. My ministry sent them all, every week, popular articles that they had to insert. Many, in any case, were ingenious in lending their collaboration with regard to some aeronautical issue. The obsession with aviation was maintained by my care on trams and in railway carriages, in feminine fashion and in the products of confectioners, pastry-makers cakes and Christmas toys!

Great aeronautical schools were opened, and it was soon accepted that a German had not completely acquitted his debt to the Fatherland until he had received his aerial baptism! Men, women and children besieged departing aircraft.

I did not neglect to set up immense factories for the construction of aircraft entirely made of metal, which, after 1920, completely supplanted the old machines of wood and canvas, and for the fitting out of modern Zeppelins that could transport 500 passengers. The success of our manufacture soon dominated worldwide construction to the point that Italy, Spain, Japan and even the United States became our assiduous clients.

Gradually, the umbrageous Entente thus had incontestable proof of the assiduity of German labor, of her desire to pay the billions in compensation, to abandon any idea of revenge, and finally to sit down in a comradely fashion at the table of Nations!

The profession of pilot soon became one of the most sought-after to which a young German could aspire. To the best of our civil aviators I had ranks attributed that put them at the same level, in the eyes of the public, as officers in the land army, and thus obliged women to make way for them on sidewalks. I imposed upon all of them a rigorous discipline that constrained them to regular exercise and made them servile in my hands. All of them were content with that constraint and that subjugation.

Your Majesty will doubtless permit me not to repeat here the minor details of a hierarchical organization that He was good enough to approve, two years ago, by Imperial Decree.

The emprise that my Air Ministry exercised over all its pilots had the official aim of making them flexible to the practical methods of the standardization of their art. The perfect knowledge of naval signaling systems and intercommunication between ships, for example, justified the frequent meeting of pilots under the authority of carefully selected leaders. Our aerial commerce gained by that discipline a bearing and a progress that demonstrated to the world, a little more every day, the greatness of Germany, and hastened our prodigious recovery by the development of our commerce.

But the ultimate goal of that emprise was, in reality, to constitute a severely selected elite of intelligent and ardent combatants hardened to all audacity. We were preparing them for a war of rapid action and surprises, overtly, under the confident eyes of the Allies.

Here, I shall give the praise that is due to one of the noblest individuals in the Empire, the Director General of Camouflage, Heinrich Mannheim, who was necessarily my confidant and collaborator. There is no brain more fertile, no merit more modest. His mere gaze transforms objects and men; at the very moments when I thought it prudent to dissimulate from him the detail of one of my projects, his psychic influence constrained me to reveal it to him in its entirety. He forced me to show him the truth laid bare, to be sincere; and thus he disguised me from myself.

If one brings the slightest common sense to the analysis of an aerial engine of bombardment, one understands immediately that the only thing differentiating it from an aerial engine of commerce is the nature of its cargo.

In consequence, the problem is limited to the solution of two problems: firstly, the rapid transformation of a peaceful cargo into a martial cargo; and secondly, a perfect knowledge of the methods of delivery of that cargo to a domicile—which is to say, the methods of bombardment.

The first element of the problem would have appeared difficult to solve if the fox with the delicate nose that Heinrich Mannheim is had not imagined his system of express delivery, which I shall describe shortly. You will see that, thanks to that, all the mechanical apparatus of aiming and release that are indispensable to a vehicle of bombardment became indispensable to a commercial vehicle. The difficulty was reduced to child's play: transformed in two hours, the meekest of aircraft could take to the air with the attitude of the most redoubtable warrior.

I am not telling the August Assembly that is listening to me anything new in reminding them that the bombs dropped by airplanes in the 1914-18 war bore no more resemblance to present engines of destruction than an explosive bullet destined for an orangutan resembles the torpedo that was reserved for the *Lusitania*! In January 1918 a miserable hundred-kilogram cooking-pot, dropped by one of our Gothas, completely destroyed a house in the Rue Geoffroy-Marie in Paris. We had thousand-kilogram bombs in 1920; we are the proud possessors of three-thousand-kilogram bombs in 1924! The explosion of La Courneuve,[50] whose ravages extended from Saint-Denis to Coulommiers, certainly did not have the power of a single one of our *Frankreichsliebs*—lovers of France! If

---

[50] On 15 March 1918 a munitions factory in La Courneuve, containing a estimated 28,000,000 grenades blew up, destroying the neighborhood completely; although only fourteen people were killed, more than a thousand were injured.

one explodes within two hundred meters of an ironclad, it sinks her completely! If it hits the ground in a city, an entire quarter is demolished, smashed and devastated; chimneys falls into cellars, electrical short-circuits ignite the gas that is flooding out of the broken mains. The Frankreichslieb treats the inhabitants of a city as a good gardener kills a wasps' nest: it turns it over with a thrust of the spade and sets fire to it.

Now, a single one of our super-Zeppelins, which ordinarily have accommodation for five hundred passengers, can transport ten of those good collaborators. You will remember, moreover, that it can rise to such a height as to be almost invisible, that it can remain in the air for three or four days without landing, and that no incendiary shell, if, by chance, any artillery piece reaches it, can reckon with it, since the gas that it carries is no longer hydrogen, but a fireproof fluid.

That example shows the excellence of the effects that we were able to expect by studying the most rapid methods of charging the cargoes of airships. The same reasons applied to the five thousand metallic postal aircraft that we possess, each of which transports fifty people, which have no more fear of bullets than a tank, and no more fear of shells than a swallow.

THE LINNETS

It is perfectly evident that one of the major causes of the formidable success that we have just obtained resides in the very character of our adversary, now disemboweled. The insouciance of the French can perhaps only be compared to that of a little gray bird, the linnet, of whose fable I shall remind you:

"One day, hidden behind the branch of a bush, a linnet saw a hunter in the plain shoot at a company of partridges. He was a young and inexperienced poacher who was making poor use of his rifle, and was fearful of gamekeepers every time he used it—with the result that the partridges suffered no more damage from his shot than the loss of a few small feathers.

"The linnet uttered a joyful cry and flew away to tell her sisters that poachers were not much more dangerous than the scarecrows that farmers stick up in their fields to frighten sparrows. 'Hunters often make a lot of noise,' she added, clicking her beak, 'but they always go home with an empty game-bag.' She demonstrated to her sisters that the danger was non-existent, and easily persuaded them, because they all wanted desperately to believe that it did not exist.

"Then, all day long, the little gray birds gathered in groups on the thickest branch of the bush, in the middle of the plain. They thought about nothing but singing, and congratulating one another on singing so well.

"One afternoon, knowing that the gamekeepers were drinking in a distant tavern, the young poacher went out into the plain, set himself at a convenient distance, calmly and unhurriedly took aim, and killed all the linnets with a single shot. He went home with a bulging game-bag, and his wife made a pâté so big that all the friends in the village were able to share it."

The French have always resembled linnets. Because the bombs of 1918 lacked precision in targeting, they concluded that aeronautics, even in 1920 and 1924, would always remain maladroit. When their Press identified "the Great Peril of the Air," they wrote to the editors of the newspapers that they would cancel their subscriptions if they continued to make them anxious. The suppressors of effort, who pullulate in that poor people, succeeded in persuading it that what was being raised up before them was a scarecrow, not a reality—just as they had demonstrated in 1913 that war was impossible, proved mathematically that it could not last longer than six weeks, that the German heavy artillery constituted a dementia, and that hostilities would always take the form of large-scale movements.

You know the facts: war broke out in 1914; it was a war of heavy artillery; and, dug into the soil to a depth of ten meters, the adversaries remained in confrontation, immobile, for four years.

Let our enemies' mortal error illuminate German consciousness forever! Let our hearts thank the Almighty for heaving attached our supreme triumph to a weapon of such simple manipulation.

How many errors our enemies heaped up! First of all, they had said to one another, during the war of 1914-18, that the airplane is much less redoubtable than the popular imagination thinks, given that, by night, the fire of the barrage is generally sufficient to stop it, and if, by chance, it gets through the fire of the barrage, the fall of its bombs is awkward, without the launcher being able to attain his intended target with any precision.

That was chloroform reasoning, good for putting the French to sleep. The truth, the truth of facts, is exactly contrary to those allegations. The truth is that the airplane is even more redoubtable, and much more so, than the popular imagination thinks. No brain can conceive all the possibilities, of every kind, that a nation possesses which has mastery over the element necessary to every human creature: the air.

The simple fire of the barrage around Paris, by night, in 1918, was sufficient to cut off the route of our squadrons? That is true. It was the case because our valiant pilots have an impressionable nervous system, like that of every human being, and it is necessary to put oneself in their place, imaginatively, in those redoubtable conditions, to understand their attitude.

In war, lacking precise reference points in the darkness, above a city whose lights are masked or deceptive, turning his head continually in order to avoid the sudden attacks of the terrible little hunter aircraft that could, in that era, send him plunging into the abyss with a single burst of machine-gun fire, always imagining that the shells of the barrage are bursting around him, the pilot, having arrived from Germany after three or four hours of anxious flight, feels his temples beating furiously before the circle of fire; he hesitates to pass through the inferno, and almost always turns away. If he has had the supreme audacity to enter the demonic circle, he gets rid of his bombs quickly, and flees...

In moments of sincerity, not one pilot seeks to deny that such contingencies overcome no matter what courage, that any human animal trembles before them. In reality, the cannons of the barrage are not firing at the aircraft, but at the nervous system of the aviator.

Those formidable contingencies are, in any case, not superior to German valor, and, when we proceed by selection, we will always find thousands of Supermen who, for the service of the Fatherland, no matter what the cost, will have no fear of entering the demonic circle with a smile!

(*The Emperor utters a vigorous "Hoch!" to which a hundred enthusiastic Hochs! respond.*)

But why talk about barrages here, since our conception of the destruction of Paris did not perceive any on the horizon? We were to pounce upon Paris at the moment when it least expected it, when, in consequence, its ring of fire would be extinct. Our bold pilots would have, for the realization of their grandiose task, the indisputable element of success: quietude. Surging forth unexpectedly, they would operate in complete tranquility. And we would see, in order to reply to the argument of the inefficacy of the aiming of aircraft, what kind of targeting a pilot is capable when he is untroubled in his preparation.

IT IS FRIGHTFULLY SIMPLE AND SIMPLY FRIGHTFUL

In reality, Your Majesty, and illustrious companions of our Emperor, there is no targeting that is simpler to make precise than that of flying machines. There is no fire that is more efficacious. For in sum, the dirigible that departs from Hamburg in order to go and drop its bombs on Creusot is essentially a cannon with a range of 2,500 kilometers. A miraculous cannon! It is a cannon that can "see" with perfect clarity that target that has been assigned to it! And it is a cannon that launches shells of a singularly higher rendition than those of its gross terrestrial comrade, since the aerial projectile does not have to resist the formidable pressure of launch, has no need of extremely thick steel walls, and is simply enveloped in a light skin of sheet metal. It is all explosive and no shrapnel!

The facility of aerial fire? But who has demonstrated that to us better than the French? Ought not a little irony season the flavorsome dish of our vengeance? Who, more than them, has perfected the methods of firing from aircraft? The relevant documentation is all of French provenance.

The amazing trials of the Aéro-Cible in 1912 and 1913 revealed the extraordinary precision that aerial targeting possesses, on the sole condition that the bombardier can operate in total tranquility. A far-sighted intelligence could already have savored one of the most beautiful military roles of the aviator: to enjoy surprise, to lull an adversary to sleep by appearances, to glide over him, with a razor up the sleeve, and with a slick thrust, cut his throat. Such is the schematic plan that, for my part, I glimpsed as one of the principal operations in the air.

Since that epoch, the progress of aerial targeting has been supported by methods that have given it a singular precision and a frightful amplitude.

During the war of 1914-18, again at the inspiration of the Michelins, an enormous school of aerial targeting was set up near Clermont-Ferrand, known as the Camp d'Aulnat. Its objective was to determine with exactitude the principles of aeronautical bombardment and, in consequence, to train excellent marksmen.

There is no need for me to enter into abstruse technical details here; it would be out of place in a lecture in which joy and incense are solely in play. I believe that I am deferring to His Majesty's desire in only tracing a sketch of the methods in question here.

After a little exploratory probing, it was recognized that the pilot of an aircraft, fully occupied with maneuvering the controls of the apparatus and the surveillance of the numerous dials, manometers and indicators that he has before his eyes, cannot be charged with the service of bombs. It is even important that he be placed under the total dependence of the bombardier installed behind him. One of the best combinations for the liaison of the two men in the din of the motor and the rush of the air seemed to consist of attaching them by means of reins, as children do when "playing horse." The bombardier directs the pilot. He is the master of the vessel. By the simultaneous means of a helmet-collimator that permits him to regulate his fire at the target, even by night, and a trigger-mechanism whose lever he has in his hand, which releases the bombs lodged under the wings one by one, he is the master of the possibilities of the marvelous machine.

The crew thus formed, it is necessary, in order to hit the target—a target placed below him—that he obtain a clear consciousness of the vertical line or, in other words, the one that extends directly above a point. The novice often makes an enormous error in imagining that he is directly over a target when he is actually some distance from it; it is necessary to find a means of showing him that error and making him acquire, by repeated trials, an intuition of rigorous verticality.

To that effect, a large circle is traced on flat ground: the target over which the aviator ought pass in the exercise is the center of that circle. At that point, a large portable *camera obscura* is installed, with its objective lens directed at the sky. One of the sides of the box is formed by a black curtain, which permits an observer to lodge his head and arms inside the box. The portion of the sky embraced by the objective is vertically projected on to a board partly covered with a white sheet of paper; a circle whose dimensions are proportional to those of the area marked out on the plain has been traced in advance on that sheet.

Thus, as soon as the aircraft begin to fly over the circle on the plain, its image appears in the circle on the paper, and the observer, by means of a pencil, traces the path it follows exactly. Imagining that he has crossed the circle exactly by its diameter, thus flying very precisely over the target, the novice, once on the ground, perceives his errors and takes a lesson therefrom. The progress he makes is extremely rapid.

But passing directly over the target is not sufficient; the projectile might fall behind or in front of the target, thus missing it. It is therefore important also to realize progress in the range—which is to say, in hitting the target itself. Numerous factors intervene here, such as the distance from the ground, the speeds of the airplane, the weight of the bomb, the strength of the wind, etc., which demand solutions to the problem that it is only appropriate to analyze in a lecture on ballistics. In any case, only the results obtained are of interest, and they are extremely interesting; as early as 1917 it was determined that the distance from the ground most favorable for aerial targeting in two thousand meters, a particularly fortunate distance since it is sufficient for the airplane to have no fear of the counterblast of the bomb exploding on the ground. At four thousand meters shots often hit the target dead on. It was determined that at five thousand meters, when the airplane is almost invisible, the bombardier, who can see the ground with marvelous clarity, can place his shot nine times out of ten on a target the size of the Gare Saint-Lazare.

Furthermore, all the conditions seem to be combined by the hand of God to make aerial fire the supreme element of destruction. The years that followed 1917 demonstrated, in fact, that such precision in direction and range is only a theoretical expression. In confrontation with an adversary, the only precision that matters is his death. What does it matter whether one kills him by striking him in the heart, as one is trying to do, or by provoking around him a shock that breaks his back? The true precision is to have the body of your enemy at your feet.

Two kinds of progress rapidly took place in destruction by aeronautical projectile. The war of 1914-18 proved that the most terrible power of a breaking shell is that of its indirect effects. The impact and the projection of the shards of a shell from the famous 75mm cannon, for example, scythed down

319

far fewer of our glorious children than the atmospheric depression determined by its explosion, which immediately permitted the gases contained in their blood to obstruct their capillaries with bubbles, and suddenly, as if in a macabre instantaneity, strike an entire section stone dead in attitudes of life.

To whom do we owe the most extraordinary improvements in projectiles? To the French. Their bombs have become ours. We have only had to ameliorate and diversity them. One alone can destroy ten houses, kill everything that breathes for five hundred meters around, pulverize all the windows, stave in all the doors and blow off all the roofs for three kilometers around, preparing the way for the efficacy of the bombs that follow! There are some that distribute an incendiary material that water only excites; there are some that spread gases so light that one neither sees not scents them; one inhalation causes death as abruptly as a lightning bolt; there are some that disperse over an entire city a fog of bacteria of paroxysmal virulence: have not typhus and plague, anthrax and glanders long pages to write in our war? There are some that, by night, suddenly illuminate the agonizing enemy with their solar glare, and descend slowly toward him, swaying!

When the French were warned in 1920 and 1921 by a few damnable prophets about the Peril of the Air, the pontiffs of the Rue Saint-Dominique advised them not to turn over on their pillow but to plunge themselves into it and pull corners back over their faces. "If the Boches bombard Paris, affirmed those terrible moustaches, they will suffer a frightful riposte! For we hold the heads of the bridges over the Rhine."

The heads of the bridges and cream tarts! A week before our attack on Paris an epidemic of encephalitis broke out among the allied troops of occupation so ferocious that the officers could not find enough moribunds to bury the dead! On the day of the attack, we had no more to do than bombard at our ease the vain "Rhine barriers." Our explosive, the commandant of the 147th squadron reported to me, fell into a kind of gigantic cemetery, around which panic stricken horses were running in all directions...

The second important progress that popularized, in a manner of speaking, the methods of aeronautical destruction was that of multiple fire, which was put into practice for the first time in France, at the Camp d'Aulnat, in 1917. I shall indicate the essential principles here,

In brief, it consists of the methodical rationalization of fire, in its discipline. It is carried out by a squadron whose commander takes the lead, and which, having arrived sat its target, releases all of its cargo on command. It is massive annihilation, irremediable pulverization by virtue of the enormity of the strike, no matter from what height it is released.

Another procedure, known as trailing, consists of operating individually, airplane by airplane, but not dropping the bombs at the hazard of caprice or aiming them; they are released automatically, in accordance with a rhythm whose cadence depends on the speed of the aircraft; it is calculated in such a way that the craters of destruction touch one another at the edges. It is applied primarily to the rupture of railways, canals, pipelines and aqueducts. It is the carpenter's saw, each thrust of which is a bomb, attacking the plank in order to cut it in two.

Finally in 1921, a supreme demonstration of the puerile facility of aerial fire was put before the very eyes of the stupid Welches; the flying apparatus for which people had been searching for thirty years, which is able to hover over the enemy, the helicopter, was found.[51] The bombardier, henceforth could remain fixed in the sky, and from a height at which he could not be perceived, rectifying his fire at his ease, could place all his strikes in the heart of the target.

---

[51] In fact, it was not until 1924 that genuinely successful flight trials of helicopters were first carried out, although inventors had been constructing experimental prototypes since the turn of the century. Etienne Ohemichen's 1921 trial only attracted a lot of attention because the machine's brief hovering was captured on film (which can now be viewed on YouTube).

The aerial cannon thus possesses an efficacy such that even precision is no longer necessary to it. Nevertheless, it puts a kind of ferocious coquetry into possessing more precision than any other cannon. That is the truth.

HOME DELIVERIES

The miraculous weapon was not yet in our hands, however. How, under the suspicious eyes of the Allies, could I ever train our postal aviation pilots to aim? Without a patient apprenticeship and frequent repetitions, how could I transform, in one day, in a few hours, the apparatus and the men and make my skillful postmen into expert bombardiers?

The impossibility of the solution appeared to Heinrich Mannheim and myself to be so evident that I almost abandoned myself to despair, when our newspapers informed us one day of the death in the United States of a man named Locklear,[52] who had the crazy specialty of jumping from one airplane to another in mid-air. They added that the unfortunate acrobat had been prompted by research of a practical order into a method of transferring merchandise from one aircraft to another without landing. Aeronautics is, in truth, endowed in such a marvelous fashion that even the demonstrations of its fantasy that seem to common judgment to be the most demented—looping the loop, the tailspin, etc.—constitute an evident progress; they create a school of adaptation that put the aviator at his ease: "at home."

Locklear suddenly showed us the way. Soon, I prescribed to the postmen a new method of "collecting sacks at

---

[52] The "daredevil" stuntman Ormer Locklear (1891-1920) starred in Cecil B. DeMille's highly successful movie *The Great Air Robbery* (1919), the chief characters in which are air mail pilots. Baudry de Saunier probably saw it. Locklear was killed while filming the follow-up movie *The Skywayman*, but the film was almost complete and De Mille hastened its September 1920 release in order to make the most of the publicity.

destination" that would singularly increase the speed of mail distribution.

On our orders, the landing of postal aircraft was henceforth authorized only at the terminal points of their itineraries; in the course of the flight they were to release their mailbags at a precise point. The localities overflown all possessed, close to their railways station, a target surmounted with metallic nets destined to deaden the shock of the bag riving on the ground. It was surrounded by a cordon of lights at night.

Every day, a chart was updated of the skill of all the postmen, recording both the number of the pilot and the cargo, and the zone, more or less distant from the center of the target, in which the sacks had fallen.

I installed an analogous system of delivery in our commercial dirigibles, at least for merchandise that could tolerate it: papers, curtains, underwear, etc.

The results were so brilliant that the Americans and the English were kind enough to congratulate me for having made such an original service practical, and they begged me to let them know the methods in order that they could apply them in their own territories.

The best recompenses that I could give my expert pilots always consisted of a twenty-four hour excursion to France, for useful purposes. Trips to France have formed German youth since time immemorial.

The Elite Intelligences that have deigned to follow me here will have divined that the slightest details of the machines employed in our civil aeronautics were submitted to the most severe checking by my engineers. The uniformity of the modes of attachment of postal sacks and bombs for example—their absolute identity—was one of the fundamental conditions of the rapid transformation of civil aircraft into military aircraft. In fact, the operation had to be facilitated to the extent that when the decisive moment came, it no longer consisted of anything but a simple change of merchandise, as I have already said. If ever standardization was rigorously applied to an item of machinery, I can affirm that it was to our no. 48 attachment hook and our no. 13 release mechanism!

BRILLIANT COMMERCE

One last stage of material preparation remained for me to complete: a redoubtable stage in which the German art of infiltration was to be affirmed in all its fecundity. Eternal glory to Heinrich Mannheim, Director General of Imperial Camouflage! All the work in this instance, is his! Without him, whose ideas are more abundant than the young eels that swim upstream from the mouths of our rivers and, like them, are able to slide between the most densely-packs stones, I would have been struck by impotence. In fact, the entire machination of my aircraft, all the skill of my pilots and all the discipline that solidly enveloped my work—the whole splendid dream—would have vanished if the fabrication of explosives and gases had remained prohibited to me by the Allies, if the bodies of the bombs and the detonators had been lacking on the day of our mobilization.

Your Majesty knows the slightest details of the miraculous conceptions of Heinrich Mannheim. I have asked him for permission not to reveal the details here, for, even if she is the Master of the Earth, Germany ought never to disarm, apprehensive of Mars and fearful of Venus. I shall only recall that the industry making pots of jam for export suddenly took on enormous proportions, that clockmaking received official encouragement, that immense cylindrical tanks were mounted in the flanks of the nacelles of our large transport dirigibles, for the delivery of soda and potash. I have said enough. Ah, God be praised again!

What does it matter if I do not reveal where the immense provisions that mechanics and chemistry poured out for us every day were dissimulated, crate by crate and drop by drop, all over the territory of the Reich? We were careful not to fall into the Romanticism of caverns, subterranean working and woods, which the Allied spies did not fail to visit, but simply to accumulate our reserves in proximity to our aviation camps and our Zeppelin hangars.

It was sufficient to deceive the Monitoring Committees. Heinrich Mannheim always had the genius to make them mistake chalk for cheese.

(*His Excellency is seized by a fit of laughter, which even spreads to His Majesty himself, which the Court accompanies with a discreet tapping of feet.*)

PETTY MANEUVERS

The Great Week was approaching. The Empire had just been restored. Your Powerful Majesty, resplendent with the Holy Spirit that descended thereinto, intended to show the Universe what a Hohenzollern can do when he allows his genius liberty. I, the humble servant of you will, the master of the hour when the Holy Flight would rise up above the Fatherland, was impatient finally to see the Orb of European domination surmounting your crows. The Holy Flight was about to make Your Majesty the Super-Emperor!

(*An explosion of* Hochs! *resounds. The great dignitaries are all on their feet, their arms extended toward the Emperor. The ladies of the court bow down, placing their fans over their breasts. Several members of the audience cannot hold back their tears, as sweet as the honey that drips from the bread of children.*)

But it was necessary to increase prudence and cunning even further before suddenly drawing the sword. It is at the moment that the athlete is about to leap the ditch that he measures its width most carefully. He makes sure of his feet so that they will not slip; he swings his arms several times as if to rehearse the leap. He bends his back to verify its flexibility. He searches for the ardor in the very fear that grips him. It was January 1924; the blow was to be delivered in April, at Easter.

325

The gravest decisions had to be made to ensure the impact of our punch.

In fact, it became evident that the enormous secret could no longer be known solely to Your Majesty, the Director General of Camouflage and myself. The intervention of our ground troops, all linked to one another by threads invisible to the Allies, constituted a necessity, since, when France's head was bloodied, it would be necessary the very next day to require our infantry and cavalry to tie up the prey. The Minister of War had, therefore, to commence an immediate secret mobilization.

Similarly, the Ministry of Foreign Affairs was also necessarily about to play its role, since, a few days before we destroyed Paris, it was necessary for some diplomatic incident, no matter how slight, to give us the right to "riposte in advance of the attack." It was important that we could once again show the eyes of the world the truth: the incorrigible militarism of France, the invariable honesty of Germany. Our own people would take a singular comfort in the demonstration thus made of our right and our virtue!

Finally, it was still necessary for me to extend a few poppy-fumes over Europe and America. While the Empire's Chancellery, weaving the commencement of a diplomatic incident with its delicate fingers, assured the Earth yet again of our frantic enthusiasm for peace, and while the Social Democrats cried out to all the socialists of all the democracies that four million of our soldiers would go on strike before any declaration of war, I was careful to provoke myself, in our own aeronautics—and I confess, by my own hands—accidents so numerous that within a month it had lost all value in the eyes of the Allies. Honor to the proud children of Germany who were immolated in those diplomatic catastrophes!

Every morning, the newspapers of Paris and London were discussing our bankruptcy in the air and depicting Germany as their readers desired to see her—which is to say, deprived of a fleet by England, deprived of an army by France, and deprived of aeronautics by German stupidity!

Even in our dear Fatherland I strove to sow panic, disbe-
lief in our serial effort, in order that the rare spies distributed
on our soil could certify in good faith to our adversaries that
Germany, demoralized, definitely had no more hope of recovery. I had it printed in all our dailies that the Minister of Aerial
Transport was about to be summoned to appear before the
Supreme Court.

How, in such circumstances, would pitiful Germany be
able to think of a revenge?

(*His Majesty smiles. The court laughs.*)

WHY EGGS OUGHT TO BE SERVED AT EASTER

During the war of 1914-18, the French newspapers repeated that the German people lacked psychology, that it
would have won battles and sympathies if it had known how
to analyze the mentality of other peoples. That was true. In
that also, we have sinned.

But in the domain of the soul, too, we have understood
the lessons of the war. We have learned to weigh henceforth
the mental factors of our enemies. If we chose the festival of
Easter as the date of the destruction of Paris, it was because
two reasons of psychology commanded us to do so.

The first is that a solemn act is best accomplished on a
day that is itself solemn. Easter is important in the minds of
men, and they judge it quite natural that great events are accomplished at Easter. All of our aviators, departing for the
assault on the French capital, heard that evening the *Hosanna*
of the Resurrection singing within him! It was a stimulant that
I could not have replaced by any other, and which cost our
treasury nothing.

The second reason for the choice of Easter derived from
the knowledge I have of the French character, as a result of
having been, for six months before the war of 1914, the principal *maître d'hôtel* in a large Parisian restaurant. A Frenchman cannot admit that a day marked on the calendar as a

327

"feast day" might be transformed into a day of misfortune by events. In his eyes, if it were otherwise, Destiny would be dishonest, and then it would simply be a farce—which is to say that the catastrophe would be delivered by tricksters.

I therefore had the certainty that in spite of the alert that had been given to France by the Schleswig Incident, and also by our preparations, which we had been unable to conceal completely, that it was on that important feast day that our enemy's defensive services would be at their weakest. I knew that on Easter Day, at least half of her aviators would have obtained permission from their superiors "to visit their aged mother."

WE HAVE GIVEN REINFORCEMENTS
TO ENGLISH DIPLOMACY

I have also been asked: "Why, on that glorious night, did you only employ 1,728 airplanes and 51 super-Zeppelins, when our forces amount in total to 4,650 airplanes and 186 super-Zeppelins? Why, at the same time as Paris, did you not strike London in its sensitive points, and even sink a part of the English fleet?"

First of all, if it is indispensable for a captain only to think in terms of great conceptions, he can only realize them by expelling from his mind the vertigo of the "immense project." Today, the Colossal demands measure. To take on Paris and London simultaneously clearly constituted a reckless design; it was sufficient to succeed in Paris.

Furthermore, psychology itself forbade us to attack England, and events have proven it correct. When it was confirmed, at the end of April, that Paris no longer existed, England turned a somersault, which was translated by a few violent diplomatic notes, but her Labor Party soon lowered the tone. She has understood, has not budged, and a fortnight later has signed the Preliminaries of the Convention that respects her self esteem but in reality puts her entirely under our tutelage.

That was, therefore, a good strategy. Protect the formalism of England! A single bomb dropped on Regent Street, even if it had only chopped the tail off a small dog, would inevitably have drawn us into war with the Peevish Lady. How many months or years would that new struggle have lasted? For how many months or years would that little dog's tail have been brandished in front of us like another "piece of paper"?[53]

It was highly preferable to confront England with an accomplished fact—a fact, furthermore, which could scarcely displease her. Since, the day after the armistice of 1918, the overly rapid recovery of France has been a continual subject of apprehension for England, have we not given the diplomacy of our insular neighbor a decisive boost by suppressing her former ally?

THE EMPEROR WEPT

The night of glory rose on the horizon, like the moon that slowly elevates her radiant face behind the hill in the darkness of summer.

It was Holy Thursday. Until my death I shall have the slightest details of that day engraved in my heart.

Your Majesty had just gathered us together in a High Council of War; it was a matter of finally fixing the great Star in the firmament.

For five hours I explained the enormous plan, the dispositions taken to ensure by aeronautics, at the same time as cutting the throat of Paris, the crushing of the Allied forces asleep on the banks of the Rhine, the sudden demolition of the great forts that, the day after the Holy Flight, might have prevented us from traversing France like a rectory garden and suddenly

---

[53] The reference is to the firm belief of the German leaders that England would not enter the Great War by virtue of the treaty obligation they had signed with Belgium in 1830—dismissed by the Kaiser's advisers as a mere "piece of paper." They were wrong.

paralyzing all the great French centers that might have opposed come resistance to us once the blow had fallen.

Then the High Chancellor spoke. The news from Europe, America and Asia did not put any cloud in the sky. The diplomatic incident, whose exact tenor I have forgotten—something in Schleswig—was treated in half a column by the most widely read newspapers in Paris. The Eternal, until the end, was favoring us with his grace.

Then, Noble Dignitaries who are listening to me, before pronouncing the decisive word that was to precipitate the future, out Great Emperor bowed his head; for a few seconds he covered his eyes with his two hands.

Then, slowly, lowering his arms, his visage raised dolorously toward the heavens, he pronounced these words, which have marked until the end of time the revolution of worlds:

"Go! But God is my witness that I have not wanted this! Go! France must be killed!"

NACH PARIS!

The next day, that of Holy Friday, the German newspapers, on my orders, demonstrated that I had put the Fatherland itself on the Cross by inflicting upon her the dolors of the aeronautical passion. The most important demanded from public opinion the twelve bullets that ought to pay for my crime.

On Holy Saturday, however, I had orders given to four thousand selected pilots to go to their respective airfields the following day, and to await with their machines for the instructions of their superiors. The reason for the convocation was entirely indicated: to examine collectively the causes of the accidents that had so profoundly discouraged the public.

Crews of fitters had been summoned, and each of the officers had received instructions in a sealed envelope that he was not to open until ten o'clock in the morning.

At nine o'clock, troops tightly surrounded all the exits from all the airfields. For twelve hours it was forbidden to anyone, under any pretext, and under threat of being immediately put up against the palisade and shot, to attempt to go in or out.

At the appointed hour, and in all the airfields of the Empire, the Emperor's message was read by the officers to all the pilots. The reports that have since been sent to me by each of the colonels of the airfields, established that on average it required two hours twenty minutes to equip a postal airplane as a bomber, and four hours seventeen minutes to make a passenger Zeppelin a transporter of Frankreichslieb.

In brief, at five o'clock in the evening on Easter Day, all our civil aviation pilots, transformed into well-trained combatants were ready to take to the air in machines of the most recent type, provided with the most powerful engines of destruction known to man.

Success could scarcely escape us, since we were proceeding by means of a surprise attack, and our aerial army was thus assured of the most important factor for the rigorous precision of its operations: quietude.

The holy squadrons were about to pounce on Paris, taking off from their respective airfields, and hence from locations that were naturally very distant from one another. They could not, therefore, all be given the signal to depart at the same time. We had taken care, throughout 1923, to exercise them, without them being aware of our plan, in aerial assemblies, which had permitted us to determine both their itineraries and their timetables.

There is no need to explain here the details of that discipline. I shall simply say that at seven o'clock in the evening on Easter Day, the aviators' officers received a sealed envelope from their colonels bearing the words: *Nach Paris*—To Paris. *Not to be opened until airborne. Maneuver no. 19*.

The order was given to them to proceed to Paris, remaining at the head of their squadron and without exceeding the speed that we had scrupulously determined for each unit. For each squadron had a very precise role to play, and it was important that the gravediggers did not arrive before the pallbearers...

German soldiers all, envy the good fortune of the aerial bombardier! He benefits from the supreme excitement of being conscious of the harm he is about to do! Each of his blows—every single one—will pulverize two or three large buildings and a hundred human beings! Successful, his four bombs will devastate an entire new quarter! How could he not operate with precision and with joy? How can anyone not aspire to his place and his feast?

(*At that moment, the Minister of Aerial Transport interrupts himself. It is evident that emotion and fatigue are overtaking him. A chamberlain approaches, and signals to him that His Majesty has granted him a few moments' rest. Five minutes later, His Excellency General Otto von Stick resumes speaking.*)

Emotion is gripping my throat. At the recitation of so much prowess, I sense my nerves giving way. Need I say how Paris was killed?

(*The minister does, indeed, seem harassed. His Majesty replies with a* Ja! *That summarizes, in its energy, all the inflexible German will. And the minister straightens up again. Supporting himself with one hand on the slide-projector table, he continues.*)

HOSANNA!

It is an indescribable dolor that Your Majesty is reawakening in my memory! To have killed Paris! But it was necessary for the immortal glory of the Fatherland! If I had to do it again, I would pray to the Lord to render me the heart that he maintained as hard as bronze for me all through the night of Easter Sunday 1924.

That evening, at the hour when joyful Paris was leaving the table—at about ten o'clock—when, in all the fashionable restaurants, the blonde women were lighting their cigarettes, when the youngest daughter of the family was playing her piano piece for grandmama, enormous flocks of birds rose up from our plains, much higher than swans or herons. They flew at high sped above Champagne, heading westwards. In their feathers they were carrying death to Paris.

The first flock arrived over the capital of France at ten thirty, unloaded over the railway stations, the ministries and the Élysée, and then resumed their flight toward Germany.

1,526 bombs had been dropped in thirteen minutes.

When the second appeared, at ten forty-five, a yellow fog under which swirls of gold were visible began, according to the reports that I received later, to cover the low-lying parts of the City; the lighting gas had been ignited by electrical sparks, stimulating the fires that our special bombs had sown.

I believe that during the passage of our seventh aerial army, three-quarters of the City of Light had been crushed or burnt. Its colonel affirmed to me that by a quarter past midnight, so much smoke was rising from the city that it was inconvenient at the regulation height of two thousand meters. Intense glows were being given off by the conflagration of the general stores, wood-yards and department stores, illuminating in red and yellow the sea whose waves were rolling in a swell higher than the towers of Note Dame. The reverberation of the heat attained such a height in the atmosphere by three-twenty, according to the report of the eighteenth army, that Commandant William Mantzel, who was manning a helicopter and remained immobile for a few seconds above the furnace, was obliged to protect his face with is map in order not to hurt his eyes.

At four o'clock in the morning our twentieth, twenty-first and twenty-sixth aerial corps, comprising 550 aircraft of large tonnage, poured into the burning fog veritable rivers of heavy asphyxiating gases. I had insisted that that work of charity be carried out in order to kill in the utmost depths of the ground those Parisians who, having taken refuge in cellars, were buried there forever; those who were still struggling under the ruins, howling, their limbs broken; and those whom the hazards of chaos had imprisoned intact, still alive, in the tangles of iron and stone. We needed to finish off all those poor people.

Our newspapers have given, a few days ago, the numbers of the results we obtained on that forever celebrated night. I can rectify them today by means of a more certain documentation. Officially, 1,473 houses remained almost intact and 187,000 inhabitants were able to escape. The elevated quarters neighboring Sacré-Coeur, the Arc de Triomphe and the Panthéon, which did not include any point that we had an interest in destroying, have been spared. 88,430 dwellings, churches and public monuments, along with approximately 1,726,000 inhabitants, no longer have a name, a face or a form.

The only problem posed today for us, with regard to the capital of the French, consists of protecting the two surrounding départements of the Seine and the Seine-de-Oise therefrom; plague might emerge from the frightful cadaver of Paris.

TWITCHES

The head crushed, France struggled for a further three weeks, as you will recall.

The police documents that I have received since the month of April establish that, on the eve of Easter, almost at the same moment that our first aerial army began to fly toward Paris, the French Ministry of War was warned, thanks to wireless telegraph, probably by a watcher in Coblentz, that we had been able to recover.

Only a cabinet secretary was on duty at the Ministry.

The news that suddenly reached him on that festival evening appeared to him at first, he later declared during an interrogation, to come from "a practical joker with no sense of humor." An army of night birds in flight toward Paris—what an implausible communication! To relieve his responsibility, however, he telephoned the three principle centers of aviation near Paris; then, leaping into an automobile, he hastened to warn the Minister, who was dining in a Montmartre restaurant and was very amused by the message. It was in the debris of the house that they were found two days later, the secretary wounded and the Minister dead.

In brief, our first army had arrived over Châlons when it was attacked by fifteen small French airplanes, extremely agile and fast, which threw themselves into an attack, as crazily and with as little success as a flock of linnets trying to overturn a locomotive.

All night long, say the reports, our aircraft, arriving over the capital in well-regulated waves, were harassed by the Chevaliers Saint-Georges of despair. The majority were hurled into the depths of the furnace by the counter-hunters mounting guard on the flanks of our squadrons.

That night, and the following days, because fury cannot defeat cold preparation, noble Germany scarcely had to shake her robe to make that vermin fall. Those stings could not alter the fact that 163 of our Zeppelins, on the afternoon of Easter, had departed to fly over French territory at an altitude so high that they were imperceptible, and all the centers of organization—Lyon, Bordeaux, Bourges, Marseilles, Saint-Etienne, Nantes, Le Creusot, Dijon—had been paralyzed during the same night as the death of Paris; that the provisions and munitions of the adversary, everywhere, were on fire five days later; that her railways were broken at vital points; that the most important wireless telegraph stations had been reduced to silence. For eight days and eight nights, without a single hour's pause, storms of shells rained down on the gatherings of men, horses or cannons that our enemies, running around like demented ants, attempted to oppose to our methodical conquest.

Thus, our aviation tied up the limbs of France, one by one, as it had crushed her head. Everywhere, all the way to the mountains, it carried our terror and our law. With a beat of its wing it opened the route to our automobiles loaded with infantrymen and machine-guns. By Easter Tuesday the rapid roadsters of our officers had already passed Tours and Nevers.

The Welches' troops had no more to do than hold out their necks, as they chose, for the knife or the yoke. The example of the headstrong of Mézilhac enlightened the French provinces: the 1,800 soldiers and peasants whom our troops had surrounded, but who refused to surrender, were lit up by our aviators, to the last man, like ricks of dry hay, in ten minutes.

Three weeks after Easter, the last twitches of our age-old enemy died away in our glory. The peoples of Europe, exhausted by the war of 1914, eaten away by social decomposition, had been unable to do anything better than drag themselves on to their balconies to watch...

We were absolute masters. We did not even grant the vanquished a treaty!

(*At these words the Emperor stands up abruptly and, in a surge of sacred anger, exclaims in a measured fashion these henceforth historic words: "Does one make a treaty with the horse over which one passes a bridle, with the ox that one harnesses to a plow? One says to them: march and pull! The crop that you prepare will be for me!"*

The eminent lecturer concludes as follows:)

Majesty,

I have finished. I have explained the patient and secret preparation of the immortal night of the twentieth of April 1924; I have stated the facts, most characteristic of the genius of our Chosen Race. I have shown the abominable and delicious horror of those festival hours; I have noted the incalculable consequences that place Easter 1924 amid the stars as the date of the most marvelous even the Universe has ever known.

The Putrid Race has disappeared. The entire German people brings back all that glory to Your august head. You are the symbol of the superiority that Providence has given the German race over all human races.

Beloved Emperor, permit the delirium of my joy to conclude with a song of praise to Holy Aeronautics.

Little mechanical birds that furrow the air, as rapid as machine-gun bullets, giant eagles whose shadow covers an entire city with blackness, frightful powers that France has created in order that we might crush her, little birds, little birds, you have given Germany the supreme wealth that Destiny has owed her for six hundred years: the Empire of the World!

Then His Excellency General Hans von Stick, his eyes filled with crystal tears, the most beautiful that any man has ever shed, ran to His Majesty, knelt down before Him, and kissed his hand for a long time.

We are incapable of even attempting to describe the scenes of enthusiasm that accompanied the Emperor's exit. The cries of "Hoch! Hoch!" shook the windows of the Hall of Mirrors, as a series of exploding bombs would have done. A delirium of love and patriotism set the entire audience ablaze. Our hearts melted in delight.

Yes, little mechanical birds that furrow the air, giant eagles, you have finally given Germany the Empire of the World!

Otto Walter.

SF & FANTASY

Adolphe Alhaiza. *Cybele*
Alphonse Allais. *The Adventures of Captain Cap*
Henri Allorge. *The Great Cataclysm*
Guy d'Armen. *Doc Ardan: The City of Gold and Lepers*
G.-J. Arnaud. *The Ice Company*
Charles Asselineau. *The Double Life*
Henri Austruy. *The Eupantophone; The Olotelepan; The Petitpaon Era*
Barillet-Lagargousse. *The Final War*
Cyprien Bérard. *The Vampire Lord Ruthwen*
S. Henry Berthoud. *Martyrs of Science*
Aloysius Bertrand. *Gaspard de la Nuit*
Richard Bessière. *The Gardens of the Apocalypse; The Masters of Silence*
Chevalier de Béthune. *The World of Mercury*
Albert Bleunard. *Ever Smaller*
Félix Bodin. *The Novel of the Future*
Louis Boussenard. *Monsieur Synthesis*
Alphonse Brown. *City of Glass; The Conquest of the Air*
Émile Calvet. *In a Thousand Years*
André Caroff. *The Terror of Madame Atomos; Miss Atomos; The Return of Madame Atomos; The Mistake of Madame Atomos; The Monsters of Madame Atomos; The Revenge of Madame Atomos; The Resurrection of Madame Atomos; The Mark of Madame Atomos; The Spheres of Madame Atomos; The Wrath of Madame Atomos* (w/M. & Sylvie Stéphan)
Félicien Champsaur. *The Human Arrow; Ouha, King of the Apes; Pharaoh's Wife; Homo-Deus; Nora, The Ape-Woman*
Didier de Chousy. *Ignis*
Jules Clarétie. *Obsession*
Michel Corday. *The Eternal Flame*
André Couvreur. *The Necessary Evil*; *Caresco, Superman; The Exploits of Professor Tornada* (3 vols.)
Captain Danrit. *Undersea Odyssey*
Camille Debans. *The Misfortunes of John Bull*
C. I. Defontenay. *Star (Psi Cassiopeia)*
Charles Derennes. *The People of the Pole*
Georges Dodds (anthologist). *The Missing Link*

Charles Dodeman. *The Silent Bomb*
Harry Dickson. *The Heir of Dracula; Harry Dickson vs. The Spider*
Jules Dornay. *Lord Ruthven Begins*
Alfred Driou. *The Adventures of a Parisian Aeronaut*
Sâr Dubnotal *vs. Jack the Ripper*
Odette Dulac. *The War of the Sexes*
Alexandre Dumas. *The Return of Lord Ruthven*
Renée Dunan. *Baal; The Ultimate Pleasure*
J.-C. Dunyach. *The Night Orchid; The Thieves of Silence*
Henri Duvernois. *The Man Who Found Himself*
Achille Eyraud. *Voyage to Venus*
Henri Falk. *The Age of Lead*
Paul Féval. *Anne of the Isles; Knightshade; Revenants; Vampire City; The Vampire Countess; The Wandering Jew's Daughter*
Paul Féval, *fils. Felifax, the Tiger-Man*
Charles de Fieux. *Lamékis*
Louis Forest. *Someone is Stealing Children in Paris*
Arnould Galopin. *Doctor Omega; Doctor Omega and the Shadowmen* (anthology)
Judith Gautier. *Isoline and the Serpent-Flower*
H. Gayar. *The Marvelous Adventures of Serge Myrandhal on Mars*
G.L. Gick. *Harry Dickson and the Werewolf of Rutherford Grange*
Delphine de Girardin. *Balzac's Cane*
Léon Gozlan. *The Vampire of the Val-de-Grâce*
Jules Gros. *The Fossil Man*
Edmond Haraucourt. *Illusions of Immortality; Daah, the First Human*
Nathalie Henneberg. *The Green Gods*
Eugène Hennebert. *The Enchanted City*
V. Hugo, P. Foucher & P. Meurice. *The Hunchback of Notre-Dame*
Romain d'Huissier. *Hexagon: Dark Matter*
Jules Janin. *The Magnetized Corpse*
Michel Jeury. *Chronolysis*
Gustave Kahn. *The Tale of Gold and Silence*
Gérard Klein. *The Mote in Time's Eye*
Fernand Kolney. *Love in 5000 Years*
Paul Lacroix. *Danse Macabre*
Louis-Guillaume de La Follie. *The Unpretentious Philosopher*
Jean de La Hire. *Enter the Nyctalope; The Nyctalope on Mars; The Nyctalope vs. Lucifer; The Nyctalope Steps In; Night of the Nyctalope; Return of the Nyctalope; The Fiery Wheel*
Etienne-Léon de Lamothe-Langon. *The Virgin Vampire*

André Laurie. *Spiridon*

Gabriel de Lautrec. *The Vengeance of the Oval Portrait*

Alain le Drimeur. *The Future City*

Georges Le Faure & Henri de Graffigny. *The Extraordinary Adventures of a Russian Scientist Across the Solar System* (2 vols.)

Gustave Le Rouge. *The Mysterious Doctor Cornelius* (3 vols.); *The Vampires of Mars; The Dominion of the World* (w/Gustave Guitton) (4 vols.)

Jules Lermina. *Mysteryville; Panic in Paris; To-Ho and the Gold Destroyers; The Secret of Zippelius; The Battle of Strasbourg*

André Lichtenberger. *The Centaurs; The Children of the Crab*

Listonai. *The Philosophical Voyager*

Jean-Marc & Randy Lofficier. *Edgar Allan Poe on Mars; The Katrina Protocol; Pacifica; Robonocchio; Return of the Nyctalope;* (anthologists) *Tales of the Shadowmen 1-11; The Vampire Almanac* (2 vols.)

Xavier Mauméjean. *The League of Heroes*

Joseph Méry. *The Tower of Destiny*

Hippolyte Mettais. *The Year 5865; Paris Before the Deluge*

Louise Michel. *The Human Microbes; The New World*

Tony Moilin. *Paris in the Year 2000*

José Moselli. *Illa's End*

John-Antoine Nau. *Enemy Force*

Marie Nizet. *Captain Vampire*

C. Nodier, A. Beraud & Toussaint-Merle. *Frankenstein*

Henri de Parville. *An Inhabitant of the Planet Mars*

Gaston de Pawlowski. *Journey to the Land of the 4th Dimension*

Georges Pellerin. *The World in 2000 Years*

Ernest Pérochon. *The Frenetic People*

Pierre Pelot. *The Child Who Walked on the Sky*

J. Polidori, C. Nodier, E. Scribe. *Lord Ruthven the Vampire*

P.-A. Ponson du Terrail. *The Vampire and the Devil's Son; The Immortal Woman*

Georges Price. *The Missing Men of the Sirius*

Edgar Quinet. *Ahasuerus; The Enchanter Merlin*

Henri de Régnier. *A Surfeit of Mirrors*

Maurice Renard. *The Blue Peril; Doctor Lerne; The Doctored Man; A Man Among the Microbes; The Master of Light*

Jean Richepin. *The Wing; The Crazy Corner*

Albert Robida. *The Adventures of Saturnin Farandoul; The Clock of the Centuries; Chalet in the Sky; The Electric Life*

J.-H. Rosny Aîné. *Helgvor of the Blue River; The Givreuse Enigma; The Mysterious Force; The Navigators of Space; Vamireh; The World of the Variants; The Young Vampire*
Marcel Rouff. *Journey to the Inverted World*
Léonie Rouzade. *The World Turned Upside Down*
Han Ryner. *The Superhumans; The Human Ant*
Pierre de Selenes: *An Unknown World*
Angelo de Sorr. *The Vampires of London*
Brian Stableford. *The New Faust at the Tragicomique;The Empire of the Necromancers (The Shadow of Frankenstein; Frankenstein and the Vampire Countess; Frankenstein in London); Sherlock Holmes & The Vampires of Eternity; The Stones of Camelot; The Wayward Muse.* (anthologist) *News from the Moon; The Germans on Venus; The Supreme Progress; The World Above the World; Nemoville; Investigations of the Future; The Conqueror of Death; The Revolt of the Machines; The Man With the Blue Face*
Jacques Spitz. *The Eye of Purgatory*
Kurt Steiner. *Ortog*
Eugène Thébault. *Radio-Terror*
C.-F. Tiphaigne de La Roche. *Amilec*
Simon Tyssot de Patot. *The Strange Voyages of Jacques Massé and Pierre de Mésange*
Louis Ulbach. *Prince Bonifacio*
Théo Varlet. *The Golden Rock. The Xenobiotic Invasion; The Castaways of Eros; Timeslip Troopers* (w/André Blandin); *The Martian Epic* (w/Octave Joncquel)
Pierre Véron. *The Merchants of Health*
Paul Vibert. *The Mysterious Fluid*
Villiers de l'Isle-Adam. *The Scaffold; The Vampire Soul*
Gaston de Wailly. *The Murderer of the World*
Philippe Ward. *Artahe ; The Song of Montségur* (w/Sylvie Miller) *Manhattan Ghost* (w/Mickael Laguerre)

MYSTERIES & THRILLERS

M. Allain & P. Souvestre. *The Daughter of Fantômas*
A. Anicet-Bourgeois, Lucien Dabril. *Rocambole*
A. Bernède. *Belphegor*; *Judex* (w/Louis Feuillade); *The Return of Judex* (w/Louis Feuillade); *The Shadow of Judex*
A. Bisson & G. Livet. *Nick Carter vs. Fantômas*

V. Darlay & H. de Gorsse. *Arsène Lupin vs. Sherlock Holmes: The Stage Play*

Séamas Duffy. *Sherlock Holmes in Paris*

Paul Féval. *Gentlemen of the Night; John Devil; The Black Coats ('Salem Street; The Invisible Weapon; The Parisian Jungle; The Companions of the Treasure; Heart of Steel; The Cadet Gang; The Sword-Swallower)*

Émile Gaboriau. *Monsieur Lecoq*

Goron & Émile Gautier. *Spawn of the Penitentiary*

Paul d'Ivoi. *Around the World on Five Sous* (w/Henri Chabrillat)

Rick Lai. *Shadows of the Opera: Retribution in Blood; Sisters of the Shadows: The Curse of Cagliostro*

Steve Leadley. *Sherlock Holmes: The Circle of Blood*

Maurice Leblanc. *Arsène Lupin vs. Countess Cagliostro; Arsène Lupin vs. Sherlock Holmes (The Blonde Phantom; The Hollow Needle); The Many Faces of Arsène Lupin; The Island of the Thirty Coffins; 813*

Gaston Leroux. *Chéri-Bibi; The Phantom of the Opera; Rouletabille & the Mystery of the Yellow Room; Rouletabille at Krupp's*

Richard Marsh. *The Complete Adventures of Judith Lee*

William Patrick Maynard. *The Terror of Fu Manchu; The Destiny of Fu Manchu*

Frank J. Morlock. *Sherlock Holmes: The Grand Horizontals; Sherlock Holmes vs Jack the Ripper*

Jean Petithuguenin. *The Adventures of Ethel King*

Antonin Reschal. *The Adventures of Miss Boston*

P. de Wattyne & Y. Walter. *Sherlock Holmes vs. Fantômas*

David White. *Fantômas in America*

Pierre Yrondy. *The Adventures of Thérèse Arnaud*

Victor Margueritte. *The Bacheloress; The Companion; The Couple*

SCREENPLAYS

Mike Baron. *The Iron Triangle*

Emma Bull & Will Shetterly. *Nightspeeder; War for the Oaks*

Gerry Conway & Roy Thomas. *Doc Dynamo*

Steve Englehart. *Majorca*

James Hudnall. *The Devastator*

Jean-Marc & Randy Lofficier. *Royal Flush*

J.-M. & R. Lofficier & Marc Agapit. *Despair*

J.-M. & R. Lofficier & Joël Houssin. *City*
Andrew Paquette. *Peripheral Vision*
Robert L. Robinson, Jr. *Judex*
R. Thomas, J. Hendler & L. Sprague de Camp. *Rivers of Time*

NON-FICTION

Stephen R. Bissette. *Blur 1-5. Green Mountain Cinema 1; Teen Angels*
Win Scott Eckert. *Crossovers* (2 vols.)
Jean-Marc & Randy Lofficier. *Shadowmen* (2 vols.)
Randy Lofficier. *Over Here*

ART BOOKS

Jean-Pierre Normand. *Science Fiction Illustrations*
Raven Okeefe. *Raven's L'il Critters; Rave's Faves*
Randy Lofficier & Raven Okeefe. *If Your Possum Go Daylight...*
Daniele Serra. *Illusions*
Randy Lofficier. *Over Here*

HEXAGON COMICS

Franco Frescura & Luciano Bernasconi. *Wampus*
Franco Frescura & Giorgio Trevisan. *CLASH*
L. Bernasconi, J.-M. Lofficier & Juan Roncagliolo. *Phenix*
Claude Legrand, J.-M. Lofficier & L. Bernasconi. *Kabur*
Franco Oneta. *Zembla*
L. Buffolente, Lofficier & J.-J. Dzialowski. *Strangers: Homicron*
Danilo Grossi. *Strangers: Jaydee*
Claude Legrand & Luciano Bernasconi. *Strangers: Starlock*
Thierry Mornet & Juan Roncagliolo. *Guardian of the Republic*
J.-M. Lofficier & others. *Strangers 0: Omens & Origins*
J.-M. Lofficier, M. Garcia, F. Blanco & J. Pima. *Strangers 1: Strangers in a Strange Land*